W

‖‖‖‖‖‖‖‖‖
W9-AOX-494

# PRAISE FOR ANTHONY JOHN'S TERRIFYING DEBUT NOVEL, *THE JUDAS VOICE*

"Spellbinding and truly frightening . . . A terrifying journey into the mind of a psychotic killer, *The Judas Voice* is a first-rate detective novel as well as a modern parable of good and evil. Anthony John is an exceptionally talented and perceptive novelist, and you'll find yourself creeping ever closer to the edge of your seat as the story moves rapidly toward its shocking climax."

—NELSON DeMILLE, bestselling author of *The Charm School* and *The Gold Coast*

# PREPARE YOURSELF FOR ANTHONY JOHN'S MOST CAPTIVATING SHOCKER, *SEE SAW*

In the tradition of *The Silence of the Lambs*, this breathtaking new thriller takes you into the minds of the hunter and the hunted—driven to the edge of sanity . . . and beyond.

ders. You'd think the world would learn. Who needs it? It's disgusting.''

''Your robe is disgusting, Rose. Murder is an international pastime, but there's no excuse for your robe. You should buy a new one, already,'' he said, still reading.

Berger watched as his wife sat down opposite him and planted her elbows firmly on the table, holding her coffee in both hands at eye level and peering at him over the brim. Berger recognized this as her favorite defensive position, unchanged after all these years—arms up like a classical boxer.

''My sister, may she rest in peace, wore this robe, Ira. It has sentiment.''

''It has holes, Rose,'' Berger said. ''Buy a new one.''

''And why, Ira? This one still looks good.''

''Your sister, may she rest in peace, probably looks better. Buy a new robe, Rose, please,'' Berger implored from behind his paper.

''New robes are expensive; you should see even the sale prices at Lerners,'' Rose persisted.

Berger put down the paper and leered. ''If you've got to wear that one, make sure the holes are in the right places. You know what I mean?'' He arched his eyebrows three times in rapid succession.

Rose buttoned the robe up quickly. ''You know perfectly well what's under this.'' She was pleased in spite of herself. She wasn't tall, only five-foot-three, but she prided herself on her youthful figure. ''Speaking of old, Ira, that reminds me. Are you going to see a podiatrist or are you happy just to cook your feet every morning?''

''There'll be no foot doctor, Rose. And that's final.''

''Ira, you promised, after all those years walking a beat—''

''Rose,'' Ira said firmly. ''Enough with the years. I came in this kitchen a fifty-nine-year-old man, and you're hocking me about old.''

''You should retire,'' Rose said.

"I promised I'd look into it. I looked and didn't like what I saw. I'm happy to do my job and cook my feet. Now, please."

"Ira," she said, changing the subject, "I'm going back to work."

Berger drained his coffee and looked at his wife, wondering how serious she was. "Work?" he asked. "What for? The Bentley needs new tires?"

"I sit too much, I wish too much, I eat too much. It's not healthy. People need exercise."

"So take up golf, Rose," Berger said.

"I'm serious, Ira. I want a part-time job. Something easy, just to get out of the house," Rose said, her tone more confident now.

"We're not going to go all over *that* again, are we?" Berger asked. They both knew what *that* meant. Rose was just forty and her biological clock was winding down. She wanted a child desperately.

"Have I made you so unhappy?" he asked, folding the newspaper into a neat square, knowing he'd have to wait until later to finish it.

"You know how I feel," she said. "There's nothing to say anymore."

"About this job," he said, shifting focus. "Where would you work? The school cafeteria retired you. You got your gold watch, your basket of fruit, and Mrs. Zarconi's knitted scarf. You can't go back, they'll repossess everything."

"Not the school," Rose said. "I was talking to Mr. Gross the other day and he needs help."

"Gross!" Berger raised his voice for the first time. "Gross the butcher?"

"Yes," Rose answered.

"Gross, the son-of-a-bitch butcher who called me a Cossack?" Berger spat the words out in disbelief. "You won't work for him, Rose. And that's final."

It had been ten years ago, Berger remembered, but he

stubbornly refused to patronize Gross's after their fight over a piece of brisket.

"We'll see," Rose said calmly. Then under her breath she whispered, "Cossack."

"What?" Berger said, suspicious.

"It's late, Ira. Your feet are waiting to be dried. I'll get you a towel," Rose said, going to the hall linen closet and returning with a frayed blue towel. She kissed him again on top of his head.

"What are you doing, Rose?" Berger said, still suspicious.

"Practicing for Mr. Gross," she answered.

"Very funny, Rose," Berger said, toweling his aching feet.

"I'm going for the mail," Rose said, clomping out of the kitchen. Ira finished drying his feet and returned to his paper.

Moments later Rose returned carrying a package, shabbily wrapped in brown paper. "It's for you," she said, placing it on the table. "Somebody left it in front of the door."

Berger took the package. "Left it in the hall?" he asked. "I'm surprised nobody stole it."

"So am I," Rose said, going back to the bedroom.

Berger studied the package while massaging his feet. He searched for a return address and found none.

Curiosity getting the better of him, he unwrapped it. Inside the box he found a wad of newspaper about the size of a bowling ball. His policeman's instincts warned him to proceed cautiously; then the ball of paper was in his hands and a feeling of wrongness came over him.

Slowly he spread the paper apart as if he were unwrapping expensive crystal. There were five sheets from the same newspaper dated Thursday, November 4, and he worked each separately, scanning the text as he progressed.

The feeling of wrongness became reality with a sudden jolt; he felt a sickening thrill. Inside the newspaper was a human hand, balled into a fist. It was dry, scaly, and bloodless, except where the shocking white bones of the wrist protruded. He caught the unmistakably sharp smell of formaldehyde as he took a deep breath to control his nerves.

Tilting the paper, he moved the hand, examining it from another angle. The kitchen's light was good, even on a gray, misty morning, and he had no trouble spotting tiny sutures ringing four of the fingers. They had been attached precisely to the thumb and palm of the hand, which was small and dainty, possibly that of a child.

Five victims, Berger thought immediately. At least five victims.

He stared at the hand intently, wondering what he should do next, when it occurred to him that whoever had sent him the hand *knew* him.

"You're still here?" Rose called from the bedroom.

The sound of her voice made Berger shudder. If the perpetrator knew him, he also knew Rose.

Quickly he began to cover the amputated hand with the frayed blue towel, but he stopped suddenly when he noticed a tiny bit of white paper poking out from between the thumb and finger.

He knew he should wait for a forensic unit, but the temptation was too great. He tugged at the paper and it slid easily from the hand's stiff grip.

Berger unrolled it like a scroll; childlike block letters covered the two-inch square. The message read: HELP US.

# 2

Nothing changes, but everything is different, Sonny LoBianco thought as he drove through the familiar streets of his childhood. The memories came: some good, some bad, some criminal. He had played on a different side of the street in those days, and he had the scars—visible and invisible—to prove it.

Brooklyn flashed past the windows of his restored 1962 Corvette Stingray, a dingy mélange of earth tones, a vivid mix of people, cultures, and colors, everything muted in the fine morning mist.

He parked in front of a two-story, brick-face structure in Bay Ridge and walked around the side of the building. A hand-lettered sign read TIP TOE INN. It was an unlicensed social club that boasted cheap booze, expensive drugs, and modestly priced whores who had much to be modest about.

Inside, several men and women lined the bar, drinking and talking as if it were 7:00 P.M. instead of 7:00 A.M. The Tip Toe Inn smelled of mice, crack, beer, sex, and oddly, hay. A barnyard smell, LoBianco thought, wrinkling his nose. He had never been in a barnyard, but he had been to the zoo as a kid. He looked over the bar's patrons with the same curiosity he had lavished on the sloths, badgers, and snakes.

He took a position at the end of the bar, just inside the

9

door, and waited. The customers made him at once: a wiseguy. The lively talk stuttered to a halt as they cast furtive glances at him.

A tall man in his late twenties, LoBianco wore his long black hair combed straight back and close to his head. His hairline formed a widow's peak that, like an arrow, pointed to his dark, hooded eyes, long aquiline nose, and strong chin. He exuded an animal intensity that the customers at the Tip Toe Inn recognized instantly: *Don't fuck with me.*

In the back room a heavily muscled black man, his bodybuilding efforts made evident by his purple tank top, was shooting bumper pool with intense concentration.

People on the street knew him as Rooster because he had a herd of women who literally worked their asses off for him. LoBianco was there for him.

Rooster saw LoBianco's stare and shot him an ugly look full of malice.

Fuck you, LoBianco thought, giving Rooster a nasty smile in return, calling his bluff.

LoBianco reached into his pocket to reassure himself that he had a roll of quarters handy and went toward the back room to take care of business.

"Hey, white ass, you got a problem?" Rooster said, stepping in front of LoBianco. He put his acne-scarred face into LoBianco's, daring him to do something about it.

LoBianco took a step to his right and pivoted, moving around Rooster and catching the man by surprise. He blew a kiss into the black man's ear before continuing on toward the men's room.

"Asshole wants to die," Rooster swore as he started after LoBianco. The men with Rooster held him back.

"Hey, bro," one of them said. "Be cool, we're just here for drinkin', not fightin'."

"Hey, Rooster," another said. "You be taking your Hulk Hogan vitamins today? That eye-talian probably carrying."

The group laughed at Rooster's expense, fueling his rage.

He pushed himself free. "No white motherfucker disrespects me," he said, charging after LoBianco.

Inside the men's room, LoBianco stood by a urinal, pretending to piss. As he waited for Rooster he read the graffiti on the wall. The main concern of the Tip Toe Inn's patrons seemed to be sucking cocks. He hefted the rolled quarters in his left hand, making a fist around it. In his shirt pocket were four vials of crack.

Rooster barged into the small bathroom, hoping to catch LoBianco with his dick in his hand. Seeing LoBianco at the urinal, he smiled and began to posture. "You're in a lot of trouble, white boy. You're in shit city."

LoBianco turned slowly. "I don't think so," he said, surprising Rooster. Then, in a move that caught the black man completely off guard, LoBianco drove his weighted fist down onto the bridge of Rooster's nose. Blood spurted onto the white-tiled bathroom walls; Rooster screamed as he fell.

LoBianco followed the black man's momentum, shifting his weight forward and shooting his left foot out in a snapping front kick to Rooster's groin. Rooster pitched forward and LoBianco pivoted as he punched down on the back of the man's unprotected neck.

That was enough for Rooster. He collapsed into a pool of his own blood.

The door opened and two of Rooster's friends tried to get at LoBianco, shouldering at each other in the narrow doorway.

LoBianco drew his .38, aiming it at them. "Back off," he shouted, holding the gun straight out.

The bartender peered from behind Rooster's two friends. LoBianco flashed his tin. "Call 911, I want cops here, lots of them." He kicked the door shut.

On the floor Rooster moaned as he dragged himself into a sitting position. LoBianco pulled the four vials of crack from his shirt pocket, wiped them clean, and handed them to Rooster.

"I want your prints on these, scumbag. Then put them on the floor." Beaten, Rooster did as he was told.

Next LoBianco pulled a butterfly knife from another pocket and also wiped it clean. Squatting, he slid the knife to Rooster. "Open it," he said.

Rooster opened the knife and placed it next to the crack vials. "I didn't know you was a cop," he mumbled.

"I always knew you were a pimp," LoBianco said. "You're under arrest for the possession of a controlled substance, resisting arrest, and carrying a concealed weapon. You have the right to remain silent," he said. "You have the right to leave Beverly Jackson alone. . . ."

LoBianco's last words struck home and Rooster suddenly understood what was happening. With blood still flowing from his nose, he nodded to LoBianco just as a uniformed cop entered the bathroom.

LoBianco gave the collar to the uniform, intentionally neglecting to finish reading Rooster his rights. Rooster would walk, but LoBianco didn't care. He just wanted the pimp to stop hassling Beverly Jackson, a schoolgirl staying at the St. Agnes Children's Shelter, in the care of LoBianco's friend, Father Franklyn Davis.

The priest and LoBianco went a long way back and St. Agnes had become his pet project. The priest had asked LoBianco to put a little heat on Rooster and LoBianco had delivered street justice with real satisfaction. Beverly Jackson, aged sixteen, mother of two, wouldn't have to hustle her stuff for this pimp just to survive. At least not yet.

The Sixty-fifth Precinct station house had been built in 1888 as a monument to municipal power and majesty, back in the days before Brooklyn—and the rest of the country—became too sensitive to use such words. Constructed of red brick and white granite in the style of a Victorian mansion, it covered the entire block, a bastion of law and order in a civilized neighborhood.

More than a century later, though, the structure of

civilization had dissolved, leaving behind a rat-infested pile of stone the color of dried blood, stubbed with useless turrets and staffed by desperate men and women. The six-five was an "A" precinct, a dangerous place in a high-volume crime area. The cops were a thin blue line attempting to keep the barbarians from the gate.

It wasn't working, but Sonny LoBianco was: the eight-to-four shift. He hurried up the worn stone steps, past departing four-to-eight guys.

A silver shield, a patrolman working in plainclothes for the Detective Division, LoBianco nodded to the desk sergeant and went up the worn metal stairs to his right, heading for the PDU, the Precinct Detective Unit. Lieutenant Santamyer commanded, with Sergeant Berger as "whip," a purely ceremonial title conferred on him because he was good at his job, and because he was old.

LoBianco found Ira Berger holding court at his desk near Lieutenant Santamyer's office.

"So you coulda knocked me over with a feather," Berger was saying. " A hand. A goddamned hand, with stitched-on fingers, no less."

The crowd around his desk murmured appreciatively; cops loved a good cop story, especially if it had body parts in it.

"What about the note?" someone asked.

"Yeah, the note," someone else said.

"The note had two words on it," Berger said, holding up two fingers. " 'Help us.' Now you know as much about it as I do," he added.

Sonny LoBianco stood at the back of the group, biding his time. He wanted the old bastards to get it out of their systems so he could find out what the hell had happened. Finally a coughing fit from the chain-smoking Santamyer ended the session. Detectives drifted back to their green metal desks to write, type, and file reports, catch whatever squeals came in, and go quietly insane from overwork and the sheer lunacy of their jobs.

Ira Berger took a bite of a buttered bagel, a luxury he allowed himself because of his morning upset, and repeated the entire story to LoBianco. "I caught the case," he said, when he was done. "And you're going to work it with me. Once the press gets hold of this, you and I are going to be famous."

"We should make '60 Minutes,'" LoBianco said.

"We should live so long," Berger said. "Borough PR people will do all our talking for us, but if we behave, maybe they'll let us mill around in the background during the press conference. Some fun, huh?"

"Yeah," LoBianco said. "But all that shit aside, why you? You think you know the creep who did this?"

"I must," Berger said. "Or maybe it's somebody I busted forty years ago or somebody who was at my wedding. Or my wife's old boyfriend. I haven't moved in years. Anybody knows me finds me."

"So what you're saying is, you don't know," LoBianco said.

"What I'm saying is, we got a lot of work to do, and we've got to do it quietly or we'll lose the squeal to some hotshot deputy inspector at One Police Plaza," Berger said, referring to police headquarters in Manhattan.

"Would that be so bad?" LoBianco asked. "Psychos are tough nuts to crack."

"A punster?" Berger said. "Just what I need. Like my bunions. But listen, I want to get this perp. He knows where I live and he—"

"Knows where your wife lives," LoBianco finished.

"And I'm not letting some *verkakhte* boss from Manhattan fuck up this investigation. This hand thing makes my feet hurt. And if you know anything about me, that's a real bad sign."

"Your feet hurt every day," LoBianco said.

"And every day's a horror, isn't it?" Berger came back. "Every single day."

"Maybe you should go to a doctor," LoBianco said.

"Maybe I need some chicken soup."

"Too bad I didn't know," LoBianco said. "I just made me some Rooster soup this morning."

At 9:30 A.M. Lieutenant Santamyer called Berger and LoBianco into his glass-walled office. It smelled like a cigarette factory.

"What is it with this hand business?" he asked Berger between coughing fits.

"That's what we're trying to find out," Berger said.

Santamyer was the most literal man Berger had ever known. He believed anything anyone told him—literally. A joke, a pun, a play on words, or an entry from the *Encyclopaedia Britannica* were all processed by Santamyer's brain in exactly the same way. If you told him you were hungry enough to eat a horse, he volunteered that he didn't like horse meat. If you said it was as cold as a witch's tit outside, he'd inquire as to the temperature of witches' breasts.

"I don't like this one," Santamyer said. "What else have you got working?"

Berger recited a list of cases that included two burglaries, four assaults, three robberies, and a score of drug cases.

"We're busier than a one-armed paperhanger," Lo-Bianco said.

Santamyer stroked his round chin, as if trying to envision such a person, then said, "I don't see how a one-armed—"

"Not too busy to take this one," Berger interrupted, giving LoBianco a dark look. "I *want* this one, Lew," he said, using police lingo for lieutenant. Santamyer's first name was Erich, but everyone called him Lieutenant, Lew, or Boss when they had to; the rest of the time they tried to avoid him.

An austere man with completely bland, regular features and thin gray-yellow hair, Santamyer was the least demanding boss Berger had ever served. He let Berger crack the whip while he mastered the paperwork. They got along fine.

"Okay," Santamyer said. "But don't spend too much time on this. No one's complained about missing fingers and hands yet."

"Right, Lew," Berger said, herding LoBianco out of the lieutenant's office.

"No one's complained?" LoBianco said when they were seated at their desks in the bullpen. "That's sick."

"That's Santamyer," Berger said. "He's the ultimate bureaucrat. A week after he retires no one will be able to remember his name. Pictures of him at police functions will begin to fade. Pretty soon it will be as if he never existed at all.

"But until then don't go out of your way to piss him off. I've worked for a lot worse bosses—and you will, too."

"What kind of name is Santamyer?" LoBianco wondered out loud. "Santa is maybe Puerto Rican and Myer is Jewish or German. He's a German Jewish Puerto Rican?"

"He's a lieutenant," Berger said. "That's a race of people you don't want to mess with."

"No, seriously," LoBianco persisted.

"Seriously I never asked him. I was afraid he'd give me eight hundred years of genealogy," Berger said.

They spent the next seven hours trying to clear their desks of current cases, checked twice with the medical examiner's office about the hand, established a working plan for investigating this bizarre case, and got nowhere in particular.

At the end of the day Berger leaned back in his green swivel chair and pushed his wire-rimmed glasses to his forehead. "You know what's bothering me?" he said to LoBianco, who was mired in a mountain of paperwork.

"No. What could possibly be bothering you?" LoBianco smirked.

"The note said, 'Help us,' yet we don't know what it really meant or who it's from. Is it a cry for help from a sick mind or is it a victim pleading for our aid?"

"Yeah?"

"So I want to know who wants help—the victims or the perp?" Berger said.

"When you find out, be sure to call me," LoBianco said, not wanting to think about the case anymore.

Berger sighed and looked at the single, badly typed sheet of paper in front of him.

### Hand Case

A. Check with FBI—similar cases.
B. Wait for fingerprint analysis and coordinate with Missing Persons.
C. Canvass my neighborhood. Did anyone see someone drop off a package at my door?
D. Does the perp know me? Rose?
E. Check with shrink for profile of perp.
F. Wait for perp to send another message to me? To kill again?
G. Buy Rose a new bathrobe.

"Let's blow this candy store," LoBianco said at seven. "We're burning up our overtime. I'll buy you a drink."

"I could use a seltzer for my ulcer," Berger said. "Give me a minute." He dialed his home number; it rang ten times before he hung up.

"Two seltzers," he said to LoBianco as they left.

Michael's was a bar two blocks from the station house. It had been there since the time when all the cops in the precinct had been named Michael, Sean, and Seamus. It had always been owned by the DiBartolo family, who knew a bar called Luigi's wouldn't have drawn such a huge crowd in those days. These days you could call it Jacob's, Washington's, or Le Bleu Moon and it wouldn't have mattered much. But Michael's it had always been and Michael's it would always be, even if the DiBartolos sold out to the Colombians.

Michael's featured two huge rooms. In the first, at the long wooden bar, scarred by cigarette burns, sat thirty cops on rickety wooden stools. A row of booths seating six small or four large cops lined the right wall. Danny DiBartolo, the present owner's father, had caused a flap in 1953 when he reupholstered the red plastic banquettes in green plastic. The cops were pissed. They didn't like change. Most of them had returned from World War II or Korea and most definitely didn't like green. Under tremendous pressure, Danny ripped out the green plastic and put in blue for the cops. It hadn't been changed since then, but nobody minded the cuts, slits, burns, and stuffing oozing through the faded and cracked blue plastic.

In the back room were twenty-five small tables and two pool tables. All the tables had matchbook covers under their legs to compensate for the floor's distinct tilt to the left. It took an expert house player to compensate for the leftward lean of the pool tables; the balls tended to gather together like sheep in a thunderstorm.

The pool room was for the younger cops in general and most of the female cops in particular. The hormone level was high and dangerous; the jukebox blared out post-1989 Rolling Stones, the occasional Run DMC, and the B-52's. Dancing slow was permitted as a good way for a cop to cop a quick feel; heavy drinking was frowned upon.

In deference to Berger, LoBianco sat at the bar in the front room. This was where the old guys gathered to drink themselves back to normal after a long tour. These were the hard-core, divorced, impotent cops who preferred the music of Frank Sinatra or doo-wop to the incomprehensible racket of Motley Crüe. The hormone level was low; the violence level was high; and drinks like white wine were frowned upon.

"I haven't been here in years," Berger said, looking around at the dark, stained wood and moth-eaten collection of animal heads on the wall. "And now I see why."

"Relax, Ira," Sonny said. "We're off duty. What'll you have?"

"Plain seltzer, I can't stay long," Berger said.

"Need a kitchen pass to get out of the house?" LoBianco said, laughing.

"What about you?" Berger said defensively. "Why don't you go home to your wife?"

"Nothing I'd like more," LoBianco said. "She doesn't live with me any longer."

"Since when?"

"Since six months ago," LoBianco said. "Threw me out of the house."

"For drinking?"

"For a better life or maybe another guy," LoBianco said. "Said I was okay, but wasn't what she wanted. No money, no status, and apparently no balls. She tells me this after three years together—two married."

A private man, Berger had never discussed his personal life with LoBianco; hearing about LoBianco's marital problems embarrassed him.

LoBianco ordered a Jack Daniel's on the rocks. Berger sipped his seltzer, wondering what to say.

"Have you tried talking to her?" Berger asked.

"Hell, no. When you go up against a perp or deal with a woman, you can't show any weakness," LoBianco said. "She'll come back when she starts to miss me."

"Then you'll take her back?" Berger asked, stirring his seltzer.

"Not right away. Let the bitch suffer," LoBianco said.

But Berger knew a lie when he heard one. The trouble with being young, he thought, is that you have to be macho, too. He and Rose had had their troubles over the years, especially over their lack of children, but they came from backgrounds where divorce was the equivalent of committing a crime. Today, neither crime nor divorce counted for much.

"I'm sorry about, uh . . ."

"Angela. And when I say it's another guy, I don't really *know* it's another guy," LoBianco said.

You know it, all right, Berger thought, or you wouldn't be blurting out these confidences so easily.

"Then there's hope?" he said.

"I'm meeting her here tonight," LoBianco said. "She called me."

"Good. A good wife is a valuable asset," Berger said. "A pain in the ass sometimes, but a valuable asset. And right now I'm worried about Rose. She may be in danger and I'm sitting here jawing with you."

"But she's not home, is she?" LoBianco asked.

"No, Mr. Detective, she's not. Or at least she's not answering the phone," Berger said.

"Another man?" LoBianco said, smiling.

"Not my Rose," Berger said, offended. But he couldn't help thinking about Gross, the butcher. "I've got to go. Don't drink too much and have a nice talk with your wife."

LoBianco watched him leave and smiled. He was a nice old guy, but he was living in the distant past, the sixties, maybe.

"Another Jack on the rocks," he said to the bartender. Angela would be there in an hour. Maybe things would get better, because right now they sure sucked.

**3**

Mother had come back. And that was bad news for Charles Maris, very bad news, as he and his mother had never gotten along. In fact, he had been positive he had seen the last of her when he had buried her in Green-Wood Cemetery.

But now she was back and he knew instinctively that big changes were on the way.

Funny, he thought, she had telephoned. Mother had never approved of telephones. She had always found them cold and mechanical; she had preferred to torture him, his sister, and his aunt in person. Found it more amusing to watch their faces as they squirmed and writhed under her barrage of disapproval.

Charles shuddered involuntarily and tightened his big, white hands around the garrote he had fashioned from piano wire and wooden pegs. It twanged nicely when he snapped it.

He had chosen a garrote for this night's work because it was neat, almost bloodless, and silent—words that might have described Maris himself. An inch over six feet, he weighed more than two hundred and sixty pounds. With his big, freckled moon face and short sandy hair, he looked stupid and harmless. He was neither. For beneath the flabby exterior dwelled the real Charles Maris—a lean, mean, killing machine—straining to get out of the fat man's body. On the outside, Charles was as blond and placid as the Pillsbury doughboy; inside, he had professional contempt for Manson and Bundy. He knew he would never be caught.

The garrote twanged again, reassuring him that the person within him was still in charge. Tonight was his first hunt; he didn't want to mess it up.

He had to replace the hands before Mother found out. He wanted to surprise her, placate her, and this was the only way he knew.

Hands, he thought, beautiful, whole, matching hands; no cutting and suturing.

For the last four days Maris had studied the woman whose hands he would harvest tonight. Originally he had wanted to take her feet, but the disappearance of the hand he had so carefully constructed made him change his mind. Why had Emily taken the hand to the policeman? he wondered. Why was she always so obstructive?

It didn't matter, he told himself. The woman he had been following had lovely hands, too. He knew her glove size was six, and that she had long, slim fingers topped with short nails. Mother wouldn't approve of the long red nails women wore today, he thought. Nor would she like chubby fingers, calluses, or the reddened, careworn hands of a housewife. They had to be perfect. Perfect for Emily.

On the principle that you don't shit where you live, Charles had left his home in Bay Ridge and had staked out a victim in Bensonhurst. These two sections of Brooklyn abutted each other, but Maris had convinced himself that Bensonhurst was somehow morally inferior to Bay Ridge. The 1989 killing of a black kid by a gang of Italian youths had upset him. The damned wops had let the nigger's two companions live and that was not neat or efficient in Charles's mind. When you kill, kill clean. That was his newly adopted motto.

He waited patiently, hidden in the shadows of the

school's graffiti-covered service entrance. The neighborhood was quiet as a grave, he thought. And that disturbed
him because Mother had become anything but quiet recently. If she could come back to haunt him, why not Maria
Parulo? That was the name of his victim, a Spanish teacher
at New Utrecht High School. She had worked late three
nights in a row, never leaving the building before seven.

He checked his watch: 7:10 P.M. Any minute now, he
thought. Patience, prudence. Those words, spoken by George
Bush, had impressed him. George Bush looked like a wimp,
spoke like a wimp, but apparently had someone else inside
him, telling him to invade Middle Eastern countries. Charles
could understand how the president felt.

Suddenly it seemed to Charles as if the world had stopped
dead. The darkness became light; the light, darkness. Like a
negative, he thought. There was an eerie silence, then a
roaring in his ears. He shook his head to clear his thoughts,
and within a few seconds the world had subsided to its usual
soft darkness.

A brain explosion, he thought. He had had them ever
since he could remember. They were as much a part of him
as his arms and legs.

He wiped his brow, feeling the sweet begin to evaporate
in the chill night air. Not now, he thought wildly. No more
brain explosions while I'm hunting. He clenched his big
square teeth, ordering his brain to refrain from interrupting.

That's when he heard the staccato beat of a woman's high
heels on the linoleum inside the school.

*Maria.*

He melted back into the shadows.

She pushed open the self-locking door, smashing it into
Charles's big body. Then, without looking behind her, she
walked purposefully down the ramp and out onto the
sidewalk.

"Damn," Charles muttered. He had missed her. But all
was not lost. He knew where she was headed. He also knew
a shortcut.

Walking quickly, but not fast enough to attract attention, Charles cut diagonally across an empty, weed-choked lot and took up position near the entrance to the subway station. In the dark, he was invisible. He felt fine and aroused to be this near his victim. Already he could hear the sound of her heels on the concrete.

She's hurrying, he thought. This is a safe neighborhood, but a woman alone at night always has to be cautious. Prudent.

Her caution made him feel powerful and in control. His skin grew cool and dry; an exhilarating tension filled his ample belly. To his shame, he began to grow hard.

He could sense her now, and felt sure she could feel the heat of his body. Her footsteps faltered, then stopped.

She knows, he groaned.

But then the rapid tap of her shoes began again and he let out his breath.

Almost there.

Charles Maris emerged from the darkness, a huge lumbering man. He tried to look contrite. "I'm so sorry," he said softly.

"Excuse me?" she said, confused. He didn't look dangerous to her, his big freckled face oddly expressionless.

Then he was behind her and she felt a searing pain as the garrote bit deeply into her flesh. She tried to scream, but could not. She attempted to fight, but her arms only jerked and flailed, clawing the empty air. Her face flushed, then turned a deep purple; her tongue lolled from her mouth, giving her a slightly ridiculous look.

Charles felt the woman's body twist, stiffen, then go limp. A foul stench rose from her as her bladder and bowels let go.

Using the garrote as a handle, he pulled her body off the vacant street and into the more secure confines of the deserted lot.

It annoyed him considerably that the woman had fouled herself. He had expected the kill to be much cleaner.

As he lowered her body beneath a covering hedge something fell from the woman's shoulder bag: an appointment book about the size of a paperback book.

He picked it up. Using his chronograph for light, he examined the entries.

He had hoped for some scandalous secrets, but the appointment book contained a young woman's predictable schedule: lunches, meetings, the date of her next period.

Reading entry after entry in Maria Parulo's tedious life made Charles wonder why women—women like his mother and aunt—lived by such predictable schedules. They led regimented lives and died regimented deaths. Except perhaps Mother. She seemed to be more unpredictable in death than she had been in life.

If Maria Parulo had varied her routine, she would be alive today, he thought solemnly.

He turned to the first page and saw words that stunned him: *Today is the first day of the rest of my life.* It was a message for him, he knew. His life would surely change after tonight. He wondered how Maria Parulo knew about him . . . and about Mother.

Carefully he closed the book and slipped it into his pocket. Then he untangled the bloody garrote from her partially severed head, put it in his other pocket, and gently arranged her body on the cold ground.

Modestly he pushed her knees together, then placed her arms across her chest. He wanted to see her body, but even in the open air he could smell feces and urine. That put him off. Besides, he wasn't after sex tonight. He was after hands. Hands for Emily.

He opened a small leather bag containing a scalpel and surgical gloves. Pulling on the gloves, Charles lifted the scalpel, taking a moment to look at the woman's contorted face. Gently he pushed her tongue back into her mouth with his index finger; her dead eyes continued to stare at him in terror.

He smiled at her and chivalrously took her left hand in his

and kissed it. Soon it would be Emily's. He saw this as a gallant gesture, a gesture right out of the stories Mother used to read to him when he was a child.

Although it was too dark to see properly, Charles felt Maria Parulo's hand all over. It was flawless. He smiled and kissed her fingertips lovingly, before twisting her hand, exposing the vulnerable underside of the wrist.

He pressed the scalpel against the skin and made his initial incision with skill and care. There was very little blood. The dead didn't bleed much, Charles knew.

He hummed as he cut.

The streets of Bay Ridge were as quiet as those of Bensonhurst when Charles, breathing hard from the long walk, trudged up the twelve steps to his brownstone. Two stone lions at the top of the stairs welcomed him home.

He needed three keys to unlock the black-lacquered door, then went into the dank, dusty foyer.

The floor of the entry hall had once been black-and-white marble; now it was a uniform filthy gray. On his left was a dead, brown rubber plant, on the right, an elephant's-foot umbrella stand that his grandmother had purchased at the turn of the century.

He tossed his keys into a tarnished silver card tray and opened the sliding wooden doors to his study. His big crepe-soled shoes left ridge marks in the dust, like the tracks of a tank.

''Mother?'' he called out cautiously.

No answer.

Good, he thought. She's not here yet.

He flicked on the dim overhead light and surveyed his private domain. Ten-foot-high oak bookshelves lined the room; thousands of rotting leather-bound books gave off the smell of genteel corruption. But it was a familiar smell, a comfort to Charles.

The twenty-by-forty-foot Persian rug, once bright and colorful, looked like gray plush carpeting. Small clouds of dust followed Charles to the ornate carved desk. He carefully put a Styrofoam box down on the leather-topped desk.

"Today was the last day of the rest of your life," he said to Maria Parulo's hands, opening the lid of the box. "But you will live again." Black clots had gathered near the severed stumps of her wrists. Charles smiled in anticipation.

"I've got them. I got them for you, Emily," he said. "I'm good to you, aren't I? I'm your loving brother. Mother will be proud of me when she comes back."

The silence in the big, dusty room was oppressive, the atmosphere thick with cold humid air and tortured memories.

"Emily? Aren't you proud of me?"

He heard only the ticking of the brass clock on the desk.

"Won't you talk to me?" he asked plaintively.

But Emily, as was her habit, kept silent.

Charles didn't expect much from Emily. He had, after all, hurt her terribly, but he desperately wanted some gratitude for his efforts to make her whole again.

He opened his mouth to berate her, but suddenly shook violently as if to dispel an inner darkness that had seeped into him. By sheer force of will, he stopped another brain explosion. He stood, taking deep breaths of the foul air.

Composing himself, he pointed angrily to the shadowy corner where the cane-backed wheelchair waited.

"If you don't want my help, all you have to do is say so," he said petulantly. "Perhaps a few days alone might make you realize what a sacrifice I'm making for you."

He waited.

"Well, all right. I'm doing it for you and Mother, then. I've spent my entire life doing things for you, and I think it's time you showed me at least a little bit of gratitude.

"Emily? You know I love you. You're my sister. I didn't mean to hurt—"

He stopped, feeling the tears well up. He had to get away from her accusing silence. Securing the lid on the Styrofoam

box, he left the study and went back into the dark foyer.
Beneath the stairs, covered with once wine-colored carpeting, now faded to the color of rust, was a massive door to
the basement. He unlocked it.

"You'll thank me for this," he said quietly. "One day."

# 4

"Is that you, Ira?" Rose Berger called from the kitchen.

"No, it's your lover, Gross, the butcher," Berger yelled back. His feet hurt worse than sin.

He shed his raincoat on the straight-backed chair in the hall, kicked off his ugly, black "space shoes," which not only hurt his feet but his pride as well, then gingerly limped into the chintz-adorned living room. He sat in his brown vinyl BarcaLounger and hoisted his feet up. Another tour completed, he thought, pushing his wire-rimmed glasses up to his forehead and rubbing his tired eyes.

Something was poking him in the kidneys. He reached behind him and grabbed a plastic doll, a high-fashion Barbie, that to Berger looked more like a hooker.

"What's with the doll, Rose?" he called out. Was this some kind of hint?

"Doll?"

"The one sitting in my chair," Berger yelled. He was too tired for this.

"I don't know what you're talking about," she said, appearing in the living room, wiping her hands on a blue apron. She looked relaxed, happy, and Berger groaned inwardly, even younger than usual.

He held the Barbie by the legs, shaking it in her direction. "This doll, Rose," he said.

"You're being contentious again," she said.

" 'Contentious'?"

"And cantankerous."

"What is it with the words, Rose?" he asked, throwing the doll on the floor.

"*Reader's Digest*. I'm improving my vocabulary," she said.

"Improve your cooking, Rose. Your vocabulary's good enough for me."

"For you I cook. For others maybe I want to improve my vocabulary," she said smugly, retreating to the kitchen.

"Gross the butcher's a Rhodes scholar, maybe?" he mumbled, but she pretended not to hear him.

"Your boss called," she said.

"Santamyer?"

"The same," she said. "He wants you should call him back."

Berger pushed the recliner into an upright position. Immediately his feet began to throb again.

"This is Detective Sergeant Berger," he said, after dialing the precinct number. "Give me the lew."

"Berger?" Santamyer said, getting on the line. "We had a squeal. A woman who was killed, the perp took her hands."

"Where?"

"With him, I guess," Santamyer said, puzzled.

"No. I mean where did this happen?"

As Santamyer told him the throbbing in his feet intensified. He wanted to kick the doll on the floor, but he knew it would hurt more than help.

The crime scene was only a ten-minute walk from his apartment. Is this too close to be a coincidence? he wondered.

"Where are you going?" Rose asked as Berger limped toward the door, shoes in hand.

"I'm going out for a hobble," Berger said. "Put that in your Funk and Wagnall's."

* * *

A twelve-year-old kid named Joey Lupo, following some logic known only to twelve-year-olds, had decided that the low hedge in the vacant lot adjacent to the subway station would make a neat place to hang out. It was a space station like in *Star Wars,* he told the cops later, a place where he could defend the universe from the bad guys. Unfortunately for Maria Parulo, he was a half hour too late to save her universe.

When he found Maria's body, he immediately forgot about alien invaders, and about telling his mother he was going to a friend's house to study, and set a record running home. His mother had threatened to spank him, a ludicrous suggestion as he was at least two inches taller than she. After a few more threats, the mother phoned the police.

By the time Berger arrived, a little after eight o'clock, a crime-scene perimeter had been established, klieg lights erected, and a group of rubberneckers had gathered to observe police procedures, hoping perhaps to see a dead body.

Berger clipped his gold shield to the lapel of his raincoat and jostled his way through the crowd. He looked for and found LoBianco. The kid's furious, Berger thought. He should be with his wife, but he looks like he could chew nails. So much for the show-no-weakness theory. He'd have a difficult time explaining to Angela why he had stood her up, Berger thought, motioning to his partner. Then he grabbed the arm of an assistant medical examiner he knew slightly.

"What happened, Jerry?" Berger asked.

"Over there," Jerry Stivers said. "Death by strangulation. The left greater horn of thyroid cartilage was broken and the left cricoid severely damaged." He gave his preliminary report in a crisp, businesslike manner. No jokes, no bullshitting. Berger appreciated that.

Using the second and third fingers of his right hand,

Stivers ran them down the left side of Berger's neck to demonstrate the site of the injuries. Berger shivered.

"Someone strangled the victim with a wire probably," Stivers said. "An extremely strong person; he almost decapitated her."

"A man?"

"Sure," Stivers said, shrugging. "Or some very butch broad."

Berger nodded and walked over to the knot of technicians who had clustered like flies around Maria Parulo's body.

She lay where Charles Maris had left her, on her back, her arms crossed peacefully on her chest. The stumps of her wrists were black with clotted blood.

"So young," Berger said to LoBianco.

"To you, everybody's young," LoBianco said. "But I know what you mean."

Ignoring his partner, Berger spoke quickly to the technicians, making sure they collected the contents of the woman's purse, went over every bit of ground searching for cigarette butts, bits of cloth, hair—anything that might lead them to the perpetrator.

"I guess there's no point in fingerprinting the body," LoBianco said, trying to lighten the mood.

"When the victim laughs, I'll laugh," Berger said sourly. "You shouldn't forget this case began in my kitchen, in my home. I can't shake the feeling that this is only the beginning. And we're helpless."

"Helpless?" LoBianco asked.

"You drive over here?" Berger said.

"Yeah, I told the bartender to look out for Angela, but with my luck she'll take a quick look into Michael's, think I stood her up, and leave," LoBianco said.

"It happens," Berger said. "Let's sit in your car and think for a minute about what all this means."

When they got to LoBianco's Corvette, Berger said, "You couldn't afford a bigger car?"

"It's big enough for me," LoBianco said.

"I don't like automobiles," Berger said. "Never owned one. How do I get into this thing?"

"You have to be young," LoBianco said, opening the door for him. "Just scrunch down and put your feet in the well."

"An instrument of torture," Berger said, groaning as he got into the low-slung Vette.

"My cousin Gene, who weighs a good two-seventy-five, says the fit in here is tighter than a virgin," LoBianco said. "It's not much of a make-out car. Though I've had some interesting times in here. Look for the ass prints on the window."

Berger snorted. He didn't like the sexual talk most cops insisted was just normal bullshit. Even when he was younger, such talk had embarrassed him. Guilt, he thought, my life is awash in guilt.

"Damn," Berger said. "I forgot to buy that robe for Rose." He had also forgotten to ask her where she had been all day. He didn't know if he wanted to know.

"Get it tomorrow," LoBianco said. "And let's get on with this. I've got to call Angela."

"It won't take long," Berger said. "I want to get home, too. Rose is alone."

"What did you mean back there," LoBianco asked, "when you said we were helpless?"

"Precisely that. Most homicides are committed for two reasons: monetary gain or some kind of family dispute. In other words, homicide for love or money.

"Those cases are cracked by traditional police work: talking to neighbors, grilling suspects, good forensic evidence, and so on.

"What we have here is—how do I put this delicately—a fucking nut."

LoBianco laughed. It was the first time he had heard Berger use the F word.

"And we ain't gonna catch him till he makes a mistake," LoBianco said. "Or he wants to get caught."

"I see you paid attention to my previous lectures," Berger said. "And you're right."

"We need a profiler, a criminal profiler from the FBI," LoBianco said.

"And we have little chance of getting one anytime soon. So we've got to use our common sense. That's all criminal profiling is, anyway. Common sense," Berger said, shifting uncomfortably in the red leather bucket seat.

"Yeah," LoBianco said. "Common sense and experience. And between us we've got forty-two years of experience. Forty for you, two for me."

"It's enough," Berger said. "I hope."

There was a tap at the window. Berger fumbled, looking for the window handle; Sonny hit the electric button in the central console.

Dr. Jerry Stivers leaned in. "We found a pair of latex gloves, surgical gloves, in the lot," he said.

"No fingerprint possibility, I guess?" Berger said.

"None," Stivers said.

"Well, unlike the movies, one piece of physical evidence does not a case make," Berger said.

"Sorry," Stivers said, walking back toward the lights and activity of the crime scene.

"Me too," Berger said softly. "We've got to think of ourselves as doctors. We look at the symptoms and try to diagnose the disease. We collect data, reconstruct the crime, develop a hypothesis, and attempt to prove it."

"Or we bang heads until we find the disease who fucking did it," LoBianco said.

"That, too," Berger mused.

Charles Maris threw open the three bolts securing the door to the basement. Inside, he pulled a light cord and a dim, fly-specked bulb poured out a feeble glow, illuminating the wooden steps and the darker shadows below.

Charles positioned his weight carefully on each step, holding tightly to the rough, splintered banister. He had nightmares about crashing through the bone-dry wooden staircase. In his left hand, he clutched the Styrofoam box containing Maria Parulo's hands.

A restless shuffling rose from the darkness. Maris greeted the sounds with a low whistling; the shuffling became agitated.

At the bottom of the stairs, Maris pulled a second chain switch, lighting a section of the basement. The damp stone walls were covered with a greenish fungus; rivulets of moisture condensed in a dry well and then drained by means of a sump pump. The floor was cement, but so mildewed as to be slippery. Maris had found it to be too much work to clean up the fungus and had crisscrossed the floor with long strips of black rubber runners. The smell would have made anyone else sick. To Charles, it was home.

The shuffling noise came from the second room, where a number of wire dog cages lined the wall in a row.

The dogs responded eagerly to Maris, pawing and pacing as he continued to whistle to them. They didn't bark because each one had had its larynx removed. They were bred for fighting, not making a racket. Besides, Emily was frightened of their loud voices, Maris thought. Now they were as silent as Emily herself.

Charles understood dogs and appreciated their social instincts. Whether in the wild or in a domestic situation, dogs, like most pack animals, lived by a simple rule: the best went first. In a dog's world the meek did not inherit the earth. More than likely a timid pup would never make it past whelping. Dogs dominated each other by size, ferocity, and intelligence.

Through obedience training Maris had made himself indispensable to his dogs. They relied on him, followed him, and loved him; he was the leader of the pack.

He surveyed the six caged dogs. They were the superb result of ten years of breeding. A devotee of the American pit bull terrier, and at one time a power in the shadowy world of dogfighting, Charles had attempted to improve the breed.

Pit bulls, he knew, where descended from bulldogs—that is, dogs bred for bullbaiting, a popular sport in the Middle Ages. The dogs were set on a bull and expected to leap up and sink their fangs into the bull's neck. They would not let go until they died or the bull collapsed from loss of blood.

The modern American pit bull terrier inherited many attributes of its ancestors: tremendous strength, agility, intelligence, and a biting power unequaled in the dog world. Bred to fight other dogs, the pit bull lived for a chance to attack an opponent. Herding dogs herded, hunting dogs hunted, and fighting dogs fought, an obvious point lost on those who considered such contests cruel. But Charles knew his dogs could never be happy unless they were in the ring. They loved it, they couldn't exist without it.

More game than a German shepherd or Doberman, a forty-pound pit bull could eat both of them for breakfast and not work up a sweat. Yet pit bulls were curiously docile in their trainer's hands. They had to be. Fighting dogs had to be ministered to during a roll, and if they took out their aggression on their masters, there wouldn't be any masters left. Although perfectly capable of killing a grown man, pit bulls, as one expert observed, were a thousand times less likely to attack a human than was another breed. But when they did, they were a thousand times more deadly.

Maris had loved the breed since he was a youngster and his reputation in the pits was formidable. But for the past few years he had shifted his interest from fighting the animals to breeding them.

Reasoning that a taller dog had an advantage over a shorter opponent, Charles had begun breeding pit bulls with Rhodesian Ridgebacks, a tough African dog noted for its ferocity and stamina. When the latter was combined with gameness and biting power, the result, Charles believed, would usher in a new era of dogfighting. He longed for a champion line bearing his name.

His favorite dog, Maris Rhody Dempsey (after the fighter), was big for a pit bull cross. At almost fifty pounds, Dempsey had a black muzzle and yellow eyes. He had a long, well-muscled neck for a good reach, a square compact body, deep rib cage, and low-set tail. Dempsey was a perfect-looking dog, but he had something more. As a nursing pup he would occasionally leave his sucking position and for no apparent reason attack a feeding sibling, driving it away from the bitch's side. Maris admired that drive; it couldn't be taught. It was innate.

Maris released the dogs from their cages. They stood, expectant, as Maris went to the slatework sink, put the Styrofoam box aside, and filled their individual bowls with water. Then he spooned out heaping portions of meat and kibble. None of the dogs moved until Maris had placed the bowls in front of them. He waited a moment to make sure they understood who was in control, then gave the signal. They leaped at the food, as they would attack an opponent in the pits.

As the dogs ate, Maris moved from one to the next, cooing their names softly, rubbing their spines where the fur grew the wrong way, and massaging the identical six-inch scars under their muzzles: proof of their silence. For money, some vets would do anything.

The dogs showed no aggression at Maris's closeness to their food. He was the master—number one in their pecking order—and they trusted him with their lives, and with their food.

The room housing the dogs also served as their conditioning area. Two treadmills occupied a corner; three spring poles were positioned in another corner. The treadmills were for roadwork; the poles, resembling small lampposts, were crossed by a horizontal metal bar. Hanging from the bar was a knotted rope. The dogs were trained to jump six feet in the air, catch the rope, and hang there until ordered to drop. The exercise was intended to strengthen their jaw muscles, but Maris knew that a champion fighter was born, not trained. The only real mistake a trainer could make was to train the wrong dog for the pits.

He left the dogs to their meal, crossed the room, and opened a heavy steel door with a large key he had stashed near the pit bulls' food. He threw a switch and bright, blinding light flooded the subbasement.

Unlike the rest of the house, Maris kept the subbasement scrupulously clean. He walked out onto the metal catwalk that rimmed the twenty-by-twenty square ring, a full story below the basement. It was up here that spectators had gathered to watch the dogfights in the pit below. Maris had accommodated as many as one hundred and fifty bettors and spectators at one time, safe from the prying eyes of the Humane Society and the ASPCA.

Maris sighed. He missed magnificent battles in which two beasts tore each other apart. It was spectacle, tradition. Like bullfighting. Except people weren't usually killed during a fighting roll. It was humane, for humans, he thought.

In turning his interest from fighting to breeding, however, Maris had developed quite another hobby. He had transformed the pit into an operating theater. He could almost imagine doctors and nurses observing his procedures from the spectators' seats, congratulating him, applauding him.

From his perch high above the pit where countless dogs had fought, bled, and died for their masters, Maris looked down on a ten-foot metal table. It was incised with blood drains, the kind of table pathologists used during autopsies. Its stainless-steel surface glinted obscenely under the spotlights. Next to it was a white industrial freezer of the freestanding variety used in supermarkets.

Maris whistled for the dogs and they dutifully followed him down the spiral staircase to the floor of his operating room.

He was drawn to the freezer, as if it had religious significance. And in a way it did. Everything he held sacred was contained within that freezer. His life's work. He ran the palms of both hands over the cold white smoothness, enjoying the tingling sensation.

He closed his eyes, but an image formed there, the image of a little girl, about four years old. She was very pretty, with dark curls and pink cheeks; she was wearing a blue pinafore and shiny black Mary Janes.

She opened her mouth to say something and Charles screamed. Screamed as if he could never stop.

Berger returned home too tired to sleep, too sleepy to do anything useful. He sat in the dark living room, amid the detritus of his life, feeling empty and dull.

The streetlight outside cast a feeble glow on the chintz-covered furniture, making it seem eerily insubstantial. Matches my life, he thought.

He had almost succeeded in dropping off to sleep when the living-room lights came on with a blinding flash. Blinking rapidly, he caught the afterimage of Rose, dressed in her disgusting pink robe, standing in the doorway.

"Ira, come to bed," she said.

"In a minute."

"Are we having a fight?" she asked.

"I'm not," he said. "How about you?"

"A struggle maybe," she said. "Not a fight."

"Then struggle off to bed, Rose. I'll be in shortly."

He watched her shrug and retreat down the hall. All these years of trying to please her had been a failure. He had rescued her from her harridan mother and harpylike sister, but he had not given her the one thing she wanted more than anything else in the world: a baby.

They had screwed themselves blue in the face, visited doctors and fortune-tellers, fertility clinics and quacks. He had read so many scientific and popular articles and books on reproduction, he felt qualified to hang out his shingle. But still no baby. And now he was too old to look forward to the prospect of changing dirty diapers and wiping snotty noses. He hoped Rose would have her change of life quickly and forget all about this baby nonsense.

He pushed these irritating thoughts from his mind and concentrated on a greater reality: his aching feet.

# 5

Sonny LoBianco woke up with a headache and a hard-on. The headache was caused by screaming sirens, the hard-on by a voluptuous civilian police aide, Lucy Velez, who slept soundly next to him.

He propped himself up on one elbow and tried to make sense of what was happening. Lucy reached for him, moving her hand up his thigh, looking, even in sleep, for his cock. He glanced at the floor and saw the melted ice cubes in a plastic bowl. Lucy had done things with the ice cubes and her mouth that made him smile even as the shrieking sirens got closer.

Groggily, LoBianco tried to reconstruct the evening before. After dropping Berger, he had gone back to Michael's, but no one had seen Angela. He had called her, but she hadn't picked up the phone. He, however, did pick up Lucy Velez.

Feeling guilty and proud of himself at the same time, LoBianco got out of bed and walked to one of the barred windows to see what was going on.

"Holy shit," he said, seeing the beat-up bus in the driveway burning like a torch.

Lucy opened one eye and leered at him. He grabbed for his clothes, his erection waving in front of him ridiculously.

"Get up," he said. "We've got a fire."

41

"Let it burn," she said, burrowing into the covers.

LoBianco grabbed a pair of jeans and a worn leather jacket and went to the door. For the past six months, since he had left Angela or she had thrown him out, depending on whose side of the story was to be believed, he had been living in a three-car garage owned by the St. Agnes Children's Shelter. The shelter was run by Franklyn Davis, a black Catholic priest, Vietnam vet, former addict, hardass, and a man who found God late in life. He had raised hundreds of kids, including Sonny LoBianco. Although he would never admit it, Sonny had come home.

"Father D!" he called out, running toward the burning bus. A pumper truck almost hit him in its zeal to get to the flames.

"Son of a bitch!" LoBianco yelled at the driver, who ignored him.

With practiced efficiency, two firemen leaped from the truck with hand-held chemical extinguishers, and within a minute had the fire under control. Five minutes later they left the smoldering wreck and went back to the firehouse for coffee and doughnuts.

A fat, red-faced fire marshal stayed behind clucking his tongue. "It was set intentionally," the marshal said. "The intense scorching inside the vehicle indicates a liquid flammable was used. A window on the driver's side was broken. That's probably where they tossed it in. Did anyone see anything?"

The fire marshal eyed the motley crew surrounding him: an enormous black man wearing a bathrobe, a young white guy with no shoes, and a gaggle of kids dressed in pajamas or underwear.

A little girl with long, straight black hair said, "Can I see the fire again?"

"It's all over, LaDonna," Davis said. "Take Shawndell back inside with you."

LaDonna, who was four, grabbed the hand of the two-year-old Shawndell, and said, "Come, Shawndell. Let's see what's for breakfast."

Shawndell went willingly.

"I saw something," volunteered a black kid named E.T. He was thirteen, a smartmouthed little bastard. "I saw guys all dressed in black come jumping off the roof. Then—"

"What are you talking about, E.T.?" Father Davis said. He loved the kid, but E.T. could be a pain in the butt sometimes.

"Yeah, they jumped off the roof, with ropes and—"

"They were ninjas, right?" LoBianco interrupted.

"Yeah," E.T. said, smiling.

"What we have here is an infestation of imagination," Davis said. "Not a ninja attack. And no more karate movies for you, E.T."

"This is arson, Father," the marshal said. "Do you have any idea who might want to torch your bus?"

"I've got several," Davis said. "But I can't prove anything."

The marshal sighed. It was like this all over the god-damned city. Who'd want to burn up a bus belonging to an orphanage?

"Well, if you want to make a statement, call me," the marshal said, handing the priest his business card. "Good luck," he said, getting into his red station wagon and driving away.

"You gonna catch him, Sonny?" E.T. asked. "You gonna blow 'em away?"

"Nope, I'm going back to bed."

"With that white chick?" E.T. asked.

LoBianco looked surprised. Father Davis laughed. "What an imagination," the priest said. "See you at breakfast?"

LoBianco nodded.

The only thing cheerful about the St. Agnes Shelter was the sound of children's voices. Structurally the gray stone buildings were dying; minor repairs postponed the inevitable, but the end was near.

Located four blocks from the boardwalk in Coney Island, it was a depressing hulk that had been built in 1907 as a Catholic orphanage run by the Dominican sisters. It flourished for twenty-five years, then went into decline, as did the neighborhood.

Surrounded by burnt-out buildings, crack dens, and shooting galleries, and infected by a transient population of pimps, prostitutes, and pushers, this ass end of Coney Island had been ignored by the constructors of luxury high rises and middle-income housing. Looking at the ruins, LoBianco thought he might as well be in Williamsburg, Harlem, or Bombay.

It wasn't much, he had decided long ago, but the only real family he had left was Father Davis. His uncle Vito ran a restaurant—along with several associated "businesses"— not a mile away, but LoBianco felt closer to the black priest.

"Hey, Luce," he said, back in his apartment, which still looked like a garage even with a bed, his weights, tatami mats, bags, and a few chairs. "Whadda you say to a little fuck?"

"Morning, little fuck," she said.

Sometimes the old jokes were the best.


"Oatmeal?" Father Davis asked Sonny LoBianco as they sat in one corner of the big kitchen while the older kids cooked breakfast for the little ones.

"How long you known me?" LoBianco asked.

"I don't know, about fourteen, fifteen years," Davis said.

"And in that time have you ever known me to eat oatmeal?"

"You've eaten enough pussy in your time. Oatmeal should be a welcome change," Davis said, spooning a gray lump onto Sonny's plate.

"Pissed off, are we?" LoBianco said.

"Damn right," Davis said. "Those fucking drug dealers torched my only means of transportation."

Davis was six-foot-four and a solid two-fifty. He was

black as coal; his hair was turning white. He had a four-inch scar on his right cheek, the souvenir of a rocket attack in Vietnam, where he had been in the Special Forces. Two tours, too much, he liked to say.

Franklyn Davis was physically, mentally, and spiritually tough. Afraid of nothing personally, he quivered with fear for his forty charges. He knew how most of them would end up. It gave him sleepless nights; it led him to carry a gun during the day. Jesus was his rock; Smith & Wesson was his staff.

"I got the damned dealers hassling the kids. I got real-estate speculators who want to turn St. Agnes into yuppie condos, I got no money, I got no bus, I got—"

"You got a lot of oatmeal," LoBianco said, toying with the gray, gluey stuff suspiciously.

"When the Dominican sisters finally had enough of this place, they turned it over to me. I changed it from an orphanage to a shelter, to get city money. But the good sisters still own the property and they want to sell," Davis said. "They want to open a shelter upstate someplace and run it themselves. I asked them what the hell they were going to do with my kids," Davis said, between mouthfuls of oatmeal.

"And with you," LoBianco said.

"And with me. But that's not important. I can always go back in the oil business," Davis said.

"The oil business?" LoBianco asked.

"Yeah, my black leather jacket, my ski mask, and my gun. 'Okay, gas jockey, this is a holdup,'" Davis said.

LoBianco laughed. "I took care of business yesterday. Tell Beverly Jackson she won't be bothered by the Rooster no more," he said.

"What did you do?" Davis asked sharply.

"You don't want to know," LoBianco said. "So, are you going to close up shop?"

"Never," Davis said.

"Even if they burn you out?" LoBianco said. "The drug dealers, the real-estate people, and the Dominican sisters."

"Yo, Sonny!" E.T. yelled, running over to LoBianco and the priest.

"Yo, yourself," LoBianco said.

"You want me to simonize your car?" E.T. asked. His name was Edward Thomas, but he had an obsession with the Spielberg movie, and in truth, he looked somewhat alien, according to his buddies in the shelter.

"How about Saturday?" LoBianco said.

"Great! Forty bucks, right?" E.T. said.

"Twenty," LoBianco said.

"Deal," E.T. said. "That lady leave yet?"

"Yeah," LoBianco said. "She ran off with the ninjas."

"Buzz off, E.T.," Davis said. "I gotta talk to Sonny."

Disappointed, the boy moved away and Davis said, "I had a run-in with some crack dealers the other day. They were recruiting a couple of my kids to sell for them. In the schools, man. They wanted my kids to sell their shit to other kids at school. Low-life bastards.

"Anyway, I straightened them out, or I thought I did. So now they straightened me out. Me and my bus."

"Your insurance will cover it. Get a rental, meanwhile. I'll pay for it," LoBianco said, shrugging.

"No insurance," Davis said. "I don't have insurance, registration papers, or valid plates. That bus was a rolling bucket of misdemeanors."

"How can you drive around like that? Suppose you got stopped."

"I'd call you," Davis said.

"Father D! Father D!" LaDonna shouted, running up to Davis and throwing herself at him. He lifted her up with one massive arm.

"Sheri's been mean to me," she told him confidentially, whispering into his ear.

"How's that?"

"Well, I was already doing something, and she told me to

do something else, so I told her, 'What do I look like to you, an octopus?' and she said I had a smart mouth. Are you going to punish her?'' LaDonna said in her rapid-fire stage whisper.

"You do have a big mouth for a little girl," Davis said. "Maybe you ought to keep it closed for a while."

"Can't," LaDonna said. "Gotta teach Shawndell his manners."

Shawndell, her shadow, smiled up at Father Davis and raised his arms. Davis picked him up with his other arm.

"Don't get into any trouble, Sonny," Davis said, his arms full of squirming kids.

LoBianco dropped Lucy Velez at her apartment in Bensonhurst, then went to work. He found a bleary-eyed Ira Berger chewing morosely on a bialy and muttering to himself.

The phone rang and LoBianco answered it. "It's for you," he said to Berger.

"Sergeant Berger."

"Morning. This is Sergeant Lopez, up to my ass in fingerprints."

"Very funny," Berger said.

"We got a match on one of those sewed-on fingers."

Berger sat up, pen in hand, and waited.

"The index finger belonged to a Marjorie Cortland, who was a cabdriver a few years back. She was printed and you're damn lucky we made a match so fast. Pure luck," Lopez said.

"Any address?" Berger asked.

"It's twelve years old," Lopez said.

"And I'm sixty, give me an address."

Lopez read him an address in Bensonhurst.

"How about the other fingers?"

"Don't press your luck," Lopez said, hanging up.

"We got a match on one of the fingers. At the Louisa

Court, not ten blocks from here," Berger told LoBianco. "Feel like a walk?"

"Let's do it," LoBianco said.

"It's the kind of day that makes you glad to be in Brooklyn," Berger said as he and LoBianco walked slowly toward Marjorie Cortland's last known address.

"It's the kind of day that makes all the ugliness disappear," Berger continued.

"Next you'll tell me you're glad to be alive," LoBianco said.

"Considering the alternative . . ." Berger breathed in a lungful of fresh, fall air and squinted at the sun. The sky was washed blue and clean; even the low buildings of Bensonhurst looked bright and sparkling.

"No more thoughts of retirement?" LoBianco asked.

"I never had any," Berger said. "Rose wants me to pull the pin."

"Why?"

"Who knows from women? Maybe she wants to wear the pants in the family for a change. Maybe she wants a job and wants me to do the housework," Berger said unhappily.

"You'd look good in an apron, Ira," LoBianco said. "A nice lacy job."

"Easy for you to say, Mr. I'm-Macho-Except-to-My-Wife," Berger said.

"Low blow. Correct, but low," LoBianco said. "Here we are."

Like a fading beauty queen, the Louisa Court clung to the memory of what it had been: the first luxury apartment house in Brooklyn to feature an elevator. Designed in a mock-Moorish style that had swept the borough in the late 1880s, the building had long ago swapped its gilt and marble for paint and plastic.

LoBianco ran a finger down the names listed in the lobby directory. There was no Marjorie Cortland. That would have been too easy, he thought, pressing the super's bell.

"Who?" a voice crackled through the intercom.

"Police," LoBianco said, and was buzzed in.

"Look at that," Berger said, when they were in the cavernous reception area. "It used to be a fountain, a fountain with goldfish in the pool."

LoBianco eyed the green travertine marble structure. "All I see is plastic flowers and dirty AstroTurf," he said.

"A sign of the times," Berger said sadly.

They spotted a handwritten sign indicating that the superintendent's office was at the end of the hall.

A squat, swarthy man was mopping the floor outside the super's office.

"You're the super?" LoBianco asked.

The man shrugged and shook his head. He turned his back on LoBianco and Berger to continue his work.

Berger sighed. LoBianco tensed, ready to unload on the mopper, when the super's door was opened by a bald man with a round, jolly face. He had a beer in one hand and a heavy wrench in the other.

"Police?" he asked.

LoBianco flashed his shield and the super dropped the wrench into a box of tools just inside the door.

"Siegfried Monk," he said, extending his hand. "What can I do for you?"

Before LoBianco or Berger could answer, Monk called to the man mopping the floor, "Hey, asshole. Mop faster or I'll turn you over to *La Migre*." The man ignored the super and continued to mop.

"Damn wetbacks," Monk said. "Hear no English, speak no English. Except on payday. Ain't that right, José, you fucking alien asshole?" Monk laughed; José laughed.

"We all got to come from somewhere," Berger said. The fat man annoyed him.

"Me, I came from Bensonhurst," Monk said. "Back in the days when you had to learn English to work, when you could leave a dollar on the sidewalk and the next day it would still be there. But not today. They'd steal your shadow if you're not careful.''

''Funny, that's just what my partner here was saying,'' LoBianco said. ''The past was perfect.''

''The past was prologue,'' Berger said. ''But what brings us here is a Marjorie Cortland. Does she still live here?''

''She don't live nowhere,'' Monk said, taking a swig of his beer.

''Let's talk some of your textbook English, Siegfried,'' Berger said.

''She's dead,'' Monk said. ''Croaked about a year ago.''

''Shit,'' LoBianco said, turning to go.

''But her mother still lives here.''

''Where?'' Berger asked, his patience with Siegfried Monk about exhausted.

''Thayer. Four-B. But you have to use the stairs,'' Monk said. ''José here washed the elevator floor yesterday and it hasn't worked since. Asshole.''

LoBianco and Berger kept their conversation with Agnes Thayer brief. The frail old lady told them her daughter Marjorie had died of cancer fourteen months ago, after a long illness. She had been eulogized at the Standish Funeral Home and buried at Mt. Calvary Cemetery in the Bronx. They thanked Mrs. Thayer and begged her to pardon them for disturbing her. It was strictly a routine follow-up.

On the way out they found José mopping the lobby. He looked up at the cops and said, ''Siegfried's the asshole,'' then went back to work, whistling softly to himself.

''What do you make of that?'' LoBianco asked as they were walking back to the precinct house.

''Her finger's pretty well deceased,'' Berger said, shrugging. ''What do you think?''

''She could be alive and missing a finger,'' LoBianco said. ''Or she could have had the finger lopped off after she was dead. Can the ME answer that?''

''We'll check,'' Berger said. ''If the amputation was

postmortem, who did it? The doctor? The funeral home? A grave robber?''

"Aliens?" LoBianco said. "Like José?"

"How about the other fingers and the hand?" Berger mused. "What's the sound of one hand clapping? What's the price of tea in China? All we have is questions."

A brain explosion had rendered Charles Maris totally incapable of working that morning. He had called his supervisor and in a strangled voice told her he could not make it in today. She had been sympathetic because Charles was a quiet, dedicated employee who rarely took a day off.

He lay in bed, his puffy body rigid, until almost noon; then he kicked the two dozen pornographic magazines from his king-sized futon and popped three Darvons for his headache.

After eating half a pepperoni pizza left over from a few nights before, he fed the dogs and went to the former pit he now thought of as his operating theater.

"I have 'hand-y' work to do," he told the three dogs, and giggled.

Charles removed the makeshift cover from the freezer. Inside, slung from rubber straps, was a Styrofoam box, six feet long and three feet wide. Lying in the box was a mannequin Charles had purchased mail order. She was unclothed and sexless, except for nippleless breasts. She was bald, but her painted eyes had said something to Charles. Take me, they said. He had.

Carefully he checked the freezer's temperature on the thermostat. Satisfied, he unscrewed the mannequin's left hand. It was smooth and icy. Then he removed the right hand and reached down into the freezer to retrieve Maria Parulo's hands. They, too, were cold and smooth, but they sent a surge of heat throughout his body.

The dogs had gathered around him, sitting quietly, waiting for instructions.

He took the human hands and the mannequin hands to the

autopsy table and lined them up. The dogs followed in their pecking order, Dempsey leading, and formed a protective ring around Maris.

Charles eyed the four hands and noticed at once that he had left a bit more flesh on Maria's right hand than he had intended. Taking a blade from its sanitary envelope, he fitted it into the scalpel. Then holding the frozen hand, as if he were shaking it, he pared away the excess flesh to ensure a proper fit. Without thinking, he flicked the scraps of frozen flesh to the dogs and watched as they jumped savagely for the snack.

The hands screwed in neatly to the mannequin's wrists and Charles felt the thrill of accomplishment. He had done more in one night than he had done previously in almost two years of work. Mother will be pleased, he thought, when she finds how far I've come.

The dogs crowded around the freezer, licking their chops. Maris wondered idly if they were developing a taste for human meat.

# 6

Sonny LoBianco gunned the Vette's 427-cubic-inch engine while he waited at a stoplight. A young couple in a Honda looked at him and laughed. He hit the accelerator and left twenty feet of rubber, about four pounds of air pollution, and the Honda behind. But it made him think that maybe he and Angela should be riding along in a Civic with the kids in the back, that he shouldn't be wheeling along—alone—in a muscle car from another era. Was he evading the present by escaping to the past? he wondered not for the first time. It made him feel as old as Berger.

"You look like shit," Father Franklyn Davis said to LoBianco a few minutes later as they sat in the priest's study, next to the kitchen. They could hear the kids laughing and shouting as they prepared dinner. "Hard day?"

"Spent eight hours looking for some maniac who likes to carve up women," LoBianco said. He and Davis were drinking Bud from the can.

"But that's not what's bothering you, is it?" Davis said.

"No. It's Angela," LoBianco admitted. "I don't know what to do. I want her back, and yet I don't."

"Does she want to come back?"

"She'll do what I tell her," LoBianco said.

Davis laughed. "Spoken like a young, young man."

Sonny was annoyed. "Spoken like a fucking priest."

"Fuck me? Hey, fuck you, man," Davis said. "I'm not the one mooning around about some piece of ass."

"Sorry, Father," LoBianco said automatically.

"Say three Hail Marys and finish your beer," Davis said. "How do you get her back? And what's to prevent her from leaving again?"

"Oh, she'll stay. Under one condition. That I quit The Job," LoBianco said unhappily.

He thought about her. It wasn't difficult to remember her right down to the last detail. She was like a dream that never quite finished: classic good looks, a unique blend of Sicilian, Corsican, and French. The daughter of a wealthy Italian banker, Angela had graduated from Vassar with everything her father's money could buy. She had leaped at life, sampling everything, finding joy in all things. For a while that included being a cop's wife.

The first time he had met her had been at an Italian wedding in Manhattan. The weather was hot and humid, standard issue for July. The reception hall's air conditioner wheezed but didn't cool. Angela had been dancing with everyone in the room, having a hell of a good time.

After several encores of "Twist and Shout," she came over to the table where Sonny and his friends had been sitting and sweating.

Angela sat down next to Sonny, looked him in the eye, and said, "It's fucking hot." Then she picked up a pitcher of ice water and poured it down her dress. The dress was sheer white cotton and Sonny would never forget what the water did to it.

He had asked her out on the spot and she had accepted. Two hours later they were lovers, two months after that they were living together, doing all the things couples do. Sonny discovered for the first time a stability he had longed for since he had been thirteen. In Angela he had tried to re-create the family he had lost when his father had been killed. He wrapped himself in their relationship, using it as a shield against the outside world. When he asked her to marry him, she had hesitated, but a month long campaign finally crumbled her defenses. That happy day had been the beginning of the end.

"She's one hot babe," Davis said. "But does your job mean so little to you?"

"I can't get her out of my mind," LoBianco said.

"Even if she's out of your bed," Davis said. "Are you confusing love and lust?"

"It's the same thing."

"If you believe that, there's no hope for you," Davis said.

"Spare me that shit, I'll work it out," LoBianco said. "Tell me about those crackhead scumbags who torched your bus. I got Rooster out of Beverly Jackson's face, maybe I can chill the dealers for you."

Davis got up from the frayed tartan-covered couch and went to the window. "Come and check out the patrol," he said.

LoBianco joined him at the window.

"Any minute now," Davis said.

A black Ford Crown Victoria cruised by slowly, stopped in front of St. Agnes, then pulled away. LoBianco could see four men inside, but it was too dark to identify them.

"They're trolling for my kids," Davis said. "Trying to line them up to sell their shit in school. The local precinct captain told me he couldn't do a damned thing about it. He busts 'em and they laugh because they know they'll be out in an hour, thanks to our wonderful land of card-carrying ACLU politicians."

"What! You mean you want to take the law in your own hands?" LoBianco said mockingly. "Put the scumbags in jail and make the neighborhood safe for kids? Radical, Father Davis, radical. And un-American. We think a drug dealer who kills children is a wonderful citizen, a bit misguided, but basically a fine human being deserving of our support and our tax dollars. I don't know about you, but it makes me feel proud to be a cop. To help our unfortunate citizens make bail and kill more kids.''

"You should have been a politician," Davis said.

"I know what I should have been," LoBianco said. "But I became a cop because you wanted me to."

"Sure, blame me. I didn't force you. Only directed you toward a socially redeeming career," Davis said. "You'd rather be some kind of wiseguy?"

"I'd still have Angela," he said.

"And a bullet in the back of your thick head," Davis said.

The priest sat down again and lit a Salem. He was wearing a Roman collar, a gray tweed jacket, and jeans. LoBianco could see the bulge of Davis's .45 under his left shoulder. At one time the tabloids had called him the "Gunslinger Priest," much to his annoyance. He now relished his anonymity.

"Tell me exactly what happened," LoBianco said. "When you decided to play sheriff."

"I caught those guys in the Ford rappin' shit to my kids, trying to sell 'em poison. I told 'em in no uncertain terms to cease and desist," Davis said.

"Told them?" LoBianco asked.

"Me and my .45," Davis said.

"You threatened them?"

"Convinced them."

"Look at your bus, Father," LoBianco said. "I don't think you convinced anybody of shit."

"What else am I going to do?" Davis said. "In this neighborhood, what's left of it anyway, you got to handle your own shit. This is 'Indian country,' not the world. Not the real world, anyway."

"Those punks who drove by," LoBianco said. "Who do they work for?"

"Everybody works for Mr. MoFo these days," Davis said. "That's short for Mr. Motherfucker, you understand. Two years ago this chump was a nowhere asshole hustling short vials on a corner somewhere. Today he's the top maggot.''

''I'm going to do something about this,'' LoBianco said.

''Don't sweat it, Sonny,'' Davis said, crushing his cigarette out on the top of his beer can. ''I know it looks bad, but we're still alive, nobody got hurt—''

''This time.''

''—so I don't want you to get into trouble,'' Davis said. ''Or I'll whup you upside your thick dago head.''

''Nobody whups my head,'' LoBianco said, laughing.

''I can whup your head good,'' Davis said, smiling. ''Always have, always will.''

''Not on your best day, you old black bastard,'' LoBianco said.

''You guys gonna fight?'' This from E.T., who peered into the study. ''Can I watch?''

''You can get the hell—'' Davis began, then said, ''What happened to your hair?''

E.T.'s hair had been shaved around the sides, then rose straight up, thick and bushy. His initials were shaved into the back of his head. The latest do.

''You look like an eraser,'' Davis said. ''If your face was yellow instead of black, you'd look like a number-two pencil.''

''Aw, Father,'' E.T. said. ''All the guys got 'em.''

''Yeah, and if all the guys was smokin' crack, you'd be doin' it, too,'' Davis said.

''Naw, I don' want none of that shit,'' E.T. said. ''Cut my wind for fighting. Right, Sonny?''

LoBianco said, ''And don't you forget it. Now leave us be.''

After E.T. had gone, Davis sighed. ''You know, when I was in the army, my lieutenant was a white dude from Elmont, Long Island. A racist bastard if there ever was one. He always told me that if they ever made him king of America, the first thing he'd do was make every black dude shave their 'fros into unusual and peculiar shapes. You know, like mushrooms.

"That no-good bigot piece of shit musta been made king without me knowing it, because it seems to have happened."

"It's just kids," LoBianco said, shrugging.

"It's the times," Davis said, sounding very much like Berger.

"In my village in Italy," Paulo said to Ira Berger as he was pouring the sergeant another cup of tea, "we didn't need all these cops, all these fancy gadgets. Some girl got raped, we—the men—found the guy that done it and strung his ass up."

"In my grandparents' village in Russia," Berger said, "*we* were the ones that got strung up. Or burned at the stake. Or run through by Cossacks."

"Well, your grandparents probably didn't rape nobody," Paulo said. "You want a doughnut?"

Berger was sitting at the counter of Paulo Tucci's diner, avoiding the inevitable confrontation with Rose. He had been listening to Paulo's vigilante talk for forty years, to variations of it every day of his life.

"Gotta run," Berger said, picking up the large shopping bag containing Rose's new bathrobe. "How much do I owe you?"

"On the house," Paulo said.

"Here's a dollar," Berger said. It was part of the ritual that made them both comfortable.

It was only 5:00 P.M. and the weather was mild enough for Berger to make a tour of the neighborhood. The uniform cops he had sent to canvass the area hadn't turned up anything interesting. Nobody had seen anything unusual. His own glimpse of the figure in black pushing a cart was too vague and insubstantial to relay to the officers assigned to the case. They would think he was losing it, so he decided to ask around himself.

Walking the streets where he had spent most of his adult life, Berger felt uncomfortable. It was the same, yet had all changed for him. Overnight the comfort of familiar surroundings had become threatening. Someone, something had come into his life, into his home, and had ruined what little satisfaction he had previously enjoyed.

"Hello, Freddy," he said, approaching a green tin newsstand.

"Hiya, Sergeant Berger," Freddy said, recognizing the detective's voice.

"How about a *Post*," Berger said.

"Right away," Freddy said, reaching behind him with unerring accuracy. He was blind, but noticed things most sighted people missed or ignored.

Berger took the paper and handed Freddy a dollar bill. He had always wondered what the news dealer would do if he handed him a single and told him it was a ten. It must have happened many times, he thought. Creeps were equal-opportunity rip-off artists. They'd steal from the lame and the blind.

"Notice anybody new on the block?" Berger asked as Freddy made change.

"A couple of niggers who don't belong here," Freddy said. Everybody needed somebody, Berger thought, to despise.

"How about someone dressed in black? Lost, maybe, or confused?" Berger asked.

"Just the usual crew as far as I can tell," Freddy said. He didn't miss much. "Is this about the broad who was killed and her hands cut off?"

"Yeah."

"I'll keep an eye peeled," Freddy said. "So to speak."

Berger stopped to speak to Old Lady Landi, who had appointed herself guardian of the block. She wore a black shapeless dress to cover her white shapeless body, black wool stockings, black shoes, and a black kerchief to cover her dyed black hair. She was still in mourning for a husband who died thirty years earlier.

"Good evening, Mrs. Landi," Berger said to the woman who was perched in the first-floor window of a two-story brick house. It was her station; she tuned into the street from the safety of her home.

"*Ciao,*" she said suspiciously. Jew cops were not to be trusted, she thought.

"Nice evening," Berger said.

"It's okay."

"You heard about that woman over by the station?" Berger asked.

"The teach," Mrs. Landi said. Any fool knew about that, she thought.

"Yes, the teacher," Berger agreed. "Have you seen any strangers around recently?"

"Yeah, two nig—"

"No, I'm looking for someone dressed in black, pushing a cart. A stranger, maybe?" Berger asked.

Mrs. Landi had to think about that one. A person in black? All her friends wore black. She stroked her not inconsiderable mustache.

"You mean like me?" she asked. "You tink I killa that teach?"

"No, no, Mrs. Landi," Berger said quickly. "I just thought you might have seen someone."

Mollified, Mrs. Landi thought about all she had seen in the last two days: the wild Franciose girl practically humping that nice Bargi boy, what was his name? Bill, Will, some kind of American name. Then there was that Greek woman who called herself Greco, but was probably not even Italian, getting out of a block-long limo, escorted by some short, dark man. Madonna! An Arab or something. The two black boys sneaking around looking for old ladies to rob. Then there was—

"Mrs. Landi?" Berger said, interrupting her thoughts.

"No. I don't see nobody like that, not that don't belong

here,'' Mrs. Landi said at last. Imagine, she thought to herself, the Jew policeman wants to arrest old ladies when the neighborhood was terrorized by *melanzana*.

Berger waved good-bye and walked slowly on, talking to Weinstein, the tailor, Rossi, the shoemaker, Gallo, the baker, and two goofy girls from Manhattan who had opened a boutique selling trendy clothes. With the area dominated by Mrs. Landi and her old-lady Mafia, the store was sure to be a bust. But who could talk sense to the young? he thought as he plodded on.

When he came to Mostel's Deli, a block from his apartment, he was overcome by the twin forces of hunger and procrastination. He would eat, he decided. He would read the paper and eat before he had it out with Rose.

Irving Mostel greeted Berger like a long-lost brother, inquiring about his health, his wealth, his sex life, and his wife.

''You know how to really piss off your wife while you're making love?'' Irving asked Berger, after the detective had ordered a pastrami on rye. Berger didn't know.

''Tell her where you are,'' Irving Mostel said, laughing.

Berger smiled wanly. ''How's business?''

''Don't ask,'' Mostel said, throwing up his hands. ''My business is like the neighborhood. Declining. Just yesterday these two *shvartzer* kids . . .''

Berger let him go on, wondering if all the eagle eyes he had spoken to could only see black people, but missed everything else. He let Mostel drone on, then said, ''Irv, have you seen anyone, an old lady maybe, dressed in black and pushing a cart or wagon?''

Irving Mostel scratched the bald spot through his yarmulke and said, ''In this neighborhood, that's the uniform an Italian women wears from the day her husband dies to the day she follows him into the grave. I see a hundred old ladies in black every day. Sometimes, if the weather is nice, two hundred. You want a pickle?''

"Sure," Berger said. "And let me use your phone. I'll see if Rose wants to join me."

Mostel handed him the phone from behind the counter. "Tell her I've got some nice chicken."

Berger dialed, but there was no answer. Damn, he thought, damn it to hell.

"Probably out shopping," Mostel said sympathetically, placing a five-inch-high pastrami sandwich in front of Berger.

Berger shrugged. "Let me have the hot mustard, Irv. Not that yellow gunk. The hot brown stuff. Tonight my ulcer performs."

The diner began to fill up with the dinner crowd and Berger was left in peace to feed his ulcer and his paranoia about Rose.

He left the deli, belching and patting his stomach, realizing he was getting too old to eat like that anymore. He had always had a cast-iron stomach, but age had rusted it through.

Without really thinking about it, he went past his apartment building, taking a path that should take him to Gross's Butcher Shop.

The wind had come up as the sun had set, chilling him. It was not an unwelcome feeling. The breeze off the ocean was fresh and bracing. He inhaled deeply, but felt the lump in his stomach, the worry in his heart, and the fear that had permeated his brain.

In twenty years of marriage he had always known where his wife was: working at the school cafeteria, staying home, or taking care of her sister. Now that she was retired and her sister was dead, he never knew where she was. He was worried about the maniac who knew where he lived and about Gross the butcher. It wasn't jealousy, he told himself, it was . . . Well, he didn't know what it was, but he didn't like it.

In front of the butcher shop, he looked through the window and saw two men behind the white porcelain display freezer. The shop was empty of customers, and the two men were smoking, talking, and leaning on brooms. Berger watched them intently, imagining all sorts of sexual possibilities between Rose and Gross. After a few minutes he gave up and slouched toward what he knew would be an empty apartment.

As he passed Mostel's he saw Irving waving to him frantically.

Inside, the deli owner said, "I think I'm going meshuga, Ira. I seem to be forgetting things right and left. I'm getting old."

"Nobody gets young, Irv. What did you forget?" Berger asked.

"The wheelchair," Mostel said, waiting for Berger's reaction.

Berger feigned an interest he had lost at Gross's Butcher Shop. "Tell me more," he said.

"This old woman, poor soul, is not tightly wrapped," Mostel said, twirling his index finger in a circle by his temple. "She was walking around pushing this old wheelchair. A big, wooden one, no less. Very early in the morning."

"She was wearing black?" Berger asked.

"Sure was. I remember now, it was real early in the morning. What, two days ago?"

"Have you seen her since?"

"No, just that one time," Mostel said. "Is that any help?"

"Could be, Irv," Berger said. "Could be."

As he shook hands with Mostel, Berger said casually, "By the way, who was in the wheelchair?"

"That was the funny thing," Mostel said. "I couldn't see who was riding in the wheelchair. Just bunched up blankets."

Berger thanked him and headed home. He trudged wearily up to his second-floor apartment and turned his key in the lock. Nothing happened; the door was unlocked.

Silently he moved away from the door and drew the service revolver from his shoulder holster.

He pushed the door open slowly with the Smith & Wesson .38, expecting the worst.

The lights were on; he could hear the TV; he pushed into the kitchen.

"Ira, you're late," Rose said, without looking up from the sink.

"Jesus Christ," he said. "Where the hell have you been all day?"

"What were you going to do, shoot me?" she asked, eyeing the revolver.

"I just called to invite you to dinner. No one answered. Where were you?" he asked, angry now, holstering the .38.

"In and out," she said.

"That a sexual reference, Rose?"

She laughed, making him angrier.

"What is it you want?" he demanded.

"You know what I want."

"Well, you can't have it. Isn't that clear by now?" he yelled.

She smiled knowingly. "Perhaps."

"What do you want from *me,* Rose? Do you want me to get down on my hands and knees and beg your forgiveness? You want I should write you an apology?" He managed to get his temper under control by clenching his fists until the knuckles were white.

"Rose. It's my fault," he continued. "You know that, I know that. A low sperm count. Shooting blanks. I'm sorry. I'm sorry I can't give you a baby," he said, the words making him cringe inside. "But it's been ten years, Rose. Ten years since we gave up. I thought you had adjusted by now."

"No," she said, turning her back on him. "I've never adjusted."

"Then I'll ask again, do you want to adopt?"

"No."

"Do you want artificial insemination?"

"No."

"Do you want me to jump off a bridge?"

She paused, considering.

"Rose!"

"I'm thinking, I'm thinking," she said, laughing.

He stalked out of the kitchen.

"I'm kidding, Ira. I'm kidding like Jack Benny, his money or his life," she called to him.

"I have no money, Rose. I have no life," he said. "And now I have no wife."

"That's a cruel thing to say," she said, following him into the living room. "Cruel and untrue."

"Is it?" he asked, sitting down heavily in his recliner. "You made me feel . . . impotent."

"Infertile."

"Screw the *Reader's Digest*. The point is, you're unhappy and you're making me unhappy."

Rose smiled mysteriously. "You did your best, Ira. Everything will work out."

"I hope so, Rose. I hope to God it will," he said.

# 7

Sonny LoBianco had never met a meaner bastard than Rotten Jack Murphy. And Sonny had known merciless pimps, stone killers, imported hit men from Sicily, child murderers, motherfuckers, and every sort of prick in the world. But Rotten Jack would do anything to anyone at any time for any reason. The fact that Jack was a cop didn't make life easier for those who screwed around in his precinct or the guys who had to work with him. He didn't care who he fucked over as long as he was fucking over someone. The most fined, suspended, and reprimanded cop in all the boroughs, Murphy was definitely on the way out, people said. But they had been saying that for ten years. He and Sonny had worked together in the South Bronx. Now Murphy worked for the new TNS, the Tactical Narcotics Squad. They had broad, citywide jurisdiction that was supposed to help to root out the bad guys from whatever rock they were hiding under.

"Jack?" LoBianco said into the phone.

"Sonny?"

"Yeah. This a secure line?"

"No."

"Meet me at the usual place. I got a deal for you," LoBianco said. "Tomorrow noon."

We'll see just how tough this Mr. MoFo is, LoBianco thought, returning his attention to the weights he had been lifting. It was 10:00 P.M., too late to be working out, but he felt kinky. Even a five-mile run hadn't burned the edge off his nervous energy. His mind was working at top speed, trying to solve four problems: Mr. MoFo, Father Davis's lack of transportation, Angela, and the scumbag who was chopping up women in his precinct.

"Men act, women react," was what his father had always told him. He decided that it was time to act.

He was toweling off when there was a knock at his door.

"It's open," he said.

"Yo, Sonny," E.T. said, poking his eraserhead around the door. "Your white chick here?"

"What do you want?" LoBianco asked, wiping the sweat off his arms and chest.

"I want to know when you want me to start on your car. The wax job."

"You should be asleep," LoBianco said, walking into the makeshift bathroom he had installed in the corner of the former garage.

"Tomorrow's Saturday. You said Saturday," E.T. said.

"Okay, but early, I'm on the road by eleven," LoBianco said.

"I'll have it shining like a gold tooth," E.T. said. "It'll look as hot as a red fucking firecracker."

LoBianco suddenly had an idea. He came out of the bathroom, a towel wrapped around his neck, his long, black hair falling in his eyes. "You know those M-80s Father D caught you with last month?"

"The ones he kicked my butt over?"

"The same. I want some."

"He got 'em all."

"I need three," LoBianco said.

"I said Father D got them all," E.T. insisted.

"Sure he did," LoBianco said. "And I'm the Holy Ghost."

E.T. was silent.

"Well, I guess maybe you and me better do some sparring. Get your equipment and I'll show you some moves you've never thought of before."

E.T. shook his head. "They got laws against that sort of thing, man. Child abuse."

"They got laws against explosives, too. Now get 'em for me," LoBianco said.

With an exaggerated show of reluctance, E.T. left the garage. He returned five minutes later and tossed three M-80s to LoBianco. "You weren't really going to beat me up, were you?" he asked.

LoBianco laughed. "You'll never know, chump. You'll never know."

E.T. smiled. "What you gonna do with them firecrackers?"

"I'm gonna make a brother an offer he can't defuse," LoBianco answered.

"Sonny, you son of a bitch. How the hell long has it been?" Rotten Jack Murphy said, grasping LoBianco's hand.

"Too long, Jack," LoBianco said, trying to extricate his hand from Murphy's viselike grip.

After paying E.T. for a first-rate simonize, LoBianco had driven to the Bronx to meet Murphy at their usual spot, the Blarney Pub on 265th Street. It was a hotbed of Irish nationalism, illegal aliens, IRA assassins, gunrunners, and NORAID officials. Just being there was bad news for a cop; Rotten Jack was a regular.

"I was just thinking about you the other day," Murphy said. "The firefucks' and the cops' boxing tournament's on this winter and we could use your help. Light heavyweight. You still in training?"

"I'm in shape, but I don't fight for trophies anymore," LoBianco said.

Murphy laughed. "Now you're starting to wise up, wiseass."

LoBianco smiled.

Unlike LoBianco, Murphy was short and stocky with reddish hair and practically no eyelashes or brows. He looked harmless—but he was as harmless as a viper. Part of his ability to survive was his innocent, almost childlike looks. Juries believed him when he lied, the brass believed him when they caught him with the goods, his wife believed him when she found him in bed with twins.

"I need your help," LoBianco said.

"Who do you want popped?" Murphy asked.

"You were never a bullshitter, Jack," LoBianco said. "So I won't bullshit you. I don't want anybody popped. I just want to make a point to a scumbag."

"You were always too much of a pussy for this line of work. Too straight in a legal sense. When you're fighting a war, everything is legal; when the other side laughs at the law, you'd better laugh, too. Or get another job."

"I want this legal," LoBianco said. "Or at least sort of legal. I need a bust on a scumbag dealer named Mr. MoFo."

He spent ten minutes filling Murphy in on what had happened at St. Agnes's. "Maybe you could set up a bust for me."

"Why don't you want to do it yourself?" Murphy asked.

"I got no real evidence to convince the local precinct," LoBianco said.

"Why not just blow the maggot away? It's simple, neat, and clean. Hell, I'll do it myself, if you want," Murphy said.

"No, I just want to know when and where," LoBianco said. "And I want five minutes alone with him to, uh, convince him of the error of his ways. He's a fucking psycho, I hear, a hardass shooter who has consolidated three major Jamaican posses by personally blowing away their leaders. I don't know if he's got a pad, but nobody wants to mess with him."

"That why St. Agnes wasn't protected? This guy got your bells shakin'?" Murphy asked.

"Fuck you, too," LoBianco said. He knew he was going off half-cocked against a lunatic by asking another lunatic for help.

"Why should you give a fuck about a bunch of kids and what's-his-name, the priest?" Murphy asked.

"Before he became a priest, when he was in the Special Forces, Frank Davis would have had that drug-dealing MoFo pissing blood, the same MoFo who's got the whole city shitting liquid," LoBianco said.

"That was then, this is now," Murphy said, shrugging. "No regular army type can survive."

"I owe him, Jack. A lot. And I want him and his kids protected. This is the only way I know how. Can you arrange it?"

"I'll call you," Murphy said.

LoBianco got up to leave.

"Say," Murphy said, stopping him. "Why didn't you go to your uncle Vito? He specializes in this sort of thing."

"I'm going to see him now," LoBianco said. "But for a different reason."

LoBianco drove south on the FDR Drive, skirting the towers of Manhattan, then through the Brooklyn Battery Tunnel. On the far side of the tunnel, he turned onto the Gowanus Expressway, heading for Coney Island.

The expressway was elevated, about three stories high, so that he could see the tops of the mixed brownstones and frame houses that stretched to infinity. This part of Brooklyn, he thought, looked like the outskirts of any rust-belt city in America. It could have been St. Louis, Cleveland, Akron, or Pittsburgh: decayed housing, decaying communities, deprived and depraved citizens. He drove on, past the once-busy Brooklyn Navy Yard, and when traffic got heavy he exited the expressway at Sunset Park. He drove past the School of Music and St. Michael's redbrick church and pushed the Vette up Fourth Avenue. As a kid, he had spent many hours getting drunk and looking to get laid in Sunset Park. But he had always been carrying when he entered this predominantly Spanish area.

It was no secret, he thought, locking the doors of the Corvette, what made a neighborhood bad. It wasn't the people or the buildings; it wasn't even money. It was hope or lack of it that ruined people and neighborhoods. Sunset Park, like Williamsburg and Brownsville and Crown Heights, suffered from this virulent disease. When eight out of ten residents were unemployed, they had nothing to lose. They had no money, no skills, no education—many couldn't even speak English. They were forced to live by their wits, by their street smarts. They stole, sold drugs, raped, pillaged, and burned. They were losers and they knew it. What the hell difference did it make if they pulled out a gun and blew you away? For a few dollars or a subway token they'd take your life because theirs meant so little.

In neighborhoods like this, he thought, the work load for detectives was enormous. If someone got shot or knifed here, there were no news stories, no weeping and wailing from relatives, no candy-assed editorials by liberal columnists decrying a world, a life-style they helped to create with their denial of individual responsibility. The system was responsible for the nine-year-old who got pregnant, the ten-year-old crack dealer, the eleven-year-old armed robber, the thirteen-year-old rapist, and the fourteen-year-old murderer.

Cops everywhere resented the philosophy, because the first time they killed a kid perp packing an Uzi, personal responsibility suddenly reared its ugly head. The cop was responsible, the fifteen-year-old with the machine gun was a victim of society.

Law enforcement in these neighborhoods was a joke. The police did their best despite being spat upon by their bosses, the press, and the crackbrained citizens.

He found an opening in the Saturday shopping traffic and

gunned the Vette around two double-parked trucks, almost hitting a shirtless man wearing a coonskin cap, then drove through Bay Ridge, Bensonhurst, and on toward the shore. To Coney Island, to a place he had avoided most of his life. Ironically he now lived within shouting distance of Uncle Vito's place.

Rosalie's Clam Bar was a family business in more ways than one. Owned by Vito LoBianco, Sonny's uncle, his dead father's brother, it served as the legitimate front for Vito's real job as a captain in Salvatore Genco's organized-crime family. Vito served good food at high prices, throwing off several hundred thousand every year. In cash. Everything Uncle Vito touched turned to green, LoBianco thought, rapping on the heavy plate-glass door with his gold-and-diamond pinky ring.

"Hey, Rosalie," he shouted through the door. "Let me in."

His uncle's wife, standing guard over the cash register, was a typical second-generation Italian, a woman with more money to spend than was good for her. She was an unnecessary woman, with dyed red hair piled up and lacquered in a beehive hairdo that had been fashionable when Sonny's Corvette was new. Diamonds sparkled on each of her fat fingers—badges of her husband's wealth—a sign that she worked only because she wanted to.

Rosalie smiled frostily at Sonny as she unlocked the door. She had never liked him, even as a child, and the feeling was mutual.

"Uncle Vito here?" LoBianco asked, pushing past her into the restaurant. The counter, tile floor, windows, and walls were as clean as an operating room. Rosalie, no doubt wearing one of her mink coats, probably insisted on cleaning up before the cleaning service arrived so they'd think she was clean. It was a dirty business, Sonny thought, smiling to himself.

"He's in the back," Rosalie said. "But he's got company."

"Good. Now he's got more," LoBianco said, walking toward the sound of the voices.

Vito LoBianco was sitting at a back booth referred to as the family table. Off limits to paying customers, it was Vito's seat of power, his red vinyl throne.

With him were two men Sonny knew well. He had grown up with them; they had pulled their first crimes together; they had been blood brothers.

"Sonny boy!" Vito said, looking up. "Is this a fucking raid?"

"Yeah, you're all going down for serving bad clams," LoBianco said, joining the three men in the booth, sitting next to his uncle.

"Hey, what's it you call an old penny?" Frankie Marcellino said. "Dirty copper?"

"Good, Frankie," LoBianco said. "You keep talking with your asshole, you'll get hemorrhoids."

Frankie's face tightened but Vito laughed, and there was nothing the younger man could do with his boss watching.

"Hello, Paulie," LoBianco said to the other man seated across from him. Paulie was confused, not quite sure if he should say hello. Paulie wasn't all that bright. He had the squint-eyed look of a boxer who had seen too many rounds. But he had never boxed; he just looked and talked that way.

"Uh," Paulie began, but Vito interrupted him.

"What are ya here for?"

"I need a favor," LoBianco said. "The kids from St. Agnes's need to borrow a bus or a van."

Vito made notes on a paper napkin. "Sure."

"And, Uncle Vito, it's okay we keep the van awhile? A good while?"

Vito shrugged.

"You still hangin' out with them fuckin' orphans?" Frankie asked. "Ya got a crush on one of 'em?"

LoBianco eyed him, thinking that Frankie hadn't always been such a shit. They had been friends once. The problem had begun with the death of Sonny's father. He had been abruptly taken away from all he had known, and after his mother had died, he had been shut up in St. Agnes's, ignored by his uncle. Frankie had somehow sucked the old man up the exhaust pipe, suddenly becoming the heir to the family business.

"There's a church law against contraception," LoBianco said to Frankie. "And the pope police are rounding up all you scumbags."

Frankie started to make a move, but one look from Vito stopped him.

"Boys, boys," Vito said. "Don't take the name of the fucking pope in vain. What we gotta have here is an understanding." A short, paunchy man with a drooping salt-and-pepper mustache, Vito LoBianco demanded and received respect. "I done a lotta work for Sal Genco in my day," he said. A lot of work meant heavy work: murder. "And I never mixed it up with nobody in my crew. That's bad business and against *our* law. And I don't want no fighting, understand?"

The three men nodded. Vito LoBianco had a reputation as a smart guy, a planner and a negotiator. "Brains beat the shit outta brawn every time," was his favorite expression. But as he admitted, he had done a lot of work for Genco; what he didn't admit was that he was scared shitless most of the time. That's why he had relied on Sonny's father to do the physical work while he did the thinking. For thirty years Vito had made all the right moves, scaled the family hierarchy, married a good woman, enjoyed a good mistress, and managed to survive. But the years had taken their toll; Vito was tired and wanted to quit. Unfortunately, if he handled it wrong, the retirement plan in the Genco family could be a permanent one. That tired, Vito told himself, he wasn't.

"So no more fighting," Vito said.

"Right," LoBianco muttered.

Vito watched his nephew and saw his dead brother's strong face, the long, thin nose, the square chin and dark eyes. Sonny was a tough kid, he thought, a stand-up kid like his father. He'd go it alone if he had to; Sonny had his old man's balls. And face.

Yet it was the way Sonny stared at him that worried Vito. He had seen that look before, the day Sonny's father had bought it. The boy had insisted on seeing his father's body at the crime scene only a mile away from Rosalie's. There hadn't been much left of his father's head; his face was only a gory mass of blood and bone. But the kid had insisted.

Sonny hadn't cried, Vito remembered. He had only looked at his uncle with cold, flat, and watchful eyes. Those eyes were even harder today.

The four men sat in silence for a moment, then they turned as one toward the sound of heavy steps on the tile floor.

"Yo, Mr. Lo," a tall, gangling black man said, greeting Vito. "How they hanging'?"

"You're up early," Vito said. "You ready to roll, Ricky?"

"Rock 'n' roll," Ricky Lewis said, attempting to high-five Paulie. It was a futile gesture. Paulie sat like a lump, Frankie scowled, and Sonny LoBianco stared impassively.

"Whoo-ee," Ricky said. "It's mighty cold in here."

"Wait outside," Vito said. "In the car." He tossed him a set of keys.

"Nice to see the family's affirmative action program in action," LoBianco said, smiling slightly.

"Hey," Vito said, after Ricky had gone. "It's hard to get help these days. He's only a part-time driver."

"A real hitter from the old country," LoBianco said.

"They fuck your women and steal you blind," Vito said. "But somebody's got to do the work. Goddamn ginzos these days all wanna lay around and get fat."

"Or join the fucking cops," Frankie said.

LoBianco ignored him. "I got to get to work myself," he said. "I'll call you about the van."

As he was leaving, Marcellino gave him one parting shot. "Sonny, how's Angela? Seen her lately?"

LoBianco stopped dead in his tracks. He started to turn slowly, then went on his way.

Driving back to St. Agnes, Sonny LoBianco gripped the wheel until his knuckles turned white. He wanted to kill Frankie Marcellino. Scratch that, he thought. He should have killed the bastard a year ago when Frankie started nosing around Angela. But he had been so sure Angela loved him, had trusted her so much, that he had ignored the warning signs: the unexplained changes in plans, the gradual loss of warmth between them, and her lack of desire for him in bed. If she was seeing Frankie Marcellino . . . The very thought made him seethe with rage.

Was it possible? he wondered. If it was, the only answer he could come up with was money. Angela, beautiful, classy, a Vassar graduate, the daughter of a wealthy banker, was used to the good life, the fast life, that made a mockery of LoBianco's pay.

He didn't know what Angela was doing now, but it involved Frankie Marcellino or he wouldn't have mentioned her name. He swore he'd find out.

Still thinking about what Marcellino had said, LoBianco drove quickly through traffic to Bensonhurst. He parked near the two-family brick house where he had lived with Angela. She had always hated that house—half a house, really—as much as she had hated the neighborhood.

"It's a make-believe world where everybody pretends they're living in nineteenth-century Italy," she had said. "It has nothing to do with New York or even with today." Eventually he had won the battle of Bensonhurst, but had lost the war.

He walked up the six steps to the door and rang the bell. No one answered, so he tried his key. Amazingly it fit. The first thing he had thought she'd do was change the locks. Either she was careless, or she expected him to arrive one day. That thought cheered him.

Then, instead of barging in, he peered through the window at the side of the door. He could see nothing through the gauzy curtains. Not wanting to intrude, yet wanting very much to see his wife, he went around to the back of the house. He hoped he'd find her in the kitchen, on the phone and unable to hear the door chimes. What he found was a silhouette of her body on the frosted glass of the bathroom window that faced the back of the house. She was taking a shower.

He stood back a few feet and watched as she soaped herself. Turning to her side, he could see her full, uplifted breasts. God, she was beautiful, he thought, feeling his balls tingle.

She lathered herself slowly and luxuriously, rubbing her fine breasts, plunging her hands down below his line of sight. He had meant to have it out with her; now all he wanted was to have her.

Waiting until she turned off the water, he used his key and opened the kitchen door, feeling like a burglar. He stood rooted to the spot, his erection straining at his jeans, when she walked into the kitchen.

"Hello, Sonny," she said casually. "What brings you here?" Although she was naked, she wasn't at all self-conscious.

"I forgot," he said, eyeing her.

"Then go away."

"I'll remember," he said. "Just let me look at you a minute."

"What am I? Some kind of peep show?" she asked, walking to the counter and taking a Salem from an open pack. She lit the cigarette, crossing her arms over her breasts.

"No," he said. "You're some kind of hot piece of ass."

"What a compliment," she said, taking a drag on the Salem.

"Come on, babe. Let's go to bed."

"I just got clean," she said.

"We'll take a shower together later," he promised. "You can see I'm hot for you." He fingered his bulging crotch.

Angela sighed. "What is this? A sympathy fuck? You having trouble scoring with the chippies you work with?"

"Something like that," he said. "Please, babe. Just one and I swear to God I won't bother you again."

"Well, come on. Let's make it quick," she said. "I've got things to do."

"That's real romantic," he said.

"I'm not doing this to be romantic. I'm here to serve. You want a blow job?" she said, stubbing out the Salem in a souvenir ashtray from Atlantic City.

"Anything, babe," he said.

He took her in his arms for a moment and kissed her roughly. She responded halfheartedly, but by this time he was thinking entirely with his dick. He unzipped his pants and pulled them down, his cock springing to attention.

She reached a hand down and felt it. "It doesn't seem to have lost anything," she said.

He pulled her toward him, crushing his cock into her belly. She moved against him so sensuously, he was afraid he might lose it right there.

"Let's go up to the bedroom," he whispered, kissing her neck, inhaling her fragrance.

"No. I don't want to get involved with you again," she said. "You'll have to settle for a blow job."

Not a bad option, he thought as she reached between his legs and held him in her cool hands.

She dropped to her knees in front of him, taking his cock in hand, stroking and fondling it. Her tongue delicately licked while her hands pumped him up and down, in long, slow strokes. Then she opened wide and took him deeply into her mouth.

Angela worked energetically on Sonny while urging him to finish. He complied quickly.

LoBianco had to lean against the kitchen table when he

was through, feeling thoroughly drained but curiously unsatisfied. Angela's had been a virtuoso performance, but merely a performance. There had been no passion.

She stood up and said, "If you're done, please leave. And remember your promise not to come back."

He hiked up his jeans and left, positive she didn't mean it.

# 8

Sergeant Ira Berger sat behind his green metal desk and wished for understanding. He wished he understood what was wrong with Rose, and he wished he knew what was wrong with himself.

It had been a week since he had surprised her in the kitchen, gun drawn. They had had a disquieting conversation, and only afterward did he realize that she had said nothing. She hadn't given up her desire to work for—or make love to—Gross. Hell, for all he knew she'd been carrying on with him for years. And he knew the reason why. A baby. A goddamned baby. She wanted to get pregnant and lie to him, tell him he was the father. He hated it when she lied to him. It humiliated them both. He didn't want to hear it.

He thought ruefully about the peace offering he had presented her the next morning. The new bathrobe went over like a pair of Jockey shorts at a transvestites' convention. Rose had looked at it, smiled, then put it back in the shopping bag. She hadn't worn it all week and probably never would, he thought.

They had settled into an uneasy truce, as married people will, each avoiding the other as much as possible. Icy civility reigned. Rose would admit nothing, even accusing him of making up the severed-hand story to keep her chained to the house. She insisted she would get a job working in the butcher shop whether or not he approved. She was an immovable object; he, it seemed, a completely resistible force.

"Anything new from that Lopez in fingerprints," Berger asked LoBianco, who looked nearly as glum as Berger felt.

"No progress," LoBianco said. "The funeral parlor, the attending doctor, and the hospital all deny any knowledge of Marjorie Cortland's finger, how it got lopped off and whether to sell short or buy."

"Well, we've got two options," Berger said. "We can start canvassing personnel at those two institutions or we can wait for this maniac to work his magic again."

"You're the genius," LoBianco said. "I got my own problems."

"Anything on the Parulo hands?" Berger asked.

"You got all the D-5s," LoBianco said, referring to the reports filed by cops investigating both cases.

"We're nowhere," Berger said, shuffling the paper in front of him. "So let's go somewhere. How about back to the hospital to see if we missed anything?"

LoBianco shrugged.

On their way out they were intercepted by Lieutenant Santamyer. "Anything new, Ira?" he asked.

"We're still looking for something. Anything. This case—"

"Is an albatross around our necks," LoBianco finished, smiling broadly.

"What the hell's an albatross?" Santamyer asked, perplexed.

"It's a goddamned smart-ass kid." Berger sighed, grabbing LoBianco by the arm and hustling him away from the lieutenant. "Damn kid," he repeated in the dark hallway. "Can't you leave him alone?"

"Hey, Ira," LoBianco said. "It's my job."

*   *   *

Bensonhurst General Hospital, a six-story brick structure built in the shape of a U, was underfunded, understaffed, and under the gun, politically and literally. The casualties of the drug wars, the victims of ignorance, the dispossessed, the repossessed, and the terminally depressed all jammed its wards. So-called community activists demanded free medical care, politicians demanded budget cuts and improved services, the unions wanted more money, and the lawyers wanted more malpractice suits. Under these circumstances it was usually safer to take out your own appendix than to put yourself under the care of a doctor from some country that no longer existed or to allow yourself to be shaved by a hulking psychopath who called himself a nurse and enjoyed playing mumblety-peg with a straight razor.

The waiting room looked like a third-world airport during a revolution. The relatives of the wounded camped out here, bringing their lunches, their religious relics, and their primitive beliefs. They prayed, howled, and shrieked to their sundry gods in various languages and dialects. Babies cried, children yelled, old ladies wept, and young ladies made time with the security guards. In the midst of this tide of human detritus, a man wearing a running suit was calmly taking a dump in a floor ashtray.

"Welcome to the future," Berger said.

"Fun, isn't it," LoBianco said.

"What was that doctor's name?" Berger asked.

"Altoon. Raymond Altoon. Head of psychiatry. Chief shrink."

"He's got his work cut out for him," Berger said, surveying the chaos of the waiting room.

"They probably call him Altoon the Loon," LoBianco said, stepping up to the reception desk and flashing his tin.

A bored woman dressed like a nurse but without a peculiar-looking cap told them they could find Altoon on the fourth floor, north.

They found the psychiatrist in a cramped office awash

with papers, files, and books. He was fortyish, completely bald, and dressed in a rumpled gray suit.

"I look like Kojak, right?" Altoon said, shaking hands with both cops.

He didn't, but LoBianco and Berger smiled.

Actually you look like shit, LoBianco thought, paunchy and soft, a heart-attack candidate.

"I'm Sergeant Berger and this is my partner," Berger said.

"Berger? Uh, yes," Altoon said. "I spoke with another officer and told them all I know," he went on affably. "Of course, I'll be glad to help in any way possible."

"I'm sure you will," Berger said politely. He knew these bastards. These psychiatrists. They wouldn't give you the time of day without a warrant.

"We'd like to know if any of your employees—doctors, nurses, attendants—might be responsible for the, uh, loss of Marjorie Cortland's finger."

"Of course not," Altoon said indignantly.

"I know it's only a wild possibility, Doctor," Berger said. "Besides, forensic tells us the stitch job on the hand was very professional."

"It could have been the funeral home," Altoon said. "It could have been an ambulance attendant, it could have been—"

"—Batman," LoBianco said. "But we're thinking some person who was fired or had a history of this sort of thing."

"I anticipated your request and pulled the files on six people who were dismissed over the last two years," Altoon said. He rummaged through the papers on his desk and handed LoBianco the six files. "They're photocopies," he said. "You can keep them, for all the good it will do you."

"Then you don't think any of these people are responsible?" Berger asked.

"They were drug addicts and petty thieves," Altoon said. "Not mutilators."

"And can you give us a profile of the type of person who might do this sort of damage to a patient?"

"Or a corpse," Altoon said. "Could your pathologists say for certain that the finger was removed before or after death?"

"They won't say," Berger said. "But they think the surgery was postmortem."

"Hardly surgery, I daresay. More like hacked off?" Altoon said.

"No, doctor. It was surgery, and very neatly done," Berger said, watching the psychiatrist's face. It registered surprise.

"You're not thinking a doctor?"

"I'm not thinking anything, Doctor. What do *you* think?" Berger said, pleased with himself for using a psychiatrist's ploy.

"I've got to think further about this," Altoon said.

"I'd appreciate that, Doctor," Berger said. "You can reach me day or night at this number." He handed Altoon a card, took the six files from LoBianco, and walked out.

"Let's stop at Michael's for a drink," Berger said as they were driving back to the six-five in a beat-up Plymouth Fury they had checked out from the motor pool.

"Ira!" LoBianco said with mock horror. "It's not even noon!"

"Just shut up and drive," Berger said, deep in thought.

They parked around the corner and pushed through the doors into Michael's. Settling in at the bar, LoBianco asked Berger if he was drinking or sipping seltzer.

"I'll have a sidecar," Berger said.

"A sidecar? What the hell is that?"

"The Harvey Wallbanger of the forties," the bartender said. "Grand Marnier, lemon juice, and brandy, shaken over cracked ice and served straight up with a twist. Right?"

"Right," Berger said. He had forgotten. The last time he had drunk alcohol was at a wedding in the 1950s. He didn't like the taste or the effect it had on him, but he felt he needed *something* to cheer him up. He took a sip of the concoction in front of him and realized at once booze wasn't the answer to his problems. It tasted like cough medicine.

"You know, this place used to be pretty tough," Berger said to LoBianco. "Look up there."

LoBianco looked up.

"Bullet holes," Berger said. "In the old days firing your piece in here was a popular sport."

"And we used to have the cleanest alley in Brooklyn," the bartender said, serving LoBianco a Jack Daniel's on the rocks.

"Why's that?" Lobianco asked.

"To accommodate the fist fights," the bartender said. "In them days the only women here were hookers and the guys enjoyed beating the shit out of each other. Keerist! You coulda eaten off that alley, it was so clean. More like a ring, you know."

"Sounds like some fun," LoBianco said. "You a major player in those days, Ira?"

"No. I always went home to my wife," Berger said.

"Doesn't sound like you missed much," LoBianco said.

"Maybe just my entire life," Berger said, bracing himself for another sip of cough syrup.

"Oh, I get it!" LoBianco said. "We're going to play 'I'm more depressed than you.' Don't be too confident, Ira. I'm real good at this."

"Well, well, Mr. I'm-High-on-Life."

"Shit, Ira. Listen to my story: I was born a poor black child in a sharecropper's shack—"

"Okay. You win," Berger conceded. "A glass of seltzer," he said to the bartender. "And take away this poison."

"That's more like it," LoBianco said. "It's not the case, is it?"

"No. It's . . . everything."

"Meaning your wife?"

"Among other things," Berger said. "And people."

"Things always get different," LoBianco said. "Better or worse, but they never stay the same."

"Thank you, Mr. Philosopher, I need advice from a kid like you like I need less hair," Berger said, running a hand through his thinning scalp.

"Maybe you *should* retire."

"And do what? Cops are always looking to quit the job and become authors, actors, or crooks. Maybe I should get a job in a coffee shop, making change. I could wear a baggy old cardigan with holes in the elbows and have everybody call me Pops."

"Watch it, Ira," LoBianco said. "I don't know if you could stand the excitement." He ordered another round.

"And speaking of excitement, I believe I see the hottest piece of ass I've had in a long while. A young woman will perk you up," LoBianco said.

"Maybe," Berger said.

"Lucy!" LoBianco called.

Lucy Velez was wearing a dark gray skirt and white blouse, the unofficial uniform she wore as a police aide. He waved and she came over to them.

"Hello, stranger," she said. Her smooth, creamy skin and dark flashing eyes turned him on instantly. "No calls, no letters, no flowers?"

"No time."

"Was I that bad?"

"No, you were that good. Nobody wants to tear off a piece of, uh, wants to eat a feast standing up. It should be enjoyed," LoBianco said.

"Mr. Valentino," Berger said disapprovingly.

"This is Sergeant Berger," LoBianco said. "He's got woman problems."

"He's cute," Lucy said, touching Berger's arm.

"You must be living with an unresolved Oedipus complex," Berger groused.

"No, but I got a cat," Lucy said.

LoBianco laughed, but suddenly turned serious when he saw Rotten Jack Murphy enter the bar and look around. "Lucy, stay here a minute and cheer Ira up. I gotta see a guy," he said. Her eyes held his, telling him things that words could not. The mood was broken when Lucy remembered her companion.

"Nice to meet ya," she said to Berger, then took LoBianco's arm and guided him over to the table where she introduced him to her friend Andy Powers. "Sonny's an old friend, too," she said.

It was obvious to LoBianco that Andy wanted to be more than Lucy's friend.

He was LoBianco's age, but short and stocky; his blond hair was shorn like a marine's. Andy Powers was bad news, a lifer, LoBianco thought. He ignored LoBianco's outstretched hand and gave him a hard look instead. LoBianco retaliated by kissing Lucy full on the lips and waving to both of them.

"I'll be over there," he said needlessly, pointing to a rear booth that Murphy had commandeered.

LoBianco could feel Andy Powers's eyes on his back as he crossed the smoky room. By the time he sat down opposite Murphy, Powers and Lucy were having a heated argument.

Rotten Jack was all business. "I'm doing this because we go back a long ways together, Sonny, and you're a stand-up guy. But you've just earned yourself a heavy marker."

"I owe you, I understand," LoBianco said, annoyed. He knew how trade-offs worked and he didn't appreciate Murphy treating him as if he were a rookie.

"Tomorrow morning, 5:00 A.M., at Broadway and Richmond. We're going to nail this sucker."

"Okay."

"You get five minutes alone with him. After that you're on your own."

"Five minutes isn't a lot of time, Jack," LoBianco said.

"Then use it wisely."

As an afterthought Murphy added, "These guys use Uzis like my old mother uses her oven. Be careful. And remember—"

"—we never had this conversation," LoBianco finished.

After Murphy had gone, LoBianco looked over to Lucy's table. Berger had joined them. Sonny smiled at them, but his smile was like a shark's. A hungry shark. Before he got halfway across the room, Andy Powers got up abruptly, grabbed his coat, and left the bar.

"What happened to your buddy?" LoBianco asked, sitting down.

"Ask *your* partner."

"Ira?"

"I told him a story he didn't want to hear," Berger said. "I told him how you were the number-one karate expert on the force and about how you maimed six people in ten seconds because they pissed you off."

"I never maimed anybody in a match," LoBianco said.

"What's the difference? Mr. Powers suddenly decided to go home to his wife. Which is what I'm going to do right now. I'm calling in sick for the rest of the afternoon."

"Thanks, Ira," LoBianco said.

"What are partners for, if not to lie for each other?"

# 9

Rose Berger felt it growing inside her: a faint movement, like the flutter of butterfly wings.

It wouldn't be long now, she thought, wandering through the boutique that had opened on New Utrecht Avenue. It was called the Baby Bazaar and specialized in clothes and accessories for newborns and toddlers. She felt at home there amid the bright clothes and cheerful mothers pushing beautiful children. It was a world she desperately wanted to join.

She picked up a pink sleeper embroidered with soft, fluffy lambs and sighed. Perfect, she thought, perfect for my little girl. She put the sleeper back and again felt the strange stirring inside her. She smiled. Ira would be so surprised.

"How much is this sleeper?" she asked a young saleswoman.

"Thirty-four dollars."

"My, things have certainly gone up," Rose said.

"For your grandchild?" the saleswoman asked helpfully.

Rose frowned and walked farther into the depths of the store. Was she that old? she wondered. Was she being ridiculous? How desperately she wanted a baby.

As she was thumbing through a rack of tiny, frilly dresses, she heard someone call her.

89

It was Josephine DeMarco, a woman she had worked with in the school cafeteria. They had been friends, comrades sharing the bureaucratic vicissitudes of the school system. Josey retired a year before Rose and they hadn't seen each other since . . . since she couldn't remember when.

"Rose! What a surprise," Josey DeMarco said. "Where have you been hiding?"

Rose smiled guiltily, feeling as if she had been caught doing something illegal or immoral. "How are you?" she asked.

Josey DeMarco was almost six feet tall in her size-eleven heels, and as big as she was tall. Cowering behind her bulk was a little girl of two, with curly blond hair. She peeked out at Rose from time to time.

"This is my granddaughter, Tammy," Josey said, propelling the little girl from behind her. "Say hello to Mrs. Berger."

The little girl grabbed one of Josey's massive thighs for support.

"She's shy," Josey said. "Didn't get that from *my* side of the family."

"She's adorable," Rose said.

"In small doses, like grappa," Josey said. "Believe me, Rose. I'm getting too old for this. My daughter had better come to her senses and move back in with her idiot husband. Some people never know when they've got it made. Like you. You never had any children to ruin your life—or your figure. You look great."

Rose smiled again and said, "Some people are so lucky."

"Not me. Just because I'm Italian, everybody thinks I'm Earth Mother. It ain't so, kid," Josey said, bending down and scooping up her granddaughter in one meaty arm. "Give Gramma a kiss, Tammy," she said.

The little girl gave her a dutiful peck on the cheek, but continued to stare at Rose with enormous brown eyes.

"What are you buying?" Josey said.

"Just some things for my niece," Rose said quickly.

"Cost an arm and a leg," Josey observed, riffling through a rack of overalls. "Say, I've got an idea. Why don't you come home and have lunch with me. I could use some adult conversation for a change."

"Well, I don't know."

"Here, you take Tammy," Josey said, thrusting the child into Rose's arms. Tammy put her arms around Rose's neck. "I just want to go next door and pick up my cleaning. I'll meet you in the parking lot around the corner in five minutes." She began walking away. Josey rarely took no for an answer.

Tammy looked fearfully at her grandmother, then turned back to inspect Rose.

"Gramma," she said.

"Yes, dear. We're going to meet her in a minute," Rose said, adjusting the child in her arms. The little girl smelled of Ivory soap and lollipops. Her chubby face and a shock of golden curls were all that showed from within the pink snowsuit.

Rose carried the child to the door of the shop, positive everyone was looking at her and admiring her child. She felt as if she was in a pleasant dream.

On the sidewalk, Rose began murmuring things in the child's ear, loving, endearing things. But instead of responding, Tammy began to fidget.

"Down," she demanded.

Ignoring her, Rose wrapped the little girl tighter in her arms and glided toward the parking lot.

Tammy began to cry, softly at first, then louder and louder. "Down! Down! Down!"

When Josey DeMarco joined them, Tammy's face was beet red, her breath coming in gasps.

"Tammy," Josey said, grabbing for the child. It took all her strength to pry the little girl from Rose's grasp.

As if waking from the dream, Rose suddenly became

aware of her surroundings. "I'm sorry," she said. "I didn't want her to run into the traffic."

"It's okay," Josey said, putting Tammy down on the pavement. "She likes to walk. Are you ready?"

"Thanks all the same, Josey," Rose said, shaken. "But I think I'll go home. I'm not feeling well."

"I'll call you," Josey said, hurrying away.

Rose turned away, sick to her stomach.

# 10

Charles Maris held her breasts in his hands, feeling the smooth hardness of her generous nipples. He took a deep breath, his groin tingling with anticipation.

Slowly he moved his hands from her breasts, down to her ample belly. He paused for a moment to finger her navel, then closed his eyes and allowed his hands to roam freely over her partially clothed body.

The pressure in his groin increased and he freed his growing penis from his pants and stroked it to full length.

With one hand on his cock and the other tracing her classical features, her breasts, and belly, he came in less than a minute; spewing his semen all over the floor of his bedroom—and on the statue of the Venus de Milo he held in the other.

He rubbed his dwindling penis on the stumps of her arms and sighed.

Arms for Emily, he thought. And he knew where to get them.

It had been a week since his first kill, and his anticipation was keen. It was made doubly keen because his mother had called again, saying he should be prepared for a visit. Or a visitation, he thought, as she had been dead for a long while. He had to hurry.

Before leaving the house, he stopped in the library to tell Emily he was going out. Although she had been voluble recently, she refused to acknowledge him this morning. She seemed to know what he intended to do, as if she could read his mind.

But he swore that no one—not Emily, not even Mother—would stop him from completing his task.

Rain fell as he left the house, a slow, steady downpour that made him pull up the collar of his dirty, tan raincoat. The wind swept sodden leaves around his feet; the sky roiled ominously.

Where's the jugular vein? he quizzed himself, imagining he was a child standing proudly before his class, answering the questions.

There are two jugular veins on either side of the neck; the external and the internal. Thank you. And wait! Their names are derived from the Latin *jugulus,* which means collarbone.

Maris smiled brightly. He had done his homework. He knew where the veins were and how much pressure it would take to cut through them.

He would do it for Emily, he thought, not for Mother.

His head began to hurt. All he had to do was think about Mother and his head began to hurt.

The rain pelted him in the face; somewhere in the distance he thought he heard thunder. Or perhaps it was only the rumble of a train on the elevated tracks.

"Charles?" he heard his mother call, in the shrill, insistent voice that always made him cringe. "You are late."

"Yes, Mother," he said, standing in the dark, airless foyer of the old house.

His mother emerged from the library. She was small and wrinkled, whipcord thin, and hard. Her mouth was a tight line of permanent disapproval. "Did you press the clean white dress?" she demanded.

"Yes, Mother," Charles answered, nodding his head vigorously to reinforce his answer.

"And are the Mary Janes polished?"

Charles nodded.

"I can't hear you," his mother snapped.

"Yes, yes, Mother," Charles stammered. "I did everything you told me."

"Very good. Now get dressed," she said.

"Mother, please." His voice was a moaning whimper.

"Don't argue with me, Charles," she said. "This is your fault, your fault entirely, and you have to be taught a lesson." Her eyes glowed with rage. "I will take tea with Emily at four. Precisely."

The humiliation of those tea parties was transcended only by the quarterly shopping sprees he had to endure. He remembered vividly the last trip to Mrs. Able's Mother & Daughter Togs, only a short walk from the brownstone in Bay Ridge.

Chattering and laughing like demented magpies, his mother and aunt looked forward to replenishing his "special wardrobe." They forced him to dress in a shapeless white frock, trimmed with little pink bows and marched him out to Mrs. Able's with a regularity that shocked Charles. But he was too young to stop them, too guilty to try.

With the absolute assurance of declining gentility, the sisters always arranged for private showings of new clothes for Charles. They were not the type of people who would fight over clothes at Alexander's or May's. No, they preferred small shops and obsequious owners bowing and scraping to their taste, position, and pocketbook.

Mrs. Able answered their discreet knock at 6:00 P.M. that winter evening. Charles was fourteen. She almost bowed to the two women and the chunky, graceless little girl.

Mrs. Able pulled the overhead chain hanging from the fluorescent lights and the dusty, neglected shop was bathed in a ghastly blue light that made Charles's pimples look like open sores.

"Tea, ladies?" Mrs. Able asked, and before receiving a reply, walked to the rear of the ship. Opening the heavy brocade curtain separating the kitchen from the rest of the store, she went directly to the teapot, kept warm by a knitted cozy.

Thinking business was business no matter how peculiar the customers, she forced a smile and poured two lukewarm cups of tea for the sisters, who had already taken up their regular positions in chairs set out for the occasion.

With a shaky hand, Mrs. Able delivered the tea, cream, no sugar, and began commenting on Charles's rapid growth and robust shape. "Not like some of the girls these days," she said. "Always dieting and ruining their constitutions."

Charles grimaced; the sisters basked in the light of false compliments.

Mrs. Able selected a garment and held it up to herself for the two women to inspect. They cooed with appreciation, and Mrs. Able had her first sale that evening. The dress, peacock blue with white-and-green trim, cost her sixteen dollars wholesale. Her normal markup was one hundred percent, but for this private showing, five hundred percent. She rubbed her hands together.

Once an armful of clothing had been chosen, it was time for Charles to try everything on. He dragged his feet like a two-year-old, pouting and whining until Mother threatened physical punishment.

Finally Charles retreated to the dressing room and, one by one, tried on the garments his mother and aunt had chosen for him. During this performance he blocked out everything from his mind, concentrating only on getting through the ordeal.

Watching from behind the brocade curtain, also wishing for the ordeal to end, Mrs. Able decided to help the process along and walked to the dressing room to help the balky girl get on with it.

Ripping the curtain open, she caught Charles between dresses, naked, prepubescent, porcine—and definitely male.

"Fuck you," Charles snarled, covering himself with a red wool skirt. "Fuck you to hell!"

Mrs. Able gasped and backed away from the fat child— the fat boy.

That's when Charles went berserk, ripping and shredding the clothes, screaming a stream of profanity at the top of his childish voice.

Mother rushed to quell the rebellion with a bony hand and punch like a fighter. But this time even repeated slaps failed to stop Charles's frenzy. He streaked out of the shop, wearing only his navy-blue coat and patent-leather shoes.

The two women followed him out of the shop and to Mrs. Able's satisfaction never returned.

Never again, Charles though as he entered Ann's Cup 'n' Saucer, a coffee shop he had been frequenting for more than a month. The coffee was weak, the toast cold, and the eggs a breeding ground for salmonella, but Ann's had one thing no other coffee shop had: Adele Woodword.

Adele was a regular at Ann's, a well-preserved, brassy blonde, who was lonely and depressed since her husband, the dentist, had run away with his twenty-two-year-old dental hygienist. He was sitting on the beach in Cozumel; she was sitting in a Bensonhurst coffee shop telling her troubles to anyone who would listen.

Charles had pretended to listen, but what he was most interested in were Adele's arms. She had solid, sinewy arms that were tanned and freckled. She was too old for Emily, he knew, but her arms were the arms of a much younger woman.

"I don't know what's wrong with this city," Adele said after Charles had settled his considerable bulk into the booth opposite her. "Rape, murder, molestation, and just last week a woman had her hands chopped off."

"Horrible," Charles murmured.

"It's enough to give me goose bumps all over," Adele said, rubbing her arms.

Charles ran his tongue over his thick lips.

"Try the pie, dear," Adele said. "You'd think with all the taxes we pay, the cops would round up these beasts and put them in jail."

"Mmm."

"Or maybe we should just give up," she said.

"'Or take arms against a sea of troubles,'" Charles quoted.

"Precisely," Adele Woodword said, smiling.


The wind rattled the panes and rain smeared the soot-darkened windows as Ira Berger sat stewing his feet in the basin of hot water.

The clock on the Brooklyn Savings Bank had stopped at 10:47 and hadn't moved in two days. Neither had Berger.

In the bedroom, Rose was getting ready to leave the house. His stomach soured at the thought of Gross.

They were two people who were occupying a small space, but they had ceased to communicate, ceased to acknowledge each other's presence. Strangers sharing an apartment, he thought morosely.

Berger had spent the past two days in his off-duty clothes: a starched white shirt with frayed cuffs and a pair of suit pants rolled at the waist. Rose had gone out all day, each day, on some mysterious business she wouldn't share with him. They were sleeping in the same bed, but they might as well have been on opposite sides of the planet.

This couldn't continue, he thought, wiping his feet on a blue towel. He would get it over with this morning. He got up and limped toward his future.

He stood outside the closed bedroom door, *his bedroom door,* and built up a head of steam. When his anger reached what he considered a convincing level, he pounded his fist against the wooden door. The sound echoed in the hallway, encouraging him. He was ready for Rose when she unlocked the door and said, "Yes, Ira." It was a voice Ira didn't recognize. She's like a stranger, he thought, saying "Rose, we have to talk."

Rose looked at her husband blank-eyed as she continued to block the doorway to the bedroom. "Not now, Ira. I'm very busy.

Berger didn't like being dismissed any more than he liked being locked out of his bedroom. "Now, Rose!" he shouted, but could not bring himself to push her back out of the way. "We've got to talk."

Anger flashed in Rose's eyes. "There's nothing to talk about, Ira. I've made up my mind."

"Made up your mind? Made up your mind about what?" Berger demanded.

"I'm leaving . . . for a while," she said.

"Leaving? Leaving here? Leaving me? Leaving everything?" he demanded.

"Yes," Rose answered. "All those."

"Why are you going?" Berger asked.

"You know why," she said, as if it were all old news to Berger. "I need to get away."

Berger's voice rose with each word as he said, "I want answers, Rose, you give me *bubkes*! Where are you going? With who?"

"Don't scream at me, Ira," she said softly.

"Where are you going, to Gross the butcher?"

"You're being asinine," Rose said, but before Berger could react, she slammed and locked the door.

For a moment Berger faced the locked door; the echoes of its slam were like a bell tolling the end of his marriage. "Rose, we *have* to talk about this," he called through the doorway. "What have I done wrong? Is it about the job?"

"No," she called back.

"Take the job, Rose. Just don't leave."

"We'll see, Ira. I have a life, you must let me live it," she said. She could feel the movements again, inside her.

"With Gross the Cossack?"

"He's just a businessman, Ira. A successful business-man," she said.

"And I'm just an unsuccessful cop," he said.

She opened the door. "Ira, if you want to talk, we'll talk. But not now."

Stunned, Ira Berger went into the living room, sat down on the recliner, and cursed himself. Then he cursed Rose. Then life. What the hell could he do?

While he sat there, head in hands, Rose emerged from the bedroom, dressed to go out. He didn't even look up; she didn't bother to say good-bye.


Adele Woodword thought it was strangely coincidental that she had run into Charles Maris almost every day for a month. He was a pleasant enough man, she thought, very intelligent, very considerate, very lonely. She had a sneaking suspicion that he was gay, but she wasn't sure. Perhaps he was a passive heterosexual, denied much contact with women because of his odd looks and—let's face it—a body that was the "before" picture in a diet ad.

"Have you ever tried Nutri/System?" Adele asked Maris as he was devouring a second helping of blueberry pie.

"What's that?" Charles asked.

"It's a weight-control system," she said, parroting the radio and television commercials.

"You think I'm too fat?" he asked.

"Generous, Charles. Generous."

Maris gave her a wan smile, but felt like killing the bitch on the spot.

Damn, she thought. I've hurt his feelings. She felt a twinge of guilt from her harsh but honest assessment of his looks. Charles Maris was, in truth, an extremely unattractive man, way below the level of the men she had dated since her husband had taken off with the bimbo. But Charles was so lonely and so darn nice, she couldn't help but consider him as a potential companion, if only for dinner sometimes.

On the other side of the booth Charles was thinking about

Adele. Not as a friend or lover, but as a source of arms. Matching, tanned arms, strengthened by tennis and shaped by aerobics. They were his to harvest.

He had always made an effort to appear to be a good listener, making eye contact when she sought it and asking well-timed, pertinent questions.

"Are you busy this evening, Adele?" he asked, pushing away his half-eaten blueberry pie. The filling leaked onto the table like clotted blood.

"Well, my girlfriend and I were going to go to a movie," she said.

"Would you like to have dinner with me?" he said, lowering his eyes demurely.

"Certainly," she said. "I want you to meet Martha. I told her all about you."

Maris felt the bile rise in his throat; he swallowed hard. *She talked about me!*

"Martha's a wonderful girl," Adele said. "Smart, funny, and beautiful on the inside, where it counts." She was also forty-five pounds overweight, had a chronic case of psoriasis, and chewed with her mouth open. A perfect match for Charles, Adele thought.

"Well . . ." Charles's insides churned.

"That would be nice," he said at last. "Some other time." His anonymity had been compromised. He might be connected to her. The police would interrogate him, hound him, search him, and seize him. These thoughts raced through his mind. "What did you tell her?" he asked, barely controlling his voice.

"Charles, my goodness, you've gotten so tense," Adele said. She lightly touched his flexed arm. He jerked it away automatically.

She smiled a knowing smile, taking it for granted it was the idea of meeting women in general that had upset him. He was *so* shy. "I only spoke in generalities," she continued. "I told her I knew someone nice she might like to meet. It was nothing definite. I just couldn't help being a matchmaker.''

She smiled sympathetically. ''You're shy with women, aren't you, Charles?''

Maris nodded like a puppy. The bitch, the self-centered cunt, the condescending whore. ''Did you tell her my name?'' he whispered. There were things he had to learn quickly; he had to put her at ease.

''Only your first name. I really couldn't tell her much more than that, could I? I don't even know where you work,'' she said.

''That's all?''

''That's all,'' Adele said, smiling reassuringly. She didn't know her bright red lipstick had coated her horsey front teeth. It looked to Charles as if someone had punched her in the mouth. The idea appealed to him.

''So? Do you want to meet her?'' Adele asked.

''Can I think about it?'' Charles replied.

''Of course, dear,'' Adele said.

''But about tonight?'' he asked. ''Just us. Then maybe you can tell me more about, uh . . .''

''Martha,'' Adele said. ''It's so difficult to meet people these days, what with this AIDS thing and all the creeps running around. You never know when you'll run into some crazy.''

''True,'' Charles said, smiling broadly, then catching himself and toning it down to a shy grin.

''Excellent,'' Adele said. ''I'll meet you tonight and we'll work out all the details.''

''Uh, Adele. Could you do me a favor?'' Charles asked.

''Certainly.''

''Don't tell her anything more about me, because if I don't meet her, she'll feel disappointed. As I would,'' Charles said.

''Sure, Charles,'' Adele said. ''If that's what you want. I won't even tell her that I'm meeting you tonight.''

"Thank you, Adele." She would definitely have to die tonight, Charles thought. Before she did any more damage.

"Agreed," she said.

"Agreed!" he said, starting to get up.

Adele looked puzzled. "My address," she said.

"Oh, yes," he said. He had almost made a serious mistake. He knew very well where she lived, knew all about her. He sat back down, breathing hard.

She gave him the address, then checked her watch and told him she had to rush off to get prepared for their "strategy meeting."

As she walked briskly away Charles tried to picture her strolling down the street without her arms. The thought made him giggle aloud.

# 11

Sonny LoBianco was too tense to think straight. Had he really turned down a night with Lucy? Was he nuts? But the importance of tomorrow's bust was paramount, he told himself. He had to be calm and clearheaded in the morning or he could screw up the entire deal. His lust would have to wait; common sense reigned.

Dressed in his sweats, he poked around the orphanage looking for E.T., but the boy had gone off to play basketball at the junior-high-school gym. Father Davis, as usual, was too busy to work out with him, so he retreated through the steady rain to his converted garage.

Just as well, he thought. There were techniques he needed to practice, ones that E.T. wasn't ready for, mentally or physically; ones that Davis was too old and out of shape to endure. As usual he would have to rely on himself.

LoBianco was not a natural athlete, but he had a fighter's heart and instincts and an intelligence that made him an extremely dangerous opponent. Sometimes he wished he had more raw talent like E.T., who could pick up fighting techniques the first time he saw them demonstrated. Even at his young age, E.T. was technically better than Sonny, but that's as far as it went. Where E.T. threw perfect techniques, Sonny threw techniques perfectly. Intuitively he knew where to strike most effectively and had the inborn desire to want to hurt an opponent. The mental side of fighting could not be taught; it was either there or it wasn't.

For almost fifteen years Sonny had trained under Tadashi Harada, a Japanese karate master. Harada, a friend of Franklyn Davis, didn't operate a conventional school. Instead he chose to teach a handful of dedicated students. Harada taught karate as a martial art and not a sport. The moves he demonstrated had no place in tournaments, for these were *budo* techniques designed for the one-strike kill.

Dressed in his *gi* now and on the mat, LoBianco began by pushing the heavy bag to get it moving. The bag he used had padded arms and legs to give it a more lifelike appearance and to facilitate his foot sweeps.

Watching the bag sway, LoBianco tapped his hand against his leg, setting up a rhythm and cadence that would trigger his lightning-fast hand-and-foot combinations. As he moved against the swinging target his focus and concentration tightened until nothing else existed for him except the bag.

Warming up, he threw various combinations in fierce, staccato bursts of energy; the bag rocked wildly under his assault.

He paused for a moment to visualize what he would do next—a kick-punch combination trapping an opponent's arm and twisting it into an arm-bar throw. The throw, as taught by Harada, was leveraged against the elbow and designed to break the arm.

LoBianco practiced the technique, as he had been taught, and tried to imagine the sound of breaking bones each time he twisted into the bag. If necessary, in a tournament or demonstration, he could make a mental switch and leverage the throw into the bend of the elbow. That would tear cartilage and leave the bone intact. But he always practiced the more vicious form of any technique because he didn't want a gold medal or a blue ribbon; he wanted his opponent finished.

Unnoticed, Father Franklyn Davis slipped into the garage. With a professional eye he observed Sonny's workout and, as always, was engrossed. There was menace in every move Sonny made, menace and brutal efficiency. Sonny wasn't pretty to watch, but he was deadly effective, and there was no doubt about the damaging power of his fists and feet. He was a machine, Davis thought, a motherfucking machine. He had learned well.

Still, it saddened the priest to see Sonny governed by the same emotions that had plagued him when he had first arrived at St. Agnes's more than fourteen years before. He had been filled with rage and hate then, Davis thought. He'd controlled it to some extent, but remained a time bomb just waiting to explode. Sonny succeeded at what he did, the priest knew, because he could call upon these emotions almost at will. Frightening, Davis thought.

"Sonny," the priest called.

LoBianco heard him, but Davis's voice didn't penetrate the depth's of his concentration. But after a second or two he brought his attention back into focus and turned around.

"There's somebody here to see you," Davis said.

Angela! LoBianco hoped wildly.

"It's your uncle Vito," Davis said. His face gave no sign of his displeasure.

LoBianco ran in place, cooling down. "Send him in."

"You don't get it," Davis said. "*He* wants to see *you*. In the driveway."

Sonny shrugged. "Give me a minute."

What the hell does he want? LoBianco wondered as he toweled down and put on a light windbreaker. This is the first time he's ever come here personally. Something's going down.

Two men dressed in navy-blue suits, white shirts, and navy ties stood flanking Vito's Mercedes limousine. They were young, hard, and probably Sicilian. American wiseguys wouldn't ruin their suits by standing in the rain, Sonny thought.

One of the men opened the backdoor for him and Sonny slid into the soft luxury of the limo.

"Santino, *minghia*. I'm glad to see you," Vito said, brushing his droopy salt-and-pepper mustache with a stubby finger. He dressed like his men: formally, expensively, conservatively.

"What can I do for you, Uncle Vito?" Sonny asked.

"Jeez, Sonny. You smell like a corpse," Vito said.

"I was just working out."

"Didn't they teach you to wash here?"

"I didn't want Romulus and Remus to shrink in the rain," Sonny said, nodding toward the bodyguards. "Now, what's up?"

"I just wanted to tell you I'm delivering the bus you wanted. Tomorrow. I got a good deal on a minibus. That way all the orphans can ride together," Vito said.

"Thanks," Sonny said. "It's nice of you." What does he want?

"It's my pleasure and my duty to help the orphans," Vito said.

"I'm sure they'll appreciate your, uh, generosity." Shit, what the hell does he want?

"That's good. Real good."

Sonny took a moment to choose his words carefully. "Uncle Vito, the priest—Father Davis—has a problem accepting charity from . . ." Suddenly he found himself drawing a blank, but Vito understood.

"Yeah. The priest don't like wiseguys. No disrespect intended, but these people get uppity when they get education. He didn't object to the envelopes of cash I sent him when you was a kid living here," Vito said. "And he won't kick at this bus neither. I got it covered."

"Yeah?"

"Yeah. I know these guys in the Bronx," Vito said. "So I had Jew writin' put on the bus. You can tell him a rabbi gave it to him." Vito laughed.

"It's real nice of you," Sonny said, mystified.

"Sure, sure, Santino. But one thing: you don't want the priest should know where it came from, right? And I don't want Frankie Marcellino to find out about it either. A deal?"

"You got it," Sonny said.

"And one more thing. I think it's time we had a sit-down. Just you and I, okay?"

"Okay. When?"

"Tomorrow?"

"Late?"

"Like a hoor's legs, I'm always open," Vito said.

"Midnight?"

"I'm an old man, Santino. Eleven? Il Bacio's?" Vito said.

Sonny nodded, thinking, Christ, something real bad is happening if he's sneaking around behind Frankie's back.

"Don't forget, Sonny," Vito said as LoBianco opened the door of the limo. "Il Bacio's, eleven."

"See ya," Sonny said, slamming the door and walking back to the garage through the pelting rain.

After showering, LoBianco stretched out on his bed, missing Angela's warm, naked body beside him. Or even Lucy's.

He put his hands behind his head and tried to get everything organized, but he kept thinking about Vito. He didn't like or trust his uncle and he had always tried to stay away from the family business. Davis's influence, he thought. But apparently Vito had been paying the priest off for years.

He closed his eyes, but sleep wouldn't come. Instead he thought about the violent and tragic events that brought him to St. Agnes's fifteen years before, when he was fourteen.

He tried to remember his mother. She had been caring and attentive, providing for him as was expected of any Italian mother. Yet there had always been something distant about Antoinette LoBianco. He had always had the feeling that whatever love his mother had given him was a leftover kind of love. Left over from her overwhelming passion for his father. She was devoted to his father, and perhaps, he thought, it was more than that, an obsessive kind of love.

His father, Santino, Sr., had always seemed larger than life to his son, his wife, his associates and enemies. A sharp dresser, fond of thousand-dollar suits, white-on-white shirts with French cuffs, and black cashmere overcoats, LoBianco, Sr., was a legend in the 1950s and 1960s—the man the media identified as the *capo di tutti capi;* the man whose very picture meant Mafia. As usual the media was wrong.

Despite the media's frenzied hype and various congressional committees' charges, LoBianco, Sr., was not a boss. Or even an underboss or captain. He was the Genco family's sole enforcer. They needed no other. With his face seemingly set in concrete, his piercing blue eyes, and cruel smile, LoBianco, Sr., was a much feared and respected man.

Sonny remembered his father as a powerful force who moved through his childhood like a freight train, rarely stopping for him. In LoBianco, Sr.'s business any sign of affection—even to his own child—was a sign of weakness, and weakness meant death.

The LoBianco family lived comfortably and stylishly in their Tudor home along the affluent Shore Road section of Brooklyn. The elder LoBianco provided well for his family, even though he rarely spent time at home. He had never taken a mistress, as his brother Vito had; instead he devoted almost all his time to "doing business" for the Gencos. This single-mindedness made him the best at his job. He knew no mercy, accepted no compromise, saw no reason to doubt anything the Gencos told him. He would have made a first-rate military commander or Jesuit, Sonny's mother said.

Until he turned thirteen, Sonny considered his father an almost mythical being, who descended magically to share his presence with his family. But just when he was beginning to question his father's authority, as was natural, it all ended. Suddenly, without warning.

Two days before Christmas, LoBianco had been awakened in the middle of the night by the insistent ringing of the doorbell. He had been dreaming about Viola Rizzo, a dark-haired beauty who sat in front of him at St. Michael's Prep School. She had smiled at him before Christmas vacation and he wondered if she liked him.

The doorbell kept ringing until he finally got out of bed and went downstairs. The Christmas tree was dark, but the ornaments shone strangely in the flashing red lights from outside.

His mother stood with her back to the door, staring blankly at him.

"Mom?"

There were tears in her eyes; she bit down on her knuckle. "Tell them to go away," she said in a whisper.

Uncertain and fearful, he stood there. Then someone pounded on the door.

"Go away," his mother managed.

"Maybe it's Dad," Sonny said tentatively.

"He has a key," his mother said, between sobs.

Then he heard the word *police* shouted from outside and he couldn't wait any longer. Gently he moved his mother aside and flipped the dead bolt. Three men entered the foyer, two detectives in plainclothes and an officer in uniform. He knew at once his father was dead.

The cops were considerate with his mother, arranging for a neighbor to stay with her and looking the other way when associates of his father arrived to maintain security and privacy. During this time his mother never said a word. She had stopped crying, withdrawing into herself. But Sonny found her wide-eyed stare more frightening than her tears.

He tried to get specific information from the police, but he was only a kid in pajamas, and they ignored him or muttered well-meaning platitudes. Although they were on the other side of the law, the cops were in the same crime business as LoBianco, Sr., and they treated his family with the respect owed to a fierce enemy.

Numb, Sonny had the feeling that this was all a dream,

that he was living in a "Twilight Zone" episode. He went to his room and put on his clothes, hoping to feel less vulnerable.

When he came back downstairs, the police had gone, leaving his mother surrounded by clucking and cooing women. On the other side of the room several of his father's friends were discussing LoBianco, Sr.'s gruesome death. They were speculating about both the killers and the technique of the hit. As far as Sonny could gather, it was a professional job, an intrafamily argument settled for good.

He heard one word—*boardwalk*—and knew his father had been killed somewhere near Coney Island; suddenly it seemed important to Sonny to see his father's body. But he shook off the notion, deciding that his place was by his mother's side. He was the man of the house now, and men had certain duties to perform. He was not quite sure what those duties were, but he knew he should be strong and supportive.

Lounging in the foyer, attempting to look grown up, he watched his mother sitting in her favorite chair, dry-eyed and tense. Then, to his astonishment, Antoinette LoBianco shook her head as if to dispel the cobwebs, looked around, and smiled.

"It must be getting late," she said, standing up. "I have to get ready."

"Ready for what?" a neighbor asked.

"Ready for Santino when he comes home," she said. "I have to cook for my husband." Her voice betrayed her annoyance at such a stupid question.

She marched resolutely to the kitchen, leaving a houseful of openmouthed mourners.

Waiting a second to see what the others would do, Sonny finally went into the kitchen and led his mother firmly upstairs to her bedroom. She went along without protest.

He remembered feeling strange standing there in the bedroom, surrounded by all his father's things and knowing he was gone forever.

He dismissed the gaggle of concerned neighbors and relatives with an unaccustomed show of authority and convinced his mother to take two Valiums. Then he sat by her bed until she dozed off, wondering how long it would be until she got back to normal. No matter how long it took, he promised himself, he would look out for her, be strong for her. He had no way of knowing she would be dead in six months.

The wind bit into him like a starving wolf, but he pedaled his bicycle manfully into the gale, looking for his father. A full moon shown down on the cold ocean, giving the wind-whipped whitecaps an eerie glow. It took him more than an hour of steady riding to find the spot where his father had been assassinated.

He recognized his father's metallic-blue Eldorado at once. It was half under the boardwalk, not far from the derelict Coney Island parachute jump. Once the premier attraction at the amusement park, the parachute jump was only a green, rusted hulk standing forlornly now in the middle of a small lot.

A crime-scene unit had set up barriers to keep the curious away, a score of cops and technicians combed the area for evidence; klieg lights augmented the moonlight, producing a hellish aura around the scene. Sonny knew then that hell was not the fiery inferno the Brothers had told him about, but a cold, desolate place like this. He fought the urge to cross himself.

Shaking from more than just the cold, Sonny dropped his bike and slipped through the tape marking the crime-scene limits. He lingered nervously in the shadows, his stomach heaving, his breath rapid and shallow. He told himself not to think too much, because it would make him cry.

"Hey, you. Kid. Get the hell out of there!" he heard someone yell. "Damn it, get that kid out of there."

He took a deep breath. The dank sand and wooden piers had a distinctive smell he would remember forever—the smell of the grave. He stepped into the glare of the lights and said, "I'm Santino LoBianco's son. I want to see my father."

Twenty pairs of eyes pinned him to the spot. His mouth went dry and he thought he would throw up. Then a big, white-haired man wearing a gold badge pinned to his overcoat stepped forward. He was red-faced and more than a little drunk, and even more pissed off at having to leave his anniversary party to supervise the cleanup of some ginzo hoodlum.

"That your father?" the man asked in a gruff voice.

Sonny swallowed; nothing went down. "Yes," he said, his voice breaking. "I want to see him."

"Take a look," the red-faced man said with a sneer. "Take a good fucking look."

A uniformed lieutenant came over and said, "Should we really do that, Chief? Suppose the papers get ahold of this?"

"Fuck it," Chief Francis X. Callahan growled. "These wops grow up with this shit. It'll be a good lesson for the boy. Maybe it will convince him to be a barber or a shoemaker instead of a goddamn gangster."

The lieutenant shrugged. He wasn't going to have it out with an assistant chief over some punk kid with the ghoulish bad taste to view his father's body before it had been properly prepared.

"Hey, kid," Lieutenant Boyd said, motioning to Sonny. "You got identification?"

Sonny reached into his back pocket and took out the wallet his mother had given him for his last birthday. He riffled through it and pulled out a St. Michael's library card.

Lieutenant Boyd regarded it seriously, as if he were stopping Sonny for a traffic violation, then glanced around. The chief, Callahan, was bellowing useless orders and issuing redundant instructions as he surreptitiously negotiated his way back to his waiting car and driver.

Boyd wondered what to do, but was spared having to

make a decision by Father Franklyn Davis. The black priest came up to him and asked what was going on.

"Kid's old man was hit," Boyd said.

"What's he doing here?"

"Wants to see the body."

"Why?"

"Don't ask me. Chief said it was okay."

"Let me talk to him," Davis said.

"*I'm* not dead," Sonny said, getting angry. "Don't talk about me like I'm dead, like I'm not standing here."

"See?" Boyd said.

"Let's take a walk," Davis said.

Sonny looked at the priest with suspicion. Davis was big, ugly, and black. Sonny could see the bulge of a gun under his left arm. Normally he would have been afraid of such a man, except Davis was wearing a Roman collar. He allowed himself to be led away.

After introducing himself, Davis said, "You don't have to do this, son. Why don't you remember the way your father was. Believe me, it'll be much better." Davis had returned from Vietnam; he knew what the hell he was talking about. Death, and the inevitable refuse of war— body parts and fluids—had been his constant companion for two tours.

Sonny looked up at the priest, allowing the black man to see some of the pain and fear behind his eyes. "I have to," he said.

Davis nodded sadly, but said nothing as he walked with the boy to the car.

Santino LoBianco lay half in and half out of the Eldorado. His legs were wedged against the steering wheel, keeping most of him inside. His upper body hung out the door, his arms reaching out as if to block his fall. The back of his head was dark and matted; a pool of blood, looking like oil in the moonlight, had gathered and congealed on the pavement. The shattered windshield was smeared with blood and bits of bone and brain.

Davis pointed to the victim's jewelry. "Do you recognize the ring and watch?" he asked.

Sonny nodded, staring fixedly at the corpse. "I want to see his face."

"No, you don't," Davis said. "Believe me, you don't." He had seen what a bullet could do to a human head. The entry wound was usually small, but when the hot lead expanded inside a confined space, such as a cranium, the result was . . .

"Let's go," Davis said.

"No," Sonny said. He didn't want to spend the rest of his life knowing he didn't have the courage to look.

"A hard case." Davis sighed, motioning to a technician. "Okay if we look at his face?"

"Sure, we're done," the police technician said. "But it's X-rated, Father. Wouldn't want my boy to see this. It's something you take to the grave."

Davis looked at Sonny. The boy's young face was tight and drawn. Davis shrugged. The technician shook his head sadly and said, "Never say I didn't warn you." He put on surgical gloves and gripped Sonny's father by the hair and pulled his head into the blazing klieg lights.

There was hardly anything recognizable about Santino LoBianco's face. The upper portion of his head, from cheekbones to hairline, had been blown outward, exposing his brain. The brain itself was bloody and glistening; large chunks of it lay in the pool of blood on the pavement. An eyeball, Sonny couldn't tell which one, hung by a gray strand and swayed back and forth like a pendulum. The lower part of his proud Roman nose remained intact, but it was clotted with blood, his teeth were clamped shut in a rictus smile; a piece of bitten tongue dangled from the clenched teeth.

Sonny turned away quickly, gagging, vomiting. As he heaved his guts out he remembered the strong hands of the priest holding and trying to comfort him.

Afterward, when Davis drove him back to Shore Road, it

struck Sonny that he had been cheated. He hadn't really seen his father, only some grotesque parody of a human face. He would never see his father again.

"I'm always at St. Agnes's," Davis had said, helping the boy unload his bicycle from the car. "If you want to talk, son—"

"I'm not your son," Sonny said, his face contorting in anger. "I'm not your goddamned son!" His shock had turned to anger, but he was embarrassed he had spoken to a priest that way.

Davis sighed. "And I'm not your father. Thank God."

They were both wrong.

# 12

Charles Maris was worried about Dempsey, his prize pit bull. Maris had encouraged and shaped the dog's aggressiveness, but Dempsey had developed an alarming habit of challenging Charles's authority at every opportunity.

On more than one occasion Dempsey had left the sit-stay position Maris had commanded to return defiantly to his cage. He would also attack the other dogs if they didn't follow him, a bad sign. Charles had a palace revolution on his hands, and the only cure was to destroy the rebel. There could only be one leader, but Charles had grown attached to Dempsey in a distant way. Dempsey reminded him of another dog he had owned. Tag had had to be destroyed and Charles didn't think he could go through the agony again. But the time was coming, he thought, when he'd have to take real action.

Maris knew that total authority was imperative. To have a fifty-pound thunderbolt of muscle and jaws turn on him would be disastrous. He had answered Dempsey's initial challenges with firm admonishments, the first step in correcting a misguided dog. But Dempsey had ignored his commands, and when Maris persisted, the yellow-eyed pit bull reacted by showing his fangs. Maris knew then he should have put the dog down, but he didn't have the heart. Instead he continued to work with Dempsey.

117

During one confrontation Maris saw the other dogs watching with interest. They wouldn't interfere if Dempsey went after Maris, but when it was over, they would readily accept their new leader. It made Charles uneasy to think what the pack might do without him to control it.

Driven by love and fear, Charles had answered Dempsey's next show of resistance with a gnarled walking stick that had belonged to his grandfather. The stick, a shillelagh, was smooth and weighty, ending in a knob four inches in diameter. Putting his considerable strength behind the blow, Maris swung it viciously, catching the dog across the jaw and neck. Dempsey went tumbling and Maris continued hitting him until the dog retreated to his cage, making a last stand. Maris locked the cage, but Dempsey rocked it on its side, trying to get out, trying to get at Maris.

It took two weeks before Dempsey settled down and stopped charging the bars of his cage, trying to chew his way out to get at Maris. It was five weeks before Charles let him out and then only on a spiked choke collar with a one-foot leather lead that could be grabbed easily and snapped, giving the dog a quick, painful choke.

It seemed to work. Dempsey became obedient and docile, acting so submissive that the other dogs began to test his mettle. To the untrained eye Dempsey looked as if he had learned his lesson, yet Charles wasn't fooled. There was something behind the dog's evil yellow eyes that refused to be tamed. He knew that despite the choker Dempsey would attack him if he allowed himself to get into a vulnerable position. While the dog bided his time, so did Maris.

After he had fed and watered the dogs, Maris went upstairs to dress for his date with death. On his way out he stopped into the library to see Emily.

"Talk to me," he said, but Emily was silent.

"Stop being such a child," he said. "If I didn't know better, I'd swear you didn't want my help."

In the dim light of the library, the huddled mass of blankets in the wheelchair seemed to shift slightly. Or maybe he just imagined it. Emily could be so stubborn sometimes, it infuriated him. You try to do something nice for people and all they do is shit on you, he thought. Like Adele. He had offered to go out with the old bat and suddenly she was trying to palm him off on her ugly girlfriend. The ungrateful bitch. Well, she'd get hers to-night.

"I've got to hurry," he said to Emily. "It's almost eight and I don't want to keep Adele waiting."

He was dressed in an outdated gray sharkskin suit that was one size too small for his huge frame. A white rayon shirt yellowed with age and a clip-on paisley tie completed the outfit. His courting clothes, he thought, slipping on a pair of worn Top-Siders, size fourteen, triple E, and struggled into his dirty tan raincoat.

Reaching into the lower left-hand drawer of the massive desk, he withdrew a worn leather case. Two feet long and a foot wide inside, it held a shiny, stainless-steel bone saw nestled in red velvet. Charles secured the lock and left for his appointment.

The rain had changed to an icy drizzle at sunset, then had turned to sleet. Charles, holding tightly to the leather case, walked carefully on the slippery sidewalk. The miserable weather only whetted his appetite for the night's work. It took him forty-five minutes to reach his destination.

Adele Woodword's house was typical of Bensonhurst, a two-story brick structure with a big bay window. He looked up and down the street. Many of the small front yards on her block featured shrines to the Virgin Mary or cute lawn animals. During the holidays, Charles knew, the whole neighborhood would be ablaze with festive lights, neon crèches, and houses done up as Christmas packages.

Charles thought the waste of electricity celebrating the birth of a dead Jew was not a responsible use of a scarce resource. He sneered at the icons of the stupid and thought about kicking the next religious statue he saw. But an inner caution prevailed, and he plodded along in the sleet, trying to look as innocuous as possible. Fortunately the bad weather had emptied the streets, making his job easier.

A block from Adele's house he stopped to catch his breath. Leaning against a big elm tree, he went over how he would kill her. His original plan was to take her out somewhere to toy with her. He knew he would enjoy watching her prattle on about this and that, not realizing it was her last night on earth. But the shocking revelation that she had mentioned him to her girlfriend made him change his mind. He'd kill her in her house. Immediately.

He walked boldly to her front door and rang the bell.

"Hi, Charles," Adele said, opening the door. She was wearing a T-shirt and jeans. "It's nasty out there. Come on in."

"A good night for a murder," Charles said, entering the tiny foyer.

Adele laughed and led him into the living room.

"I've got a surprise for you," Charles said, holding out the leather case.

"Wonderful," Adele said. "And I've got a surprise for you. Let me take your coat."

"Really?" Charles said, taking off his filthy raincoat and handing it to her. "A surprise?"

"Absolutely. Sit down, Charles," Adele said. "How about a drink?"

"Aren't we going out?" he asked.

"One of us will," Adele said mysteriously. Then: "Martha, he's here."

A tiny, toadlike woman came shyly into the living room. She wasn't five feet tall, but she was about five feet wide, Charles decided.

"Charles," Adele said. "This is Martha Collins. I was telling you about her."

Maris couldn't have been more surprised if he had been hit in the head with a sledgehammer. The room suddenly turned bloodred and began to spin as he felt a brain explosion overwhelm him. He staggered to the blue velvet-covered couch and collapsed.

"I've had guys run out on me before, but they never fainted," Martha Collins said. She was dressed in a black sacklike dress that she imagined made her look thinner. Her lank brown hair had been freshly permed into a lacquered helmet to give her more height.

"Charles!" Adele said, rushing to his side. "Are you all right?"

Maris gave a strangled cry and gripped his head to keep it from exploding.

"Okay, so I'm no Miss America," Martha said. "But you're not exactly Tom Cruise."

"Martha, please," Adele said. "I think he's having a heart attack."

"That's novel," Martha said. "Usually they remember a pressing engagement. Thanks anyway, Adele. I think I'll go now."

"*Martha!* Call a doctor," Adele said, really worried now.

"No," Charles said in a hoarse whisper. "I'm all right." Still holding his head, he struggled to sit up.

"Goodness, Charles," Adele said, relieved. "What's wrong?"

"I don't know," he said, knowing full well. "Could I have a glass of water?"

"Of course, poor thing," Adele said. "How about a brandy?"

Charles closed his eyes and nodded.

"This is all my fault," Adele said. "I shouldn't have surprised you." Then to Martha: "Charles is a sensitive man."

"More like terminal," Martha said.

Charles looked at both women with a bleary-eyed hatred, waiting for the room to settle down. That stupid bitch had really fucked up his plans. Martha was an ugly surprise. But he had a surprise for her, too. A surprise for both of them.

*  *  *

"I'm singing in the snow, just a-singing in the snow,"
Charles crooned to himself on the long walk home. In his
right hand was a Samsonite suitcase that had belonged to the
late Adele Woodword. Inside the suitcase were her arms and
Charles's bone saw. The arms were fresh and bloody, the
bone saw dull from the unexpected amount of use it had
seen. He couldn't wait until the police found out what he
had done, and for a moment considered making an anonymous call. But that was dangerous, he knew, what with all
the new tracing devices the cops had. No, he would bide his
time.

In the absence of wind, the snowflakes fell straight down,
a curtain of white to hide his journey back home to Bay
Ridge. It was late, well after midnight, and the streets were
deserted.

Charles felt washed by the snow, purified, as he trudged
up the thirteen steps to his brownstone and unlocked the
door.

"Hi, honey. I'm home," he said to no one in particular.
He knew Emily would be furious with him, so he decided to
ignore her and went directly to the basement, where he kept
the dogs.

He flicked on the dim lights and checked the pit bulls.
They shuffled nervously in their cages, wondering why he
was paying them a late-night visit. In truth he didn't know
why he was down there, except he felt the need for an
audience. And it would be a perfect opportunity to set up a
test for Dempsey. He had been letting the dog out of his
cage with the other pit bulls for the last two weeks,
removing the choker for longer and longer periods of time.

With the collar Dempsey was a model of obedience,
eager and willing to comply with Maris's commands. But
when the collar was off, Charles detected a certain insolence
he couldn't abide.

Hefting the suitcase in one hand, he released Dempsey
from his cage and told him to sit-stay. The dog obeyed

slowly, almost grudgingly. Charles smiled to himself. The confrontation approached.

Before opening the steel door to his operating room, he reached into the bottom drawer of the cabinet and took out the stun gun he had purchased for this very occasion and jammed it into the pocket of his raincoat.

"Come," he said to Dempsey, opening the door to the subbasement. The dog looked at him warily and finally complied.

In the pit Charles gently put the suitcase on the autopsy table.

"You know, Dempsey," he said, "that woman pulled a nasty trick on me. She should have minded her own damn business. She should have obeyed me."

He unsnapped the suitcase and looked lovingly at his twin prizes: Adele Woodword's tanned, tennis-strengthened arms. He had used the bone saw to sever them at the shoulder. A neat job, he had to admit. Though he hadn't been as careful with the rest of her, and he was downright sloppy with Martha Collins. They deserved it, he thought, taking the arms from the suitcase and putting them on the stainless-steel table. Then he picked up her left arm and held it out to Dempsey, who was watching him carefully.

"Here, boy. Shake." Maris said, laughing. "Want to meet the bitch for you?"

The dog didn't move.

"Not feeling friendly?" Maris said. "Well, I have a hunch you're feeling real mean, aren't you? You want to get at me, don't you, boy? Yeah, that's what you'd really like. But I got a surprise for you—just like the one I had for Adele. It's a night of surprises, isn't it?" He smiled.

The dog remained still.

"Not in a talkative mood, are we?" Charles said. "Never mind. This is going to be a night we'll both remember."

He commanded the dog to stay, then went back upstairs. It was part one of his plan to regain control of Dempsey. From the cabinet he took his scalpel case and a new blade for the bone saw. He also took the knotted wooden walking stick.

When he returned to the basement, Dempsey was up on the autopsy table licking the blood from Adele Woodword's torn shoulder. He looked up quickly, and seeing Charles, he put on his war face, yellow eyes ablaze with hatred.

"So you *do* like the lovely Adele," Maris said, his smile matching the dog's in ferocity. "I'm sorry, but she's mine."

The dog's hackles rose at the sound of Charles's voice; then he attacked. His powerful shoulders hunched, his head low, Dempsey launched himself off the autopsy table straight at Charles's throat.

Charles knew that if his timing was off by a fraction, he'd be in deep shit. With his left hand he pushed the cudgel into Dempsey's muzzle to block and distract the animal, with his right he pressed the stun gun into the dog's stomach.

Dempsey took the forty thousand volts of power; it sent him falling to the floor. He landed on his side, a mixture of foam and blood leaking from his mouth. He lay there panting, stunned and confused. Then Charles bore down on him and hit him twice with the stick. If he had possessed a larynx, Dempsey would have whimpered. But all he could do was drag himself to his feet and retreat upstairs to his cage. Maris followed.

The beaten dog looked through the bars, seeing nothing but Maris and the cudgel. The twisted walking stick was the only thing in the world he hated worse than Charles Maris.

"And so to bed," Charles said, locking the cage.

# 13

The Tactical Narcotics Squad was a political creature born of the drug crisis and nurtured by great gulps off the federal teat. But like all hybrids, it was, in the end, sterile and ineffective. Sixty dedicated men and women risked their lives so that coke-sniffing, grass-toking politicians could convince their pill-popping, crack-smoking constituents that they were on top of the drug situation. It was a joke, but the cops didn't get it. Most of them thought they were doing good; they didn't know they were only cannon fodder in the laughable war on drugs.

Rotten Jack Murphy, of course, was not fooled. He didn't give a damn if eight-year-olds turned their brains to mush; he craved the action. Like a junkie, he needed the rush to get him up. Without combat he felt dead. Worse then dead, useless.

Dressed in fatigues, his pants bloused at the top of his spit-shined jump boots, flak vest tied down, M-16 clean and ready, Murphy felt the familiar tension ease as the squadron readied themselves for the assault on Mr. MoFo's headquarters.

"Tozirelli, Burke, Sanders, go around back and shoot any fucking cockroach who tries to scuttle away," Lieutenant Riker said. He was the boss and even Rotten Jack admired his guts. "You lead, Murphy," Riker said. "These bastards are probably asleep, so I don't think we'll have to kill *any* of 'em."

"Shit, Lew," Murphy said. "I need the notches." This brought a few nervous laughs.

"Lock and load," Riker ordered. The squad silently ringed the storefront MoFo used as his hangout.

Riker nodded and Murphy checked his watch. It was one minute to four, one minute to go.

According to plan, Murphy and two other men would make a frontal assault on the store, driving its occupants to the rear, where they would be disarmed and cuffed. Intelligence said there would be at least five heavily armed men inside, plus whatever women they were screwing at the moment.

Murphy had studied mug shots of MoFo, whose real name was Clyde Walker, and would do his damnedest to keep him alive for Sonny LoBianco. It was a sacrifice, but he had given his word.

*Thirty seconds.*

Murphy bent down to touch the 9mm Glock automatic strapped to his waist. It gave him the firepower of the M-16, but was considerably lighter. He flicked the safety off his rifle and set it on rock 'n' roll, full automatic. You could seriously ruin someone's day in less than three seconds if he stepped into the spray of an M-16 on rock 'n' roll.

*Twenty seconds.*

Murphy had memorized the building plan. Riker wanted him to attempt a silent entry into the store, then burst in MoFo's living quarters at the rear. The lieutenant had said that there was a guard out front, but if he could be disarmed quickly, they could bag the whole bunch without a fight. Damn bad news, Murphy thought.

*Ten seconds.*

Contrary to orders, Murphy toyed with the idea of popping the guard as loudly as possible, hoping to spark a good firefight. *Yeah.*

*Go.*

Murphy and his two men broke cover and plastered themselves against the brick wall of the store. Carlyle was supposed to force the door, but Murphy waved him away and tried the knob. It turned easily. Terrible security, Murphy thought, releasing it. He gave a thumbs-up to Carlyle and Moody, then walked boldly into the store and turned on the lights.

A huge bald-headed black guy looked up in surprise. He had been dozing in an armchair, his Uzi out of reach.

"Morning," Murphy said pleasantly. "Stand up."

The guard began to rise; Murphy hit him in the side of his neck with the M-16

Carlyle raised a questioning eyebrow.

"He stood up," Murphy said, slamming a fresh clip into his rifle. "Let's get 'em."

They smashed down the door separating the store from the living quarters, and found themselves looking down a short corridor lit by red bulbs. The carpeting, also red, was thick and plush. There were three doors, two on the right, one on the left. Murphy assigned the two on the right to Carlyle and Moody and took the one on the left for himself. He wasted no time, simply kicked in the door and sprayed the room with the M-16. He reloaded and fired again, his back against the wall.

"Want some more?" he asked.

"Don't shoot, man," came the reply.

"Come out on your belly," Murphy said. "Crawl like a snake."

Two shots rang out to Murphy's right, and he saw Carlyle drop his rifle and grab his arm.

"Son of a bitch," Murphy said as a guy dressed only in bikini underwear darted out into the hall and headed for the backdoor. Murphy shot him, almost casually, then called to Moody.

"Son of a bitch," Moody said.

Turning his attention back to the room, Murphy asked, "Who else is in there?"

"Don't shoot no more." It was a woman's voice.

"Tell that motherfucker to start crawling out right now or I swear to God I'll kill you both. Real slow," Murphy shouted, using his command voice.

"Who are you, mon?"

"Police."

"You sure?"

"No, we're the fucking Red Cross. Now, get out here or die. I'm losing my patience real quick," Murphy shouted.

"It's only the police," Murphy heard MoFo say to the woman. It was that kind of attitude Murphy hated, an attitude he was out to change. Reeducation at the barrel of a gun. It had worked in North Vietnam.

"I'm comin' out," MoFo called. His voice was calm, controlled. He had little to fear from the law. He'd be back on the street before noon.

"Crawl!" Murphy roared.

"I ain't got no clothes on, mon."

"Crawl!"

Murphy pointed the M-16 down toward the threshold. A black head appeared at his feet. He thought about giving the drug dealer a whack on the head, but stopped when he realized it was the woman. MoFo had sent her out first to see what would happen.

"You're next. If you try the window, you're dead meat." He grabbed the woman by the hair and yanked her out of the doorway.

"Comin' out," MoFo said.

By now all twelve members of the TNS team were in the cramped hallway, surveying the damage. One dead man, one wounded cop, a lot of lead expended in the effort. One naked black woman, a prisoner. Mr. MoFo crawling on his belly like a snake. It was 4:05 A.M.

Murphy really wanted to pop this guy, but a promise was a promise.

Clyde Walker, alias Mr. MoFo, stood up slowly. He was six-three and skinny. His arms were skinny, his legs were skinny, his neck was skinny. In fact there was only one part of him that wasn't skinny.

"Holy shit," Murphy said, looking at Mr. MoFo's equipment, which hung down almost to the drug dealer's knees. "If you ever got a hard-on, all the blood would rush from your head and you'd faint."

"I sense he'll be very popular with the guys at Attica," Lieutenant Riker said. "Wrap it around your waist and put on some clothes."

Lieutenant Riker surveyed the damage and shrugged. "Toss the place, get your stories straight, and be prepared for a press conference. We'll make the six o'clock news."

"I'll take care of Mr. Motherfucker," Murphy said.

"Not literally, I hope," Riker said.

"Won't harm a hair on his fine head," Murphy said, his eyes shining like an evil choirboy's. "Come on, Clyde. You and me got an appointment."

"Where we goin'?" Mr. MoFo asked as he was led, hands cuffed behind his back, out the front door. "And where's my guys?"

"One, we're going to see a friend of mine. Two, in custody, where they belong," Murphy answered.

Sonny LoBianco was sipping coffee from a paper cup, watching the operation go down. There was something about their quiet professionalism that made him envious of the TNS. It seemed to him that guns and guts were what police work was all about. He had offered to join them, but Murphy had been adamant.

"We're a team, Sonny," Murphy had said. "You're an outsider. Keep playing the Lone Ranger, it's your style, and let us be the cavalry."

LoBianco supposed Murphy was right, but when he heard the first shots, he threw the coffee away and walked to the alley where he had arranged to meet Murphy. He heard more shots, the sharp popping of M-16s, then it was over.

Minutes later he saw Rotten Jack emerge from the storefront with a single prisoner: a tall, lanky black man with his hands cuffed behind his back. The prisoner wore an insolent sneer that LoBianco knew wouldn't last long.

Murphy nudged Mr. MoFo with the barrel of his Glock and brought him to a halt in front of the unmarked squad car that would eventually take him to Brooklyn Borough detectives for questioning.

"Just listen, Sonny," Murphy said hoarsely. "I'm going to take a five-minute piss, so watch my prisoner for me. When I come back, I want you gone."

"You got it."

"Listen again, Sonny," Murphy said. "Be as convincing as you have to be, but I want this scumbag in good condition when I get him back."

"Right."

"Be convincing, but be cool, Sonny boy." Murphy opened the backdoor of the car and shoved Mr. MoFo inside.

"Hey, mon," MoFo said as he sprawled out on the backseat, making himself comfortable. "Mr. MoFo gets the treatment: a private car with two honky chauffeurs." He laughed at his own joke.

LoBianco nodded to Murphy and got into the front seat.

"On the way we have to stop for my *a-turn-knee*, boy," MoFo said, laughing again. He missed seeing LoBianco leaning over from the front seat to back-fist his face with a blow that echoed inside the closed car.

Then in one fluid motion, LoBianco pulled the prisoner forward until his head was over the back of the seat. Using his free hand, LoBianco peeled an eight-inch strip of adhesive tape he had stuck to the inside of his jacket.

"Keep quiet," he said.

Clyde Walker, alias Mr. MoFo, was by his own admission a man of violence. From his feral youth in the stinking slums in Kingston to his lofty perch as a crack king of south Brooklyn, Walker had shown a total disregard for human life. He had never hesitated. He would kill men, women, or children if it pleased him. In fact, he found killing as enjoyable as sex. He had personally killed seventeen people in the past fifteen years, including an uncle, two cousins, and a six-year-old niece who was in the wrong place at the wrong time. He slept peacefully every night; he had no dreams, no conscience.

Walker understood, intuitively, the nature and use of violence. He also understood, looking into the cold blue eyes of the guy in the front seat, that he had met an equal. The thought that he might well be killed inside a stinking police car threw his instinct for survival into high gear. There would be no bullshitting this honky asshole. He had to deliver whatever this guy wanted or die.

He threw LoBianco a wide-eyed, innocent look he hoped would buy him some time. If he got out of this alive, he'd make this white man beg for his life, then he'd kill him slowly. Very slowly, a piece at a time.

LoBianco grabbed Walker by the chin and pulled him over the seat until the drug dealer's head was wedged under the steering wheel.

"I have three M-80s, each equivalent to a quarter stick of dynamite," LoBianco said in a voice that was neither loud nor threatening. "I've wired them together and hooked them to a one-minute fuse."

All Walker could see was the underside of the dash, a tangle of colored wires.

"I'm going to shove this down your pants and light it."

Walker made muffled pleading sounds through the tape. What he had between his legs he prized as much as his drug business.

"Here, take a look," LoBianco said, holding the firecrackers so that Walker could see them. Each stick was three inches long and red in color; LoBianco had placed the fuse in the center of the middle firecracker. It would make quite an explosion.

"I'm lighting it," LoBianco said. Then he shoved it down Walker's pants.

"You got one minute, give or take," LoBianco said.

Walker tried to twist, but LoBianco hit him in the gut, calming him down. "Less than a minute!" he said. "I'm going to make a few requests. If you agree, grunt; if you don't agree, you don't have to grunt."

Walker could hear the fuse burning slowly, feel the heat as it worked its way down his shirt to . . .

"If you grunt just right, I'll pull the fuse," LoBianco said. "If not . . ." He left the sentence unfinished. "I can't hear you," he said.

Walker grunted for all he was worth.

"You know the priest at St. Agnes, Father Davis?"

Suddenly Walker understood. This must be the fucking cop who had set up Rooster. Although Rooster had avoided arrest, the incident had been an insult to Walker. Rooster was his main man.

"You torched his bus," LoBianco said.

Walker grunted.

"You harass his kids."

Walker was silent.

"Your balls don't have much time left."

Walker grunted.

"I want you to make a donation to St. Agnes. Say a nice Plymouth Voyager, fully loaded. This is no time to cheap out. I want it registered in the priest's name and with a full tank of gas."

The fuse finally burned through Walker's shirt and he could feel it sizzling on his skin. He screamed.

"Is that a yes?" LoBianco asked.

Walker screamed again.

"Good. And if any of your goddamned posse goes near Father Davis or his kids, we'll do this again—with a grenade."

Walker was grunting and screaming like a pig being

slaughtered. He didn't realize for a moment that LoBianco had opened the door and left the car.

"By the way," LoBianco called to him. "Father Davis's favorite color is black."

When Rotten Jack returned, he found Walker bouncing up and down on the front seat, humping it, trying to put out the fuse.

"Jeez," Murphy said. "Don't you ever stop? Of course, if I was hung like you—"

Walker screamed through the tape.

Expecting the worst, Murphy hauled his prisoner into a sitting position. Except for the tape across his mouth and a scorched shirtfront, Walker was in good shape. From the rubber mat he picked up the three M-80 casings.

"What's this?" he asked Walker, after removing the tape from his prisoner's mouth. "It's a dud, no powder."

Staring at the empty casing, Walker screamed again, this time in anger at being suckered. He was so crazed with hate for LoBianco he failed to notice he had wet his pants.

# 14

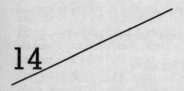

On Sunday morning Ira Berger sat at his desk and reviewed the Parulo murder. He had finally returned from sick leave, glad to get out of his damn apartment and back to the PDU. Rose remained cold and distant; Berger felt like a stranger in his own house. He wondered if he should get help for her, professional help. But his hatred of psychiatrists made him dismiss the idea.

He cracked the black shade that covered the window and looked out at the snow. It was already turning to brown slush. Like his life, he thought. It couldn't be normal for a woman to change almost overnight. Maybe she was going through menopause. Maybe she was possessed. Maybe he didn't have any damned idea.

The PDU was as busy as ever, snow or no snow, Sunday or no Sunday. The wire-mesh cage was occupied by two Hispanic men who had been caught raping a sixty-four-year-old woman. They were laughing and speaking in loud voices. None of the other cops seemed to notice, but their callousness grated on Berger's nerves.

I should be used to this by now, he thought.

He opened the brown, legal-sized folder marked "Parulo" and reread the D-5s and his own cryptic notations. The case was floundering in a predictable fashion. So far he had no answer from the FBI regarding serial killers who mutilated their victims, no witnesses had come forward to identify Parulo's murderer, and that dirtbag in fingerprints, Lopez, had gone on vacation without identifying any of the other fingers on the hand delivered to Berger's door.

I should be used to this by now, he thought again.

He tossed the file on top of the others on his desk and took out a pad of yellow legal paper. Closing his eyes, he let his mind wander for a few seconds, then pictured Parulo's corpse lying near the subway station. He tried to imagine her face. Was it bruised, cut? No. He remembered her wide-eyed stare. Her face was undamaged. Surprised. That probably meant she did not know her killer. Facial beating generally indicated the victim and killer knew each other. He wrote *strangers* on the empty pad.

The type of weapon came next. Knives and other cutting tools, because of their intrusive nature, usually introduced a sexual subtext to a homicide. The piano wire or whatever it was that had killed Parulo might indicate the reverse. Perhaps the killer was not interested in sex at all; a garrote would distance him from his victim. That, of course, was negated by the postmortem amputations. *Not a sex crime in the usual sense,* he wrote. *Perp organized. Smart?*

But why would he take souvenirs? Would he keep the body parts in a jar and relive the crime every time he looked at them? Would he keep them on ice? A picture of Parulo's gray, rigor-stiffened hands neatly stacked in the refrigerator next to the horseradish, ketchup, and milk popped into his brain. *Has Alka-Seltzer for brains,* Berger wrote.

"Feeling better, Ira?"

Berger looked up and saw Lieutenant Santamyer standing over him. "Yes, thanks, Lew," he said automatically.

"Anything on Parulo?"

"Just working on it now," Berger said.

"Good, good." Santamyer stood there, his face expressionless.

"Something I can do for you?" Berger asked.

"How's your wife?" Santamyer said.

"Fine."

"Good, good." The lieutenant still stood there, as if he had something on his mind.

"How's *your* wife?" Berger asked in desperation.

"Fine."

"Good, good," Berger said.

"Somebody said your wife—uh, Lilly?—was no longer living with you."

"It's Rose and of course she's still living with me. Where would she go?" Berger said.

"Good, good. A man's wife should stay at home," Santamyer said, and walked back to his office.

What the hell was that all about? Berger wondered. Sonny LoBianco must have been shooting his big mouth off. The kid didn't have the sense God gave a camel, he thought. Then he returned to thinking about Parulo.

Motive, Berger thought. The motive puzzled him. Did the perp have a dog who gave him instructions? Was this another Son of Sam? Was he the latest David Berkowitz, tormented by inner voices? Berger knew he'd probably never be able to decode the killer's inner logic, but he also knew it was there someplace. Trying to decipher a psycho's logic was like taking a color-blindness test. People with normal vision read one word, those who were color-blind saw a different word. He could stare all day and still not come up with the right answer. *Nutbar,* he wrote.

Opportunity. Was the perp a local resident? Or did he commute from Clinton, Colombia, or Connecticut? Berger had to assume that the man, and it was almost definitely a man, lived in the metropolitan area. He wrote, *Local.*

He knew from FBI crime profiles that the killer was almost certainly a white male, between the ages of twenty-five and forty years old. If this perp fit the profile, he would live by himself and had probably committed a string of murders, only a few of which had ever been recognized as his MO. He had probably been interviewed by the cops, somewhere, but he had never been a real suspect. Berger wrote, *Sociopath.*

He leaned back in his chair, then, wrote: *An asexual sociopath with Alka-Seltzer for brains . . . an organized local who attacks strangers for some nutbar reason.*

That narrows it down to a million people, he thought. But how the hell does he know my name?

He turned his attention to the severed-hand case and worried with that for an hour, but got nowhere. So he signed out and hitched a ride with a blue-and-white. The uniformed cops dropped him at his door; it was almost 11:00 A.M.

"Oh, Ira, I'm glad you're home," Rose said.

"That's a change," he said.

"I'm going out," she said.

"Going where?"

"Just out."

"Then why does it matter if I'm home? You leave all the time and don't tell me," he said.

"Good-bye."

"Are you coming back?"

"Of course," she said, getting her coat out of the closet.

She left him feeling like an impotent old man. His feet hurt, his head hurt, and most of all his heart hurt.

Bundled against the cold, Rose Berger hurried to the subway station to catch the B train to Manhattan. She had an appointment in Chinatown with a certain Dr. Chin. The most important appointment of her life, she thought nervously.

She stared out the filthy windows of the equally filthy car and thought about the baby. It would be a girl, of course, blond like herself, but with Ira's intelligence and her sister's strong will. Her baby would be special; Dr. Chin had guaranteed it.

A drug addict lurched toward her, making her flinch, but he ignored her and moved on. He and the other unwashed insects that inhabited the trains should not distract her attention. Only the baby mattered.

Stepping around a sleeping bum who had urinated on himself and the subway car, she walked up the garbage-strewn stairs to the gray, fetid air of Canal Street. Orientals, smoking, swearing, and sweating, jabbered in high-pitched voices, but Rose cut a path through them. She had an appointment with destiny.

Sonny LoBianco hit the heavy bag with brutal force and bad intentions. He was still worked up from his morning confrontation with Mr. MoFo and needed some kind of physical release. He battered the bag with his hands, following up with vicious knee strikes and kicks to finish the combination.

E.T., coming in at the end of LoBianco's workout, watched in amazement. More than anything, E.T. wanted to be like Sonny. He worshipped the cop and continually measured himself against his hero. Sonny, in turn, was flattered that the boy wanted to learn from him. He tried to steer the kid in the right direction, just as Davis had done for him, but he sometimes felt the strain of unsolicited responsibility.

After his workout Sonny draped a towel over his head and rested on the mat, cooling down.

"You're lookin' good, Sonny," E.T. said, joining him on the mat. "But you look like nobody I ever seen on TV or at the matches I been to."

"If you can win in the streets, you can win on the mat," LoBianco said. His personal style was heavily influenced by Harada and had none of the flash and dash of American sport kick boxing. To LoBianco, fighting wasn't a sport. It was survival.

"Yeah, but how about Bruce Lee?" E.T. asked, leaping up and giving a demonstration of Lee's flamboyant style.

"You look like a ballet dancer," LoBianco said. "A mental midget like you would never understand."

E.T. stopped in midkick, stung. "I ain't no mental midget."

"You ain't no Einstein. Maybe you're too young."

That hurt worse.

"Now, don't go getting all teary-eyed," LoBianco said seeing the boy's face. "What I mean is you've got the physical moves down, now you gotta get the mental moves perfected. It's a matter of being able to summon up, instantly, your optimal state of functioning."

"Huh?"

"It has to become automatic, like breathing," LoBianco continued. "A street fight is simple and direct. You combine defense and offense into one action. This takes mental as well as physical training. You don't go leaping around squealing like a bad sound track from a Bruce Lee movie. You will yourself to win—and you do."

"I don't understand," E.T. said.

"I know you don't," LoBianco said. "That's why I'm going to teach you."

E.T.'s face lit up. "Yeah?"

"Yeah."

"To fight like you?"

"No, to fight like you," LoBianco said.

"Thanks!"

"Don't thank me yet," LoBianco said. "It won't be easy."

The boy barely heard him. All he heard was talk, but what Sonny did to the bag was awesome. Pure and simple, LoBianco was bad and that's what E.T. wanted to be. He didn't give a shit about all the mental jive. He gave away his attitude when he asked Sonny how a particular low kick could be adapted to a jumping technique. The idea of kicking to the head in a street fight made as much sense to LoBianco as punching to the feet. But E.T. liked the gymnastics of jump kicks.

"Get your stuff and get on the mat," he told the boy. "I think you need a lesson in listening."

While Sonny was waiting for E.T., LaDonna and her constant companion, Shawndell, arrived to pay him a visit. He got a kick out of the little kids and indulged them.

"We're here for fightin' lessons," LaDonna informed him.

"You and Shawndell?" Sonny asked.

"Both of us," she said with four-year-old gravity. "We want to be Teenage Mutants."

"Well, you're halfway there," LoBianco said. "But I'm afraid you're a bit young for karate."

"You're teaching E.T. You can teach us," LaDonna said. "Show him, Shawndell."

Using his straight-arm handshaking technique, Shawndell launched himself at Sonny, trying to run him through with an outstretched arm. Sonny had to dodge to prevent the two-year-old from hitting him in the groin.

"Nice move, Shawndell," Sonny said, a hand on the little boy's head; Shawndell continued to flail away at him mightily. "Whoa, Shawndell. " he said. Then to LaDonna: "How do you turn him off?"

"Chill out, Shawndell," LaDonna yelled, and the boy stopped in midpunch, dropping his arms to his side.

"I'm training him," LaDonna said confidentially.

"I'd like to help you out," LoBianco said. "But I've got my hands full with E.T."

LaDonna gave him an arrogant look, saying, "Come, Shawndell. Father D will teach us." They walked out together, arm in arm, their disdain for him as great as their disappointment.

When E.T. returned wearing his black, ninja-style *gi*, he put on a show for Sonny. He juked, jived, shuffled, and even moon-walked, keeping up a stream of raplike invective against his invisible opponent.

"Sit down a minute," Sonny said, but the boy was so caught up in his routine he didn't hear. So LoBianco stepped up to him, and while E.T. was skipping backward like a boxer Sonny gave him a sweeping kick that snapped across the back of the boy's legs, sending him flat on his ass.

"I said, take a break."

"What you do that for?" E.T. asked, still sitting.

"Have you ever been in a fight, a real fight at school or in the neighborhood?" LoBianco asked.

"Sure. Hundreds," E.T. said proudly.

"What happens? How does it go down?"

"Well—"

"I'll tell you," LoBianco said. "Two guys start mouthing off to each other. One guy says, 'Fuck your mama.' Right?"

E.T. nodded.

"Then the other guy says something clever like, 'Oh, yeah. Well, fuck your mama, too!' Then the first guy says, 'And your sister, too.'"

"And your aunt, brother, and goldfish," E.T. added, laughing.

"Right," Sonny said. "Then they glare at each other and get real mad. After that they start pushing each other; then a punch is thrown, a big roundhouse that misses. Then they grab each other and wrestle around on the ground like two faggots in love. Am I right?"

E.T. thought about it. "I suppose."

"Unless things have changed, that's about the way it goes, and I'm telling you neither one of those guys wants to fight."

"Somebody say, 'Fuck my mama,' I'll fight 'em," E.T. said, his chin jutting out.

"You don't have a mama," LoBianco said. "What does it matter?"

"He dissed me," E.T. insisted. "I kill him."

"We'll talk about that later. But the point is: Neither of the guys I described was serious. They did a lot of stupid talking, useless pushing, and wound up rolling around holding on to each other so tight neither one of them could throw an effective move," LoBianco said. "When you fight, fight. When you talk, talk. Understand?"

"No."

"Well, instead of calling the guy's mother a name, he should have just moved right in and hit his opponent. There's no need for a pushing contest. Just attack," LoBianco said. "Stand up."

E.T. stood.

"Come at me," LoBianco said.

E.T. feinted left, then came at him with a high-flying kick. LoBianco grabbed E.T.'s ankle with his left hand and hauled the boy off his feet. With his right hand he hit E.T. in the stomach, hard enough to hurt. He dropped the boy to the mat and backed away.

Anticipating a follow-up attack, E.T. recovered quickly and came at Sonny, a flurry of arms and legs. Instead Sonny ripped a well-aimed left hook that caught E.T. in the ribs. It was the pinpoint accuracy more than the power behind the punch that brought E.T. to his knees. He wrapped his hands around his middle and rocked back and forth in pain.

"That's what's called street fighting," LoBianco said. "You can learn it in a dojo but it has to be perfected on the street."

E.T. moaned again, and LoBianco, thinking he had hit him too hard, went over to see if the boy was all right. Bending down to check him out, Sonny was caught off guard as E.T. grabbed the sleeve of Sonny's *gi* and pulled him off his feet.

"And you don't learn that from no honky cop," E.T. said, jumping up and running away as fast as he could.

LoBianco wanted to shout something after the boy, but was laughing too hard.

After he had showered, Sonny came to a decision. He called Angela. The sound of her soft voice raised a longing in his heart and did as much for his dick.

"Angela," he said, feeling as if her were talking to a stranger.

"Sonny? How are you?"

"Good. How are you doing?" he said. The banality of their conversation was embarrassing; he wished he had thought up some interesting things to say.

"I'd like to see you," she said.

"Me too." His heart was hammering. "When?"

"This afternoon?" she asked.

"Four?"

"Fine. You've got some clothes here you might want," she said.

"Catch you then," he said, knowing that the clothes routine was an excuse to see him. He couldn't wait.

Whistling tunelessly, he splashed on some English Leather after-shave she had given him last Christmas. Eleven months ago, he thought, and my whole damn life was different.

Smelling like a used saddle, he went outside to survey the snow that had fallen overnight. He was also looking for an opportunity to ambush E.T. with a couple of ice balls, but thoughts of revenge were short-circuited by the sight of a large yellow bus standing proudly in the driveway. Father Davis, E.T., and several kids surrounded it with wide-eyed wonder as it were a UFO that had landed at St. Agnes.

Vito had delivered, but the lettering on the side of the bus gave LoBianco a twinge; he had to find a way to explain it to Davis. The thought of a black priest driving a yellow bus with Hebrew lettering while kids of all colors hung out the windows made him smile. Maybe he could sell the idea to television.

"Nice and roomy," Sonny said to Davis as the priest opened the door and peered inside. "You won't have to tie them to the roof."

"A hundred dollars," E.T. said, running a hand over a worn seat. "A hundred dollars, and I'll clean it like new."

"For a hundred dollars I could hire five kids," Davis said to E.T. Then to Sonny: "This is great. Where did it come from?"

"Well, obviously not from Catholic Charities," Sonny said. "It's only a loaner. My partner, Ira Berger, arranged it."

"It's a mitzvah," Davis said. "A blessing."

"Right." He had to remember to clue in Berger in the unlikely event that the two men ever met. "And I'm working on another deal for you," Sonny continued. "A permanent replacement."

"What kind of deal?" Davis asked suspiciously.

"Trust me."

"I trust in Jesus," Davis said. He looked at the bus. "But you only get the benefit of the doubt. For now."

"And, E.T.," Sonny said, "I got a present for you."

The boy's face lit up before he was doused by the handful of snow Sonny threw at him.

"Boys, boys," Davis said. "Play nice."


Dr. Chin's office was on the third floor of a building owned by the J&A Trading Company, Ltd., importers of sunglasses, hats, costume jewelry, and heroin, China White to be exact. The cops knew it, the locals knew it, Dr. Chin knew it. Rose Berger was completely in the dark.

Climbing the narrow stairs, she could feel her heart pound with anticipation. She rested for a minute on the dimly lit landing, catching her breath, before knocking on the frosted glass door marked "Private."

A short, stocky Chinese woman wearing a white nurse's uniform buzzed her into the comfortable waiting room. By the door was a four-foot-tall bronze Buddha, looking suspiciously like a pregnant woman. Rose touched its belly for luck and sat in one of the three gold brocade easy chairs placed strategically around a black-and-white marble cocktail table. Despite Dr. Chin's unusual address and even more unusual medical practices, he had the usual out-of-date issues of *Newsweek* and *National Geographic* littering his waiting room. But Rose was too excited to read, so she sat on the edge of the chair, twisting her hands together.

Except for the scratching of the nurse's pen and the muted tick of a bronze wall clock, there wasn't a sound. Rose could hear her heart beating furiously, and thought perhaps she heard a second, smaller heart fluttering within her. If it were true—it had to be true—then she owed it all to Dr. Chin and his holistic approach to medicine.

The regular doctors and specialists she had consulted had been so pessimistic about her chances of conceiving that she had almost believed them. Then she had read about Dr. Chin and his remarkable track record helping women and she had contacted him six months before. He had listened patiently to her story, then prescribed his own patented fertility pills, made, he said, of natural ingredients. He had also given her a supply of grayish powder she mixed into Ira's food. Her medication, she was told, was the yin; Ira's the yang. They must mesh, and when they did, a baby was the inevitable result.

It made such good sense, she thought, and although the cost was high—more than five thousand dollars in the past few months—Dr. Chin wasn't much more expensive than the high-and-mighty specialists who charged for their electronic gadgets and gloomy forecasts. What was money?

"Mrs. Berger?"

Rose looked up to see the tall, almost cadaverous figure of Dr. Chin standing in the doorway of his examination room.

Rose stood up quickly. The look on her face was beatific. She glowed.

Sonny's groin tingled in anticipation as he gunned the Vette through the plowed and salted streets toward Angela's house. The posi-traction on the restored car worked perfectly, gripping the dry spots on the road and ignoring the ice.

Things were finally looking up, he thought, but he didn't want to press his luck. He should be cool and not look like he couldn't wait to get into her pants. Play it cool, he told himself. The last thing you ever wanted a woman to know was that you were hot for her. Let her make the moves, then give in and do her a favor.

He smiled. Jesus, it was going to be difficult not to jump her in the hallway. He could almost feel his hands caressing her fine, firm breasts, stroking her dark nipples into hard buds that . . . He had to stop thinking like that, he knew, and concentrated on finding a parking place a few blocks from his destination.

By the time he reached her door, he had regained control. Planning to surprise her, he tried his key. Son of a bitch, he thought, she's changed the locks! What did that mean? He pushed the bell and heard a faint chime.

She came to the door wearing a T-shirt, no bra, and jeans that looked like they had been sprayed on. Her face, devoid of makeup, looked to Sonny like it should be on the cover of a fashion magazine. Her hair was as dark and lustrous as always. Her black eyes were full of surprise.

"You're early," she said.

"Hello to you, too," he said, grinning like an idiot. "I'm ready for another sympathy fuck."

"You'd better come in," she said. "It's cold outside." She was shoeless.

He walked into the house he had shared with her for two years and was amazed at the changes. She had completely redecorated; it was her house now, in every sense of the word. He had missed that the last time he'd been there; the kitchen was the same as ever.

She noticed his surprise and said, "It's better, but it's still not right."

"I'd like to help you make it right," he said, moving to take her in his arms.

She evaded him, slipping sideward. "There's nothing here for me anymore. I'm moving," she said.

"Where?"

"Manhattan. I hate goddamned Brooklyn," she said. "Look, let's get on with this."

Things weren't going the way he expected.

"Sit down a minute, baby, and tell me what's going on," he said.

"Let's go upstairs," she said.

That was better, he thought.

They entered what had been their bedroom, and again he was surprised. Nothing was the same; he was depressed and excited at the same time.

"We had a lot of good times here," he said, again moving to embrace her.

"And a lot of shit times, Sonny," she said. "Don't go getting all nostalgic. We're finished."

It was a slap in the face that left him numb and confused.

"There's nothing left?" he asked.

"There wasn't anything to begin with, you knew that. I told you when I married you it wouldn't work. But you're too damn pigheaded to listen to anybody. You know it all."

"Listen, baby," he began.

"No, you listen to me for a change. I'm not your fucking baby. I'm not your wife. I'm not your girlfriend or your mistress. I'm my own person. You failed, Sonny. You thought your macho bullshit would turn me into some kind of Italian housewife who washes your socks and is thrilled when you stop home long enough for a quick screw.

"Well, that sort of crap doesn't work with me. I told you it wouldn't and it didn't."

"What the hell do you want?" he asked, feeling the rage build up inside him.

"I want what you could never give me," she said. "A life. A real life, filled with real people, parties, clothes, and a bit of respect."

"Just because I don't have the money, doesn't—"

"It's not the money," she said. "It's an attitude. Your idea of a great night is a pizza and a blow job. That's not my ideal evening, but you wouldn't know or like what I want."

"I could try, Angela," he said. This was definitely not

going as planned, he thought. He was on the defensive; in a moment he would be begging.

"No, you couldn't," she said. "Oh, you'd probably try, but you'd just end up hating me because I made you change. No, Sonny. We're finished and the sad part is that I should have never let it get started."

"Who's the guy?" Sonny asked suddenly.

"What's the difference? It doesn't have anything to do with you anymore," she said, crossing her arms over her breasts.

He lunged for her, grabbing her by the shoulders. "Tell me, damn it!"

"What are you going to do, Sonny? Rape me? Beat me up? Is that the way you'd change for me?" She was completely limp, indifferent to his touch. He let her go.

"Get yourself a nice girl who'll worship you, have your children, and cry at your funeral," Angela said.

"Bitch," Sonny said.

"Always have been, always will be," she said. "Just take your clothes and leave, Sonny."

He looked at the pile of cardboard boxes in the corner.

"Yours are marked 'X,'" she said. "An appropriate letter of the alphabet."

"Shove 'em up your ass," Sonny said, turning on his heel and leaving.

"And an appropriate final word from a real classy guy. Good-bye, Sonny," she said.

# 15

Sonny LoBianco drove aimlessly through Brooklyn, feeling pissed off and pissed upon. He replayed the scene with Angela in his mind, thinking of several stinging retorts and snide comeback lines, but they were useless now. On the verge of making himself completely nuts, he suddenly realized how late it was getting. No one kept Vito LoBianco waiting.

It was almost eleven when he parked up near Il Bacio's in Coney Island.

Inside, Vito LoBianco fretted over a snifter of Sambuca and an espresso. It had become irritatingly obvious to him that he had been sitting on his ass too long and that the scumbag Frankie Marcellino was getting ready for some kind of move.

He had no one to blame but himself, he knew. He had wanted to take the easy way out, to retire gradually, but Marcellino had sensed his weakness and was now taking advantage of him.

Vito noisily sipped his Sambuca and looked up to see Sonny standing there. For a moment he thought it was his dead brother, Santino.

"Sonny boy," Vito said. "Sit. Have a drink."

Sonny sat and ordered an espresso from a waiter, who hovered over his uncle like an anxious mother.

"Nice place," Sonny said. Like Rosalie's, Il Bacio's restaurant was mobbed up, a home for the neighborhood wiseguys. *Il bacio,* Sonny knew, meant the kiss in Italian, but a kiss in this joint could mean your ticket had been punched.

From the window he could see the sinuous loop of the Cyclone roller coaster at Astroland Amusement Park. The Cyclone, one of the last wooden-track roller coasters, had been rebuilt and pronounced safe; it had even been awarded landmark status, but it was a relic, he thought, just like his uncle Vito.

"You know, Santino, when my mother and father, your grandparents, may they rest in peace, came here, this was all farmland. Would you believe it? Vegetables grew on Mermaid Avenue! Now look at it. Nothing can grow here now."

Sonny looked around the dark café and said, "You're wrong. They still grow shit here, especially on this block."

Vito sighed and ignored Sonny's remark. Rosalie's was only a few doors away. "When we first got made, me and your father," he continued, "we were with Old Man Genco's two sons in the same crew. Now Old Man Genco had this *consigliere* named Tommy One Eye. Unocchio was his nickname and Genco loved him. But Unocchio was about a thousand years old, and he was getting buggy in the head. Maybe he had that disease, what's it called . . . old-timers' disease? But in those days we weren't smart like we are now, we didn't know these things.

"Anyway, we learned a lot from Unocchio when his mind was working right, but we took turns watching him, you know, driving him around, shopping for him. Things like that." Vito paused to sip his espresso, and looked into Sonny's cold blue eyes before he continued.

"Anyhow, one day Unocchio tells me he wants me to drive him to visit his friend's grave. I say okay and the next day I pick him up. No problem. So we start to drive. And we drive and we drive. Now, I told you the old guy had had his good days and his bad days and you hadda look out for them. But this day he looks like he's good, but we don't seem to be gettin' nowhere.

"Finally we wind up in Canarsie. I took the Belt Parkway. Then he starts moving me through the streets. 'Go this way. Go that way. Turn here. Turn there.' So I says, 'Sure.' But I'm getting a bad feeling about this.

"We drive for maybe half an hour, forty minutes, in and out, up and down, until we get to this neighborhood with new houses, and I'm thinking this guy's *pazzo*. There ain't no graveyard in a housing development. But I keep drivin', 'cause like I said, I liked the old guy and Genco loved him.

"I'm about to suggest we go back when all of a sudden he makes me stop in the middle of the street, and he gets out and looks around like he's checking his bearings.

"*Marone!* I'm thinking he's gonna get killed by a truck and Genco will have me whacked for it, so I open the door to grab him, then you know what happens?"

Sonny, still irritated, said, "*You* get hit by a truck."

"No, Santino. Pay attention," Vito said. "Right out in the middle of the street he drops to his knees, genuflects, blesses himself and starts to pray. Holy Mother of God, I think, seeing the traffic on both sides of him swerving out of the way like he's some kinda rock in a river. This is the fucking end.

"Next thing I know, there's people looking out from their houses and yards. Everybody's out, it was a nice day. So I grab him and say, 'Tommy, what's goin' on? This ain't no cemetery. I'm takin' you home. I bet you forgot to take your medicine today.'

"'Let go of me,' he yells. 'Fuck the medicine. Fuck the cemetery, you fucking *gavone*. My friend is buried here.' He points to a spot in the middle of the street. 'I should know. I put him here.'" Vito began laughing and coughing at his own story; Sonny just sat there.

"The point is," Vito said when he had calmed down.

"The point is just because a guy is old don't mean he's got no brains."

"What's that supposed to mean?" Sonny asked.

"It also means that business is business and friends are friends, but business comes first."

"What's *that* supposed to mean?" Sonny said. "Is that a threat?"

"No, no, Santino. Just listen and remember business comes before friends and before family."

"Thanks for the lesson," Sonny said, getting up. He'd had enough of this crap.

"Sit down." Vito's voice was harsh for a moment, then softened. "You know, kid, you're the spitting image of your father, may his soul rest in peace. You're *testa dura* just like him."

"I hardly remember my father, he was always too involved with *business* to pay much attention to me," Sonny said. "His *business* killed him."

"Your father was too tough for his own good, Santino. He wouldn't listen, he wouldn't be reasonable. Business was always personal with him. He never understood that business ain't ever personal. When . . ." Vito paused for a moment, as if he were afraid of saying too much. Then, deftly, he changed the course of the conversation. "Your father, my brother, would have wanted you in with me in *our business.*"

"I'm a cop," Sonny said, loud enough for the dozen customers and the staff to hear. Cops were about as welcome as roaches here.

"You're family," Vito shot back. "Let's remember that." He put up both hands, palms out, and gave a furtive look around the room to see who was watching. Everyone was.

"Sure, Uncle Vito," Sonny said in a low, dangerous voice. "We're some fucking family. I remember how you took me in and helped me. I remember that—like shit. All I remember is a fucking orphanage and not one fucking visit from you. Now, get to the point. I'm tired, I had a bad day, and I'm a cunt's hair away from busting this whole damn place. I see one of your buddies who's got an outstanding warrant on him.''

Vito saw his brother's stubbornness in his nephew and didn't doubt for a minute that Sonny would make good his threat. He spoke quietly and urgently. "I want you with me, Sonny, but I also respect your wishes. I got a problem, you got a problem. Maybe we can wash each other's back.'' Vito leaned back and stroked his droopy salt-and-pepper mustache.

"I don't got no problems," Sonny said.

"You got a black motherfucking problem named MoFo,'' Vito said. "I can take care of him."

"He's already taken care of. I took care of *business* myself.''

Vito shrugged. "Problems have a way of getting out on bail.''

"Then I'll take care of it," Sonny said. "What kinda problems you got?" He was annoyed but intrigued by his uncle's unusual behavior.

"You need that orphan home protected," Vito said. "I need my back watched.''

"Frankie Marcellino," Sonny said. He had known it all along, but he couldn't believe that a punk like Frankie could get his uncle upset. "Marcellino's a bag of shit. You know it, I know it, but how can I help you? Is he in with the Gencos?''

"Not the Gencos. I can handle the Gencos, but what if he's making deals with the cops? You can find out for me."

"I could," Sonny said. "But how are you going to help me? Send a bunch of Sicilians armed with *luparas* to walk the perimeter of St. Agnes?''

"Uzis," Vito said. "We don't use no shotguns no more, and I don't intend to put soldiers in the joint, but I can negotiate with your friend Mr. MoFo when he gets outta the slam.''

"He's cool. I told you, we made a deal."

"What you done was start a war, Santino," Vito said. "I can arrange a lasting truce."

"How?"

"I have ways. Let's just say this *strunzo* needs us more than we need him."

Sonny studied the red-and-white-checkered tablecloth. Vito had just admitted to being MoFo Walker's drug wholesaler. He should walk away right now, he knew, but having Vito as an ally instead of an enemy made sense. "Let me think about it," he said.

"Sure, sure. Think about it, but think about it quick. I gotta make some moves pretty soon," Vito said.

"Why don't you just pop him?" Sonny asked. "In the Sicilian tradition."

"I can't," Vito whispered, leaning over the table so no one could hear. "Not yet."

Sonny nodded. Vito wasn't as tight with the Gencos as he had boasted.

"I'll call you," Sonny repeated, getting up to leave.

"You do that," Vito said softly. "Blood. You are my blood, Santino. Remember that always."


"Love can turn to hate as quick as a rat," Father Franklyn Davis said, flipping a cheese omelet.

"Well, she packed my stuff into boxes marked with an 'X.' I'd say that rat made a U-turn," Sonny said.

Davis laughed, but he knew how much Angela had hurt Sonny. They were in the rectory kitchen. It was after midnight.

"By the way," Sonny said as Davis deftly slid the omelet onto a plate. "I need a favor. Would you pick my shit up? I don't want to go back there again."

"Sure," Davis said, dividing the omelet and pushing the plate in front of Sonny. "You want to talk about this?"

Sonny shrugged and the priest took it as an invitation. "Who do you blame? In your heart?" Davis asked.

"She's got a boyfriend, Father. Who do I blame? The mailman?"

"You might start with yourself," Davis said.

"I don't believe what I'm hearing. You sound like her. I thought you'd be on my side," Sonny said.

"You know exactly what I mean, and I *am* on your side. Stop being so Sicilian," Davis said, chewing a mouthful of eggs.

"What the hell are you saying?"

"That you haven't changed since you come here as a snot-nosed punk," Davis said, still eating. "You still act like a greaseball just offa the boat."

"Jesus Christ!"

"No swearing," Davis said automatically. "You were always a whiny little shit, except then you had nothing to back up your bad attitude. Now you got a gun, a badge, and a small amount of hand-to-hand training."

"Hey, screw you," Sonny said. "'A small amount of training,' is it? I've spent fifteen years training and I could beat your ass in about two seconds."

Davis laughed. "See? You still got an attitude."

Sonny calmed down when he realized Davis was teasing him. He had never been sure when the priest was kidding or being dead serious.

"When you first came here, you couldn't fight a lick. All gangly arms and legs. You had more zits than smarts," Davis said.

"I never had zits," Sonny said.

"Well, you did have a problem matching a bad attitude with a worse fighting style," Davis said.

"Yeah, but that book you got me—"

"*Sergeant Rock's American Combat Jujitsu Manual,*" Davis said.

"Taught me everything about fighting. I owe a lot to Sergeant Rock," Sonny said.

"What about the mattress and the see-ment weights?" Davis asked.

"You mean the mattress and the cement-filled coffee cans? You know, the first time I saw you tying that mattress around a pillar, I said to myself, now there's a man who don't know where a mattress goes, and if he don't know where a mattress goes, how can he teach me anything about fighting," Sonny said.

"O ye of no faith a-tall," Davis said. "And that was before the Rocky movie."

"I suppose you taught him to fight, too?" Sonny said.

"You'd better watch your mouth, wiseass. Or I'll show you a few moves I've held back."

Sonny laughed. "This is a conversation for drunks, but I have to admit you taught me everything I know."

"About fighting," Davis said. "But not about emotion."

Sonny knew where they were heading and tried to change the subject. "What about Harada? We just forget what he taught me?"

"That vicious bastard?" Davis said. "Oh, yeah. He taught you lots. A lot of stuff that maybe no one should know."

"Come on, Father. *You* know that stuff and you can handle it."

"Can I?" Davis asked. "Can you?"

"Sure I can. But what I think about mostly is that you showed me a way to handle almost everything. We both know how I'd have turned out otherwise," Sonny said.

The priest shrugged off Sonny's words. "You weren't much different than the others."

Sonny laughed again and pointed at the priest's face. "Hey, I made you blush."

"Look at my face," Davis said. "You see a blush?"

"Nope. I see a big, fat, ugly, black face," Sonny said. He felt comfortable joking with Davis, uncomfortable being serious with him.

"This ugly old face has seen it all, Sonny," Davis said. "It's seen a terrified kid, whose father had been killed and whose mother had gone insane, reaching out desperately for help. It's seen that kid build a wall around himself to keep others out. It's seen a skinny kid turn into a dangerous man whose shell is impenetrable. Nobody gets in now, do they?''

"Except you."

"Except me," Davis said. "Sometimes. What about her?''

"Who?''

"Angela. Your problems with her can be traced right back to the suppression of your childhood emotions. It's like following a road map," Davis said.

"I don't believe this," Sonny said. "What are you? Some kind of Sigmund Fucking Freud? The woman screws around on me and it's my fault because I had an attitude as a kid?''

"Trouble is, the only emotion you're good at is anger, and anger and love don't mix," Davis said, shaking his head sadly.

Sonny was incensed. He stood up and jabbed the table with his finger. "The broad was a cunt. She was fucking another guy, probably in my bed, while I was working. So fuck her!''

"Did you ever tell her you loved her?''

"And fuck you!''

Davis sighed and watched Sonny stomp out of the kitchen. Too bad there was no *Sergeant Rock's Manual for Marital Arts,* he thought.

# 16

"Two lonely words on a field of white," John Sanford said. "Not much to go on."

Sanford was a handwriting analyst on retainer to the police department. He had been trying to analyze the note Berger had found clutched in the dead hand delivered to his door.

"'Help us,'" Berger quoted.

"I'm trying, but mostly it's pure guesswork," Sanford said. He was a stooped man who looked as desiccated as his work.

"Guess away," Berger said, looking at his watch. LoBianco was late.

"Well, as you know, the notepaper was ordinary bond probably pulled from a six-by-eight memo pad. The manufacturer produces millions of pounds of that paper a year and sells it to thousands of customers. It is virtually impossible for us to trace. At least that's what the lab says," Sanford said. He was interested in more than handwriting; he had studied paper, pens, pencils, and typewriters.

"The pen was a Papermate, one of billions sold," he continued, sounding like a hamburger commercial. "So there's no help in that direction."

Berger nodded patiently. Experts in all fields, he knew,

liked to impress cops with the breadth of their knowledge before they actually told you anything of value.

"Much of what goes on in a person's mind is translated into his writing," Sanford said. "People lie, but it's much more difficult to lie about yourself when you write."

"As I said, there's not much to go on, but the letter forms are correct in structure, indicating a basic education. The block letters are obviously an attempt to disguise the handwriting." Sanford paused.

"Go ahead, Mr. Sanford," Berger said encouragingly.

"I can posit two tentative conclusions. First, the writer is either a sloppy person and not particularly concerned with appearance. Or perhaps he or she was in a hurry. There's not enough material here to analyze," Sanford said.

"A man or a woman?" Berger asked. "Can you tell me that?"

"That's my second guess. It was a man, I think, but one at war with himself," Sanford said. "The writer seems to have a violent conflict within himself. I sense this because the letters vary in pressure and structure."

He held up a photocopy of the note and said, "Look at the *E*'s. They are different in *help* and *me*. It is as if two people collaborated on this note."

"A split personality?" Berger asked skeptically.

"I'm not a psychiatrist, but I can detect a tension between two competing personalities." He put the photocopy down.

"I wouldn't swear to it in court, of course," Sanford said. "Because whoever wrote this might have been doing it clandestinely. You know, trying to get a message to you before his—or her—captor returned."

"So it is the victims who want help?" Berger asked.

"Or the killer's cry for help?" Sanford asked. "It's open to interpretation."

Berger thanked the handwriting expert and hustled him out the door. Another dead end, he thought, checking his watch again. LoBianco was late. He sat back down at his desk and called LoBianco's home number. A woman answered.

"Officer LoBianco, please," Berger said.

"He no longer lives here," Angela said.

"Sorry," Berger said. "I must have an old number."

"Who the fuck's that?" Berger heard a man's voice.

"Wrong number," Angela said, hanging up.

It didn't take a detective to figure out what was going on, Berger thought. We're both in the same boat while our wives are out screwing around.

He shuffled through the pile of papers on his desk and found LoBianco's new number, but before he could dial, Sonny walked into the squad room.

"You're late," Berger said, without looking up.

"Yeah," LoBianco said, sitting down opposite Berger.

"'Yeah'? That's all you got to say, Mr. I-Don't-Know-What-Time-It-Is?"

"Back off, Ira," LoBianco said. "You were out for days and I'm worn-out."

"Your lack of progress indicates you sat on your duff the whole time."

"Jeez, Ira."

"Santamyer says we only got a couple more days to develop some leads or we're history. Borough is foaming at the mouth," Berger said.

"Fuck them," LoBianco said without emotion. He had been up all night thinking about Angela. Father D was on his case, and now Berger was riding him. He just wanted to be left alone.

"Oh, that's the kind of talk that really helps," Berger said. He was getting angry at this young man's cavalier attitude.

LoBianco shuffled some papers on his desk in an overt attempt to end the questioning.

Berger grumbled and returned to reading the D-5s he had read a hundred times before. They ignored each other for twenty minutes, then LoBianco got up and went to the back of the PDU bullpen and poured himself a cup of coffee. The phones were ringing off the hook, detectives were talking over the din, and outside, a fire engine, siren wailing, horn blaring, roared by.

What a fucking hole, LoBianco thought. This place makes a slum look like a luxury hotel. Maybe Vito was right. He *should* join the family business. A cockroach marched across the wall; LoBianco crushed it with his thumb and left its remains twitching on the green wall.

"LoBianco!" Berger called across the room.

Sonny turned and saw Ira heading for the door, his overcoat over his arm.

"Get a move on it," Berger said. "We've got a squeal."

Mrs. Iona Iorio sat on Adele Woodword's porch, huddled in a green loden coat. She could feel her heart hammering and taste the sour bile rising in her throat. Mrs. Iorio was sixty-one and led a quiet life, but what she had seen in Adele's kitchen would haunt her forever.

"How do you spell that?" Berger asked her. He and LoBianco had arrived before the lab guys, before the crime scene had been established.

"Ten R Ten," Mrs. Iorio said. "That's what my late husband used to say: Ten R Ten, the *I*'s and the *O*'s are the tens." She blinked at them, confused and terrified. Her eyes were red and glassy from crying; her nose ran.

"You called the police," Berger said. "What did you see in there?"

Mrs. Iorio gulped back the vomit. "In there," she whispered. "Jesus, Mary, and Joseph."

"You saw, uh, what?" Berger persisted.

"Don't go in there," Mrs. Iorio said, in a whispery, shuddery voice. "Not in the kitchen."

A blue-and-white patrol car pulled up to the curb and Berger told the two uniforms to take care of the woman.

"She's really spooked," LoBianco said.

"So am I," Berger said. "Let's get this over with."

LoBianco followed Berger up the stairs to the front door. Mrs. Iorio's keys were dangling in the lock. As they would discover later, Adele Woodword and Iona Iorio had had plans to attend a concert that evening at the Brooklyn Academy of Music. But when Adele hadn't answered Iona's numerous phone calls, Iona had gone over to see what was wrong. Adele had given her a key some years ago, and Iona hadn't hesitated to use it. She would forever wish she had.

Berger steeled himself for the expected scene of horror and pushed open the front door.

The room was neat and untouched. Nothing seemed out of place.

"We ought to wait for the crime-scene unit," LoBianco said. "I don't want to screw up the investigation."

"You're right," Berger said, moving into the living room, his eyes hard behind his glasses. He used his elbow to push open the swinging door to the kitchen.

Avoiding a yellowish pool of Iona Iorio's vomit, he looked around. The kitchen too seemed in perfect order. A half-filled coffee cup and saucer on a kitchen table was the only item out of place. Adele Woodword was a very neat woman.

"What are we missing?" Berger asked aloud.

"Some kind of nut, that Mrs. Ten R Ten?" LoBianco asked.

"Could be," Berger mused. "But she saw *something* in here." He went to the cabinet beneath the sink and opened it. Nothing unusual. He checked the cabinets above the refrigerator, but they contained only the usual canned and packaged goods.

While Berger was carefully nosing around Adele Woodword's kitchen LoBianco idly examined the partially filled cup of coffee on the table. He tipped the cup slightly to examine its contents.

"That woman must be crazy," Berger said. "I can't find a damned thing."

"This might be something," LoBianco said in a quiet voice.

"What?"

"This," LoBianco said, motioning to Berger.

"What's that?" Berger asked, looking into the cup. LoBianco took a pen from his pocket and stirred the murky contents. A human eyeball rolled gently to the surface and stared at the cops.

Berger felt a sudden revulsion; he hoped he wouldn't lose his breakfast.

"Cheer up, Ira," LoBianco said, noting Berger's gray-faced shock. "Coffee's always a good eye-opener."

"Let's get out of here and wait for forensic," Berger said. Inside he felt the cold chill of death. "A whole woman lived here and now all we have is an eye. Where is the rest of her?"

"Tell forensic to go on an Easter-egg hunt. Putting Humpty Dumpty back together again isn't in my job description," LoBianco said as they retraced their steps to the front door.

A uniformed sergeant named Testerelli shook a meaty finger at them as they emerged from the house. "Now, don't go ruining my crime scene," he said. He waved them to the front yard, where he had a logbook that would record all police and technicians who entered the house.

"So, Sergeant Berger and friend, come on down!" Testerelli said. "And sign in please. Let me guess your occupation and win valuable prizes." Testerelli thought of himself as a game-show host, though he constantly confused one show with another.

Berger and LoBianco dutifully signed in and waited for the lab guys to show up.

"Let me guess what's behind door number one," Testerelli said. "A murder victim?"

"You're part right," LoBianco said.

"Which part?"

"An eye."

"For an eye?" Testerelli said.

"Nope."

Testerelli rubbed the black stubble on his chin. "And the answer is: Huh? What's the question?"

"The question is, what are you, some kind of nut?" Berger said.

"Good answer," Testerelli said, clapping his hands.

"Meshuggener," Berger said, retreating to the sidewalk. LoBianco followed.

The lab van pulled to the curb, joining a half-dozen blue-and-whites and two unmarked PDU cars.

Berger and LoBianco were issued plastic shoe guards and surgical gloves, then with four technicians, they went back into Adele Woodword's house.

"Will we need some M-18?" one of the technicians asked, referring to the crystals cops broke under their noses to cut the stench of death. The crystals smelled like violets.

"Yes," Berger said, remembering the pool of vomit in the kitchen.

"Where's the body?" Dr. Jerry Stivers, the assistant medical examiner, said as he joined the six men in the living room.

"All over, I'm afraid," Berger said, explaining the situation.

"Christ, and I could be back in a warm autopsy room carving out some guy's heart," Stivers said. "How do you want to do this?"

"You and LoBianco check upstairs and the rest of us will work downstairs," Berger said, leading the forensic team into the kitchen. He pointed out the eye in the coffee cup, then began a methodical search.

Upstairs, LoBianco volunteered to take the bathroom, figuring there weren't a lot of hiding places for body parts. Stivers and two lab men took the bedrooms.

The bathroom was spotless; its black-and-white tiles shone brilliantly. The opaque shower curtain, a white-on-white design of flowers and birds, was closed. Sonny thought he could see a large dark shape hiding behind the curtain, so he took a deep breath and yanked it open. "Trick or treat," he said aloud, but all he found was a woman's woolen coat hanging from the shower nozzle. It took him a few seconds to realize that there were feet sticking out from the sleeves.

"Christ," LoBianco said. The coat was damp with blood, fluids, and water; it gave off a strangely feral smell, like a wet dog.

LoBianco stared at the coat, and once the shock wore off, he began to see the glimmerings of a pattern behind the perp's widely creative murders. He went to the medicine cabinet and opened it. A severed hand clutching a bottle of Tylenol fell into the sink with a bony rattle.

I'm certainly glad I volunteered for the bathroom, LoBianco thought, peering at the hand with morbid curiosity.

"One bedroom's clean," Stivers said, leaning into the bathroom. His voice made Sonny jump.

"Look at this shit," LoBianco said.

Stivers shook his head. "At this rate it will take us a week to put her back together."

"You want to open the toilet?" Sonny asked.

"No way. I don't like this treasure-hunt stuff," Stivers said. "I like 'em whole and on the table."

"You chicken?"

"Yeah. Are you?" Stivers asked.

"No."

"Then *you* open the toilet seat," Stivers said.

LoBianco borrowed a tongue depressor from Stivers and put it under the lid. He lifted it slowly, expecting the worst. The lid slipped backward and banged against the water tank with a hollow sound.

"Nothing," LoBianco said thankfully. The water was crystal clear.

Stivers shrugged and went back to join the search in the other bedrooms. LoBianco unzipped his fly and pissed into the bowl, thinking he should reduce his coffee consumption.

He pushed down the handle to flush the toilet, but it was jammed. He forced it, causing a gurgle of water. "Fucking thing," LoBianco swore. Then he saw the trickle of water that had leaked into the bowl was red. Bloodred.

"Shit," he said. "Doc!" He zipped up, and waited.

Stivers reappeared; LoBianco pointed at the bowl. "Look at this."

"Having kidney problems?" Stivers asked, looking at the bloody urine.

"It's in the tank," LoBianco said.

"What?"

"That's what we're about to find out," LoBianco said, lifting off the top of the tank. Adele Woodword's head was jammed inside; she didn't look happy about it.

"I don't think I want to play this game anymore," LoBianco said.

Downstairs, Ira Berger opened the refrigerator. At first everything seemed normal, but then he noticed a large jar of dill pickles. Floating in the brine were pickles and fingers. Berger called the technicians over and they carefully removed the jar.

"Looks like five fingers," one of the forensic men said.

"Give me five!" his buddy said, laughing.

Berger shuddered and went back to work. A half box of eggs attracted his attention. He opened it and found . . . six eggs. But as he was putting the carton back the top of one of the eggs slid off, revealing a second human eye. The perp had emptied the yoke and inserted the eye; Berger handed the carton to the technicians and kept on exploring.

He expected the worst and soon found it. Picking up a bottle of orange juice, he noticed it looked too orange. He shook it. A hand, severed at the wrist, gently waved to him. Berger said, "If I smoked, I think I'd go outside and have one right now."

"This ain't nothing," one of the technicians said. "Why, last month we—"

"Spare me the details," Berger said. "I'm a thirty-year

man and I used to be able to handle the job. But I'm too old for this."

The technicians took the bottle of orange juice from the refrigerator and lined it up with the pickles, coffee cup, and egg carton.

"Berger!" He heard LoBianco's voice from upstairs.

"I'll be back," Berger told the technicians, and went upstairs.

LoBianco was standing in the bathroom. "Check this out," Sonny said.

Berger looked in the tank. Adele Woodword stared at him.

"She's got eyes," LoBianco said.

"Two bodies, four bodies, an entire block of murdered women," Berger said.

"In here," Dr. Jerry Stivers called from down the hall. His voice sounded shrill.

Glad to leave the bathroom, they went to the second bedroom, where even the lab guys looked a little pale.

"Look at this?" Stivers whispered. He was having trouble speaking.

Two female torsos, clad in bras, were resting side by side in the queen-sized bed; dried blood covered blue satin sheets with a rusty patina. One of the torsos had a head attached; the mouth was open; hanging from the mouth was a hand, middle finger extended in the universal "fuck you" sign. LoBianco winced. In the closet, open for inspection, Martha Collins's stumpy legs had been jammed into a pair of high heels. They stood rigidly like the gateposts to hell.

"Thank you, boys," Berger said. "I believe I've seen enough."

"Yeah," said LoBianco. "I'll wait for the book. I don't like this movie."

# 17

The phone call came at noon, waking Charles Maris from an uneasy sleep. It was his day off and he had been up all night working on Emily's new body. He had hands and arms, a very good start, he thought.

He let the phone ring ten times, but the caller wouldn't give up. On the fifteenth ring he picked it up and listened.

"It's time, Charles," a woman's voice said.

Charles gasped. "Mother," he whispered.

"I'm on my way and you know what you must do."

"Yes, Mother."

"Remember, none of your foolishness."

The line went dead; Charles wiped the nervous sweat from his brow. He kicked the dirty sheets and blankets from his bed, sending a flurry of pornographic magazines tumbling to the floor.

Lurching to the bathroom with a sudden blinding headache, he drank a glass of water with a handful of Percodans and tried to get his head together, for it threatened to fly apart again. Why couldn't Mother stay dead? he asked himself. What had he done to deserve this?

Actually he knew very well what he had done. Neither Emily nor Mother would ever let him forget.

He dressed quickly and went to the basement to feed the

dogs. It took great effort to prevent himself from visiting the mannequin in the subbasement. He wanted to stroke the arms and hands and figure out which body part he needed next. Legs? Feet? A head? Hair? Breasts? The last thought embarrassed him, so he concentrated on mixing the dogs' food.

Dempsey stood in the back of his cage, hackles up, mean as ever.

"You know, I could put you down, should put you down," Charles said to the dog. "But I'm giving you a second chance. Just like Mother gave me, and I hope you suffer like I have."

He brandished the cudgel at Dempsey and the dog shrank back even farther, its yellow eyes betraying fear and hatred.

"Maybe you're smarter than I am," Maris said. "Maybe you know the hell you'll have to go through to . . . to atone for your sins."

*Charles!* He could almost hear Mother's voice. *Charles, where is Emily?*

He said he didn't know, but he was lying. It had been his fault. Emily had found Tag, his first pit bull, and . . . He didn't want to think about it. He had big plans today.

Charles walked to Third Avenue, toward one of his favorite spots. It was a restaurant called Norge, a holdover from the days when Bay Ridge had been predominantly Norwegian. The Dutch had originally settled the area in the mid-1600s, giving way to Norwegians in 1825, when sailors, shipbuilders, and their families flocked to the area like flies to *kransekake,* the traditional Norwegian wedding cake.

The interior of the restaurant was dimly lit by bronze ships' lamps; the walls were paneled with dark wood, and the floor covered with a thick brown carpet. He felt instantly at home, inhaling the rich aromas coming from the kitchen.

"Mr. Maris," Carl, the maître d', said. "Welcome back. It's been a long time."

"I've been busy, you know. Since Mother, uh, died," Charles said.

"I was so sorry to hear about that," Carl said. "Your mother was such a . . . proper lady."

"And more," Charles said, thinking, *bitch*.

He was seated near the fireplace, and at his request a waiter lit the cedar logs. They gave off a perfumy smell that relaxed and calmed him. He rubbed his hands over the stiff white damask, took a drink of water from a crystal goblet, and wondered how life could be better.

From a basket on the table he took a piece of *vortelimpe,* a rye bread flavored with molasses, anise, and orange; he slathered it with fresh Danish butter and shoved it in his mouth. It made him dizzy with pleasure.

He had demolished the basket of bread by the time the waiter came to take his order, so he asked for more *vortelimpe* and some *grisellebred,* which was twice baked for an extra-crispy crust. And more butter, of course.

Charles studied the menu and selected creamed herring for an appetizer; the famous yellow pea soup; *lapshous,* which were meat cakes with onions; and *sviskergrot,* a prune compote with cream, for dessert. He told the waiter to save him a piece of Norge's famous apple cake in case he wanted it with the *sviskergrot.*

He felt warm and secure in the restaurant. They treated him like an old friend and a valued customer. Perhaps that was because his father had first taken him here before Emily arrived and Poppa departed.

Unbidden, the memories of his father swept back, overloading his senses. Paul Maris had been big and blond, Charles remembered, a gentle man, a hardworking man who spoke broken English and worked with his hands. He and Mother had been happy together even though, Charles supposed, Poppa wasn't exactly a suitable husband as far as Mother's rich family was concerned. But Charles had loved him with an uncritical, perfect love—until Emily came. Then it all changed. Poppa left, left him at the mercy of a furious mother, a timid aunt, and a baby that was the object of Mother's affection and his affliction.

Leaning back in the brown leather chair, Charles wallowed in anticipation of the magnificent meal to come when he saw something that shocked him to his soul.

Emily walked into the restaurant.

Tall, about five-foot-nine, she had wavy blond hair and a face he knew instantly. He felt the familiar tingling at the back of his scalp. He closed his eyes and willed the brain explosion away, for this was no time to be incapacitated. He had to have her head.

She moved gracefully, her hand placed lightly on Carl's arm, to a table near Charles's. As she passed him he could smell her perfume, a spicy, flowery scent that made him instantly hard. With a shaky hand he took another drink of water, hoping to quench the fire in his brain and groin. It was Emily, he thought wildly, the way he had always imagined her. He had seen that face in his dreams for decades and now the owner of that face was less than ten feet away from him. It was a sign, an omen. He couldn't take his eyes off her.

The young woman, unaware of his scrutiny, became deeply engrossed in the menu while Charles planned her murder. He was woefully unprepared for this stroke of luck, he knew, but he couldn't let the opportunity get away.

He had always been worried about reconstructing Emily's face, thinking he would have to get an eye here, a nose there, a mouth somewhere else, but now he could save a great deal of trouble. God knew, he had to hurry. Mother was coming home soon.

Charles slurped the creamed herring and practically inhaled the yellow pea soup, his eyes never leaving the back of the woman's head. The hair, of course, would have to go, he thought. Emily had dark, lustrous hair. The rest of the woman's body was superfluous. It would be discarded like the neck and feet of a chicken.

The woman must have sensed Charles's penetrating stare because she turned around suddenly and looked him straight in the eye. Quickly he dropped his glance and concentrated on his plate. When he looked up again, stealthily, she had gone back to eating her meal. But she had seen his face and he knew he couldn't let her go. He declined the apple cake the waiter had saved for him, paid the check, and hurried out of the restaurant.

The ocean breeze was damp and cold; the sun hid behind the lowering clouds.

Basically Charles had two choices: follow the woman home and kill her, or follow her home and go back later. Not having a detailed plan made him nervous, but he decided to let circumstances shape his decision. He pulled up the collar of his dirty tan raincoat and waited, pretending to window-shop up and down the street. In the old days a beat cop would have noticed and questioned him, but nowadays you had to machine-gun a church congregation to elicit a police response. That sort of scrutiny was anathema to Charles, who, despite his bizarre crimes, had sunk into the anonymous sludge of a bankrupt, unmanageable city filled with savages. At least there was a method to his madness, he thought. Though the madness of his method never occurred to him.

The woman with the blond hair left Norge thirty minutes after Charles and walked east. He followed her at a distance, wondering if he would have to be satisfied with simply discovering where she lived. That was the safe way to operate: stalk, identify, establish routine, prepare, and attack. Still, it would be so good to feel his hands around her pretty neck. That thought made him hard again and he found it painful to hurry after the woman, who strode confidently ahead of him.

Ten minutes after leaving the restaurant, the blonde led Charles to a block of neat, five-story apartment houses.

Each building was attached to its neighbor and each had similar glass-and-cast-iron front doors, leading to well-kept foyers.

He hung back, noticing that even the garbage cans that lined the street were in orderly groups, individually lined with black plastic bags, the buildings' addresses painted on the sides. Charles appreciated both the symmetry and the cleanliness of the neighborhood. It was just the sort of place Emily would like.

The blond woman walked up the stairs to a building at the end of the block and fumbled for her keys. That was Charles's signal. He moved with a rapidity that belied his bulk, reaching her just as she was opening the foyer door. His two hundred sixty pounds plowed into her, knocking her to the polished terrazzo floor. Before she could scream, he put his big hand over her mouth and began dragging her down the hall to the basement door, marked by an exit sign.

With one hand he opened the black metal door, with the other he dragged the struggling woman down the stairs. Though she had taken self-defense classes, the blonde, whose name Charles would discover later was Sarah Goldman, was no match for Charles's vicious, surprise attack.

When he reached the bottom of the stairs, he took his hand from her mouth and wrapped it around her exquisite neck. She gagged and fought, but lost consciousness within a minute. Charles hefted her onto his shoulder and looked for an operating theater. He found it at once. The empty boiler room. His luck was holding.

The boiler, huge and barrel-shaped, was old and loud and, to Charles's horror, covered with asbestos. Cancer, he thought, goddamn cancer. What was wrong with the people in this building? Did they want to die?

He took a handkerchief from his pocket and tied it around his nose and face, in the hope of mitigating the effects of the carcinogen. If he hadn't been determined to help Emily, he would have left this place of death immediately.

Furious because there would be no time to enjoy this, he

snapped Sarah Goldman's neck like a twig, then searched the boiler room for some sort of instrument to complete his task before his lungs became clogged with the killer dust.

Although he hadn't done any research on decapitation, it didn't strike him as being too complicated a procedure. The best way, he thought, would be one blow with a very sharp instrument. That was the way a guillotine worked, but the quick blow was designed to spare the victim extended pain. The woman lying on the gray cement floor, however, was past any pain, and he supposed he could afford to be less humane in his technique.

A search of the boiler room turned up no sharp instruments, forcing him to explore the rest of the basement. He peered down the dimly lit hallway and spotted a wire-mesh cage that had once been used by tenants for storage, but now housed the super's equipment.

Cautiously he walked to it, finding it padlocked. But upon closer inspection he noted that the hasp securing the lock was a makeshift affair. He reached into his pocket and took out his key ring. Using a long silver key, he pried the hasp away from the dry, splintery wood frame. It took him only seconds to gain entry; only a minute to find a hacksaw, similar to his bone saw, but rusty and badly kept. He sighed. It would have to do. He also took a black plastic garbage bag and returned to the boiler room.

Charles could feel the motes of asbestos swirling around him in the hot and stuffy room, trying to invade his lungs. He took a breath through his handkerchief and touched the dead woman's neck. He wanted to cut it as low as possible, saving the final trimming for later when he had the proper instruments. This, he thought, was only the rough cut.

He lined up the hacksaw and began sawing off Sarah Goldman's head.

Returning home, the severed head in the garbage bag over his shoulder, Charles couldn't wait to get to the subbasement. He released the dogs, except Dempsey, and descended the metal stairs to his operating theater. All in all it had been a magnificent day, he thought, gently putting his package down on the stainless-steel autopsy table.

For several minutes Maris flitted around Sarah Goldman's head like an insane hairdresser. He secured the head, faceup, on the table so that he could freely cut away the ragged skin of her neck. Never perform major surgery with a hacksaw, he told himself. He put the scraps in a pile for the dogs.

Then he began to cut away her long, blond hair with the same pair of surgical scissors he had used on her neck. Sarah's hair was fine and cut easily. In less than ten minutes he had it down to a stubble. Whistling, he lathered her scalp with hot shaving cream and opened a package of Good News disposable razors.

The dogs watched in rapt fascination as Maris crisscrossed Sarah's scalp with professional razor strokes until her head was as smooth as a politician's rap. The dogs drooled.

As Maris stood back to admire his creation a sudden thought struck him. He had heard that hair and nails continued to grow after death. Would he have to shave her again? he wondered. He caressed the bald head.

Maris looked at her closely, noticing that her lips were beginning to curl into a sneer. A sneer on Emily's lips would never do, he thought. He'd have to sew her mouth closed.

Leaving the subbasement, the dogs following him, he went up the steps to the kennel area. There he found what he was looking for, the sterile surgical needle attached to eight inches of chromic gut. Perfect for the job. He also took the needle holder, a scissorslike device used to push the needle in and out of the flesh.

Humming to himself, he cast a wary eye on Dempsey, still locked in his cage. The big pit bull stood and wagged his tail, a sign of submission. Stopping, Maris took a moment to consider the dog's unusual behavior. Then, making a decision, he retrieved the walking stick and stun gun and let Dempsey out.

With slow, almost tentative steps, Dempsey left the cage and joined the other dogs, staying behind them, not disrupting their new pecking order. Maris shook his head in disbelief. Dempsey had either reformed or was a great actor.

Congratulating himself on being a skilled trainer, Maris went downstairs to begin the work of keeping Sarah Goldman's mouth shut.

# 18

Ira Berger arrived home at 6:00 P.M., feeling his stomach upset and his ulcer doing a tap dance in his duodenum. What he wanted was peace and quiet, what he found was Rose sitting in the living room surrounded by her luggage.

"Taking a trip?" he asked. His feet hurt like hell.

"I'm leaving you," she said.

"Just like that?"

"I waited to tell you in person," she said.

"What an honor."

Rose stood up to grab her black Samsonite carryon when Berger interrupted her. "We should talk," he said.

"We talk all the time."

"Not about us," he said.

"There is no us anymore," she said.

His stomach dropped to the cellar.

Looking at her closely, he noticed for the first time that she had dyed her hair, a brown color with reddish headlights. With her soft figure, she looked years younger than forty.

"I have a life, Ira. I'm allowed to make my own decisions," she said.

"I see." He couldn't think.

"You don't see, Ira," she said. "You've never seen.

You've made me into some kind of person that suits your purposes, but not mine. I'm not included in your agenda.''

''Are you sleeping with him?'' Berger asked, finally able to say the words.

''Would you believe me if I said no?''

''No.''

''Ira, I've been faithful to you all these years because I owe you so much. You took me in when no one else would. You've given me more than any person in the world, except maybe my sister.''

''You didn't answer my question,'' he said, dry-mouthed, stomach heaving.

''I had a choice to make,'' she said.

''I mean so little to you?'' he asked in a whisper.

''You mean a lot, Ira,'' she said. ''But I should have done this a long time ago. The only reason I stayed was that I had no reason to leave. I would have had to get a new apartment, a new job, and as I said, you were always good to me.''

Berger was too stunned to speak.

''I'm glad you're taking it so well,'' she said, moving across the living room to kiss him.

He shied away as if she were a snake. ''Fucking Cossack!'' Berger shouted. ''Fucking, goddamned Cossack!''

But she was gone.

Pacing back and forth, his mind reeling, Ira Berger attempted to make sense out of what had just happened to him. And to Rose. He tried to think where he had gone wrong, how he had failed her. Had he been that bad in bed? Had he kept her too much under his thumb? Was it the goddamned baby, or lack of one? After twenty goddamned years suddenly it was over.

He tried to visualize her face as it had been when he had first met her, but the best he could come up with was Grace Kelly. Rose hadn't been as pretty, he supposed, but she had had Kelly's regal bearing and ingenuous quality, which had appealed to him, a thirty-nine-year-old bachelor. She was only nineteen when he had married her, taking her away from her crazy sister. Nineteen. It seemed incredible to him now.

Rose had never talked much about her childhood, saying only that her parents had died when she was eight and her older sister had taken their place. After a year of trying to get along with the sister, Lois, Berger had given up. The woman was a first-class bitch, if the truth be told. He had been glad when Rose resumed her relationship with her sister without him. Rose doted on her niece and nephew, lavishing upon them love and presents, he supposed, to make up for her own barrenness.

Berger had been just as glad they had never had children, but maybe that was why Rose had left him. Maybe she wanted to adopt; maybe she had found a doctor who could make her fertile; maybe she couldn't abide having *his* child.

That thought made his ulcer do cartwheels and he went into the bathroom to drown his sorrows in Maalox. Then he turned on the television to watch the news.

Seated in his vinyl recliner, he tried to concentrate on the blond anchorwoman, but the silence in the rest of the apartment was oppressive.

"So this is the way I'll spend the rest of my life," he said out loud.

Then the tears came.

Sonny LoBianco found a brand-new Plymouth Voyager parked next to the yellow school bus when he returned to St. Agnes that evening. The sleek, futuristic lines of the black van contrasted strangely with the boxy bus and the neoclassical architecture. Mr. MoFo had delivered. E.T. sat behind the wheel, pretending to drive himself to California.

"It's mint!" the boy shouted to Sonny. "Fully loaded. It's got everything: A/C, CD and cassette, power windows, and power brakes. Stereo's awesome; I can listen to my tunes while we're cruisin'."

"You sound like a commercial," LoBianco said, pulling past the minivan. E.T. got out of the van and raced after him.

"Hey, Sonny," E.T. shouted breathlessly. "How about head-to-head, a quarter mile? Your Vette against my Black Beauty."

"Your Black Beauty?"

"That's what it's gonna say when I pinstripe it, man," E.T. said, his eyes alight with joy. "It's gonna say 'E.T.'s Black Beauty' and it's gonna blow the doors off your old Vette."

"If you don't stop messing around with that van, I'm going to pinstripe my shoe on your butt," LoBianco said.

E.T. laughed. "Where did it come from? Father Davis has had his balls in an uproar all day about it. He told me he wants to see you right away."

"Tell him I'll be there when I'm there," LoBianco said sourly.

"Yooo," E.T. said. "Vexed."

LoBianco ignored him, unlocked the garage, and closed the door in E.T.'s face. Fuck 'em both, he thought.

"Yo, you step to me correctly" E.T. called through the door.

Ira Berger couldn't take it any longer. He had to do *something* and most especially he had to get out of the apartment. Not a violent man by nature, he felt his control slipping and that worried him. For the past hour he had been thinking of ways to shoot Gross the butcher and not caring if he got away with it.

Finally he made a call and got an equally disgruntled LoBianco on the phone.

"You want to do an old man a favor?" he said to his partner.

"Like what?"

"Like maybe we could play some gin?" Berger said.

"Or drink some?"

"Whatever. You got the time?" Berger said.

"I got nothing but time. Unfortunately," LoBianco answered. He was still angry with Davis for messing with his mind, furious at Angela, and confused by his uncle. Life was suddenly too complicated. "You want to go to Michael's?"

"No," Berger said.

"You want me to come over there?"

"No. I'll come for you. Give me the address."

Berger wrote St. Agnes's address in his pocket notebook, then called a cab. He was at the door of the shelter in twenty minutes, glad to be anywhere but home.

He introduced himself to Franklyn Davis and was surprised when the black priest shook his hand like an old friend.

"I can't tell you how much we appreciate your lending us the bus," Davis said sincerely.

Berger stared at him blankly. "What bus?" he asked.

"The one in the driveway—" Davis stopped, realizing Sonny had done it again.

"I'm sorry," the priest said. "I think we have a case of mistaken identity. I keep mistaking that miserable son of a bitch Sonny for a human being."

"I have no idea what you're talking about, Father," Berger said in his best ecumenical manner. "But is that miserable son of a bitch Sonny around?"

"Oh, he's around, all right, and I believe I'll have me a talk with that young troop. Why don't you wait in my study?" Davis said, leading the way. "I'll be right back."

"You and I need to have a talk," Davis said, pushing his way into Sonny's garage apartment. "A vee-hicular talk." He sat down on the bed.

"Come in, Father. Welcome to my house," LoBianco said. "Please make yourself comfortable."

"Cut the crap, Sonny. Where the hell did they come from? The van and the bus?" Davis asked.

"I already told—"

"—lied to me. Tell me the truth."

"Look, Father," LoBianco said. "All you're going to do is bust my onions about this, so why don't you just enjoy them and save the questions."

"Tell."

Sonny shook his head in disgust. He knew he was in for a battle he couldn't win.

"The van is from the people who torched your bus. They're replacing what they destroyed. You don't have any cash, you don't have any insurance. And you don't have any other options. Just take it and let your morals look the other way."

Davis rubbed his scarred face and was silent, but just when LoBianco thought the priest would drop the whole subject, he said, "I don't believe my ears. I've been fighting these drug-dealing maggots all my life and you're taking gifts from them? You're unbelievable."

"It's not a gift, Father. It's a reimbursement. A replacement, with an apology."

"Sure," Davis said. "They volunteered it, right?"

Sonny dropped his gaze. "Something like that."

"I'll bet, man," Davis said. "Listen, it's not that I don't appreciate it, but the van was bought with drug money. I can't deal with that. I won't!"

LoBianco was silent, trying to control his temper.

"And what about that yellow bus?" Davis continued, pressing his advantage. "Drug dealers donate that one up, too?"

"I told you—"

"You *lied* to me. Sergeant Berger's in my office right now. He doesn't have a fucking clue about the bus."

"Shit," LoBianco said. "Okay. It's a loaner from my uncle."

"Vito LoBianco?"

"Yeah."

"What were you thinking?" Davis said. "The van was

bought with drug money and the bus with mob money. No matter how much you coat it with bullshit, it's blood money and I won't have it.''

"Money's money, Father," LoBianco said.

"Balls," Davis roared, getting up off the bed. "Haven't I taught you different."

"You didn't mind it when Vito sent over envelopes of cash when I was a kid," LoBianco shot back.

"How did—"

"Vito told me, Father. So much for your theory of 'blood money.' You're on the fucking pad like everyone else, so don't get on your high horse about this. It won't wash with me.''

"Let me try to explain," Davis began.

"Just leave me alone," LoBianco said.

"I—"

"Fuck off, Father," Sonny said, closing the door on the priest.

"Goddamn it," he said out loud, punching the swaying dummy. "Goddamn it to hell.''

After twenty kicks and punches he managed to cool off. He went to the phone, and after getting two forwarding numbers, he reached his uncle Vito.

After a minute of being polite Sonny said, "You can have the bus picked up.''

"You got another one?" Vito asked.

"Yeah.''

"Good. But tell that priest next time trouble starts, let us know in the beginning and not to wait until it's too late. We can help, tell him. Now, Sonny, what we discussed, did you think about it?''

"Not really. I've been busy.''

"Santino, this is important. It's business, you gotta give it priority.''

"Your business is not my business, Uncle Vito. You keep forgetting I'm the law.''

"And you keep forgetting who your family is . . . you

keep giving all your time to that nigger priest.'' Vito's voice had a hard edge to it.

Sonny let a silence grow between them until it became unbearable. Then he spoke. ''He's black, Vito, not a nigger, you got that? And for a good part of my life *he was* my family, my only family. I didn't sign myself into this orphanage, somebody dumped me here. Somebody signed a piece of paper that said 'take the kid, I don't want him.' You have any idea whose signature was on that paper, *Uncle Vito?*''

''You don't understand what was going on then, you don't understand what I was up against. Alone. Without your father.''

Vito took a long breath that ended in a sigh. ''Look, I know what you're thinking, what you've been carrying around inside you all these years. And I know what the priest did for you, all he did for you. You gotta excuse my mouth sometimes. When I call him a nig—you know what I mean, sometimes my mouth goes faster than my brain.''

Sonny wasn't buying anything his uncle said, but he needed a question answered; it was the reason for his call.

''How can I help you?'' he asked his uncle.

Vito spoke low. ''Frank Marcellino, he's making deals with the, uh, blacks.''

''And?'' Sonny asked.

''I told you, I need to know what he's up to. You got informers out there. They can get answers for me without him knowing I'm the one asking.''

''You want to know what he's cooking up, if anything?''

''That's it,'' Vito said.

''I'll put the word out,'' LoBianco said. ''Whatever Marcellino is doing, I'll find out.''

''You and him were good friends once,'' Vito said.

''Once, yes. No more.''

''He's changed, Sonny. He's a *gavone* now. A greedy son of a bitch.''

''People change, Uncle Vito. Sometimes more than you can guess,'' LoBianco said.

He took a shower and then called Lucy Velez, before walking over to the rectory to collect Berger.

Ira Berger looked around Davis's study and found it comfortably, if cheaply, furnished. He recognized the plaid-covered furniture; he and Rose had bought the same chair, couch, and love seat at Levitz more than fifteen years ago. It made him sad. *All those years, all those goddamned years.*

Unable to sit any longer, he got up and began pacing, trying to force all thoughts from his mind. He walked to the window, turned on his heel, and almost bumped into a little girl dressed in pink overalls and a pink shirt. She was, Berger guessed, about four, but he wouldn't swear to it in court. What he knew about children could be inscribed on the head of a pin with enough room for a score of angels. Her dark hair was braided; he guessed she was Spanish. She looked up at him curiously.

"Hello, little girl," he said.

"'Lo," she said. "I'm LaDonna. Who are you?"

"I'm Detective Sergeant Ira Berger."

"Do you have a penis?"

"Not according to my wife," Berger said, shocked and amused.

"Does she have one?"

"Perhaps."

"Will you show me yours."

"No."

"Okay," LaDonna said. "Do you want to meet Shawn-dell?"

"Why not?"

She ran from the room and returned almost immediately with a little boy in tow. He was perhaps two years younger than LaDonna and wearing nothing but diapers.

"This is Shawndell," LaDonna said.

"Pleased to meetcha," Shawndell said, holding his left arm straight out for Berger to shake.

Berger bent down and pumped the boy's small hand twice.

"I'm teaching Shawndell manners," LaDonna said.

"And doing a very good job," Berger said. "Hello, Shawndell."

"Shawndell has a penis," LaDonna said.

"How nice for you," Berger said.

"Hey, you kids," Davis said, entering the room. "Leave Sergeant Berger alone."

"They're not bothering me," Berger said. "We were just getting acquainted and trying to sort out our sexual identities."

"LaDonna," Davis said, understanding at once. "Enough of this penis business. Now scoot. Sergeant Berger's here to see Sonny."

"Does Sonny have a—"

"*Basta!*" Davis roared, and the two kids scurried out of the room, screaming in mock terror.

"I'm sorry," Davis said. "And at the risk of sounding like a mother, it's a phase she's going through."

"Life is a phase we all go through," Berger said, shrugging. "Until we die."

"That's what I like," Davis said. "An upbeat cop."

"Don't say 'beat' to a detective," Berger said, managing a smile.

Davis laughed. "Sonny'll be a while. He's trying to make himself as angry as possible."

"Angry at who?" Berger asked.

"At me, among others," Davis said. "You have to chew his ass out, too?"

"Me? No. I'm just a lonely old man looking for a gin game," Berger said, feeling sorry for himself.

"Then you've come to the right place," Davis said. "I'm a gin-playin' fool. I'll get the cards."

Berger moved over to the chair by the desk and sat. When Davis returned, he tossed a deck of cards on the table. Each featured a Walt Disney character. "Three of a Goofy beats a Dumbo straight," Davis said. "I think we've got a full deck here, but small fingers tend to get sticky and so do the cards."

Davis dealt and they played a hand in silence, feeling foolish staring at the jelly-covered cartoon cards. Finally Berger said, "So. How long have you known my erstwhile partner, Mr. Macho Wapo?"

"Since he wasn't so tough," Davis said. "And right now he's about as down as he's been in years."

"His wife?"

"He told you?"

"Not in so many words, but I called his old number. I could hear a man in the background," Berger said.

"He knows it, but he won't admit it," Davis said. "It's tearing him up and there's nothing I can do about it—except tell him the truth. Now he's mad at me."

"No one likes to hear the truth," Berger said. "Especially me. It's amazing how blind we can be to our own problems."

"You sound like a man with a problem yourself," Davis said, shuffling the cards.

"Should we go to the confessional?" Berger asked. "On second thought, I'd be afraid of lightning bolts if I entered your church. I'm a Jew."

"Jesus was a Jew," Davis said. "A Jew with an attitude."

Berger smiled. "You don't look like a—you should forgive the expression—a priest."

"I suppose not," Davis said. "But I'm not sure what a priest should look like. Barry Fitzgerald? Bing Crosby?"

Berger tossed in his hand and said, "You know, Father, I think I like you."

Davis threw his hand down and looked Berger in the eye. "What's the problem?"

"It's that obvious?" Berger asked.

"As obvious as a wart on the end of your nose."

"Not my heart on my sleeve?" Berger said gently.

"I'm a good listener," Davis said. "And to tell you the truth. I'd like to hear some adult problems for a change. I screwed up with Sonny, maybe I can help you."

"Nobody can help me," Berger said gently. "I'm responsible for my own plight and I'll live with it."

"It's a woman, isn't it?" Davis asked.

"What else?"

"Your wife? Girlfriend?"

"Thank you for your confidence in my magnetic charm, Father. But just my wife," Berger said.

"Just?"

"Former wife, I guess. She left me tonight," Berger said.

"Is she coming back?"

"Who knows? I don't think so. She has a lover," Berger said, amazed that he was opening up to a stranger. "I'm sorry to burden you with my petty problems," he said. "No doubt you have your own."

"Nothing that a couple of mil couldn't fix," Davis said. "Confession's good for the soul."

"Catharsis, thy name is vanity," Berger said, still embarrassed by his newfound intimacy with the priest. "I really should be going."

"Why? Because you're being honest with yourself? Because the cards stick together? If I didn't know better, I'd swear you're Sonny's father."

In the end Berger stayed until Sonny LoBianco, showered and changed, stuck his head into the study.

"Ira. Ready to go?"

"Go where?"

"Out. Away from here," LoBianco said pointedly.

"See?" Davis said. "I'm the twelve-letter word we're all familiar with."

Sonny wouldn't even look at Davis, but disappeared down the hall.

"Take care of each other," Davis said to Berger. "And come back to see me. LaDonna and Shawndell are terrible gin players."

# 19

"This is a real challenge, crime-wise," said the earnest young man from the FBI. His name was Arthur Tillman and he was an attorney with a J.D. from Georgetown. Tillman was twenty-eight and knew everything about criminology, the law, and the FBI. He made Ira Berger doze off.

"You want to wake the old guy up?" Tillman said to Lieutenant Santamyer, who, with three other detectives of the Sixty-fifth Precinct PDU, had gathered around a battered table in the corner of the bullpen.

LoBianco shoved an elbow into Berger's ribs; Berger woke with a start, staring at the assembled group as if they were not quite real.

"You okay, Ira?" Santamyer asked.

"Yeah. Go on."

"Thank you for your undivided attention," Tillman said.

Berger coughed. "Sorry. Too much sex, drugs, and rock and roll," he said, sitting up straight and adjusting his conservative blue tie. All the men around the table laughed except Tillman. They knew Ira Berger was almost monastic in his habits; they didn't know that he had been out carousing half the night with LoBianco. Well, LoBianco and Lucy Velez had been carousing; Berger, a third wheel, had been along for the ride.

"The perpetrator is sending us mixed signals," Tillman began. "On the one hand, he exhibits the classic profile of a serial killer. On the other hand, he could also fall within the parameters established to identify the sexual murderer."

"Maybe he's a sexual serial killer," Berger said.

"Not likely. They seem to be different sort of—"

"—animals," Berger finished.

"Correct. We all know that sexual murderers are generally white males, with average-to-above average intelligence. They are usually unemployed, unable to get along with coworkers. They grew up in a single-parent family, were psychologically or physically abused as children, disliked or feared their fathers, loved and were dominated by their mothers, and were probably treated as adolescents in a psychiatric setting. They—"

"I don't care if his mommy didn't potty-train him correctly," Detective Second Class Bobby Green said. "I don't want to live next door to an ax murderer."

"Of course not," Santamyer said humorlessly. "Now, please allow Special Agent Tillman to finish."

LoBianco smirked; Berger frowned.

Tillman cleared his throat and continued, "The sexual murderer has a high rate of suicide attempts, comes from a home that has criminal, psychiatric, drug, or alcohol problems. They are interested in pornography, voyeurism, fetishism, but are generally sexually dysfunctional."

"That's nice to know," Berger said. "But what makes you think the bodies we've found were victims of a sexual murderer?"

"Good question. Glad to know you're paying attention, Mr. Berger," Tillman said condescendingly.

Berger felt too tired to draw his gun and shoot the snotty fuck, so he settled for removing his glasses and rubbing his burning eyes.

"The hand that was delivered to Mr. Berger's door—"

"That's Sergeant Berger's door," Sonny interrupted, feeling he should defend his partner.

"Correct. *Sergeant* Berger's door," Tillman said, making *sergeant* sound like a dirty word. "That hand has to be discounted. It is simply too bizarre for us to deal with. We have to have a crime scene, intact, to be able to work our magic."

He waited for a laugh; he got a cough from the chain-smoking Santamyer.

"Lay it on us, Houdini," Bobby Green said. He was a short, nasty, black detective with little tolerance for bullshit and bullshitters. "Pull out that fucking rabbit and let's nail this scumbag."

"Bobby, please," Santamyer said, his bland face creased with disapproval.

Green smiled wickedly at Berger and Tillman continued, "If we are indeed dealing with a sexual murderer, we—"

"There's been no semen traces on the victims," Green said.

"No. But that does not preclude the possibility that the perpetrator is a sexual murderer," Tillman said. "We have to examine the entire crime scene. For example, take the bodies of Adele Woodword and Martha Collins. They were found in bed together; a hand, middle finger up, had been inserted into Collins's mouth. That sounds pretty sexual to me."

"Then you should get out more," Bobby Green said. "Date."

Santamyer covered his eyes with his hand.

"He's got a point," LoBianco said. "Both women were wearing bras, and Parulo was dressed and unmolested. That doesn't sound to me like a sex maniac at work. But then I'm no expert like you."

"In fact, I'd say you were off base," Berger said. "This nut is collecting body parts. That's his psychosis or whatever you call it. He wants the *parts*, Mr. Tillman, not sexual intercourse with his victims."

"Have you considered what he's doing with these parts?"

Tillman said, stung. It had seemed a good theory when he had studied the case in his office. Damn cops think they know everything, he thought.

"Of course I've thought about it," Berger said. "But I don't have a glib answer."

"Ah," Tillman said.

"Ah, your aunt Milly," Berger said. "This is all speculation. Valuable, perhaps, but it won't catch this guy."

"It could help," Tillman said.

"Chicken soup could help, too," Berger said.

Tillman looked crushed; Santamyer looked away. Green and LoBianco were suppressing their laughter.

"Relax, kid," Berger said to Tillman. "You'll get an ulcer. Just leave your report. We'll study it."

Tillman gathered up his notes and stuffed them into his FBI-issued briefcase and slunk out of the office.

"That wasn't very nice, Ira," Santamyer said, after the agent had gone. "He seemed like a nice young man."

"Old age and treachery will overcome youth and skill," Berger said, adjusting his glasses. "Every time."

"Why don't you go home and rest, Ira?" Santamyer said.

"I've got things to do," Berger said. His head hurt worse than his feet.

"Come into my office," Santamyer said to Berger, dismissing the meeting.

When both men were seated, Santameyer said, "I just got the word from Borough. They're yanking the case from us on Friday. They're setting up a task force, assigning fifty detectives from all over the city. It's going to be run by Deputy Inspector Boynton, out of the Brooklyn Navy Yard."

"That klutz," Berger said. "He couldn't find an elephant in a studio apartment."

"Really?" Santamyer said. "I thought he was an experienced man."

For an instant Berger considered turning in his shield and

gun. It was just too much trouble to go on. He was right on the point of pulling the pin when he heard LoBianco knock on the frosted glass wall of Lieutenant Santamyer's open office.

"I got the six-oh on the line. They got a headless corpse in the basement of an apartment in Bay Ridge. You want to look at it?" LoBianco said.

Berger stood up. "Still in charge till Friday?"

Santamyer nodded. "Take care of yourself, Ira. You don't look well."

"I may not be well, but this is about as good as I get," Berger said.

"You were pretty funny last night," LoBianco said as they worked their way through traffic to Bay Ridge.

Berger closed his eyes and pretended not to hear.

"Lucy likes you a lot," LoBianco continued. "You want me to fix you up?"

Berger opened his eyes. "I married a young woman once. That was a mistake. I won't make it again."

LoBianco laughed. "Hey, Ira. Wake up. This is the nineties. You don't have to marry her. Just fuck her."

Berger closed his eyes again. "That's not a nice thing to say."

"It's up to you," LoBianco said. "Sitting home alone doesn't help. I ought to know."

Berger suddenly found himself thinking about Lucy Velez: her long black hair, her creamy skin and big . . . He had to stop that kind of thinking. He was too old for Rose and this girl must be fifteen years younger than his wife, thirty-five years younger than he. Good God!

"Give it a shot, Ira," LoBianco said. "We all have to do our part to prevent this decade from becoming the Gay Nineties."

"Thank you no very much," Berger said.

LoBianco laughed, thinking Ira might be coming around.

Last night he had listened with unaccustomed patience to Berger's version of his split-up with Rose. There was nothing more boring than other people's love lives, he thought, but Ira had really seemed broken up, so he had listened quietly. The parallel between their situations had been too close for him to miss. What it proved, he thought, was that no matter how old you got, women got up and went. Davis was an asshole if he thought anything else.

"Pull up over there," Berger said, pointing to a row of blue-and-whites from the Sixtieth Precinct. "Oh, God, here we go," he added, seeing three news trucks and a dozen print reporters crowding around the outside of the building.

"Are we going to be famous, Ira?" LoBianco asked. "Like you promised?"

"No, we'll be roasted alive if we open our mouths. Leave those vultures to the flacks."

"There goes your chance for promotion," LoBianco said. "You need headlines."

"I need some Mylanta," Berger said, getting out of the car stiffly. They shoved their way through the reporters and rubberneckers, trying to remain inconspicuous.

"What's happening in there?" a reporter shouted.

"More mutilations?" yelled another.

"How many bodies? The same guy?"

A petite, dark-haired woman in the uniform of a deputy inspector was fielding questions. Sally Silver was a former TV reporter herself and knew all the tricks. The new police commissioner had tapped her as his chief spokesperson, the face and voice of the NYPD. Her face was drawn, her voice hoarse.

"We have no connection between this murder and the double homicide the other day. It would appear that we're dealing with a different perp," she said unconvincingly.

"Shit, Sally," said a reporter. "Tell us the truth, will ya? We're buddies, right?"

She sighed and repeated her pro forma announcement.

They knew she was lying; she knew they knew she was lying. It was business as usual.

Berger and LoBianco identified themselves and went into the building, knowing all the time that what lay inside would do little to further their investigation.

# 20

Clyde Walker, a.k.a. Mr. MoFo, was dressed in white: white shoes, white silk socks, a white linen suit, a starched white shirt, and a white panama hat. Standing in an empty warehouse in Crown Heights, Brooklyn, he was looking forward to a good game of cricket. He hefted the heavy wooden bat and cracked it against the palm of his left hand. The sting sharpened his senses, countering the effects of the *ganja* he had been smoking all day. Cricket was the very thing to improve his spirits, he thought, taking a sweeping practice swing.

"Is my team ready?" he asked.

Three men dressed like their boss stepped forward.

"Is my opponent ready?"

That wasn't a fair question because Mr. MoFo's "opponent" was a small-time crack dealer called Pogo, who was hanging upside down, naked, chained by the ankles. Pogo made a terrified trilling noise.

"I take it that is a yes," MoFo said. "For, you see, when you play in my game, you play by my rules." He motioned to Rooster, who felt ridiculous in his white threads, but you had to play by Mr. MoFo's rules. Pogo, for example, had no license to sell in MoFo's territory and would now pay up—with his life.

Rooster took a running start and, swinging the cricket bat with a vicious golfing motion, smashed the hanging man in his ribs.

"Good shot," Mr. MoFo said. "One run." He had to speak loudly to drown out Pogo's agonizing screams.

The second player, known on the street as Boxcar because he was as big and about as smart as one, ran at the swaying body and launched a crashing blow to Pogo's testicles. Pogo started to scream again, but the vomit that poured from his mouth dampened the sound.

"Good show," Mr. MoFo said approvingly.

The third man in whites, called Arsenio because of his small teeth and enormous gums, launched his attack. The solid wooden bat, aimed at Pogo's neck, missed. He smashed the crack dealer on the nose, crushing cartilage and bone.

"Foul!" Mr. MoFo screamed. "His head belongs to me."

Arsenio mumbled an apology, hoping his boss wouldn't use *him* for cricket practice. But MoFo graciously accepted the apology. He motioned Arsenio out of the way, then stepped up for his turn at bat.

"You remember that runt, what was his name?" Mr. MoFo asked.

"Lewis?" Rooster volunteered.

"That's the one," Mr. MoFo said. "He had a scrawny little neck."

"And you took his head off right at the shoulders," Rooster said, grinning. It was quite a sight to see Lewis's head fly across the warehouse like a well-kicked soccer ball.

Mr. MoFo poked Pogo in the neck with his cricket bat. "You think I can do it again?"

"He looks pretty sturdy, man," Boxcar said, then hurriedly added, "but you can do it."

"You bet I can," Mr. MoFo said, standing back from his victim. He wound up and swung a solid blow that flattened what was left of Pogo's face. Pogo swung wildly from the chains attached to his ankles, but his head remained attached to his shoulders. The body swung back, spraying Mr. MoFo with blood.

"Damn," Mr. Mofo said softly. He swung again, denting the top of Pogo's skull; again the bloody body swung erratically, this time leaking gray brain matter with the crimson blood.

Mr. MoFo attacked for the third time, opening Pogo's head from just above the eyes. The top of the cranium yawned open, held to the rest of the head by a flap of skin; Pogo's brown cow eyes rolled out of his head, attached tenuously to the greenish optic cords.

"I believe we've had our innings," Mr. MoFo said, stepping back from the ruined corpse. Hearing no response, he said to Boxcar, "Cut off his hands and dump him in the ocean." Then he reached into his blood-splattered suit pocket and took out a small silver chalice. He knelt by Pogo's body, filling the cup with the crack dealer's blood.

"But first come with me. All of you," Mr. MoFo said. He led his cricket players to a small office in the corner of the cavernous warehouse.

The windows had been painted black to keep out every bit of light. Inside, the ten-by-twelve-foot room had been painted black; a black carpet hid the cracked wooden floors underneath. On a black-draped crate sat a human skull and a single black candle guttering in the darkness.

"We will pledge our devotion to our brothers," Mr. MoFo said. "We will drink to the success of our next venture."

He reached out and took the skull from the makeshift altar, turned it over, and poured the blood from the chalice into it.

"Rooster, you have been beaten and dissed by this white pig LoBianco," Mr. MoFo said. "What do you say?"

"Death to the white pig," Rooster said vehemently.

"Boxcar, Rooster is your brother. What do you say?"

"Death, man."

"Arsenio?"

"Same, man."

"Then we drink the blood of the last fool to fuck with us and pledge to repeat our success," Mr. MoFo said, looking at his wide-eyed men. They were stupid men, he thought, who needed all this mumbo jumbo to steel their nerve. They were weak and had to be reminded often who was the boss, who had the brains, who was the strongest of the pack. Years ago he had invented quasi-religious rites like this one to impress his superstitious posse.

"We swear by the gods of our birthplace and the gods of our ancient home in Africa," Mr. MoFo intoned. "If we fail to kill this man who needs killing, we will offer our eyes, our balls, and our hearts to appease our gods. *We will not fail.*"

"We swear," the three other men said in unison.

"Go then and kill this . . . pig," Mr. MoFo said. "And remember what happens to those who fail."

Rooster, Boxcar, and Arsenio stepped forward, each taking a sip of blood from the skull.

Stupid men, Mr. MoFo thought. Stupid, but exceedingly dangerous, if given the right motivation.

Rooster, Arsenio, and Boxcar had been cruising south Brooklyn all morning waiting for the call. It came a few minutes after noon.

Rooster picked up the car phone and waited. A voice said, "Nick's. Bay Ridge." Then the connection was broken. Rooster shook his head. That MoFo had eyes and ears everywhere.

He drove with assurance and intimate familiarity with the territory, keeping within the speed limit and using his signals for each turn. In an hour he'd take the car to a chop shop and pick up a cool fifteen large. Life could be good, he thought, except for one thing: the bats.

Mr. MoFo insisted that the three men beat LoBianco to death. Rooster ran his hand over the Louisville Slugger resting between his legs; it made him nervous. He had gone toe-to-toe with LoBianco before; he didn't want a second go at him—up close. A drive-by shooting was more what he had in mind, blow the cocksucker away at twenty miles per hour. LoBianco was too dangerous for hand-to-hand combat.

But MoFo wanted the cop's death to be slow and painful, and after witnessing what had happened to that poor sucker Pogo, Rooster was more afraid of his boss than of LoBianco.

His thoughts leaking to his mouth, Rooster said, "Damn. I ain't no motherfucking baseball player."

"You a good cricket player," Arsenio said.

"Shit. I ain't no ballplayer and here I am with this here piece of wood smaller'n my dick, lookin' to hit a motherfucking armed cop."

"No guns. Mr. MoFo say no guns," Boxcar said. He was a former boxer who had sparred with the best and had lost to the worst.

"You're one bright motherfucker," Rooster said. "So you can be the first to go at that fucking eye-talian fuck."

"Okay," Boxcar said.

"Damn," Rooster said. "You got shit for brains. I seen this guy fight."

"Don' say nothin' 'bout my brains," Boxcar said. He swung his bat with a flick of his wrist and smashed off a portion of the Buick's padded dash.

"Okay, man," Rooster said quickly. Boxcar was all muscle, but if he had a brain no one had found it yet.

"This dude bad?" Arsenio asked from the backseat.

"Real bad," Rooster said. "We got to hit him fast and hard. We won't have no time to fuck with him—or he'll fuck with us. Got it?"

Boxcar and Arsenio nodded, but Rooster touched his broken nose and wondered if they did get it.

He pulled the Buick within a half block of Nick's Diner in Bay Ridge and waited. Twenty minutes later he saw

LoBianco and an older man, who looked like an accountant, emerge from the diner, deep in conversation. A cold fear gripped him; he touched his nose again, then turned to Boxcar. "Go get him, champ," he said.

Boxcar Brown shrugged and got out of the car, the Louisville Slugger pressed against his leg. For a moment he studied LoBianco and could detect nothing ferocious about his intended victim. The white man was cruiser weight at best, and Brown figured he had a good sixty pounds on him. Shit, he thought, I don't even need a piece of wood for this dude. But MoFo had ordered bats, and Boxcar Brown followed orders.

LoBianco and Berger were discussing the decapitation of Sarah Goldman as they walked toward the maroon Buick. Suddenly LoBianco spotted Brown's stiff-legged gait. "We got trouble coming," he said to Berger just as Boxcar Brown brought the bat up to swinging position, covering the short distance between them in two long, loping strides.

LoBianco tried to push Berger out of the way as Brown's first swing came down, but the bat grazed the older cop's shoulder and slammed him into the brick wall of an apartment building. Berger hit his head and sprawled on the sidewalk, stunned.

Brown cocked the bat back quickly for another swing and let it fly. Reacting instantaneously, LoBianco stepped inside Brown's arc of power, twisting into the path of the attacker's arms. By harmonizing with the force of the attack, he let it wrap itself harmlessly around him.

He was so close to Brown he could smell the man's bad breath and terrible body odor. It nauseated him, but the closeness of their contact rendered the bat useless. LoBianco trapped Brown's right wrist with both his hands, then twisted it savagely. Boxcar's wrist snapped loud enough to stop Rooster and Arsenio in their tracks.

Holding his shattered wrist, Brown dropped to his knees, moaning and cursing. Nothing in boxing had ever caused him this much pain.

LoBianco straightened Brown up with a jolting knee strike to the boxer's face. Brown crumbled into a heap and prayed he'd pass out. He got his wish when LoBianco's second kick found the big man's exposed rib cage.

Shaken out of his momentary torpor, Arsenio tried to blindside LoBianco, but the cop was one step ahead of him. He grabbed both of Arsenio's sleeves. Then with one fluid extension of force and power, he pushed his hips back, into Arsenio's stomach. Still holding Arsenio's sleeves, he pulled the man across his hip and extended a leg, in a throw called *O-soto-gari* in Japanese. Arsenio spun over LoBianco's body into what looked like a cartwheel gone sour. At the last possible second LoBianco yanked at Arsenio's sleeves, slamming the man's head straight into the cement. Arsenio's head made a louder sound than the bat clattering into the gutter.

Rooster suddenly found himself in the position he had feared from the beginning. He was facing LoBianco alone, with nothing but a piece of wood in his hands and a switchblade knife in his pocket. His mouth went dry; his muscles turned to jelly, as if they were being drained by the sweat that poured from his body. LoBianco smiled, recognizing him. The smile made Rooster quiver with fear, but he held the bat across his body, shortening up his grip. He circled LoBianco, muttering to himself, cursing MoFo. Only the bat stood between him and LoBianco's fists, and the cop had just wiped out two big men holding the same weapon, without breaking a sweat. LoBianco waited patiently, the smile gone.

Rooster charged, the bat held in an overhead position. LoBianco met the charge with a cross-arm block, fists balled. He could have put Rooster away with a kick to the groin, but in an unaccustomed show of arrogance he pivoted on his right leg, getting behind Rooster. He snapped off a *shuto* chop to the bodybuilder's neck. Like a rock in a sock, the blow slammed into the base of Rooster's skull. Moving upward, it was designed to shake the brain inside its protective cranium. Rooster gagged, then dropped quietly to the pavement. LoBianco looked around. Three men down. Any more? he thought.

But by the time LoBianco had turned his attention back to Rooster, the situation had changed. Rooster had grabbed Berger by the collar of his suit coat and lifted the smaller man off the ground. With his free hand he put the switch-blade to Berger's throat.

"Move, motherfucker, and I kill him," he said in an unnaturally high voice.

LoBianco stopped dead. He knew Rooster wasn't bluffing; he also knew he couldn't shoot faster than Rooster could draw the blade across his partner's throat.

While he hesitated Berger came awake suddenly and stepped down hard on Rooster's Air Jordans, simultaneously spinning out of his captor's grasp, leaving Rooster holding his jacket.

While Berger tugged at his .38, LoBianco threw himself at Rooster. But he was too slow. Rooster had gone into a crouch, handling his eight-inch blade expertly, taking short horizontal slashes at LoBianco's belly. Without a weapon LoBianco was forced to retreat.

"Get away from him," Berger shouted, cocking his Smith & Wesson Police Special. LoBianco, the blood roaring in his head, didn't hear him, but continued to stay as close to Rooster as he dared.

Timing one of the cutting arcs, LoBianco followed it with a crescent kick to the side of Rooster's head. The blow stunned Rooster long enough for LoBianco to sweep the man's feet out from under him, sending Rooster's heavy body to the sidewalk.

As he fell Rooster kicked out viciously with the agility of a trapped animal. It was a desperate move, but successful, catching LoBianco in the sternum, sending him reeling.

Berger took aim, but couldn't get a clear shot around LoBianco. Rooster leaped to his feet and practically laid rubber getting the hell out of there.

*  *  *

Rooster slunk back to the warehouse in Crown Heights, a whipped dog. His broken nose still oozed blood, his left arm hung limp and useless at his side. Normally slow to think things through, he knew he had no choice but to go to ground. He had to hope Mr. MoFo would give him a break; perhaps the sacrifice of Boxcar and Arsenio would somehow placate him.

"What happened?" Mr. MoFo asked. He had changed his bloody whites for a black, open-neck silk shirt and black linen pants. To Rooster's bloodshot eyes he looked like a vision of the devil.

In his slow-witted way, Rooster spat out his tale: eight white men had jumped them. They had been wielding baseball bats and flashing Uzis. They were eye-talian, the mob, the Mafia.

Mr. MoFo snorted. "You are a total incompetent. That damn cop beat the shit out of the three of you, didn't he?"

Rooster looked at the floor.

"Come, Rooster, mon. Tell the truth and I shall be merciful. Lie and die," Mr. MoFo said soothingly. "I know it is difficult to admit defeat, to lose to a stronger man. But this policeman is a special case, I see. A special case requiring special care."

Whether from fatigue or in supplication, Rooster dropped to his knees before the black-clad figure and poured out his story. Except for hiding his cowardice and highlighting his bravery, it was mostly the truth. As he talked he felt Mr. MoFo's cool hands on his head, stroking his short-napped hair as if he were massaging the truth from his lieutenant.

Suddenly Rooster was silent, having told all he could tell. Mr. MoFo dropped his hands to Rooster's chin and held it up. "I am very proud of you. You told the truth."

Rooster tried to smile, feeling the warmth of the man pour over him like sunshine.

"You shall be rewarded, my friend," Mr. MoFo said.

Rooster lowered his eyes modestly, which is why he

didn't see the flick of MoFo's razor as it slashed through the muscles of his neck. He didn't feel anything for a second, only a slight burning.

"You shall be rewarded in hell," Mr. MoFo said, swinging the razor backhanded. Blood fountained from Rooster's neck in powerful spurts. He tried to scream, but blood, not words, poured from his mouth. He toppled over sideways, not sure what had happened to him, but it was too late for him to care.

Mr. MoFo watched the blood slowly stop pumping from Rooster's ruined neck and shook his head in disgust. Wasn't there anyone who could be trusted for even the simplest tasks? In a sudden fury he kicked Rooster's corpse. He had lost too many men recently; it had to stop. And he knew what he had to do.

Wiping the blood off his shirt, he went to the office at the back of the warehouse that served as his inner sanctum and called three more of his men to clean up the mess in the warehouse. Then he dialed a number he had committed to memory. It was to be used only in emergencies.

"I need a favor," he said without identifying himself.

"Shoot."

"There is a Plymouth Voyager, black in color, parked in front of a place called St. Agnes in Coney Island," he said.

Silence at the other end.

"It needs to disappear as soon as possible," Mr. MoFo said.

"And how will you pay for this?"

"Quid pro quo," MoFo said. "As we discussed. The old man is history."

A click.

Mr. MoFo smiled. Let the fucking Italians take care of Davis first, then LoBianco.

# 21

The Golden Eagle was a hot-sheet motel on Gaffrey Road near Bay Ridge. A hundred and one rooms of down-and-dirty sex, it gave sanctuary to philandering husbands, wayward wives, lecherous lesbians, and horny homosexuals. There was no sexual act, perversion, or deviation that had not been practiced within the pastel-green walls of the Eagle.

Night manager Billy Casco had seen it all: old broads with teenagers of both sexes, drooling dopers with kids, nervous businessmen with black hookers, guys and their household pets. You name it, Joe Casco had seen it and it had ceased to interest him.

That's why he was shocked to his socks when a nice-looking, middle-class lady with no companion walked through the jungle of plastic plants that grew out of the lobby and inquired about weekly rates.

"Jeez, lady. You sure you could stand seven days?" he said to Rose Berger. He leered at her, his busy eyebrows arching with Groucho Marx lewdness.

Rose pretended not to understand and stood her ground.

Casco rummaged around under the black Formica desk and came up with a flyspecked sheet of yellow paper. He told her the rates and accepted her Visa card.

"Through the parking lot, to the left, and past the lounge. Second floor," he said.

Blushing, Rose took the key from Casco, trying not to touch his blunt, hairy fingers. Only when she had left the green vinyl hell of the lobby did she notice that the key ring was in the shape of a voluptuous woman.

Her suitcase gripped tightly in her hand, her mouth set in a determined line, Rose found her room at the top of the stairs. When she entered, she entered a world she had never dreamed existed.

The walls were covered with red-and-gold velvet, the furniture was black plastic, and the bed was . . . round. Rose stared about in disbelief. Reproductions of ancient Japanese porno prints ringed the room, a thirty-two-inch TV stared at her accusingly, and a rack of X-rated tapes made her feel queasy.

She sat gingerly on the round bed with the black velvet headboard and closed her eyes.

"Fool," she said aloud. "Stupid fool."

A tear ran down one cheek. Stupid man. All she had ever wanted from Berger was a baby, a child to raise as her own. Hadn't she been wonderful with her niece and nephew? She would be a wonderful mother. She only needed to have a child.

And that liar Chin. She would show him. She *knew* she could get pregnant.

Wiping away the tear, she patted her stomach reassuringly. She would have a baby, no matter what it took.

## 22

Charles Maris leaned over his monstrous creation and found it good. In the freezer Sarah Goldman's head, shiny and bald, stared up at him in adoration, assuring him everything was just fine.

Legs, he thought, two legs, a torso, and some hair. That was all he needed to complete Emily's new body. How foolish he had been to move so slowly at first, a finger at a time, stealing body parts from the morgue. His new technique was paying off better than he dared hope. He could actually visualize the day Emily got out of her wheelchair and walked. What a triumph for him; Mother would be proud and forgive him.

Reluctantly he closed the lid to the freezer and walked up the metal stairs to the basement. The dogs rested placidly in their cages, awaiting their morning meal. Even Dempsey seemed calm. Charles brandished the wooden stick, but the dog barely moved. Acceptance, Charles wondered, or defiance? He mixed their food and allowed them out of their cages. All except Dempsey.

At his command they dug into their chow, gulping it down as if it were their last meal. Charles watched, satisfied. The he returned them to their cages and got the short leather lead for Dempsey. Docilely the pit bull allowed himself to be chained around the neck. He eyed the bowl in front of him, but made no move for it. Charles made him wait until a pool of saliva had formed under the dog, then gave the command. But Dempsey just stood there, rooted to the filthy cement floor, drooling.

"Goddamn you," Charles said, giving the signal again. This time Dempsey approached the bowl and sniffed at it. He cast a baleful eye on Charles and began to nibble at his food.

"Damn you!" Charles screamed, bringing the cudgel down on the dog's ridged back, again and again.

Dempsey cringed under the blows, but stood his ground. Finally, with a yellow-eyed glare, he retreated to his cage. The dog had won the battle of wills, proving to Charles that he could not be bribed by food or force. It was Dempsey's death warrant, Charles thought, locking the cage door in disgust.

Upstairs in the library, he spoke to Emily for a few minutes; but not eliciting a response, he soon tired of the game and prepared to go to work. Then the phone rang, sending a chill up his spine. He watched the noisy instrument without blinking; finally he reached for it. He knew who was calling; it was an easy guess.

He picked up the phone and listened.

"Charles. What have you been doing?"

"Nothing, Mother," he answered.

"You've been killing people, Charles. You've been killing women."

"Well—"

"Don't lie to me, Charles."

"Well, it was supposed to be a secret," he said, a whine in his voice.

"Why have you been killing women, Charles?"

"To make a new body for Emily," he said. "It's almost ready."

"Charles, you've been very bad. And very stupid," Mother said.

"Stupid? Stupid!" Charles stuttered. "You dare call me stupid?" He had been very smart and very crafty.

"How old was Emily when your dog attacked her?" Mother asked. "Think, Charles."

"About, uh, I don't know, four?" He knew.

"Right, Charles, four. She wasn't a woman, was she?" Charles was staggered by this insight. "But she's a woman now," he said hesitantly. "Isn't she?"

"No, Charles. She'll always be my little girl. I want her back. As she was. My lovely little girl."

"But she's not a little girl," Charles insisted.

"She will be, Charles. When you're done. Everything will be as it was," Mother said. "Unless you want to be Emily again."

"Nooo!" Charles shrieked, seeing stars dance behind his eyes. "No!"

"Are you sure, Charles? You used to look so cute in those darling little dresses. You were always so ladylike, Charles. Don't you want to be my little girl again?"

Charles dropped the receiver and grabbed his head; the pain behind his eyes was intense. Color, all the colors of the spectrum, flooded his senses, driving him to the floor. He kicked his feet and pounded his hands on the thick gray carpet of dust. In his mind he could see himself, a chubby twelve-year-old, wearing a white dress with a blue ribbon around the waist, a straw hat, patent-leather Mary Janes, and white ankle socks embroidered with pink flowers. Underneath the frilly dress he wore pink silk underpants. Girl's underpants! He bit his tongue, drawing blood.

When his head cleared, he found himself on the floor, coated with dust. He had wet himself. From his vantage point the phone's receiver dangled over his head, gently swaying like a black cobra ready to strike. He thought he could hear a small, insistent voice still speaking to him.

He dragged himself closer to the phone and put an ear to it.

"Charles. Listen to me," he heard.

"No!" he screamed. "I won't kill a child! You can't make me!"

"Listen closely, Charles," Mother said.

" 'Humpty Dumpty sat on a wall,/Humpty Dumpty had a great fall,/All the King's horses and all the King's men,/ Couldn't put poor Humpty together again.' "

Charles gave a strangled cry and collapsed back to the floor, unconscious.

When he woke again, he was no longer Charles Maris. Of that he was certain. He was afraid of Charles, deathly afraid. He stood up and was horrified to find himself covered with dust and urine. And the clothes he was wearing! Men's clothing. It was all so strange.

"Emily," he said in a curiously high-pitched voice. "Is he gone?"

He thought he saw a slight nod from the huddled bundle wrapped in blankets, sitting quietly in the high-backed wheelchair.

"Good. But we don't have much time. We must stop him before he kills a child."

Charles Maris, who was no longer Charles Maris, left the study and went upstairs to change. There was no time for a bath, even though he had wet himself, so he shucked off his clothes and poked around in the back of the closet. From a wire hanger he grabbed a black dress, a large shapeless affair that slipped easily over his gross body. He tied a black scarf over his head and bent down to pull on a pair of size-fourteen low-heeled pumps. Downstairs, he fished through the desk in the library and retrieved Maria Parulo's appointment book. He slipped it into an empty manila envelope and wrote *Sgt. Ira Berger* on the outside.

"Are we ready, Emily?" he asked.

"Yes, Mother," came the reply.

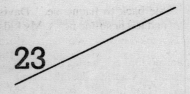

# 23

"Sergeant Berger. What a surprise," Father Franklyn Davis said, ushering Berger into the rectory. "Come back for revenge at gin?"

"Actually I came to see Sonny, but he's locked himself in the garage and I can't get him to come out. You heard?"

"Yes, I heard, and I can't say I approve. But I'm glad he's all right." Davis led Berger into his office and motioned for him to sit down.

"Why does he act like this?" Berger asked.

"He's always been like that. Since he was a kid. He was lucky today, I guess. Nobody fights with their hands anymore. Now scores are settled with nine millimeters. So I guess you could say Sonny's old-fashioned, and a little bit softhearted," Davis said.

"He's one of the toughest kids I've ever seen," Berger said. "Perhaps too tough for our business."

"That's where you're wrong. But I suppose I can't convince you or anyone else who's seen him fight," Davis said. "It must have been a great show."

"It was, uh, instructive," Berger said. "Like watching a lion battle hyenas. He won this time, but there are a lot of hyenas out there who'd kill their own mothers for ten dollars worth of crack."

"That's why I carry a gun," Davis said. "I carry it to protect my kids in a neighborhood like this, where even the roaches and rats are packing."

"I read your notices," Berger said. "The Gunslinger Priest."

"So that old crap has come back to haunt me," Davis said, sighing. "I carry a gun and it's headline news. My kids eat spaghetti three days a week because we can't afford meat and nobody writes about that. I swear to God, I'd dance naked in Macy's window if I could get some contributions and publicity. But the sad fact is nobody cares about a bunch of black kids who are doomed to grow up bad."

Berger shook his head in sympathy.

"Let me tell you how all this gunslinger stuff started," Davis continued. "There was this twelve-year-old girl who came to me a few years ago. Her pimp had burned his initials on her chest with a cigarette. She came to me because she was scared and had no other place to go. The police got involved and I said some things in anger, something like the only way to deal with an animal like the pimp was to take off my collar and strap on my .45.

"The next day the headlines called me the Gunslinger Priest, Father Fast Draw, and all kinds of other crap. They played me up big and wrote only a little about the girl who was suffering. No one asked what could be done to help her and others like her.

"For a month contributions came in, then faded away to a trickle. Nobody wanted to know what was happening here, only about me, my .45, and the pimp."

"It made good reading," Berger said.

"It made me realize I had a choice to make. Become a media-star phony or sink back into obscurity, trying to help these kids and serve my God," Davis said.

"Did you do the right thing?" Berger asked.

"Sometimes I wonder," Davis answered. "If I had the

kind of clout Covenant House used to have, I could help more kids in more ways.''

"And sell your soul for a mess of pottage," Berger said.

"Oh, my efforts have been a mess, pottage be damned. I'm under the gun here, literally and figuratively. The dealers want my head, the good sisters want my land, and even Sonny wants me to go away. I'd say that's not much of a life." Davis rubbed his scarred cheeks. "After two tours in 'Nam, I must have been spared for *something*."

"Perhaps one of your children will become a saint," Berger said.

Davis laughed. "I'd settle for a couple of them avoiding jail, drugs, and prostitution."

"Perhaps that's enough," Berger said. He had felt an affinity for this ugly black priest the moment he had met him. It was like talking to a friend, a friend he hadn't seen in a long while.

"Come on, let me give you a tour," Davis said.

As they walked around the old buildings Berger could see the damage time and neglect had inflicted on St. Agnes. Floors rolled and creaked, cracks spun like a web through the plaster, ceilings were water-soaked and mildewed, doors hung out of line. The entire complex was sinking slowly into the shifting sands of Coney Island.

Davis kept up an optimistic patter that Berger found comforting background music; the priest's knowledge of Coney Island's past was impressive.

"There are a lot of Jews here," Davis said as they completed their tour. "Though some of the beautiful old synagogues have suffered the same fate as St. Agnes."

"The water and boardwalk," Berger said. "Sometimes I think some of us would live in a PLO camp as long as we could be near water."

Davis smiled.

"What are we going to do about Sonny?" Berger asked, when they had settled back into Davis's study.

"I knew him as a ninety-pound bundle of rage. I tried to

direct that rage into something more positive and now I have a hundred-and-ninety-pound bundle of rage. But, as the Bible says, 'This too shall pass.' I've done all I can, it's up to him now.''

As Davis talked, Berger could see that this old father-and-son relationship—a black renegade priest and an Italian cop with a chip on his shoulder—was based on love and respect. It made him a little jealous, now that he had no one.

"Father D, Father D," E.T. yelled, bursting into the study. "You said we could go cruisin'!"

"Can't you see I've got company?" Davis said. "Be patient. All things come to those who wait."

"But I've been waitin' all day," E.T. said. He stood first on one foot then on the other, bursting with energy.

Davis rolled his eyes and said to Berger, "I do have to do food shopping."

"You go ahead," Berger said. "I've taken up enough of your time."

"Do you want to come with us?" Davis asked.

"No, but I'd like to make a contribution to St. Agnes," Berger said, reaching for his wallet.

"No need," Davis said, raising his hand.

"A great need, I think," Berger said, fishing out the folded one-hundred-dollar bill he carried for emergencies.

"Bless you," Davis said.

"You yourself are a blessing . . . to your children." Berger said.

"Yeah," said E.T. "Thanks for the dough. Can we get Devil Dogs?"

"You are a master of the inappropriate," Davis said.

"I think I'll look in on Sonny," Berger said. "Any messages?"

"Yeah," E.T. said. "Tell that son of a bitch to go to hell."

"What he do to you?" Davis asked.

"Told me he wasn't going to help me anymore, told me I was a no-good pr—"

*"E.T."*

"—guy," E.T. finished. "What's wrong with him, anyway?"

"Life," Davis said. "He's got a serious case of reality."

"Huh?"

"You'll understand in about thirty years." Davis sighed. "Tell Sonny I'll pray for him."

Berger nodded and walked to the front door. "Everything will be all right," he told the priest, not really believing it.

Sonny LoBianco lay on his narrow bed, fully clothed. His ribs had been bandaged. He felt drained, but in spite of the pain, it had been good to mess up the scumbags who had attacked him. Direct action was somehow more satisfying than almost everything else. He decided the pain was purposeful. It reminded him that he had violated his own rules for street fighting. Instead of putting Rooster away, he had played with him like a bullfighter taunting a bull. The result was a cracked rib and a missing perp.

"Mr. Karate, you awake?" Berger called through the door.

LoBianco groaned inwardly. He wanted to be alone.

"It's open," he said at last.

Berger came in and walked over to the straight-backed chair next to LoBianco's bed.

"Don't say it," LoBianco said.

"Say what?"

"That I let that Rooster get away."

"Okay. Thank you for my life. How about that?" Berger said.

"They didn't want you, they wanted me."

"I was a witness and they didn't look like the kind of men who leave a lot of witnesses around," Berger said. "Does it hurt much?"

"No."

"I guess you'll live," Berger said, getting up.

"You were worried?" LoBianco asked.

Berger frowned. "No. But your friend Father Davis and that kid, E.T.? They're both worried about you."

"The hell with them both," LoBianco said. "As soon as I'm well, I'm moving out of this loony bin."

"Whatever," Berger said, moving to the door.

"I mean it!" LoBianco insisted.

"Of course you do," Berger said. The insincerity dripped like venom.


LoBianco had been asleep for less than an hour when Berger woke him.

"I thought you left," LoBianco said groggily. The painkiller had dulled his brain and left his mouth dry and foul.

"Wake up," Berger said, his face grayer than usual.

"What is it?"

"There was an accident," Berger began.

"Yeah?" LoBianco was dizzy with pain; the words weren't getting through. "You okay?"

"Not me. Father Davis—"

LoBianco opened his eyes, suddenly alert. "What happened?"

"An explosion. The van. It was no accident. There was a bomb," Berger said haltingly.

Sonny bolted upright in bed, ignoring the searing pain. "Where? Is he alive?"

"They took him to Bensonhurst General. He was at the Shoprite with E.T.," Berger said.

"And E.T.?"

"Dead."

"Jesus. Oh God, no," LoBianco said, struggling to get out of bed.

"There's nothing you can do," Berger said.

On his feet, LoBianco said, "I've got to see him, Ira."

Berger sighed. "I should drive," he said.

Without argument, LoBianco reached in his pocket and handed Berger the keys.

Berger cast a dubious eye on the Corvette. It was so low
to the ground he feared it would bottom out if he hit a
pothole. Groaning, he lowered himself into the driver's seat,
stretching his legs into the well.

"I've never driven a car lying on my back before,"
Berger said, fumbling for the ignition switch. He found it
and the car roared into life.

Berger put it in first, revved the engine, then popped the
clutch. The Vette juked and jived like a spastic guard on a
basketball court. LoBianco didn't notice.

Driving in second gear, never going more than thirty-five
miles an hour, Berger nursed the Vette toward Bensonhurst
General. They drove in silence.

Father Davis was in the intensive-care unit and it took
some shield flashing for Sonny to gain admittance. He
looked down at the priest, wondering how such a big man
could look so small and helpless; wires and hoses stuck out
of every orifice; a small Oriental nurse sat by his bed
reading *Modern Romance* magazine.

"How's he doing?" LoBianco asked her.

Looking up from her reading, she asked, "You a rela-
tive?"

"Yeah, he's my illegitimate father," LoBianco said.

She shrugged. "Internal injuries, lost a lot of blood, has
bits and pieces of metal embedded all over his body. He's
leaking faster than we can fill him up."

"What's your opinion?" LoBianco asked.

"He's sour. He'll go quickly."

LoBianco felt his stomach heave; suddenly he had trouble
drawing a breath and had to move away from the bed to lean
against the glass partition separating the ICU from the
nurses' station.

"You all right?" the nurse asked, more with curiosity
than concern.

"Yeah," he said, staggering to the door.

"What's he wanted for?" the nurse called after him.

"So many things," LoBianco said under his breath.

LoBianco found Ira Berger sitting on a yellow, plastic-covered couch in the waiting room. Sonny sank into the sticky cushion, feeling as if he would never get up again.

"He's dying, Ira," LoBianco said. "And it's my fault. I might as well have put a gun to his head and blown him away."

Berger didn't know what to do or say. He knew he wasn't good at this sort of thing and he also knew that the platitudes he had learned on The Job didn't fit this occasion. It was one thing to tell a stranger his wife was dead, it was another to console your partner. LoBianco looked so young and helpless to his old eyes that Berger felt an almost fatherly duty to say or do something comforting. He settled for patting LoBianco on the shoulder.

Sonny was silent, lost in his own thoughts.

"Do you want to stay or go?" he asked after a moment.

"I want Father D to live," LoBianco said. "I'm the one who should die."

"Stop this melodramatic nonsense right now," Berger said. "You're supposed to feel sorry for him, not for yourself."

"But it's my fault," LoBianco insisted.

"You don't go until it's your time," Berger said. "Maybe this is his time. Besides, he's not dead, is he? And from what you've told me and what I've seen with my own eyes, he is one damn tough man. If anybody can pull through, he can."

Numb, LoBianco nodded. He needed something, no matter how insubstantial, to hold on to.

"Let me take you home, you can keep in touch by phone," Berger said, hoping to move LoBianco while he was still dazed.

"But I want to see where it happened first," LoBianco said.

Berger nodded. He understood.

They drove to the Shoprite parking lot on Cushman Road, ten blocks from St. Agnes. Although it was still light, the kliegs were already on and the area taped off. A dozen blue-and-whites, vans, and a fire marshal's red car were in attendance.

Sonny had a sinking feeling that he had been through this before, not far from here. This was the first time since his father's assassination that he had visited a crime scene with personal interest. He felt distanced, drifting, an unseen observer able to float above the confusion.

In one corner were the skeletal remains of the Voyager, a charred husk of the beauty that E.T. had shined to perfection. Like a man in a trance, LoBianco walked toward the wreck. He was intercepted by Rotten Jack Murphy.

"I thought you'd get here sooner or later," Murphy said, physically preventing LoBianco from getting any closer to the Voyager.

"What are you doing here?" LoBianco asked.

"I have my sources," Murphy said.

"Sergeant Berger," Berger said, introducing himself to Murphy.

"Yeah," Murphy said, ignoring Berger.

"What have you got?" LoBianco asked, the words bringing up the bile from his stomach.

Murphy produced a notepad from his jacket pocket and began reading. "Forensic had no trouble identifying the explosives," he said. "It was Semtex, a plastic explosive from Eastern Europe. It's not run-of-the-mill shit, Sonny boy. You gotta have connections to come by this heavy-weight stuff. The feds are sending a man just to look at it."

LoBianco was standing stone quiet, his hands in his front pockets. Neither Berger nor Murphy wanted to know what Sonny LoBianco was thinking at that moment.

Murphy continued reading from his notes. "The explosion could have been triggered by the ignition switch or electronically by remote control. The device was placed under the carriage of the van and designed to explode upward. The way the bomb was framed, there's no doubt the priest was the target. Unlike a pipe bomb that goes off in different directions, this device was situated in such a way as to clearly target the driver. There was a message being sent here.''

LoBianco turned to Murphy and Berger, and while they stared back, his eyes changed to those of an assassin with complete concentration and dedication. ''Not a long list of suspects, is there, Murphy?'' he said as he walked to the blown-out van. It gave off a strange, lethal smell—the smell of death Sonny knew well. The van had been blown outward; three doors had been ripped off, the roof burst upward. A single Nike basketball sneaker was half-melted and stuck to the twisted A-frame. LoBianco tried to view the damage with a clinical eye—a cop's eye—but he couldn't because he was crying.

A uniformed cop approached Sonny from behind and said, ''Hey, be careful. Lots of little nigger kibble and bits around. You could step on some and get your shoes fucked up.''

Sonny turned slowly and in a detached, workmanlike fashion did sufficient physical damage to the cop to warrant an emergency ambulance call. Despite the circumstances Rotten Jack had to laugh.

# 24

"Father B! Father B! When are we gonna eat?'' LaDonna yelled to Berger.

"Don't call me that,'' Berger said, stirring a huge pot of sloppy joe mix. "My name's Ira.''

"Please ta meetcha,'' Shawndell said, holding out his left arm, board straight.

"Children, please,'' Berger said.

"When's Father D coming home from the hospital?'' LaDonna asked.

"God willing, soon,'' Berger said. He had had to drag Sonny off the uniformed cop and drive him back to St. Agnes. Then, instead of returning to his empty apartment, he had decided to stay at the shelter for the night. The two older girls who normally assisted Father Davis had been too shocked and too upset to be of much help, so Berger had taken over command of St. Agnes. Ten minutes after he had arrived, the forty-seven children who lived there had accepted him as Father Davis's temporary replacement. The little ones called him Father B, much to his chagrin.

"Where's E.T.?'' Shawndell asked.

"Blowed up,'' LaDonna told him.

"Oh.''

"Children, why don't you help set the tables?'' Berger suggested. They ignored him.

"Is Sonny blowed up, too?"

"Nope. He's beat up," LaDon... weary patience of an overworked moth...

"Is he dead?" Shawndell persisted.

*"Children!"* Berger raised his voice, sudd... the peace and quiet of his lonely apartment.

"Father B, is Sonny dead?" Shawndell was trying the events of the day straight.

"No. He's resting," Berger said. "Now, LaDonna, take Shawndell into the rec room and watch TV until dinner."

"Come, Shawndell," LaDonna said with the gravity and authority of a duchess ordering her coach. "We must leave Father B to his cookery."

Sonny LoBianco couldn't sit still. The image of the charred Voyager had been burned into his memory. The sight of Father D on what would surely be his deathbed had cut Sonny to his soul.

With total detachment Sonny pummeled the workout bag. Punch after punch, kick after kick, he very slowly worked out the anger and impotence that were tearing him apart.

He felt the pain of his bruised muscles and cracked rib spreading into his arms and legs. His shoulders and knees cried out against his repeated jabbing and snap kicks. With one final movement, his fingers straight out, stiff as steel, Sonny thrust at the bag. The old canvas gave way, and as he worked to extract his hand from the torn bag, he realized what his next move would have to be. Without even toweling off, he left the apartment.

Rotten Jack Murphy sat with two IRA gunmen on the lam from Ireland. They had killed three British soldiers, ambushing them with Soviet-made AK-47s, leaving their bodies looking like bloody Swiss cheese. Murphy was enjoying their description when Sonny LoBianco walked into his Bronx hangout.

"'Scuse me, fellows," Murphy said. "I gotta see a man

Shawndell asked.

na answered with the

er.

denly missing

to get

arm and led him

sliding into a dark

.

,"

y you are. Somebody

d of getting even, you

ne."

aid.

for this dance, so you're
gonna have                          ," Murphy said.

LoBianco sank deeper                gloom, but his black eyes
were fierce.

"Some fucking Sicilian you are," Murphy continued.
"Sitting there whining like a kid. You sure your name's
LoBianco? Your old man would be real proud of you. Even
your fat uncle is more a man than you."

LoBianco just stared at Murphy and let him finish.

"I told you before, you're too much of a pussy. You
thought you were going to bluff that nigger with a bunch of
bullshit, but he cut right through your shit because he's
tougher than you'll ever be. He didn't climb to the top of the
dung heap because he knew any of that bullshit Jap fighting
crap. He made it because he's mentally tough. He'd cut off
his own dick if he could cause you even more pain.

"He outgutted you, Sonny boy. That karate stuff wrecked
three of his soldiers and it's good for keeping your weight
down. But on the street it's your brains and balls that pull it
off."

"I once told a kid that same thing," LoBianco said.

"Did he listen?" Murphy asked.

"No. He didn't understand."

"Nor do you, Sonny. Your big, bad act has crapped out.
What are you going to do next? Threaten Mr. Motherfucker
with a parking citation?"

"I'm gonna kill him," LoBianco said without emotion.

"Bullshit!" Murphy said. "It's not in you. Your father was a shooter. You're a peace officer."

"Put him in front of me and I'll show you," LoBianco said.

"Get him yourself," Rotten Jack taunted him.

"I need your help to find him," LoBianco said.

"You need my help to kill him."

"Okay."

"How you gonna make him pay?" Murphy asked.

"I'm gonna get a throwaway and blow his brains out."

"Too easy and there's no justice in it. Your friend the priest suffered. The kid suffered, you suffered, so that scumbag should suffer, slow and painful. He should know why he's dying, and how he's dying, and not be able to do a fucking thing about it."

"How do we do that?" Sonny asked. He was interested now; it was why he had driven all this way.

"I don't know," Jack said. "Let me think." He was smiling. It was a menacing smile. Rotten Jack Murphy was having fun sorting out and considering ways to make Mr. MoFo die.

LoBianco waited impassively.

Murphy finally spoke. "When dealing with scumbags, Sonny boy, there are no half measures. You and I weren't lucky enough to be spit out of highfalutin' cunts. We was born in shit town so we gotta play by shit rules. You had no business leaving that bastard breathing."

"You said that already, Jack," LoBianco said. "What do I do?"

Rotten Jack signaled a passing waiter for a double bourbon. The waiter, seeing how drunk Murphy was, thought about eighty-sixing him, but then he thought about his own fragile facial bones and changed his mind.

Jack held up his drink. "I'm gonna give you one more chance, you wop asshole. I'm gonna show you how to cross over the line and get away with murder, and if you give me any of that 'I can't do it because I'm a cop' shit, then you can go bury your friends, stick your badge up your ass, and stay out of my way.''

Instead of going back to his apartment, Sonny LoBianco made an unusual detour. He went directly to the chapel of St. Agnes. Genuflecting unconsciously, he walked down the short, cold aisle to the altar. For a moment he stood there, staring at the crucifix hanging above him. Christ's unendurable pain, captured expertly by the artist, failed to move him. He knew all about pain, mental and physical. It could be conquered; it could be defeated.

He knelt before the image and bowed his head, but his thoughts weren't of supplication and mercy, they were of death and revenge. Inside, he could feel his resolve hardening, feel the restraints ripping from his mind. The teachings of Christ and those of Father Davis hadn't touched him deeply; they were merely a veneer that could be scraped away, exposing the raw, brutal power of his instincts. His bruised and bloody knuckles clasped before him in mock prayer, he swore that if there was a God, they were now enemies.

He rose shakily when he heard the door to the chapel open suddenly. Outlined in the dim light was a solid, blocky figure.

"Ain't that touching," the figure said in a rough growl. "Prayin', are we?"

LoBianco squinted at the man in the doorway. "Who the hell are you?" he asked.

"Sergeant O'Banion. You're under arrest."

"What the fuck for?"

"Assault with intent to kill."

"Kill who?"

"Three of our darker citizens and one patrolman."

"Shit."

"You got it, asshole. You're in deep shit. Are you

coming with me or do I have to call for the goddamned TNS
to smoke you out?''

"I'll come.''

"Put your hands on your head and walk slowly toward
me," O'Banion said.

When LoBianco got closer, he could see that O'Banion
had had a 9mm Glock trained on him the entire time.
O'Banion threw LoBianco up against the doors of the
chapel, frisked him expertly, then cuffed him.

"That's the first smart move you've made all day,"
O'Banion said, pushing Sonny roughly out the door. Two
cars were parked in the drive, five plainclothes cops with
shotguns had the place surrounded. "I was kinda hopin' you
were a tough guy. It's one thing beating the crap out of
helpless young cops and stupid niggers. It's another to fight
a man.''

"Hey, O'Banion. You speak Italian?" LoBianco said.

"Some.''

"Well, fuck you.''

O'Banion hit LoBianco in the gut with all his power—
once, twice, a third time. Sonny could feel his cracked rib
breaking; he couldn't breathe. Then O'Banion clipped him
in the face with his knee, sending him tumbling down the
stairs; his face smashed into the gravel; the pain made him
black out for a moment. He woke an instant later, wishing
he had stayed out.

"Trip?" O'Banion asked.

LoBianco spat out a mouthful of gravel.

"What's all this?" Berger asked, hurrying toward the
police cars.

"What's it to you, Pops?" O'Banion answered.

Berger adjusted his glasses and reached for his shield.

O'Banion pointed the Glock at him. "Not so fast," he
said.

Gingerly Berger pulled out the wallet containing his gold
shield. "That's Detective Sergeant, you putz," he said.
"And I asked you what the hell was going on.''

"Got a warrant for this scumbag," O'Banion said.

"Let me see it and let me see your identification," Berger said.

Grudgingly O'Banion produced the documents.

"Ah," Berger said. "Internal Affairs. I thought I smelled something foul. Get Patrolman LoBianco to a hospital at once. Then I'm going to file charges of police brutality myself."

"File away, Pops," O'Banion said, putting his shield and warrant away. "It's six against two. You lose."

O'Banion grabbed LoBianco by his cuffed wrists and yanked him to his feet. "Let's put this asshole on ice," he said to one of the men. "Night, Grandpa. You'd better get inside before you catch your death, if you know what I mean."

"I'll have you out in a couple of hours," Berger called after them, wondering if it were true.


Sitting in the back of the unmarked car, LoBianco tried to relax. This is one more nail in the coffin, he thought. My life has changed completely, as of today.

Not feeling up to having his ribs rearranged for the tenth time that day, LoBianco was content to ride in silence. He was surprised when they pulled into the driveway of Bensonhurst General.

"I want a complete medical report on you before we begin our conversation," O'Banion said, hustling Sonny through the crowd of moaning, crying, screaming wounded who inhabited the waiting room twenty-four hours a day.

O'Banion grabbed a dark, scrawny doctor and hauled him into an examination room with LoBianco.

"Oh, my goodness," said Dr. Patel. "What on earth is going on here?"

"Give this asshole a quick check, then I'll get him out of here," O'Banion said.

"How are you feeling?" Dr. Patel asked LoBianco.

"I'm feelin' real bad, doc," LoBianco put in. "I'm dyin'."

"You shut up," O'Banion told him.

Dr. Patel worked quickly and efficiently, probing LoBianco's broken ribs. Sonny howled with fake pain, figuring a night in the hospital beat a night in lockup.

"I want to X-ray his ribs and keep him overnight for observation," Dr. Patel said, when he had finished his examination.

"Oh, God, it hurts," LoBianco moaned.

"He's faking," O'Banion said.

"He is *not* faking," Dr. Patel said, pulling up LoBianco's shirt. The bruises were purple, yellow, and brown.

"All right," O'Banion said at last. "But I want him cuffed to the bed and guarded."

"It shall be as you say," Dr. Patel said, not wanting to excite O'Banion further. "Uncuff him so I can treat his facial cuts and contusions," Dr. Patel said.

LoBianco turned around to make it easier for the Internal Affairs Division sergeant to take off the cuffs. But instead of freeing him, O'Banion brought two huge fists down on LoBianco's head.

"I guess he ain't goin' nowhere," O'Banion said, unlocking the cuffs from an unconscious Sonny.

"Oh, my goodness," Dr. Patel gasped.

Sonny woke up to a world of pain. The handcuffs chaining him to the hospital bed allowed him only minimal movement and he began to itch in places he couldn't reach.

Outside his room a black policewoman sat with her chair tilted against the wall, reading the *New York Post*. He thought about calling to her, but decided against it. He didn't need any more hassles. He closed his eyes again; the next time he opened them morning had come and Ira Berger stood looking down on him.

"How are you feeling?"

"Ira, my left side, under the bandage. Scratch it for me," LoBianco said, his voice hoarse and dry.

Like a man reaching into a basket of spiders, Berger scratched him tentatively.

"Harder," LoBianco said. "I'm coming, Ira."

Berger pulled his hand away. "Get a nurse to do that," he said. "Suppose someone saw us?"

"Does that mean you won't give me my enema?" LoBianco said, stifling a laugh that hurt like hell.

"I see they didn't dent your peculiar sense of humor," Berger said. "Your doctor wants to keep you here a few more days, but the IAD wants you out by noon. You're in real trouble, Sonny."

"What have they got?"

"Enough to send you away for a couple of years, dismissal at the very least. You just can't go around punching out people," Berger said. "You can shoot and kill them, but God help you if you rough them up."

"That's the truth," LoBianco said. "I'm sorry about the cop."

"He deserved it morally, if not legally," Berger said. "I brought a PBA lawyer with me. He's not keen on defending you, but you'd better see him." Berger went back out in the hall and returned with a thin, shrunken man. He wore a blue polyester sport coat, tan cords, and Reeboks. The collar of his jacket was sprinkled liberally with dandruff.

"Patrolman LoBianco? I'm Nelson Sutter, from the PBA," he said, reaching out his hand. Then realizing LoBianco was chained, he made an odd limp-wristed movement as if he were trying to disguise the attempted handshake as something else.

"I'd like to be alone with my client," Sutter said to Berger.

"I'll be outside," Berger said, leaving. The policewoman continued to read the *Post,* bored by the proceedings.

"You're charged with three counts of assault with intent

to kill, battery, riot, and several minor charges. In other words they're throwing the book at you,'' Sutter said.

"And it looks like it landed on my head," LoBianco said. "Can I have a sip of water?"

Sutter reached for the glass by the bedside and held the straw near LoBianco's swollen lips.

"Thanks," LoBianco said. "What do you suggest?"

"Well, beating up that cop ends your career," Sutter said. "Beating those three dealers will no doubt produce some civil and criminal suits."

"Thanks for the good news. What's the best I can do?"

"Resign, then hire a good lawyer and try to put the inevitable off as long as possible," Sutter said, scratching his thinning brown hair and sending a flurry of fresh powder cascading down his sloping shoulders.

"What happens next?" LoBianco asked.

"You'll be interrogated by the IAD, none too gently, I gather. I'll be there if you want. Then you'll be brought up on charges, dismissed, and flung out into the street to suffer whatever criminal and civil charges pop up."

"Wonderful," LoBianco said.

"So long," Sutter said, again reaching out to shake hands, but ending in a curious kind of wave.

LoBianco closed his eyes, trying to shut out the world. He felt totally adrift, completely alone. First one family was ripped away from him, then Angela, then Father Davis, and now his last home, the department, had turned its back on him. *The department takes care of its own.* That had whole new meaning now, he thought. They were really going to take care of him.

Berger returned looking hopeful, but when LoBianco told him what Sutter had said, he frowned. "Whatever I can do, you know I will," he said.

"I know, Ira," loBianco said. "But it looks pretty bad."

"I checked on Father Davis," Berger said. "He's hanging in there, much to the surprise of his doctors."

"That's something at least," LoBianco said.

"I'll let you rest," Berger said. "All the kids are asking about you. They want to come to visit you."

Before Sonny could say anything, he heard a commotion in the hall. Three men in formation approached the police-woman in the hall. The youngest one handed her some papers while the leader and his assistant walked purpose-fully into LoBianco's room.

"I'll need a few minutes with my client," Alfred Barre said. He was tall and distinguished looking, wearing what Sonny judged to be a twenty-five-hundred-dollar suit, white shirt, and a red silk tie. His briefcase would have cost Sonny two months' salary.

"I've already got a lawyer," LoBianco said as Berger again left the room.

Barre introduced himself and said, "I work for your uncle's employers. I can have you out of here and into the private ambulance I have waiting in less than ten minutes, if you like.

"I like," said LoBianco. The Gencos, he thought. This guy's their hotshot lawyer.

"All you have to do is nod and not say anything stupid until we're outside. Is that clear?"

LoBianco nodded.

Barre snapped his fingers, and his assistant turned and walked out of the room. When he returned, he had a uniformed police captain and two sergeants in tow. The policewoman who had been lounging in her chair stood up quickly to attention.

"Release him," the captain said, and the policewoman practically ran to LoBianco's bed and unchained him.

Once freed, LoBianco started to scratch himself.

"Where are your clothes?" Barre asked.

LoBianco shrugged.

"Then put on a robe. We're leaving right now."

LoBianco did as he was told. "I'd like to stop in ICU to see a friend before we leave."

Barre shook his magnificent head. "There's no time.

Someone is waiting. I'll get you a full report on the priest later.''

LoBianco eased himself to the floor, not really under-standing what was going on, not really caring at that moment. All he wanted was to get out of the damned hospital.

# 25

Vito LoBianco paced across the wide veranda of Woodlane, a private sanitarium on the north shore of Long Island. The bare trees surrounding the mob-owned estate made him think of claws reaching for him. A thin trickle of cold rain fell intermittently; the sky was as dark and troubled as Vito himself. Inside the enormous Georgian house Salvatore Genco himself was holding court. Vito knew big things were about to happen; he just hoped he could survive.

Vito had known about the explosion before Sonny, and he had mixed feelings about what it meant. Almost immediately he began calling in favors to get information. A plan was forming in his mind, one that would allow him to retire in peace and pass along the family business to a LoBianco. It would also be a convenient way to rid himself of Frankie Marcellino, before Frankie Marcellino could get rid of him.

As underboss of the Genco family, Vito LoBianco knew his calls carried weight, enough weight to surprise even himself. It reminded him that he had gone soft by pushing off the day-to-day operations on subordinates like Frankie. He wondered if he had become nothing more than the fat, old owner of a restaurant named after his wife. It was time to change all that.

There was a sudden flurry of activity a half mile down the

driveway. Vito could see the flashing lights of an ambulance and watched as the high, iron gates swung open electronically. The ambulance, preceded by a tan Lincoln Continental and chased by a Cadillac limousine, sped up the driveway to the main building. Whatever else you said about him, Vito thought, old man Genco had the power to get things done. Their three-car procession came to a halt in front of Vito. Alfred Barre and his assistants got out of the limo and walked past Vito without saying a word. They reported to Genco directly and didn't have time for a mere underboss.

Three sharply dressed young men, part of Genco's inner circle of soldiers, got out of the Lincoln and helped the attendants unload Sonny from the ambulance. He was protesting bitterly, but they ignored his complaints and carried him up the stairs to the clinic.

"Tell them I'm okay," Sonny said to Vito as he was marched past his uncle, belted to the stretcher.

"Relax, Santino," Vito said. "Mr. Genco wants you checked out."

"Screw him," Sonny said as four men rushed him through the doors.

Vito winced. It wasn't smart to curse Mr. Genco. "I'll be with you in a minute," he called after Sonny.

LoBianco was deposited on an examination table at the rear of the building. Almost immediately a short balding doctor entered the room and introduced himself as Dr. Tedesco. "Let me have a look at you," the doctor said.

Sonny accepted his fate and lay back on the table while Tedesco removed the bandages from his ribs and face. The doctor pursed his full lips and made a clucking sound.

"How do you feel?" he asked.

"Just fucking wonderful," LoBianco said. "How do you think I feel?"

"I want X rays of those ribs," Dr. Tedesco said to a middle-aged nurse who had slipped into the room unnoticed.

"Any more X rays and I'll have mutant children," LoBianco said. He wasn't going to make it easy for anyone.

The doctor ignored Sonny's comments and spent fifteen minutes examining him, testing his reflexes and generally probing where LoBianco didn't want to be probed.

"You need some rest," Dr. Tedesco said, washing his hands. "But you're in good shape. The ribs can be taped; your nose is broken, but it will heal. You'll be as good as new in a couple of weeks."

"I ain't got a couple of weeks to fuck off," LoBianco said as the nurse swooped down on him to carry him off to x-ray. Neither the doctor nor the nurse wanted to discuss it with him.

After the X rays and a rebandaging, the nurse sent him to a richly decorated consulting room. He pulled the blue hospital robe around his ribs and sat in a brown leather chair. Wearing only Jockey shorts under the robe, he winced at the coldness of his seat.

He waited only a few minutes before Vito came in and tossed him a pile of clothes. "I had somebody get these for you," he said.

Sonny recognized his own clothes.

"In our business you don't always need keys," Vito said, sitting down behind the massive desk.

Sonny dressed in silence, then sat back down in the leather chair. "Well?"

"Mr. Genco wants to see you. At my request," Vito said. "I need you, Santino. *He* needs you."

"Nobody fucking needs me," LoBianco said.

"Your friend Frankie is fucking up the organization," Vito said. "He's doing his own deals with the, uh, blacks, and Mr. Genco ain't happy."

"So what's that to me?"

"Who do you think blew up that priest?" Vito said.

"Frankie?" LoBianco pushed himself forward in his chair, his eyes blazing.

"As a favor to his friends," Vito said. "That MoFo gets gas, Frankie farts."

Sonny sat back. "I figured that." He knew he had to keep his cool and let whatever happened, happen.

"Your friend Frankie is also fucking your wife," Vito said.

LoBianco tensed, feeling the blood rise to his face. He took a sharp breath. "I figured that, too."

"I'm glad you got it all figured out," Vito said, stroking his bushy salt-and-pepper mustache with a thick finger. "Because you're gonna do something about it."

"Why the hell should I?" LoBianco said.

"A man fucks your wife and you walk away? A man kills a kid and probably kills your best friend, the priest, and you ask why you should care?" Vito asked.

"I didn't say I was walking," LoBianco said. "I'll take care of my own problems."

"Like you took care of MoFo?" Vito asked.

LoBianco twisted in his chair. He knew he was being sucked into something he had always sworn to avoid.

"We can help each other, Santino," Vito said. "We *must* help each other."

There was a knock at the door and one of the young hitters stuck his head in. "Mr. Genco will see you now."

Both Vito and Sonny rose, but the soldier said, "Just him." He pointed to Sonny. Vito sat down heavily. It was not a good sign.

He was ushered into a large wood-paneled room at the rear of the building. Ten-foot-high bookcases lined the walls on three sides; the tall French doors looked out on the grounds, now brown and dreary in the winter rain. A cheerful fire burned in a walk-in fireplace.

Genco was alone, sitting at the end of a large conference table. Salvatore Genco was called the Boss, and no other title suited the thin, blue-eyed patriarch of the Genco family. He was past seventy, but the brilliance of his eyes made Sonny aware that the old man had lost none of the cunning that had brought him from the slums of Palermo to the heights of power.

Salvatore Genco smiled sincerely, staring for a long time at Sonny's bandaged face. "You're your father's image," he said at last. "So much of him I see in your face. But what is in your heart?" His voice was hardly more than a whisper, forcing Sonny to pay close attention to every word.

"Why did you bring me here?" Sonny asked.

"Did you enjoy being chained to a hospital bed?" Genco said. "Some kind of perverted pleasure." The way he said it made LoBianco think this old man had spent a lifetime taking his pleasures, perverted and otherwise.

"No," Sonny answered.

Genco made a gesture with his thin-lipped mouth. It meant, "Well, there you go."

"There's gotta be more to this," Sonny said. Genco's eyes seemed to be piercing him to his soul.

"Of course, Santino," Genco said. "There is always more to everything."

Sonny sat in silence. If they were going to play mental chess, he had a few moves of his own.

He watched Genco warily, his head cocked like an arrogant street punk. But Genco wasn't fooled, the young man in front of him was no punk; he was his father's son and that was the point of the meeting.

Genco stared out the French doors at the misty grounds, his hawklike nose seeming to smell out Sonny's ruse. "I need a LoBianco at my side," he said softly.

Sonny remained silent.

"The Gencos have always relied on the power of the LoBiancos. They—your father and uncle—were the steel in the fabric of my family. I have many people in my organization whose loyalty to me will remain only if it is guaranteed by a LoBianco. You are a LoBianco."

"You want my name?" Sonny asked, feeling stupid.

"I want you."

"I'll sell you the fucking name. How much?" Sonny said.

"Do not joke about a name," Genco said.

"I'm a cop," LoBianco said.

"You were a cop," Genco said. "Now you are nothing. I'm giving you a chance to be something again. You have a choice to make."

"What kind of choice?"

"Join me or I'll throw you to the wolves," Genco said, smiling slightly.

"Don't you think the wolves have got me already?" Sonny asked.

"I can fix all your problems."

"Just like that?"

"No, not just like that," Genco said. "It will cost me money and favors. I want to make sure you are with me first. What is in your heart, Santino?"

"Pain," Sonny answered. If the old guy wanted that *gombah* shit, he'd get it.

"We all have that," Genco said.

"Pain and revenge," Sonny said. He felt it. "But what can you do to help me?"

"I offer you a new life. A better life."

"I don't have much choice, do I?"

"No. But not for the reasons you think. You're Sicilian, you will always be Sicilian. To those who respect your name, that is something special. But to the *pezzonovanti* who control the police department, you are a gangster, an outsider," Genco said, leaning over the table, looking directly at Sonny.

"You are a Sicilian, a LoBianco," Genco continued, tapping the polished mahogany table with his middle finger. "And *this* is where you belong."

For a moment LoBianco thought he saw a flicker of warmth in Genco's cold blue eyes, and suddenly he felt something new, a sense of legitimacy, of belonging, that he hadn't felt in years. It felt good to be wanted again.

Genco seemed to read his thoughts. "Then we have an understanding?" he said.

LoBianco nodded. "Yes, Mr. Genco." He was committed and it felt good.

"*Bene, bene,*" Genco said. "You are welcome to stay here and get your strength back. You have my hospitality and good wishes."

"No, I think I'll ride back to Brooklyn with Vito," LoBianco said. "Assuming he's going there."

"Vito goes where I tell him," Genco said.

"Yes, definitely," Sonny said. "I'd like to go home."

Genco shrugged. "You are home, Santino. I will send for you soon and we will talk again."

Sonny stood, ready to leave the smiling old man. He wondered if it was his imagination or if Genco's smile looked more malevolent than sympathetic.

As Vito and Sonny drove back to Brooklyn, Salvatore Genco sat at ease, his elbows resting on the conference table, his fingertips touching. He waited for the knock on the door; he didn't wait long. Frankie Marcellino entered the room, oozing confidence. He sat without being asked and stretched his long legs under the table.

"Everything go all right?" Marcellino asked.

"As expected. He fell right into our hands," Genco said.

Marcellino laughed. "I know you're not supposed to get involved with this shit, but I can't tell you how much I been looking forward to wasting that asshole and his fucking uncle."

"The plan?" Genco asked.

"Covered," Marcellino said. "Our Jamaican friend is on the job."

"See that nothing goes wrong and you'll be a very rich man," Genco said. "You'll have Vito's business."

"Nothing can go wrong, Boss," Marcellino said. "Don't worry about a fucking thing."

"When people tell me not to worry, that's when I begin to worry," Genco said.

Marcellino stood up. "It will all be over soon," he promised.

Genco went back to tapping his fingertips. Youth, he thought, always so confident. Good luck to you . . . both.

The cold wind seemed to bite through her as Rose walked down the overgrown cemetery path. It had been several months since she had come here, months during which thoughts of her dead sister and her family had haunted her. Damn her, Rose thought. Two children, *two* children, and I'm all alone. But the baby, the poor, poor baby, if only she hadn't died. Then she could be all mine, all mine to love.

She would have the baby, Rose knew. As surely as the sun would rise in the morning, Rose Berger would become a mother. It was all coming together. Even the liar, Chin, and her stupid husband couldn't stop her.

Before she left, she pulled some of the weeds away and read the carved lettering. *Beloved sister . . . beloved daughter.*

Beloved daughter, Rose thought, then rose to leave. She had plans to make.

# 26

Sonny was surprised to find Ira Berger sitting at Father Davis's desk playing solitaire with a deck of kid's cards.

"What the hell is going on?" Berger asked him without preamble.

"I got a new job," LoBianco said, sitting down on the plaid couch. "How is he?"

"Davis? I just checked. He's still hanging in there," Berger said. "In fact, the doctors are amazed."

"He's a tough son of a bitch," LoBianco said. "E.T. wasn't so tough."

"No," Berger said. "What are you going to do?"

"Work for my uncle," LoBianco said.

"You stupid bastard."

"I got no choice, Ira," LoBianco said, relating what had happened to him that day.

"You're a good cop," Berger said, when Sonny had finished.

"No, I was a bad cop. I didn't have my heart in it."

"And you'll have your heart in being a killer? A gangster?" Berger was outraged.

"You gotta do what you gotta do," LoBianco answered calmly.

"Truly a brilliant answer, Mr. Philosopher," Berger shot back. "Isn't there another way out?"

"You think of one, be sure to let me know," LoBianco said, rising. "You taking over the shelter?"

"As a matter of fact, I'm just leaving," Berger said. "The Dominican sisters sent two nuns to close up the place."

"Davis will shit," Sonny said.

"Davis will be lucky to evacuate his bowels ever again," Berger observed. "And when he gets better, he'll kick your ass for what you're doing."

"He'll have to stand in line," Sonny said.

Berger got up and walked across the room. "Please, Sonny. Don't do this." He wanted desperately to make Sonny listen to reason.

"It's too late, Ira," Sonny said. "I enjoyed working with you, but I won't miss the department. They fucked me."

"Can you throw it all away so easily?" Berger asked.

"Watch me, Ira. Just watch me."

After Sonny had gone, Berger sat at the table for a long time, worrying. It seemed to him that he had worried all his life—about everyone and everything. And all that worrying had been justified. Nothing had ever worked out the way it should.

A memory from his childhood suddenly struck him. It was Friday evening, the Sabbath had begun. He could see his father, mother, and sister. God rest their souls. Such a long time ago, he thought. Such a long time since religion had played any part in his life.

Always the detective, Berger realized what had triggered the memory: trouble. When people were in trouble, they turned to God. But who listens? he wondered. His faith, like his hair, had disappeared over the years, without his really noticing it until it was almost gone.

If there really were a God, you'd think He'd be big enough to run all the religions.

"Such a thought," he said out loud, taking off his glasses and closing his eyes. He felt a tap on his knee.

"Don't cry, Father B," LaDonna said.

Berger looked down at the four-year-old. "I'm not crying," he said. "But I'd like to."

"I'll tell you a joke," she said. "Why did the cookie go to the doctor?" She paused for two seconds, then said, "Give up? Because he felt crummy!" She laughed hysterically.

Berger smiled and patted her on the head. "I guess we all feel pretty crummy tonight."

"But you liked my joke?" LaDonna asked.

"Joke, schmoke," he said. "I like you."

There were twelve cops standing around Ira Berger's desk at the precinct. Seven wore plainclothes, five were in uniform. Three were women. Together they represented more than one hundred and seventy years of experience, yet not one of them knew how the manila envelope containing Maria Parulo's appointment book had ended up on his desk.

Berger glared at the embarrassed group while two technicians from the police lab carefully examined the book. "I realize I'm only a thirty-year hairbag," Berger said, his tone unusually nasty. "But in the old days the police department had this policy that encouraged officers on duty to keep their eyes open. Yet what I have here is some kind of supernatural envelope. It appeared out of nowhere. No one saw a damned thing. This is security? Suppose it was a bomb?"

There were a few murmurs, but everyone was too ashamed to speak.

"By the way," Detective Bobby Green said, breaking the tension, "your wife stopped by to see you this morning."

"Rose?" Berger was stunned. He must have just missed her.

Somebody laughed.

"My wife," Berger said scathingly. "My wife didn't deliver this envelope, did she?"

"No, I don't think—"

"That's the point. None of you think. My wife you

remember—a couple hours later. But a homicide suspect waltzes in here carrying a package and nobody sees a thing. Frankly, if I had my way, I'd ship all of you back to the academy for a refresher course.''

"Sorry, Ira," Green said.

"Sorry don't make it, Bobby. We are obviously incapable of running a homicide investigation." Berger twisted his mouth into a grimace that was difficult to look at; the group dispersed, abashed.

Frustration, personal and professional, was making Berger a nervous wreck. LoBianco was running around somewhere playing godfather, Berger's newfound friend Father Davis was hanging to life by a thread, he had virtually been called incompetent by the bosses at One Police Plaza, and now Rose strolls into the precinct and he was asleep in his lounge chair at home.

"Get this thing to the lab quickly," he told the two technicians. "Print it, search it, field-strip it. If this book has secrets, get the data to the special task force immediately." He got up from his chair and invaded Lt. Santamyer's office.

"Tough morning, Ira?" Santamyer asked.

"The toughest, Lew," Berger replied. "I'm sorry. I've screwed things up royally."

"Really?"

"Yeah. The people I relied on have messed up everything," Berger said.

"Don't be so hard on yourself," Santamyer said, his bland face calm and collected. "I'm sure you did your best."

"But it wasn't good enough, was it?" Berger said bitterly. "Maybe I'm too old for The Job."

"Nonsense, Ira," Santamyer said. "You have many good years left."

Berger sighed. Santamyer was a pleasant, ineffectual man who wouldn't show a hair out of place in a hurricane.

"Have you got the records together for Deputy Inspector Boynton?" Santamyer said.

"All packed up," Berger said. Three cardboard cartons were stacked in front of his desk. "The whole magilla."

"Good," Santamyer said, looking at his watch. "He'll be here any minute. Wants to talk to you, probably to ask you to join the task force."

"Should I?" Berger asked. He didn't feel like making any more decisions.

"It's up to you," Santamyer said unhelpfully. "It's your call."

While Berger was thinking, Deputy Inspector Boynton, three men in plainclothes, and two in uniform burst into the PDU. "Where's Santamyer?" Boynton said in a loud commanding voice. The entire bullpen looked up.

"Santamyer!" he yelled. Boynton was imposing. Standing six-foot-six, he had the barrel chest of a wrestler, grayish hair swept back and oiled, a square face, and a pugnacious jaw. He was dressed immaculately in a custom-made black pinstripe suit, a trench coat thrown over his wide shoulders. Berger thought he looked like a movie star who specialized in cop and gangster roles.

"Over here," Santamyer called weakly from his pathetic cubicle.

"We're here for the records," Boynton said, striding across the floor. He motioned to the uniforms who stood ready to do his bidding.

"Over there," Berger said, pointing.

The uniforms rushed to seize the cardboard boxes as if they contained gold.

"I understand there was a first-class fuck-up here this morning," Boynton said, his voice penetrating the farthest corner of the PDU squad room. "That's why we're here. To make sense of this muddle."

The detectives, who had been staring openmouthed at Boynton and his entourage, quickly looked away and buried their heads in the paperwork on their desks.

"Who's Berger?" Boynton boomed.

"That's me," Berger said, standing.

"This is the guy," Boynton said, pointing to him. His three plainclothesmen, all big and expensively dressed, smiled sarcastically. Berger blushed.

"Heard about your partner," Boynton said. "You a tough guy, too?"

Tough enough for an asshole windbag like you, you schmuck, Berger wanted to say. But he controlled himself. He stood silently.

"You got nothin' to say? That's good. Let's get outta this dump," Boynton said, looking around. "Go back to busting five-dollar crackheads and leave the big cases to the professionals." He turned on his heel and with his men in his wake exited the PDU. Those in the room breathed a collective sigh of relief.

Berger could feel every eye in the room on him, pitying him. He couldn't stand it any longer and turned to leave.

"That's funny," Santamyer said absently. "He didn't ask you to join the task force. It's usual."

"With Boynton in charge, they've got enough incompetents," Berger said. "One more won't make any difference."

# 27

Charles Maris woke suddenly, knowing something was wrong. He opened his eyes slowly, expecting the worst. It was pitch-black, and for a moment he had no idea where he was. He shook his head slowly, feeling the concrete beneath his naked body. Then he knew. The basement. He whistled softly and was rewarded by the sound of the dogs shuffling in their cages. He was home; everything was all right. But where had he been and where were his clothes?

Groaning, he pushed himself to his knees before attempting to stand. His head throbbed, the pain of a receding brain explosion. He began to shake from the damp cold of the basement as well as the terrible pounding in his head.

Finally he stood, wriggling his toes in the fungus. It felt like the muck at the bottom of a lake.

He fumbled his way across the room, following the rubber runner until he found the light switch. The dim light flooded the foul basement; the dogs moved forward in their cages, anxious for food and attention. But Maris ignored them, searching for something to wear. All he found was a rumpled black dress, and that wasn't suitable at all. In a rare show of neatness he picked up the dress and walked slowly up the creaking stairs.

The heavy door at the top of the stairs was ajar. He shook

his head slowly. He *always* remembered to lock it from the inside. Something was definitely wrong. He pushed it open as if he expected someone to leap through the doorway and attack him. But everything was quiet. He walked awkwardly, his fleshy thighs rubbing together, his big feet pointed outward in a duck waddle.

Holding the dirty black dress in front of his privates so that Emily would not be embarrassed, he entered the library and sat behind the ornate desk. A streetlight shone feebly through the black curtains. It was night and he had lost a day. The feeling of wrongness overwhelmed him as he switched on the desk light.

"How are you, Emily?" he asked automatically.

When she didn't respond, he looked up and stifled a gasp. Emily was gone! The wheelchair was empty. Well, not empty. In place of the bundled blankets sat a small silver picture frame. Frozen in a sunlit moment on a long-ago afternoon was Emily. In the photograph she smiled at him winningly, her dark hair cascading down her shoulders.

The phone rang, causing his stomach to churn. He looked at it as if it were an alien artifact. Finally he picked up the receiver.

"Peek-a-boo, I see you," Mother said. Charles suddenly remembered he was naked. He blushed.

"Humpty Dumpty sat on a wall," Mother began. Charles slammed the phone down, suddenly unable to get enough air into his lungs. He tried to scream, but a shrill whistling was all that escaped his thick lips.

The hunt was on. Charles Maris needed children. He had to do what Mother told him, that was painfully obvious. He had fought her, but she had won.

As he had done when he was stalking women, Charles had to avoid looking in his own neighborhood. Many of the children there knew him, anyway, and most feared him, ugly hulk that he was.

Charles didn't particularly like children. He hadn't enjoyed being one, and he hated the way the other children had always treated him. Still, he knew killing them was wrong, and he hated Mother for forcing this upon him. Where, after all, was he going to find enough children to help Emily?

Thinking about the problem in a purely analytical way, he narrowed the source of his prey to nursery schools and playgrounds, the natural habitats of four-year-olds. But they would be guarded during the day and it was night now. He had to prove to Mother that he was seriously trying to fulfill her wishes.

Then a thought struck him: the shelter, the orphanage or whatever they called it now. St. Agnes in Coney Island. Maybe he could find what he—what she—wanted there. He pulled a fresh pair of surgical gloves from the desk drawer, took his scalpel case, and laid out the rest of his equipment. Then he went upstairs to dress. He never noticed that Maria Parulo's appointment book had disappeared.

Half an hour later he had paid the car-service driver and was walking parallel to the boardwalk on his way to St. Agnes. It was a beautiful evening, cold and clear. The stars twinkled brightly, sending their cold fire to guide him.

The farther he got from the rides, the more depressing the neighborhood became. Derelicts, dirty and dangerous, made him wish he had brought one of the pit bulls along for protection.

He walked past the burned-out buildings, seeing the flicker of cigarette lighters as addicts ignited crack pipes, saw discarded heroin rigs crushed by automobiles, and stepped around used condoms.

It took him only three minutes to reach St. Agnes. The dark, forbidding buildings made him shiver. He could see only three lights: one downstairs, one in the garage, and one upstairs. He rested his head on the rusty iron gate, trying to decide what to do. The wind from the ocean whistled down the side streets, moaning eerily as it whipped through the silent stone buildings.

He pushed tentatively at the gates, and to his surprise they squealed open. Fools, he thought, if I lived here, I'd have the gates chained and the dogs running loose on the grounds.

Half expecting floodlights and alarms, he walked boldly into the courtyard, getting a feel for the place. There was something wrong here, he thought, something tense about the atmosphere. He shrugged off the feeling and crept silently to what he imagined was the rectory and tried the door. It opened easily. Thinking of a cover story in case he was detected, he closed the door softly and went to the stairs. The first step groaned under his weight, but he ignored it.

"Harriet? Sister Harriet?" He heard a female voice call from his right.

"Yes, Sister," came an answering voice from his left.

He had caught a flash of movement from below and ran up the stairs, taking them two at a time.

Peering over the balcony, he saw two women, one short and fat, the other tall and fat. They were wearing blue dresses, white blouses, and odd headpieces. Nuns, he thought.

"Oh, it's you," said the short one, with a face only a mother superior could love.

"Of course," the tall one, Sister Harriet, said. "You were expecting St. Dominic?"

"It's this creepy old house," Sister Valerie said. "I'll be glad to get back upstate. I don't know why we've allowed this to go on so long."

"The Lord will protect us," Sister Harriet said.

"In this neighborhood I think I'd prefer Saints Smith and Wesson."

Both nuns laughed and went into Father Davis's office.

Maris breathed a sigh of relief and looked up and down the long corridor, trying to decide which way to go.

With exaggerated care he crept to his right and moved halfway down the hall. He chose a door at random and, opening it, looked inside. Two triple-decker bunk beds flanked the walls. Six kids. He closed his eyes, waiting for them to adjust to the dark. When he opened them, he saw at once that the occupants of the bunks were black; worse, they were all boys.

He closed the door softly and tried another room. This time he saw four girls, teenagers, also black, unsuitable for his purposes.

A third door opened on a row of cribs. This was more like it, he thought, entering the room. The first two babies were too dark; the third, much lighter than the rest, was a definite possibility. The baby had blond, fluffy hair. She was too young, he thought, but he knew what he must do. He had loomed over the crib to get a closer look when the baby woke up and began to cry.

Flustered, Maris backed away from the crib; the baby whined and fussed for a moment, then went back to sleep. Charles waited for his heartbeat to slow, then left the room. He was thinking about a safer way to abduct the baby when he almost stumbled over a small girl who, dressed in a Simpsons nightgown, was on her way to the toilet.

"Hi," LaDonna said to Charles. "How come you aren't wearing your red suit?"

Charles, his eyes wide with fear, gasped.

"And where's your beard?"

"Beard?" Charles whispered.

"You are Santa Claus, aren't you?" LaDonna said impatiently, her hands on her hips.

"Uh, well," Charles began.

"I've been real good this year," LaDonna said. "I want a Barbie Soda Shoppe, a Play-Doh Fun Factory, My Little Pony, Dress and Dazzle, and—"

"Be quiet. Or I won't bring you anything," Charles said, appraising the four-year-old. She had dark hair and a light complexion. Spanish? He didn't know. Or care. She was the one. He knew it.

"Would you like to come to the North Pole with me?" he asked.

"Nope," LaDonna said. "Too cold. I'm not dressed for it. Just bring the presents."

"I'll give you all the presents you want," Charles said, licking his thick lips. "And candy. And ice cream."

"Nope," said LaDonna. "Too fattening."

"Come with me, damn it," Charles said, grabbing the little girl. She eluded his grasp and ran down the hall to the bathroom.

"Gotta pee," she said, locking the door.

"Who's making all that racket up there?" Sister Harriet called from below.

Charles pressed himself against the wall.

"Don't make me come up there," the nun said.

Charles looked around wildly; his eye caught an exit sign at the end of the hall and he ran for it. As he was pushing open the fire door he heard LaDonna say, "Bye, Santa."

He pounded down the concrete steps and found himself outside the shelter; the cold wind dried the sweat on his brow, but his mouth was desert dry. What was he doing? he thought savagely. I can't kill a child like that. Mother had always told him what to do. He never got to do what he wanted. It wasn't fair. His mother's overpowering influence terrified him.

Gulping great quantities of damp night air, he walked toward the lighted garage, hoping to stop there for a few minutes before he began his long trek back to Bay Ridge.

He looked in a side window and what he saw made him forget all about children and Mother. There, inside the garage, was the most beautiful woman he had ever seen. She was stark naked, straddling a man, rocking back and forth. He had to blink twice to believe what he saw.

Lucy Velez threw her head back in ecstasy as she approached her climax; the movement caught Charles's attention. The hair. Black, long, lustrous hair. Emily's hair. How he wished he could have that hair, but Mother would be angry at him.

He watched with undisguised lust as the dark-haired

woman raked her nails down the man's chest, oblivious to everything except her own wild passion.

Charles had never seen anything like it. In his porn magazines and videos the girls were attractive enough, but they all looked bored or were bad actresses. This girl, however, was not acting. She had abandoned herself to the pleasures of the man she was servicing.

He reached into his pants and freed his own penis, pretending the dark-haired girl was his own. Maris dared not blink as he watched the girl grind her hips into the man's groin, making little moaning sounds he could hear through the window.

Charles came in less than a minute, spraying his semen over the garage wall. His knees buckled, and for a moment he thought he'd faint, but he thrust out a hand and caught himself. Breathing ragged, knees weak, Charles Maris forced himself to stop watching the live sex show. It was too dangerous.

But he would be back soon. That was a certainty.

# 28

Sonny LoBianco rolled over and grabbed Lucy's breast. She moaned in her sleep, and in truth he was glad she didn't wake up. She had exhausted him the night before. He dressed quickly and left her snoring softly.

The morning was clear and cold; the Vette roared to life. He smiled to himself, thinking about Lucy.

Slamming the Hearst shifter into reverse, he pumped the gas pedal, enjoying the deep-throated roar of the engine. He turned on the stereo, ready to hit the road. He had things to do.

As he was backing out of the driveway he saw a small figure rocketing toward him.

"Where ya going?" LaDonna asked.

"Out," Sonny said.

"Can I come?"

"No."

"I saw Santa Claus last night," LaDonna said, reaching out a finger to touch the Vette's candy-apple-red finish.

"I got a present, too," LoBianco said. "Watch out now. I gotta go."

LaDonna stood back and waved like all little kids, by clenching and unclenching her fist. LoBianco tapped the horn and gunned the Vette into the early-morning traffic.

His destination was an almost empty warehouse in Crown Heights; his target, Clyde Walker, also known as Mr. MoFo. He had to meet Rotten Jack Murphy by 8:00 A.M. This wasn't work, he thought, this was pure pleasure.

LoBianco parked in an open lot five blocks away from Mr. MoFo's hangout and walked down a side street. Murphy was waiting for him. He was twirling a big, navy-blue gym bag.

"Don't bounce that shit around," LoBianco said.

"Don't sweat it," Murphy said. "The guy I got this from told me you could drop it off a roof and it would go *splat,* not *bang.*"

LoBianco rolled his eyes. Plastique deserved more respect. "Yeah, but this guy's not here, is he?"

Rotten Jack stopped in his tracks and purposely let the bag slip from his hand.

LoBianco winced.

"Listen to me," Rotten Jack said. "I got this shit from an explosives expert. A genius. This guy's been fucking around with this stiff since 'Nam and he's still got some of his fingers. He showed me how to make it work. It's got a detonator and a big red button. All you gotta do is press the button down and the detonator is primed; you release the button and you got ten seconds to haul ass somewhere else. Now both of us know everything there is to know about it. Satisfied?"

"Who's this expert?" LoBianco asked, not satisfied. "Do I know him?"

"They call him Peg Leg," Murphy said, deadpan. "For obvious reasons."

LoBianco smiled nastily.

"It's me, you dickhead," Murphy said. "I know more about explosives than Alfred Nobel."

"Who?"

"Forget it," Murphy said. "This is prime stuff, used by Arab terrorists, IRA patriots, and the CIA."

"And used on Father Davis?" LoBianco asked.

"You might say that," Murphy said. "You got a problem?"

LoBianco shook his head, but he didn't mean it. "Let's get on with this. Two white guys in this neighborhood are like a neon sign in a church."

"Put this on," Murphy said, reaching into the gym bag. He pulled out an oversized pair of coveralls. Embroidered on the back was "Murphy's Pest Control."

"That's for sure," LoBianco said, pulling on the coveralls; Murphy put his on.

"We're just a couple of exterminators," Murphy said. "Let's put the vermin out of its misery."

They walked the remaining blocks to Mr. MoFo's warehouse and climbed the two-story fire escape to the roof. It took Murphy only a minute to snip off a rusty padlock that secured the skylight. He put the lock cutters back into the gym bag and retrieved a flashlight.

The powerful beam cut through the darkness; all was quiet, although LoBianco expected a hail of bullets at any moment.

Murphy reached into his seemingly bottomless bag and took out a length of rope with a hook at one end. He attached the hook to the skylight frame and dropped the rope into the warehouse.

"A few feet short," Murphy said. "Remember that. Now to test my theory." He dropped the gym bag into the darkness.

"Jesus," LoBianco said, shying away. But all he heard was a clang.

"Nobody home, Sonny boy. Didn't I tell you that?" Murphy said.

"Christ, Jack," LoBianco said. "No, you didn't."

Murphy shrugged, then lowered himself down the rope, hand over hand. "Come on in, the water's fine," he called to LoBianco.

Sonny was down the rope in seconds, standing next to Murphy in the oppressive darkness.

"What do we do next?" LoBianco asked.

"Wait," Murphy answered.

Clyde Walker gave the bitch one last look before he got out of bed. He liked white women, but considered them a secret vice. It didn't look good in his profession. His men tended to get upset when he preached the virtues of black sisters while he himself screwed only ofay bitches.

He gave the hooker two hundred dollars and told her to get her saggy whore butt out of the apartment that belonged to Rooster. The place was a pigsty, appropriate for a man named after a barnyard animal, he thought, kicking empty beer cans out of his way.

He dressed in a salmon-colored linen suit, a lime-green silk shirt, and white leather shoes. Feeling cool and refreshed, despite not having bathed, he went out into the cluttered living room to await his men.

They arrived together. Two men imported recently from Jamaica. They were called the twins and indeed they could have been. Both were young, dark, and dressed in conservative blue blazers and gray slacks. They could have passed for businessmen or security guards in upscale white establishments. MoFo eyed them appreciatively. Where they were going, it paid to be neat.

He gave them their instructions and with a grand flourish produced a pair of Uzis. The way the twins checked their weapons reassured him. These men were professionals, he thought, veterans of many hits.

"Be careful, but be thorough," MoFo said, handing the twins two photos. "They'll be at Rosalie's."

The twins nodded in unison, without saying a word. Once Vito LoBianco and his shithead nephew were out of the way, he could expect even more business from Frankie Marcellino—and Salvatore Genco. By tonight he'd be bigger than both of them. He rubbed his hands together appreciatively.

An hour later, feeling on top of the world, Clyde Walker

unlocked the door of his warehouse and ran straight into the arms of Rotten Jack Murphy.

Without wasting a word, Murphy brought the barrel of his 9mm automatic down on Mr. MoFo's head. The stunned dealer crumpled to the floor, feigning unconsciousness. Even in the dark he recognized the two cops. A bust, he thought, smiling inwardly. They'd beat him up and let him go, those sad, soft policemen. Before the day was out, LoBianco would be dead and the other asshole would be next.

Murphy grabbed MoFo by the collar of his lime-green shirt and dragged him to the middle of the empty warehouse.

"Get in the chair, asshole," Murphy said. "You ain't dead yet."

"I'm bleeding, mon," Mr. MoFo whined.

"I can improve on that if you don't sit in the chair," Murphy said.

Walker pulled himself up, crying piteously. It didn't affect Murphy; LoBianco kept E.T.'s face in his mind.

"Cuff him," Murphy said to LoBianco.

"I got my rights," Mr. MoFo complained. "You can't arrest me. I ain't done nothing."

"By God he's right," Murphy said, slamming the barrel of the automatic between MoFo's eyes. "So I guess we gonna have to do something else if we can't arrest him."

"My nose, my nose," Mr. MoFo cried.

"Hurts, don't it," Murphy said. "How about this?" The pistol whipped MoFo again, opening the flesh of the drug dealer's cheek.

LoBianco flinched. He looked at Rotten Jack, but he saw no emotion.

Handcuffed to the chair, Mr. MoFo suddenly realized that these two cops weren't planning to take him to the station house. Fear crept into his stomach as he began to sort out the deals he could make to save his life.

Rotten Jack unloaded the contents of his gym bag so that

MoFo could savor every moment of his execution. That distracted the drug dealer long enough for LoBianco to wrap two strands of wire around MoFo's legs, pinning him securely to the chair.

As Jack fiddled with the plastique and the detonator MoFo began shaking. The Italian cop was a pussy, Walker thought, but this red-haired honkie was a devil. He could feel it. He wanted to scream, but the sight of Murphy's automatic, covered with his own blood, kept his lips sealed.

"Listen, mon. We can get past this," Mr. MoFo said. "How much will it cost?"

"How much you got?"

"Six hundred thousand?"

"Not enough," Murphy said, holding up a chunk of Semtex plastique explosive and its detonator.

"How about a million. A cool million, mon. You can't say no to that."

"This is Semtex, an explosive manufactured in Czechoslovakia before its recent conversion from godless communism to freedom and democracy," Murphy said. "You know what's really special about it?"

"No," Mr. MoFo said. "No. Don't use it. We can deal."

"What's special about it," Murphy continued, "is that it is the same type of explosive used to kill a little boy and almost kill a priest."

"I didn't have nothing to do with that, mon," Mr. MoFo protested.

"Damn," Murphy said. "Here I was about to explain the irony of this situation to you and you add an ironic twist. Irony of ironies, you're an innocent man."

"Two million. For God's sake. Take the money. Don't kill me!" Mr. MoFo screamed. "It was Marcellino. He did it. He had the guy with the explosives."

"It was your hit," Murphy said in a matter-of-fact voice, dismissing the drug dealer's denial. "You gotta pay."

Murphy held the detonator close to Mr. MoFo's bleeding face. "This is how it works," he said. "Push the button down and it starts ticking. Let the button up and twenty seconds later it goes boom. Open your mouth.''

MoFo's eyes grew to the size of golf balls, but he had the presence of mind to keep his mouth shut.

Murphy laughed. ''Since there's some doubt about your guilt, if only in your mind, I'm going to give you a better shot than the kid you killed. I'm going to let you keep the detonator in your mouth. If someone shows up before your jaw gets tired, you made it. If not . . .''

Murphy mashed the chunk of plastique to the underside of the chair. ''Don't move around too much. A vibration will set this thing off even if you're still chowing down on the detonator,'' he lied.

Mr. MoFo looked at Murphy in disbelief. ''You and the guinea are dead men. You don't know it, but you'll both be dead by tonight.''

''Open your fucking mouth,'' Murphy said. ''Or you'll be dead in twenty seconds.''

Slowly Mr. MoFo did as he was told. It was his only option. He knew someone would arrive within the half hour; if he could only hold out, he would enjoy playing cricket with these bastards. He bit down on the detonator and mentally prepared for what would be the toughest thirty minutes of his life.

LoBianco and Murphy walked casually out the front door and down the street. They hadn't gone a hundred feet when the warehouse exploded into an orange inferno that broke windows two blocks away.

''Jeez,'' LoBianco said. ''He didn't last very long.''

''That's because I coated the detonator with battery acid,'' Rotten Jack said, laughing.

The Sons of Italy Social Club. That's where Sonny LoBianco knew he'd find Frankie Marcellino. As teenagers, they had tried to join; Frankie had made it, Sonny had joined the department instead. It was, as it had been, a hangout for Genco's soldiers, a place to meet and conduct business.

He parked a block from the club and noticed two things that amused him. An electronics service truck was parked outside the club, indicating that the Gencos were having the place swept for wiretaps. And across the street was a battered red van, seemingly empty, that LoBianco knew belonged to the FBI. The feds were taping the debugging of their own handiwork. What a joke, he thought.

Normally he wouldn't have dared invade the social club, but he was wired from the morning's kill, and he reasoned that the constant vigilance of the FBI gave him a measure of security. Frankie probably wouldn't whack him out with the feds watching. He went directly to the door of the club and tried the knob. It opened. The assholes inside had forgotten to lock it after letting the electronics technician in.

The interior of the club was dark, bare, and smelled of stale Italian cooking. Four men sat at a round table, drinking espresso laced with anisette and playing whist. The four men wore expensive suits and each had draped his suitcoat over the back of his chair. They looked at LoBianco impassively.

"This is a private club," one of the men at the table said. Sonny recognized him as Sal Galina, a semiretired soldier in the Genco family. Sal was almost sixty, but was built like a wrestler. He was smoking a DiNobili cigar and flicked the ashes toward an overfilled ashtray on his left.

"I'm looking for Frankie," LoBianco said.

"My English that bad?" Galina said to his companions. The other three laughed.

"This is police business," he lied.

They laughed harder. He wondered if he had made a fatal mistake. Any one of these men was capable of killing him on the spot with no more remorse than stepping on a cockroach. He changed his approach.

"Vito wants to know," he said.

That didn't carry much weight, he could see, but at least they stopped laughing.

"He's not here," Sal said.

''Damn it, Sal. We gotta clean this place up. It smells like pig shit in here,'' one of the other men said.

He was getting nowhere, LoBianco decided, and left the club with as much dignity as he could muster. The Sons of Italy were sons of bitches, he thought, but it was his own fault. He had been too impulsive, too high from MoFo's execution to think straight. Still, he had to find a way to get to Marcellino. Perhaps news of his appearance would provoke Frankie.

Outside, he suddenly wanted to go back in and break heads, but he figured he'd used up his stupidity quota for the week. He flipped his middle finger at the FBI van across the street and walked back to the Vette.

As he sat in the car wondering what to do next, a black Cadillac Fleetwood double-parked in front of the social club. LoBianco watched as the driver got out and opened the curbside door.

Angela emerged from the car with the grace of a dancer and the attitude of a high-priced call girl. She wore a full-length fur coat, something much more expensive than mink, Sonny thought.

In the hard winter sun she was ablaze with diamonds; her hair gleamed and the coat reflected the light in an ever-changing pattern. Sonny felt a longing that caught in his throat. But when Frankie Marcellino got out of the car and stood next to her, the longing turned to disgust, envy, and hatred. Frankie reached under Angela's coat and massaged her ass. LoBianco clenched his teeth.

This was not the ideal place for a face-off with Marcellino, in his own backyard, with the FBI taping away, but LoBianco had to make the challenge. He got out of the Vette.

Marcellino had the same snot-nosed sneer on his face that LoBianco remembered from long ago. It had gotten them into more than a few jams back then and Sonny knew why. Just looking at Marcellino made him want to blow holes in the man's windpipe.

"Hello, asshole," LoBianco said.

Marcellino turned. The perpetual sneer on his face turned to a nasty smile. "Well, if it ain't the ex-cop," he said. "Looking for a job?"

"I got a job," LoBianco said. "With Vito, which means you work for me."

Marcellino laughed. "Yeah, right."

Marcellino's driver moved to Sonny's left, but LoBianco caught the movement and pointed a finger at the man. "Far enough, scumbag," he said, freezing the driver in his tracks.

The four men from the social club came out into the street.

"You got problems with this *strunz,* Mr. Marcellino?" Sal Galina asked.

"*Mister* Marcellino?" Sonny said. "Doesn't that piece of shit know you were born under a rock, Frankie?" Then he turned to Angela. "If you're going to hoor around, you can do better. Good-looking cunt like you."

Angela glared at him. "Just go away, Sonny. Leave us alone."

For a few seconds they faced each other, Sonny against Marcellino and his crew of five. Six, if he counted Angela.

Sonny figured the standoff would go on for a while, then Marcellino would walk away. But his faith in the deterrent value of the FBI stakeout team was misplaced. Sal Galina lunged for him. LoBianco spun away from the frontal attack and landed a devastating, stiff-fingered punch to the old man's neck. Galina went down like a sack of shit; LoBianco smashed Galina's face with a well-placed kick. One down, he thought, ready for the rest of them. But Frankie raised his hand to stop the others.

"Fucking fancy, Sonny," Marcellino said. "But this ain't the time or the place." He gestured to the van. "We got a problem, we should solve it."

"A sit-down?" Sonny asked, not believing it. A setup was more likely.

"We can work it out," Marcellino said.

"Work this out," LoBianco said, stepping forward and slapping Angela across her carefully made-up face.

"You know where I'll be, asshole," he said. "Coney Island. Tonight. Bring your fucking troops, bring your fucking hoor, I don't give a fuck. Just show up, don't make me go looking for you."

He looked Marcellino in the eye, but he didn't see fear. He saw amusement.

"Run back to your uncle Vito," Frankie said. "But ask him who whacked out your old man. You'll be surprised by the answer." Marcellino put his arm around Angela and guided her to the social club.

Once they were inside, his driver asked Marcellino why he hadn't just popped LoBianco, FBI or no FBI.

"It's taken care of," Marcellino said. "After tonight Sonny LoBianco is a bad memory."

# 29

The lunch crowd was just leaving when Sonny walked into Rosalie's Clam Bar. Rosalie was at the cash register making change. For the next two hours she would pore over the luncheon receipts to make sure the waiters weren't stealing. On days when everything balanced out, she was disappointed, because she knew all employees stole and her failure to catch them at it was a lapse of vigilance. She was wearing a wine-colored dress with a flower sewn at her ample hip. It looked to Sonny like she had used a caulk gun to apply her makeup. She nodded to him, but said nothing. Her sneer said it all.

He found Vito at the family table drinking grappa.

"Santino," he said, brightening when he saw his nephew.

"I'm ready," LoBianco said, sliding into the booth, facing his uncle.

"Good, good," Vito said. "Can I get you something? Some clams? Some linguine?"

"Nothing but a few answers," LoBianco said.

Vito shrugged.

"First, what's with Frankie?" LoBianco said.

Vito shrugged.

"Me and Frankie get down to serious business tonight," LoBianco continued. "But what I need to know is where he stands with you, where I stand with you, and where we all stand with the Gencos.''

Vito sipped the powerful drink. ''Frankie's dealing with the niggers. Independent. I'm not getting my share,'' he said.

''He won't be dealing with them anymore,'' LoBianco said. ''I just heard Mr. MoFo retired.''

''Yeah? I ain't heard that,'' Vito said.

''You will. Was Frankie cutting in the Gencos?'' Sonny asked.

''No. I don't think so.''

''Does Genco know it?'' LoBianco asked.

''That old bastard knows everything,'' Vito said.

''You been holding out on him?'' Sonny wanted to know.

''Santino! I'm a Sicilian. I believe in honor. I'm surprised to hear you talk to me like that,'' Vito said.

''There ain't no honor left in this world,'' Sonny said. ''There's only power. And power comes from guns and a willingness to use them.''

''Frankie's using MoFo as an outside crew,'' Vito said. ''A gang of maniacs with automatic weapons to enforce his decisions and throw Genco off the trail. His own crew's got lily-white hands, see?''

''Yeah. I see,'' LoBianco said. ''Not a bad idea. Mr. Gotti did okay with the Westies.''

Vito sipped grappa, looking glum.

''Does Genco want you out?'' Sonny asked.

''Who knows? He read a book once about Franklin Roosevelt; you know, the president? He told me that this book said about how Roosevelt always assigned a job to two or more of his crew and then sat back to see which guy did best. He's like that,'' Vito said. ''Like F.D.R.''

''So he's got both you and Frankie doin' the same job?'' LoBianco asked. And me, he thought.

Vito shrugged again. ''That's why I need you, Santino. Together we can get rid of Frankie and get back in good with Genco.''

Sonny watched his uncle. The old man was like an insect skewered on a pin. No matter which way he moved, he was a dead man. It was time to ask *the* question.

"Who killed my father?" LoBianco asked.

The question hit Vito like a punch. "What?"

"You heard. Answer me."

"Why now, Santino? It's water under the bridge. It's finished. What good will it do now, these things you ask?"

"Tell me, or I swear to God, I'll walk out that door and you'll never see me again," Sonny said, getting ready to leave.

Vito knocked back the rest of his drink and said, "Your father, may he rest in peace, was a loyal soldier. But he was stubborn, like you."

Sonny settled back in the booth.

"He was stubborn and he was stupid," Vito said. "He allowed his pride to interfere with business."

Sonny could feel the blood rise within him. He wanted to lash out at his uncle, but he steeled his nerve to listen.

"Your father had a friend, his name was Joey Stabilio. The three of us grew up together, did our first work together. Joey was a good man, a stand-up guy like your father, but he wasn't as smart as he thought he was.

"Joey got caught dirty by the Feds and he got indicted. The case against him was as tight as a crab's ass, and that's waterproof. Joey got convicted and faced heavy time." Vito stroked his droopy mustache and watched Sonny's reaction. He couldn't read a thing in his nephew's face.

"Old man Genco tried to buy some favors, to cut Joey's sentence, but the fucking feds wouldn't move a cunt hair on his time. Not nothin'.

"Genco wasn't surprised they had a case of the ass at Joey. I guess he sorta suspected it, so he takes care of Joey's family while Joey's in the slam. End of story."

"End of story?" Sonny asked.

"Right. Not the end of story, but it shoulda been. Genco pays, Joey keeps his yap shut. But after a while we start to smell a deal brewing between Joey and the feds. A deal we're not part of. Then the smell turns into a stink and Genco tells your father to reach out to this man and tell him he should think about his family.''

Sonny interrupted. ''You threatened the man's family?''

''We were sending his family a lot of money. We just wanted him to think about it,'' Vito said.

''Bullshit! You wanted my father to threaten the man through his family and he wouldn't do it. Why the fuck didn't you do it yourself?''

''Because coming from me it wouldn't have carried much weight. But your father . . .''

''My father told you to go fuck yourself,'' Sonny said. He wanted to lean across the table and smash Vito's face to a pulp.

Vito remained silent.

''Because he wouldn't hurt a man's family, my father was killed,'' Sonny said, clenching his teeth. ''Is that the honor you wop bastards are always bragging about?''

Vito shook his head. ''There's more to the story. You want I should go on?''

''I'm listening,'' Sonny said.

Pointing a finger at his nephew, Vito said, ''We understood your father's problem, so we backed off. We used up a lot of favors getting Joey moved to a place it was easy to reach him. Then Mr. Genco told Santino, your father, to take care of business.''

Vito stopped talking and looked defiantly into Sonny's eyes. ''No one's family was involved. Just one guy against another guy. It's the way we do business,'' Vito said.

Sonny sensed what was coming next. ''He still wouldn't do anything?'' Sonny asked.

''He wanted to wait,'' Vito answered. ''To be sure.''

''This Joey was my father's friend? A good friend?'' Sonny asked.

Vito held up his hand. ''Joey was no friend. He was a fucking stoolie, but your father couldn't understand that. He lived by his balls and his honor and couldn't understand anyone close to him turning rat. He pretended Joey was still a stand-up guy, but he was just stalling.''

"So?"

"So your father stood up for a friend, who was not a friend, and he was killed because he couldn't see the truth when it was right in front of his eyes. Joey was in bed with the feds, opening his ass for them and fucking us at the same time. He sold us out, almost put us out of business.'' Vito signaled the waiter for another grappa. His mouth was suddenly very dry.

"Your father's job wasn't to wait. He was the enforcer. If he liked waiting so much, he shoulda drove a cab. Your father went down with his friend—a fucking stoolie.''

"Who killed him?" Sonny asked.

Vito took the fresh glass of grappa from a waiter and drained it. He waited for the man to move away and said, "Your father was my kid brother, but I loved him like a son.''

"Who, Vito?"

Vito put his hands to his eyes; he was crying. "I killed him, Santino," he said. "I killed your father.''

"You killed your own brother?" Sonny managed to whisper.

Vito nodded. "I couldn't let anybody else do it.''

Sonny left without a word. Vito wiped his eyes with a napkin and hoped no one had seen him cry. He took a sip of water and wondered if he had told Sonny too much or too little. He hadn't told the boy about how he almost shot himself after he had killed Santino. He hadn't told him how his ulcers reacted whenever he saw the boy, how he couldn't bring himself to adopt Sonny. Maybe he should have explained all this, he thought. Maybe he should have had Davis explain it years ago. He certainly paid the black priest enough for keeping the boy safe.

If Sonny is half the man his father was, he'll be all right,

Vito thought, pushing himself out of the booth. He walked to the front of the restaurant, past Rosalie, who was still going over the lunch receipts.

He was a little surprised to see two black men enter the restaurant. Rosalie's was a mobbed-up place that welcomed blacks like it welcomed Feds. But these two were well dressed and seemed to be from some foreign country. Perhaps Santino was right, he was behind the times.

"Can I help you?" Vito asked.

"A table for two, sir," one of the men answered. Vito recognized a Jamaican accent. He made a quick decision and said, "Follow me. Someone will be right with you."

The two men, who looked like twins, followed Vito to the back of the restaurant.

"Pardon me," one of the Jamaicans said.

Vito turned around and noticed both men were smiling. The last thing he ever saw was a mouthful of gold teeth and a handful of Uzis.

The twins' smiles broadened as they stitched Vito LoBianco from head to foot with automatic fire. Vito did an unchoreographed dance of death as the blazing Uzis jerked him backward across the restaurant and into the family booth. The two Jamaicans calmly turned and left Rosalie's as the shouts and screams began.

Still numb from talking to Vito, Sonny walked slowly down the crowded Brooklyn street, wondering if he should act like a man and go back and whack out his uncle. He wondered if that would make him as bad as Vito. Suddenly all his plans were shot to hell. He was no longer a cop, he couldn't work for Vito, and now Frankie was gunning for him. Vito had just gotten off the seesaw and slammed him back into reality. He was fucked. No place to turn.

The sound of sirens brought him out of his funk. He stopped in his tracks and watched three blue-and-whites and an ambulance tear down the street. Looking back, he saw they had gathered in front of Rosalie's.

Curiosity overcoming dread, he went back the way he had

come. The cops hadn't yet established a crime scene and it was easy for LoBianco to enter the restaurant.

Rosalie was screaming and clawing at the bodice of her wine-colored dress, howling like a starving dog. Vito, his white shirt now a shade of red, sat slumped in the family booth, his eyes open, his head thrown back. His expression was one of surprise.

Rosalie spotted Sonny and screamed, "Santino! Help me, please!"

Like you helped me, he thought. The cops looked at him. He shrugged.

"Never saw her before in my life," he said, walking away.

Vito had just had his last sit-down and things were finally looking up.

# 30

"I've seen that abomination in the basement," Mother said.

Charles Maris cringed. She was back, condemning him, criticizing him.

"Dispose of it, and pray to God for forgiveness."

"I only did what you wanted," Charles said lamely.

"You did what *you* wanted, Charles," Mother said. "You like to hurt people, don't you?"

"No, you made me," Charles said.

"You know what I want," Mother said.

They were in the study, Charles behind the desk, Mother sitting primly on a straight-backed chair near Emily's empty wheelchair. Mother had stolen Emily and now wanted him to destroy his nearly completed creation. He knew he had two choices, fight her and risk her wrath, or pretend to do her bidding and bide his time.

He smiled. There wasn't much difference between him and Dempsey. They were both skilled actors, and extremely dangerous when they saw an opening.

A crash brought him back to reality.

Mother had smashed the frame containing a picture of Emily.

"Pay attention, Charles," Mother said. She removed the

picture from the frame. "Bring me Emily," she said. "Now."

Charles stood and approached Mother warily. He took the five-by-seven snapshot of Mother and four-year-old Emily.

He looked back and forth between the picture and Mother. Something was wrong; Mother looked different somehow. Of course, she had been dead, and the photo had been taken years ago, but . . . something.

"Go," Mother commanded.

Berger had debated calling in sick again today. But he'd already missed Rose once at the station. What if she came back? So he'd gone into the precinct and pretended to get some work done. LoBianco's desk had been cleaned and bare, as if a school of piranhas had been at it.

The special task force hadn't left him even a scrap to work on and Berger felt at loose ends. He gave Rose until after lunch to show up and then retreated to his empty apartment, picking up the accumulated mail.

But Rose hadn't returned home, hadn't called, hadn't written so much as a postcard. And two days of silence had been enough to open more holes in his stomach and convince him something was desperately wrong.

It was now almost 7:00 P.M. Berger turned his portable radio to an all-news station. He heard the words *LoBianco* and *shot* and almost had a heart attack. He called into the precinct. The news was disturbing, but at least Sonny didn't seem to be involved.

The sales clerk at Toys "R" Us smirked.

"It's for my niece," Charles said hurriedly.

"That's nice," the clerk said. "All the girls love Wet and Wild Barbie."

Child molester, the clerk thought, looking at the lumpy marshmallow of a man in the dirty tan raincoat.

"Have fun with it," the clerk said, putting the doll in a plastic shopping bag.

Charles grunted. Next stop, St. Agnes.

* * *

Sonny LoBianco sat in his Vette, the motor idling roughly, the heater working heroically, but unable to take the chill off his soul. In his hand was Franklyn Davis's army-issue Colt, which he had taken from the priest's study. Like Davis, it was an antique, a big, bulky gun of undeniable power—a .45-caliber slug could knock down a telephone pole at ten paces. But technology had passed it by, as time had passed Davis by. Modern weapons, like the 9mm Glock under the seat, could fire thirteen shots in seconds, and unlike the Colt, the Glock was compact and required little skill to fire. A .45 would break the arms of half the police force since the elimination of the physical requirements for the job. An eighty-nine-pound policewoman couldn't even lift the old Colt. Sonny oiled it carefully; it was a part of his childhood, and an extension of Davis himself.

He checked the clip and rammed it home. Then he put it under the seat with the Ruger and pulled a .32-caliber automatic from the pocket of his leather jacket. He had taken it from a small-time dealer months ago and kept it as a throwaway piece. It was notoriously unreliable, with little stopping power, but it was easy to conceal. He slid it into a pancake holster in the small of his back.

He was ready for Frankie.

Hitting the accelerator, he gunned the engine for a moment, then slowly joined the traffic. Next stop, Elmhurst General Hospital.

"It's me, Santa Claus," Charles whispered. "I brought you a present."

LaDonna regarded him with a critical eye. He really didn't look much like Santa Claus, as she had first thought, but he had something for her in the shopping bag. A present. She had never actually received a present before, as far as she could remember. She had been at St. Agnes for less than a year. Her life before that had been a blur of pain and tears.

"Are you sure it's for me?" LaDonna asked.

Charles reached into the pocket of his raincoat and pulled out the picture of Emily. ''This is you,'' he said, handing her the photo.

They were standing in the southeast corner of the shelter's front courtyard. Charles had waited for the other children to go inside before he had caught LaDonna's attention.

She looked closely at the photograph. It was hard to see in the dark. ''That's not me,'' she said.

''Sure it is. You just don't remember. Besides, this is for you,'' Charles said. He handed her the Barbie doll.

LaDonna hugged the box to her thin chest. She couldn't wait to open it, but suddenly Charles jerked it out of her hands.

''This is just one present. I have ten presents for you,'' he said.

''Ten!''

''Maybe more.''

''Where are they?'' she asked.

''At the North Pole,'' he said. ''Don't you want to see my sled and reindeer?''

''Yeah!'' LaDonna said.

''Come on, then,'' Charles said, taking her hand.

He had almost made a clean escape when a small figure in a snowsuit, an elf hat on his head, raced out of the rectory, yelling, ''LaDonna! LaDonna!''

LaDonna turned to see Shawndell running as best he could in the bulky snowsuit.

''Dinner, LaDonna!'' Shawndell yelled.

''Shawndell wants to see the reindeers, too,'' LaDonna said.

The small boy, panting in the cold night air, grabbed LaDonna's arm, trying to drag her away from Charles.

''Enough of this shit,'' Charles said, scooping LaDonna up.

''Hey!'' she yelled, reaching for Shawndell. The little boy grabbed for her, too, but only managed to tear the photo out of her hand. He fell on his ass. Like a turtle on its back, Shawndell was unable to get up because the snowsuit weighed him down. He watched, fascinated, as Charles carried LaDonna away.

"*Not* pleased ta meetcha," Shawndell said, struggling to get up.

Berger drove around aimlessly, trying to drain himself of all emotion. He had always prided himself on his ability to stand away from his personal problems. It was funny, but sometimes a stranger could see the obvious. He tried to be a stranger to himself.

Facts, he told himself. What are the facts? One thing that was painfully clear to him was that Rose was serious about staying away. But why she had so suddenly gotten fed up and left him remained a mystery.

He was mulling over the situation when he heard the dispatcher get all cranked up about something happening in Coney Island. The address was St. Agnes Children's Shelter.

Berger hit the siren and put his orthopedic shoe to the metal.

Little kids were sobbing, big kids were staring, wide-eyed and afraid, the Dominican sisters were praying at a rapid-fire pace, and the police on the scene at St. Agnes were wondering how to interrogate this mob. Berger felt he had arrived in some obscure circle of hell.

Flashing his gold, he pushed past the milling minors and knocked on Sonny's garage apartment. No answer. He tried the door. Locked. No lights. Berger rejoined the confusion.

Lieutenant Sam Cibulsky of the local precinct was attempting to bring his Polish charm to bear on the witnesses, but was having about as much luck as Richard Nixon at a gathering of socialists. No one paid him much attention.

"Dear God," wailed the short, fat nun. "Deliver us from this evil."

"I told you we should have never come," the tall fat nun said, clutching her rosary beads, clacking off a prayer a minute.

"Pleased to meetcha," Shawndell said, shaking the left hands of all the cops.

Berger took Lieutenant Cibulsky aside and said, "What happened, Lew?"

"Damned if I know," Cibulsky said. "What are you doing here, Ira?"

"I, uh, know this place. Once I almost donated a bus to St. Agnes," Berger said.

"The priest here, Father Davis," Cibulsky said. "He's in the hospital, and all hell's broken loose."

Berger nodded. "Maybe I can help."

He waded through the crowd of confused children, finding Beverly Jackson, the girl LoBianco had saved from Rooster, and asked her to calm down.

"Oh, it's terrible. Terrible," Beverly cried, putting her head on Berger's shoulder.

He patted her shoulder tentatively. "I can't help you until I know exactly what happened," he said.

"LaDonna," Beverly said. "She's run away."

"She's only four," Berger said, as if that negated the problem.

"She's run away or been stolen," Beverly said.

Berger pursed his lips. "Have you searched?"

"We looked everywhere, but she ain't here," Beverly said, sobbing.

"There, there," Berger said, in his ineffectual way, patting her again.

"Nobody's seen her since an hour ago," Beverly said. "Then she just disappear."

Berger felt a tugging at his coat. He looked down to see Shawndell, dressed in his blue snowsuit, his long knit cap askew. "Pick up," he said, reaching out his arms. Berger picked him up.

"Father B, LaDonna's all gone," Shawndell said.

"Where'd she go?" Berger asked.

"Bye-bye, with a man."

Berger felt his guts tighten. "Do you remember what the man looked like?" he said.

"Big," Shawndell said, holding out his arms.

"Was he white or black, this man?"

Shawndell thought about that for a moment. "White," he said. Then: "When's LaDonna comin' back?"

"Soon," Berger said, putting the boy down.

"Picture," Shawndell said.

"That's nice," Berger said, easing around the boy.

"No," Shawndell said. *"Picture."*

"You can show me your picture later, Shawndell. Right now I'm busy," Berger said, working his way back to the rectory. But Shawndell was attached to his leg like a blue tumor.

*"Picture!"* Shawndell screamed, hurling himself to the ground in a tantrum.

"Beverly, please," Berger said, nodding to the screaming boy. "Help me out, will you?"

The girl went to comfort Shawndell while Berger plowed into the tight knot of cops on the steps of the rectory.

"It's a missing kid," Lieutenant Cibulsky said. "All this fuss. She's probably hiding under a pew in the chapel."

"I'm not so sure. I got a witness says she was snatched," Berger said.

"Where?" Cibulsky asked, grabbing Berger by the arm.

"Not a reliable witness, I'm afraid," Berger said. "He's only two."

"For God's sake, Ira," Cibulsky said.

"But the little girl, LaDonna, is his best friend," Berger said. "I believe him."

"Well, it's better than nothing, just about," Cibulsky snorted.

"Father B!" shouted Shawndell, hurling himself at Berger. "Picture!"

Berger sighed and hauled the boy up in his arms again.

Cibulsky turned away, peeved, and went to search the shelter.

"Let's see your picture," Berger said, resigned.

Shawndell held the black-and-white photo to Berger's face, forcing him to take it from the boy and hold it in the light.

Berger blinked and stared hard at it. He heard a buzzing in his ears and felt as if he were going to faint. He staggered, almost dropping Shawndell.

Gasping for breath, he leaned against the cold, damp stones of the rectory.

*He knew and he was afraid.*

# 31

Father Franklyn Davis lay in the semidarkness of his hospital room listening to the screams down the hall. Drifting in and out of consciousness, he lived in a twilight world where reality and illusion melded into one sustained nightmare. For a time he thought he was on a hospital ship headed for home, and that cheered him. To be leaving the 'Nam was a fine thing. Later he realized it had been twenty years since he had been medevacked from Vietnam, and that was also a fine thing. The drugs kept him high for a while, but like the people he knew, they let him down in the end. The pain returned.

He prayed his rosary and read his breviary, when he was awake long enough to remember. His faith, like his body, had been assaulted and crushed. Why had he been spared and E.T. killed? Sometimes he thought he saw the boy hovering over his bed; sometimes he saw Sonny. But in truth he saw nobody he wanted to see.

Life had never been fair to Franklyn Davis, and he didn't expect it suddenly to reward him for his faith, but he felt he wasn't strong enough to absorb the shocks anymore. His world had turned ugly and black, and this time black wasn't beautiful.

A uniformed patrolman sat outside Davis's door bemoaning his fate. Of all the duty to pull, guarding some broken-down black priest was probably the most boring in the world. He almost wished for a group of armed scumbags to charge the room. Anything to break the monotony. The screaming of a patient down the hall was beginning to get on his nerves. He shifted in his chair.

The patrolman made LoBianco for a wiseguy the moment he saw him coming down the long corridor from the elevator. Something too self-assured about the way he moved gave him away. The patrolman, whose name was Floyd Warren, welcomed an opportunity to bust some balls.

He stood up. "You supposta be here?" he asked.

"You supposta be guarding Father Davis or playing with your dick?" Sonny answered.

LoBianco took a moment to savor the young cop's confusion. He wasn't used to being disobeyed. In fact, he had used his uniform as an excuse to bust heads. Warren put a meaty hand on LoBianco's arm.

"I wouldn't do that," LoBianco said.

"Why not?" Warren asked.

"Because," Sonny said, taking Warren's wrist and snapping it painfully around the startled officer's back. "Because I'll break your goddamned arm."

"What's going on here?" A sergeant in uniform came running down the corridor.

"This asshole's in my way," LoBianco said, still restraining a furiously squirming Warren. "If you'll look on the list, you'll see my name. LoBianco. This douchebag can't read."

"Let him go," the sergeant said.

Reluctantly Sonny complied.

Warren went for his gun, but the sergeant restrained him. "For Chrissake, Warren," he said. "Would you cool it?"

After a moment's search the sergeant found LoBianco's name on the authorized visitors' list, and allowed him to enter Davis's room.

Davis seemed to be sleeping, so LoBianco bent over the priest to make sure.

"You get any closer, we're gonna have to kiss," Davis said, his eyes still closed.

"Shit?" Sonny said, startled. "You awake?"

"Yeah. Some dumb-ass in the hall was making a racket. Woke me up."

"You must be feeling better," Sonny said, sitting in a chair by the bed. The mechanical clicks, beeps, and burps made him uncomfortable; the sour smell of sickness and blood set him on edge. Unless he was lucky, he'd be on a slab like this in a few hours or a colder one in the morgue.

"I came to give you this," LoBianco said, pulling an oilcloth-wrapped package from his coat pocket. "Your .45."

"So I can blow what's left of my brains out?" Davis asked. "Am I that bad?"

"You're the baddest dude I ever met," LoBianco said. "But I thought you might like to have it.

"Besides, with those two nuns from upstate running the shelter, who knows what might happen? They'd probably blow the habits off each other the first time they heard a noise."

In the dim light of the room Davis caught a subtle change in LoBianco's face, a certain hardness he had seen many times. He knew what it meant; it meant trouble. "Talk to me," he said.

"Nothing big," Sonny said. "I want you to hear my confession."

"Nobody lives that long," Davis said. "Give me the *Reader's Digest* version."

The priest watched for a smile, but Sonny's face remained strained and rigid. He noticed for the first time the cuts and bruises. "What are you up to, Sonny?"

"Nothing."

"Liars lose their tongues in hell. Do you remember me telling you that when you were a kid?" Davis asked.

"Just do me this favor without any questions or lectures."

"Sure. But tell me what you're up to."

LoBianco was silent. The idea that had seemed so good an hour ago was falling apart. He was seeking salvation while planning to kill a man.

"Vito was smarter than you," Sonny said. "He knew what I was, you never did. He knew what I was deep down inside. You were just shoveling shit against the tide trying to change me."

"What are you, then?" Davis asked, his voice weak. He closed his eyes. He knew the answer.

"I'm not a cop. I'm . . . the son of Santino LoBianco and it's time I accepted it and started acting the part," Sonny said.

"Who are you going to kill?" Davis asked, his will to continue this conversation suddenly gone.

"I'm going after the piece of shit who did this to you," LoBianco said, "the man responsible for killing E.T." He couldn't look Davis in the eye. It had been a mistake to come here, he realized. His rage was just too great.

"It might go the other way," Davis said with a reasonableness he didn't feel. "LoBiancos have a knack for getting themselves shot up."

"Damn you," Sonny said.

"No, Sonny. Damn you. You didn't come here penitent. What you want is absolution for what, God forgive you, you're about to do. We don't operate that way."

"I came for a favor," LoBianco said.

"You came to cover your ass."

"It doesn't matter," Sonny said. "I'm gonna blow Frankie Marcellino's brains out all over Coney Island."

"Don't do it," Davis pleaded.

"What do you want me to do? Turn the other cheek so he can shove his dick up my ass? It won't work, Father. He's gotta pay."

"Vengeance is mine," Davis said. "You think you can

make the sign of the cross then go out and kill a man and call it business? You're not Vito. You're not your father.''

"I know who I am," Sonny said.

"Get out, Sonny," Davis said. "You want to be a LoBianco, then get the hell out of my sight and be a LoBianco somewhere else."

Davis's words stung. "I thought you were my friend," Sonny said, leaving abruptly.

"I am your friend," Davis whispered to himself. "God help me, I am your friend."

Rose Berger stood motionless amid the jumble of marble and granite monuments covering every inch of Holy Ghost Cemetery. Lugubrious angels, heroic Christs, death's-heads, and maudlin putti vied for her attention; Greek Revival mausoleums strove for pastoral dignity in this tenement of the dead.

In the dark, with the wind blowing the first flakes of snow, she knelt on the cold ground and began to pray to the Holy Spirit. A sudden feeling of well-being came over her after a few minutes, a rosy glow of certitude that would make her task much easier, her life more complete.

When she had finished her prayer, she stood regarding the towering obelisk, a dark blot against a black sky.

"Things will be all right now," she said, speaking to her sister, gone a year now. "You'll see."

The snow began to fall more steadily and Rose felt a clammy sensation, as if someone were touching the back of her neck with a dead, chill hand. "I'm going to have somebody to love me, somebody I can love."

The wind stirred a few sere brown leaves into a miniature tornado at her knees. "It's what I want and need," she said in a voice that was quickly lost in the wind moaning through the stone monuments.

She got slowly to her feet, standing for a moment to take a long look at the cold gravestones. Then she turned her back on all doubt and strode resolutely away.

## 32

After the overheated hospital room the frigid night air cleared LoBianco's head and focused his rage. He parked near Frankie Marcellino's apartment in Coney Island, more determined than ever to bring his problems to an end.

Sleety snow stung his face as he looked up at the twenty-four-story tower that dwarfed the surrounding buildings. It looked to LoBianco as if the massive structure was giving the finger to the neighborhood.

He knew he had a slim chance of catching Marcellino alone and for a moment considered simply waiting for him on the street. But the inaction gnawed at him. Somehow he had to flush the rat out of whatever sewer he was hiding in.

The lobby of Frankie's building looked like a tropical rain forest. Waterfalls, pools filled with floating vegetation, and even a half-dozen screaming macaws contrasted grotesquely with the snow falling outside.

"How may I help you?" the concierge asked from behind a huge service desk.

"Marcellino," Sonny asked.

"Your name, sir?" the concierge asked, picking up the house phone.

"Franklin," LoBianco said, fishing a hundred-dollar bill out of his pocket. "Ben Franklin."

The concierge, a slope-shouldered bald man, looked around carefully, then pocketed the bill. "Penthouse," he said.

LoBianco took the phone from the concierge's hand and put it in the cradle. "It's a surprise," he said.

The bald man looked into LoBianco's dark eyes and decided silence was better than permanent injury. He retreated from the desk, suddenly remembering something important to do.

The walnut-paneled elevator took LoBianco to the top floor. There were only six apartments on the penthouse level. Marcellino's was at the far end of the plushly carpeted hall.

Angela answered the chime. "What the hell are you doing here?" she demanded, trying to close the door on him.

"Where is he?" LoBianco asked, pushing past her, his hand on the 9mm in his jacket pocket.

"He's not here," she said sullenly.

"Where'd he go?" LoBianco asked, scanning the enormous apartment. The furniture was black, the deep-pile carpeting was white, the tables were chrome, and the view was worth six grand a month. He stared out at the ocean, watching the snow swirling in the fierce wind.

"Tell me," he said.

"How do I know where he is?" Angela said. "I'm not his secretary."

"Just his whore," he said.

"Fuck you, Sonny," she said.

"Not anymore, babe," he said. "Not even with somebody else's dick."

"I can see why you hate me," she said. "But what's Frankie ever done to you?"

"He killed a young boy, a friend of mine, and just about killed Father Davis," LoBianco said. "That's the kind of man you're spreading your legs for."

Angela looked shaken. "I don't believe you. Now, get out of here before I—"

LoBianco grabbed her by the arm and squeezed hard. "You'll do nothing except deliver my message," he said. "He's going to pay for the kid and Davis—with vig."

The look on Angela's face told him how much she despised him, but it didn't hurt nearly as much as he expected. In his mind Marcellino was already dead and Angela was only a bad memory.

He pushed her away. "Better find another sucker, Angela," he said. "Because when I'm though with that piece of shit, your days of trolling for AIDS with Frankie are over."

Something flickered in Angela's eyes. A wild, almost insane hatred distorted her beautiful face. She went for him. Her maroon-lacquered nails were like claws, her lips twisted in a snarl.

"You low-life bastard," she screamed, scraping her nails down the sides of his face. "He'll kill you."

"Let's give him a reason to try," LoBianco said, side-stepping her renewed attack and slapping her twice with his open hand. Red welts appeared on her cheek.

Angela retreated, holding her hand to her face. "You're dead, Sonny," she said.

"And you're a fucking hoor cunt," he said. "Enjoy it while you can."

Ira Berger drove at a sedate pace that belied the fear and turmoil within him. He had the photograph tucked in the pocket of his overcoat, but the black-and-white image was indelibly imprinted in his brain. It was at once a memory of the past and an omen of the future.

He thought about looking at it again to make sure he hadn't misinterpreted what he had seen, then changed his mind, with the frequency of the traffic lights he passed.

By the time Berger reached his destination, the roads were beginning to get slick and the photograph was on the seat next to him. He sat for a moment, the engine off, wishing the snow would cloak his fears as it was obscuring the windshield. More than anything, he wanted to drive away, but it wasn't in his nature to quit.

He removed the Smith & Wesson .38 from his shoulder holster, checked it, and put it in the pocket of his overcoat. Turning up his collar, he got out of the car and went to face his worst nightmare.

The crash took Sonny LoBianco by surprise. One minute he was driving down Surf Avenue, the next his Corvette was a small, red target for two dark brown Lincoln Continentals. He downshifted to second and gunned the Vette away from his pursuers, but he could smell burning rubber. They had caved in the back of the Stingray; the tires were rubbing against the fractured fiberglass.

Taking a hard right, he sliced around the corner, but the two Lincolns were right on his tail. A sharp left, then another left failed to shake them.

"Son of a bitch," he said, wrestling with the wheel, trying to keep his speed up and the Vette on the road.

One of the Continentals moved ahead of the other and again smashed into him. The right rear tire blew, and the Corvette skidded left, doing a three-sixty on the icy street.

Going with the slide, LoBianco managed to keep from smashing into an oncoming truck, but the skid had allowed the Lincolns to catch him. Together, they herded him off the road and into a vacant lot near Astroland and the boardwalk.

Sonny was out of the car in an instant, running for his life. He had been looking for Marcellino, but Marcellino had found him first.

The snow was an inch deep in the sandy lot, just enough to hide the odd bricks, stones, and tin cans he stumbled over. It was like running an obstacle course.

"Get that fuck," he heard Frankie shout. Then there was a popping noise that sounded trivial in the tearing wind, but meant they were shooting at him. LoBianco zigzagged over the uneven terrain, praying he didn't fall. Once he was down, he was dead meat.

It was blacker than a hooker's heart; the wind from the ocean drove the crystalline snow into Sonny's face. He was panting now, his face numb, his breath coming in gasps. He had to calm down, he told himself, trying to remember all the meditation techniques he had taught himself over the years. But in an actual combat situation, theory was subsumed by terror.

LoBianco looked behind him and saw the figures stumbling after him. He darted to his left, looking for a place to make a stand, but all around him was a flat, desolate killing ground.

On the verge of panic, LoBianco suddenly made his choice. He spotted the hulk of the once-famous Tornado roller coaster, shut down for years. If he couldn't escape them by outrunning them, he'd hide from them, hoping they would lose him.

With renewed energy he ran toward the massive black shape that blotted out the sky. In the fury of the storm he could just make out the three arcs of the roller coaster in front of him, each one higher than the next. Beneath the roller coaster was a two-story structure, used to store equipment.

LoBianco looked up at the hundred-foot height and decided to head for the house.

A wrecked 1974 Cadillac guarded the entrance to the green-shingled structure. LoBianco dodged around it and hit the door full force with his shoulder. He caromed off and fell on his ass in the snow.

Cursing, he got up and saw that the door was steel: two huge padlocks secured it. LoBianco ran around to the side of the house and found a small window. He tried it, but it wouldn't budge. Using his elbow, he smashed the glass, then crawled through.

The pitch-black room was cold but oddly silent after the

screaming wind outside. It smelled of dust, rot, and machine oil.

Quickly LoBianco searched the room, looking for something to block the window. The smashed glass was a dead giveaway. He found a stiff piece of canvas lying on what had been a kitchen sink, but had somehow migrated to the center of the floor. Using his hand, he found several nails that had pushed out from the Sheetrock walls and jury-rigged the canvas over the window. He did the best he could. He hoped it was enough.

Retrieving the 9mm from his pocket, he flicked off the safety and worked his way through the detritus littering the room. He smashed his shin on a chunk of metal that looked like an engine and almost hit his head on a metal sign advertising the roller coaster, but eventually he reached the hallway and the stairs to the second floor.

Taking the stairs one at a time, LoBianco reached the landing and looked around. There were two doors off the hallway; bedrooms, he guessed. Light seeped in from holes in the roof, the floor was damp with snow and weak with rot. This was the place, he thought. He would make his stand here.

He chose the bedroom on his right and immediately found what he was looking for: a battered but solid chest of drawers. He hauled it out onto the landing, tipping it over to form a barricade at the top of the stairs. Then he sat down.

He didn't have to wait long. Below, he heard soft cursing and heavy footsteps. They had found the broken window and were coming for him. He figured four guys in the house and two or three outside to cut off any escape attempt.

"He's gotta be here." The voice sounded like it was right in his ear. LoBianco gripped the 9mm Glock with both hands and rested his arms on the bureau.

"Check upstairs, Paulie."

"*You* check upstairs," Paulie said.

"Chicken shit."

"Fuck you," Paulie said.

"Quiet."

"Fuck you twice," Paulie said.

"Oh, all right, I'll go."

LoBianco tensed. He couldn't see a damned thing, and he hoped it worked both ways. He lined up the shot, left of center, assuming the hood who was coming for him would use the banister.

When he heard the stairs groan twice, he fired two rounds. The flash from the 9mm was like lightning, giving him a quick glimpse of a middle-aged man grabbing his throat as the second round took him in the stomach, jerking him backward. One down, LoBianco thought.

Suddenly bullets were splintering the chest. Paulie and another man were firing blindly from the safety of the doorway below. LoBianco lay prone, waiting for the first frenzied shots to subside, then he carefully squeezed off three shots. He was rewarded with a scream. He had hit someone.

There was silence for several minutes, then Frankie Marcellino called out, "Give it up, Sonny, and I'll let you die quick."

LoBianco wanted to empty the clip at Marcellino, but he had to conserve his ammunition.

"Fuck you, then," Marcellino said. There was a whispered conversation, then the entire house erupted with light, noise, and smoke. The chest Sonny was hiding behind disintegrated in a hail of shotgun pellets.

"Shit," LoBianco said, the splinters of wood impaling themselves in his face, chest, and arms. He lurched to his left, turned, and fired four times before disappearing into the small bedroom. He didn't think he had hit anyone, but it might slow them down.

There was only one way to go, he thought: up. Ripping the metal slats from an abandoned bed, he smashed through the leaky roof, opening a hole big enough to crawl through.

The wind howled savagely and the tar paper on the roof was as slick as a skating rink, but LoBianco managed to

reach the wooden superstructure of the roller coaster. He
hooked an arm around a strut and hung on, waiting for the
first guy to put his head through the hole. The 9mm felt as
if it weighed a ton; it was a cold lump in his freezing fingers.
He cursed himself for not wearing gloves. He had four shots
left and two thirteen-round magazines in his pocket, as well
as the .32 automatic six-shot. They had shotguns, Uzis, and
as far as he knew, tanks. This wasn't going at all the way he
had planned it.

A dark shape appeared from the hole in the roof. In the
snow LoBianco held his fire until he was sure of what he
was seeing. The dark shape waved about, then disappeared.

Assholes, LoBianco thought. They had put a coat through
the hole to draw his fire.

A moment later someone hauled himself up on the roof,
figuring it was safe. LoBianco aimed for the man's chest,
but before he could fire, the hood staggered, fell, and slid
down the roof, yelling and clawing for purchase on the slick
tar paper. He went over the side as smoothly as if he had
been on the water slide. He hit the Cadillac in the yard with
a crash that LoBianco could hear above the wind. It was
comical, he thought, wanting to laugh.

A head popped up through the hole, then disappeared.
LoBianco pushed as much of his body as he could behind
the thick timbers of the roller coaster. He was ready for the
worst, and he got it.

Two hands attached to Uzis appeared through the hole in
the roof, and suddenly bullets were as numerous as snowflakes. Uzis on full automatic could make Swiss cheese out
of almost anything, and the men below weren't bashful
about using them.

LoBianco climbed away from the deadly fire, hoping to
get an angle on the hole and kill the bastards who were
firing at him.

Forty feet up the roller coaster, he balanced precariously
on a two-foot-thick wooden beam. The wind was even
stronger, and he could barely see the roof, twenty feet

below. As cold as it was, he was sweating. He pumped four rounds into the hole on the roof and immediately the Uzis were silenced. LoBianco let the empty clip fall into space and slammed home another magazine.

The beam on which he stood creaked dangerously, so LoBianco lay down to spread out his weight and lower his profile. He looked desperately for a more sheltered perch, thinking things couldn't get much worse, when suddenly they did.

Two powerful halogen searchlights lit up from below.

''Goddamn it to hell,'' he said out loud. Marcellino was on a search-and-destroy mission and he was the target.

The lights crisscrossed around him, passing over him twice without nailing him. But they'd get him eventually, he thought. He had no choice but to climb.

On the ground, oblivious to the commotion he was causing, Frankie Marcellino shouted orders to his remaining five men. Six to one, he thought, if we can't blow his ass away we don't deserve to live.

Level by level, the lights began a systematic search pattern. Seeing their plan, LoBianco continued climbing.

More than eighty feet above the ground, he found a maintenance platform and a small wooden toolshed. He opened it to see if there was anything he could use. Something unfriendly was living inside. LoBianco caught the gleam of red eyes in the searchlight; he used the butt of his automatic to smash the rat back into its box. Looking down, he attempted to get off a shot at the probing lights, but the glare blinded him and the angle was too steep for an accurate shot.

A barrage of Uzis fire erupted from below, ripping away at the wooden beams and struts, ricocheting off the metal tracks of the roller coaster. Sonny was too slow to change his position. A bullet smashed into his left thigh, making him drop the 9mm. His scream was lost in the wind.

The lights closed in on him.

# 33

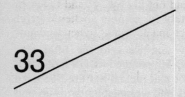

Ira Berger had given up ringing the bell and tried knocking on the front door of the brownstone. Peering into a window, he saw it was covered by a thick, black material. Blackout curtains? he wondered.

He put his ear to the lacquered wood of the door, but he could hear nothing. Using his shoulder, he tried, gently, to force it open. He failed.

Wiping the snow from his glasses, Berger felt foolish. Then he heard a long, strangled cry from inside. He drew his .38 and, using the butt, began rapping on the door, denting the hard wood. No one answered.

Desperate, Berger pulled away from the door, forcing himself to think calmly, like a cop, as he had been trained to do. He had taken two steps down the stairs on his way to the basement door when he heard the creaking of rusty hinges. He whirled around, gun in hand, and saw the front door yawning open. The interior of the house was like a black pit.

Slowly he pushed the door open all the way, making sure no one was hiding behind it. Then he walked inside.

His nerves taut, the hair on the back of his neck erect, he tiptoed through the thick carpet of dust. The house smelled like a funeral parlor, he thought. There was the cloying odor of some kind of perfume covering the powerful scent of death and corruption.

To his left he could see a ribbon of light coming from under a sliding oak door. Taking a breath, he slid the door open.

It took a moment for him to adjust his eyes to the badly lit room. Sitting in an old-fashioned wheelchair, covered with blankets, LaDonna was eating ice cream from a porcelain bowl.

"Home now?" she asked, looking up at him hopefully.

Berger put his .38 away and went to the little girl, relieved to find her unharmed. He put the bowl of half-eaten vanilla ice cream on the floor and picked her up. She gave him a sticky kiss on the cheek and wrapped her arms around his neck.

*"Put her down!"*

Berger turned, his heart racing.

"What are you doing here?" Charles asked.

"I've come for the child," Berger said.

"Put her down or you'll be sorry," Charles said, advancing on Berger.

"Why did you take her?" Berger asked.

"*She* says she's Emily," Charles whispered. "But she isn't."

"Who says she's Emily?" Berger asked, backing away warily.

Charles went silent.

"You'd better tell me what's going on," Berger said, using his authoritative cop's voice. "Who's Emily?"

"No matter what *she* says, it was an accident," Maris said. "Emily is my sister. When she was small, she got hurt. I've been trying to help her ever since."

Berger considered these remarks. "Emily is dead, isn't she, Charles?"

"No!" Charles yelled, standing up from behind the desk. "She's only hurt. She'll be fine when I'm through."

"She's dead and you killed her," Berger said as calmly as he could. He had to shake Maris, get him to admit the truth.

"No. Tag killed her," Maris said, slumping into the chair.

"Tag?"

"My pit bull Tag." His voice was suddenly that of a boy. "I wasn't supposed to keep him, but I did."

"And you feel responsible," Berger prompted. "For Emily's death."

"No. She's going to be fine," Charles said.

"You just admitted she was dead, Charles, that Tag had killed her," Berger said.

*"No!"*

"Let me talk to her," Berger said.

*"No!"*

"Why did you kill those women?" Berger asked.

"To help Emily," Charles snapped.

Jesus, Berger thought, I was right. "How, Charles," he said. "How can you help her?"

"By giving her a new body, a perfect body," Charles said, as if it were the most obvious thing in the world.

"But she's dead," Berger insisted. He had to get Charles to admit it.

"No. She's here," Charles said, shaking his head back and forth, as if to keep out Berger's words.

"Show her to me," Berger said. "Show her to me and I'll leave."

Charles put his head in his hands, blotting out the world. He was tired of this game. "No," he whispered. "She won't let me."

"Who won't let you?" Berger asked.

A look of terror passed over Charles's face. His mouth opened in a silent scream, he pointed to the doorway.

Berger whirled around, and what he saw made him gasp. A woman in a pink bathrobe ran at him. Her hair was wild, her eyes wilder; she wielded a large kitchen knife.

"Rose," was all he had time to say before the knife sliced into his shoulder.

* * *

"He's hit!" Paulie yelled over the noise of the storm. He was excited. They were closing in for the kill.

"Where?" Frankie Marcellino asked, shielding his eyes from the driving snow.

"There, there!" Paulie pointed upward and the lights zeroed in on LoBianco, pinning him to the spot. A barrage of gunfire arced through the snow, spattering all around him.

Dragging his wounded leg, LoBianco knew he had to get out of their range or die. He turned his back on his attackers and leaped out for a looping section of rollercoaster track. Landing with an excruciating bolt of pain, he slid down the tracks, cleaning off twenty feet of steel rail with his face and hands before he could stop.

The lights and gunfire were moving upward and away from him, thankfully going in the wrong direction. LoBianco closed his eyes for a moment; he put his head down on the freezing track and just wanted to go to sleep.

"Fucking amateur."

The voice jolted LoBianco awake. He reached for the .32 automatic, but a size-eleven combat boot ground his hand into the steel track.

"You got more balls than brains, Sonny boy," Rotten Jack Murphy said. He was dressed in a black commando jumpsuit.

"Where the hell did you come from?" LoBianco asked, easing his hand from underneath Murphy's boot.

"It's kind of hard to miss this shindig. Marcellino's making more noise than a division of troops," Murphy said. "Fucking amateurs, all of you."

While Sonny got painfully to his feet, favoring his wounded leg, Murphy moved ten paces down the track and unslung the modified M-16 sniper rifle from his shoulder. He screwed in the customized silencer and peered through the light-enhancing scope. In five seconds he had taken out two of Frankie's men, leaving their bodies bleeding in the snow.

LoBianco began inching down the track toward Murphy, but Rotten Jack waved him back. "Not yet; three more to go."

Murphy took careful aim and shot two more of Marcellino's men, proud of himself. Head shots at this range and under these conditions were extremely difficult.

There was only one searchlight now, and Paulie was too dumb to realize he would be the next to die. Rotten Jack Murphy didn't keep him waiting long. Paulie was dead in seconds, the halogen searchlight lying on the snowy ground, smoking, destroyed.

Murphy slung the M-16 over his shoulder and made his way back to LoBianco.

"You get 'em all?" LoBianco asked.

"All but your buddy Frankie," Murphy answered.

"Where is he?"

"That's your problem, Sonny boy," Murphy said. "Mr. Genco sent me to even up the odds in this amateur production of World War Three. I did my job. You wanted Marcellino, now do your job."

"But I'm hit," LoBianco said, regretting his words immediately. They sounded whining and pleading.

"You're a tough guy. Use some of that Jap crap you're so famous for," Murphy said. "It ain't my problem no more."

"But Jack—"

"By the way, I left you a present," Murphy said. "About twenty feet above you." Then he was gone, moving as swiftly and silently as a ghost.

LoBianco shook the sweat and snow from his eyes and, dragging his useless leg, climbed up the tracks to find out what Murphy had left for him. An M-16 with a couple of clips would be welcome, he thought, but at this point a peashooter would improve his arsenal. When he got to the spot, another maintenance platform, he was disappointed to find two six-packs of Guinness Gold.

"Shit," he said aloud. That fucking Murphy had a strange sense of humor. "Great fucking present."

He sat down, thinking the last thing he needed was a cold beer. A doctor, maybe. A Stinger missile, certainly, but not a brew.

"What the hell?" he said, reaching for a beer. That's when he saw the MAC-10 behind the cans. He laughed.

Before starting his climb down to finish off Marcellino, he examined his leg. The blood had dried, or frozen, around the wound. It had been a clean shot; he could feel the exit wound at the back of his thigh. No permanent damage.

Working his way carefully down the tracks until he was only ten feet above the house below the roller coaster, he swung out onto a wooden ladder.

He had only taken two steps down the ladder when all hell broke loose. Bullets smacked into the wood all around him. One creased the back of his head. The blinding pain turned to darkness as he fell from the ladder and slid down the tar paper roof.

Frankie Marcellino threw away the Uzi, and like a wolf spider popping up from its lair to grab its prey, he dragged the unconscious LoBianco through the hole in the roof and into the house.

"Humpty Dumpty sat on a wall, Humpty Dumpty—"

Charles Maris put his hands over his ears and screamed, "No!"

"Listen to me, Charles," Rose said.

"No! You've killed him and now we're all going to die!"

"Calm yourself. He's not dead," she said.

"You're not Mother. You're Aunt Rose," Charles said, suddenly seeing Rose clearly for the first time.

"Does it matter?" she asked. "You were like a son to me."

"Get out of my house," Charles said. "Or I'll—I'll—"

"You'll what, Charles? Kill me like you killed all those women?" Rose said.

I might have to, Charles thought.

"Charles, help me with Ira," Rose said. Berger lay crumpled on the floor, the butcher knife in his shoulder, the blood leaking slowly from him. LaDonna, paralyzed by fear, lay in the corner, moaning.

"Stop telling me what to do," Charles said, low and nasty. He was losing control. The only way to reestablish it was to be his own boss again. And that meant Rose had to go. He inspected her critically. She was only a bit over five feet tall, her face was heavily made up, her hair a tangled mess. He remembered the pink bathrobe. It was Mother's. She must have stolen it, he thought.

"You'll do as I say or suffer the consequences," Rose said, her voice hard and even.

Still he refused, thinking wildly that he should kill her quickly.

Rose walked over to LaDonna, who was curled up on the floor like a broken doll, her breathing shallow, her moans intermittent.

She picked the child up and sat with her in the wheelchair. "It doesn't matter," Rose said. "I have my Emily. You can go to hell."

Charles felt the room shift; everything was suddenly crimson. He staggered.

"She's not your sister, you know," Rose said, stroking the little girl's dark hair. "She's your half-sister. Your father was her father, but she's my baby."

Charles was swaying, the pain in his head unbearable.

"You tried to kill her, but you brought her back to me," Rose continued, rocking LaDonna in her arms. "You can go now."

With a scream that rattled the loose panes of glass, Charles launched himself at Rose. His charge slammed the woman and the little girl she held into the wheelchair against the wall. Plaster cracked and the cane-backed wheelchair broke apart under the ferocity of his attack.

With one massive blow of his big fist he broke Rose's

jaw; a second hard punch to her midsection cracked her ribs. She gasped in pain. He hit her a third time, breaking her cheekbone. She was quiet. At last.

The spittle drooling from his thick lips, Charles pushed himself up from the wreckage beneath him. He looked blankly at Rose, then focused on LaDonna. *Emily.*

Maris scooped the little girl into his arms. Her head lolled, her eyes were closed. He blew into her face to wake her. His foul breath made the injured girl open her eyes slowly, until she recognized Maris. Then they froze wide open for a moment. Then closed again.

"I hate you, Emily," Charles said softly. "I've always hated you. It was your fault. Why did you have to come along? You drove my father away. You ruined everything. Everything!"

He carried her out of the study, saying, "Now it's time to feed the dogs. You want to feed the doggies, don't you, Emily?" Maris grinned. His big, square teeth looked like tombstones.

The dogs were at ease, but sprang to attention when Charles and LaDonna came down the metal stairs to the subbasement. Charles ignored them and placed the little girl on the autopsy table. When she moaned, working her way back to consciousness, Maris placed a meaty hand on her stomach to hold her down.

LaDonna felt the cold stainless steel under her, but she was so frightened she couldn't cry.

"Those who do not learn from the past are forced to repeat it," Charles said. "Well, I'm smart, Emily. Smarter than anyone ever knew. The last time they thought it was an accident, that *Tag* killed you. But you and I know different." He reached for his collection of scalpels and saws.

"I starved him. Starved Tag. Then I made some tiny cuts on your arms and legs." He giggled. "The rest, of course, is history.

"Tiny cuts. No one ever noticed. It was a tragic accident," he said. "Tragic for you. Good for me. I had Mother to myself. And Father."

He ran his finger along the wickedly sharp edge of a surgical saw. "Then things got worse. That was your fault, Emily. No matter what I did, Mother wouldn't forget you. Wouldn't let me forget you."

He smiled dreamily. "Oh, how you screamed and cried. 'Humpty Dumpty,' you yelled. That was what you called me. Humpty Dumpty. Just because I was a little overweight. But Humpty Dumpty wouldn't save you, would he?

"Want to play now?" he asked. "We'll play seesaw, Marjorie Daw. You'd like that. You always liked that."

He brought the saw down to LaDonna's neck and nicked her soft skin. A drop of blood appeared, shockingly red against the whiteness of her neck.

LaDonna was awake, but she kept her eyes shut tight. It was her only defense against Charles's insanity.

He knew she was faking and slapped her hard in the face, but the pain of the blow only served to deepen her resolve not to open her eyes.

"Damn you!" he screamed. "Wake up!" He was furious now, knowing her ploy—he had used it himself often enough—but unable to bend her to his will.

Understanding the purpose of LaDonna's manipulation sent Maris into a frenzy. He stomped around the subbasement, screaming incomprehensible curses, raging at the world.

One of the dogs was too slow getting out of his way. He kicked it savagely. LaDonna was pretending to play hide-and-seek with Father Davis, that's why it was so dark. She kept her eyes screwed tightly shut. She didn't want to be "it."

Upstairs, Rose opened her eyes. She tried to get up, but the cracked ribs were like a burning brand across her chest. Her mouth hung open. When she swallowed, she swallowed her own blood.

Across the room Ira was also coming to. What was he

doing here? she wondered. Then she remembered. *Emily*. Charles and Emily. She had to save her child from that monster.

With a superhuman effort, fueled by her long-dormant mothering instincts, Rose got unsteadily to her feet and, like a drunk, her breathing torture, made her way to the basement door. Even at the top of the stairs she could hear Charles screaming and raving. She hoped she was not too late.

By the time she reached the basement, Charles was quiet, and that was a worry. She looked around the filthy room, shuddering in fear and pain. More afraid of the dogs than of Charles, she searched for a weapon. Any weapon. She spotted the walking stick made of gnarled wood and picked it up. It was heavy, but she felt a righteous power building in her broken body.

Calm now, Charles put a fresh blade in the scalpel handle, preparing to make thin cuts along the child's legs and arms. Although the wounds would be superficial, they would bleed profusely, and that was the purpose. The blood was to enrage the dogs.

So intent was he on his preparations, he didn't see Rose until it was too late. With all her strength she brought the cudgel down on Charles's shoulders. He howled in pain, dropping the scalpel.

Rose hit him again with the heavy wooden stick, driving him to the floor of the basement. He screamed like a woman, raising his arms to protect his head. He could feel the bones breaking.

With a desperate lunge he tried to escape the blows raining down on his head. Rose, in pain, struck out at him, but her cracked ribs burst under the exertion, puncturing her lungs. Bloody foam appeared on her lips; she dropped the walking stick and staggered to the autopsy table, throwing her arms protectively around LaDonna's inert form. She'd die before she let him harm her child.

Suddenly aware that the attack had ceased, Charles dared

to uncover his head. His left arm was broken, his head felt swollen to twice its size, breathing was difficult. He was crying.

Wiping away the tears with his good hand, he saw Rose's body covering the child, and his fury returned. She wouldn't get away with it, he thought, she'll die right now. Then Emily.

Painfully he raised himself to his feet, staggered, and went to the table. He reached for the scalpel, but it hurt too much to bend down, so he grasped the surgical saw, holding it to the light, enjoying its stainless-steel glint. Then he grabbed Rose by the hair and exposed her neck.

"Hold it."

Maris looked up. At the top of the stairs Ira Berger stood unsteadily, the .38 in his hand.

"Uncle Ira," Charles breathed.

"Drop it, or by God I'll kill you where you stand," Berger said, with more confidence than he felt. His shoulder was on fire. He had lost a lot of blood.

Berger took two steps down the metal stairs when he saw Charles smile evilly and run the saw across Rose's neck. The blood fountained out, spraying Maris and LaDonna. A dark red grin appeared on Rose's neck, matching the one on Charles's face. Her head was almost ripped from her body.

Berger fired twice before he fainted. He tumbled down the stairs, his gun clattering uselessly to the floor.

Maris, unharmed, threw Rose's lifeless body behind him and called to the dogs.

"Dino! Kiss, Dino! Kiss!"

When LoBianco came to, Marcellino was standing over him, smoking and smirking. He prodded Sonny with his shoe.

"Wake up, cocksucker. We got business to take care of."

He kicked LoBianco in his broken ribs again. The pain made him vomit; vomiting made the pain worse.

"Don't puke on my shoes," Marcellino said. "They cost more than you make in a month."

"Fuck you," LoBianco gasped. The words were impotent, but it was the best he could manage. He tried to get up, but Marcellino said, "That's far enough, tough guy. I want you crawling, begging me to kill you. It's a special request from Angela."

LoBianco wasn't listening; he was trying to figure some way out of this. He spotted his .32 automatic less than five feet away on the bed, but it might as well have been in another state. Frankie had always been thorough, he thought.

"Tell me, Sonny," Marcellino said. "What hurts worse? Those bullet holes or Angela sucking my cock?"

LoBianco was silent. If he was going to die at Marcellino's feet, he would do it with as much dignity as possible. He wouldn't give the bastard any satisfaction.

As if reading his resolve, Marcellino kicked him between the legs. "You won't need those no more," Frankie cried, kicking him in the balls again.

LoBianco gagged and drew himself into a fetal position. A thousand points of light swam before his eyes, but he remained conscious.

Marcellino kicked him again, and that did the trick. He blacked out.

But it only lasted a moment, then he swam back to consciousness, cursing his luck.

"Shall I cut your cock off?" Marcellino asked. "I'll give it to Angela for a Christmas present. She'd like that."

LoBianco closed his eyes.

"Or how about this?" Marcellino asked.

LoBianco opened his eyes and saw the barrel of a 9mm automatic through a red haze. Marcellino squeezed off a round into Sonny's undamaged thigh. The blood spurted out in a geyser. The pain was a living force, racking every inch of LoBianco's body. He blacked out again.

"Wake up, cocksucker." LoBianco heard Marcellino's voice, but it sounded far away and unimportant. The sting of snow on his face, however, brought him out of the comfortable darkness and into a world of pain.

"I can keep this up all night," Marcellino said. "How about you?"

He took aim at LoBianco's crotch, then pulled the gun away. "No," he said. "I'll save that for later. How about an arm? Or a knee?"

LoBianco waited patiently for the next shot. The pain had short-circuited his nervous system. He couldn't feel anything except a great thirst. He wished he had one of Rotten Jack's beers.

"I got it," Marcellino said. "A foot. One foot at a time." He laughed, taking aim.

"You move, you die."

Marcellino looked up to see a huge .45-caliber army-issue Colt aimed at his head from the doorway.

"Lower the weapon," the voice said.

LoBianco recognized the voice and the gun. Father Davis. He wondered if he was hallucinating.

Davis, wearing a coat over his hospital gown, was holding the .45 with both hands. He looked feverish and weak; his face was blotchy and covered with sweat.

Marcellino regained his control quickly. "I thought you were dead," he said. "Or shoulda been."

"No one's dying, 'cept maybe you, you don't put that gun down," Davis said, his voice thin and unconvincing.

"Before I die, I'll take care of Sonny," Marcellino said, the 9mm trained on LoBianco's stomach. "What we got here is a Mexican standoff."

"Put the gun down," Davis said.

LoBianco tried to focus on the priest, but even through his pain he could see that Davis was out on his feet. Only willpower had gotten him this far.

"You're a fucking priest," Marcellino said. "You won't kill nobody."

Davis smiled grimly. "I was killing people before you were born." He paused for effect. "I like it, God help me."

Marcellino tried to see if Davis was bluffing, but the priest's eyes were wild and unreadable.

"Kill me, kill your buttboy," Marcellino said. He watched Davis lick his lips. The priest was having trouble keeping his eyes open and his mind alert. The adrenaline had worn off, the painkillers were reasserting themselves. The .45 he had always hefted with ease felt as if it weighed a thousand pounds. He fought to keep it aimed at Marcellino, but gravity dragged it toward the floor.

Marcellino didn't miss the wavering gun and took a chance. He snap-fired the 9mm, getting off two quick rounds.

On the floor, LoBianco screamed the single word "No," as he watched the slugs rip the life out of Davis. At the same time he rolled toward the .32 automatic on the bed.

As Marcellino turned to finish him off LoBianco, left-handed, from a sitting position, fired twice.

The small-caliber bullets entered the forehead side by side, adding a second set of eyes directly over Marcellino's own.

All four eyes looked shocked as Marcellino fell over backward without a sound.

Covered with Rose's blood, Charles Maris ordered the dogs to kill Berger. They hesitated.

"Dino! Kiss!" he screamed. But Dino ignored him and looked to Dempsey. The big pit bull bared his fangs and Charles knew instantly Dempsey had reasserted his authority over the pack.

"Shit," he said. It was a groan. He felt the dog's yellow eyes coolly appraising him.

The dogs got up silently, following their reinstated leader. The walked slowly, their bodies tensed, their hackles raised, their mouths curled back, their fierce yellow teeth bared.

They came within two feet of Berger as he lay there stunned. He could smell their bloody, fetid breath.

"Kiss! Dempsey!" Maris roared, and the pit bull, hearing

his name, turned. Again he eyed Charles as if he were a steak.

Maris slowly reached down for the walking stick Rose had dropped. He had just reached it when Dempsey recognized it. He didn't hesitate, he attacked.

Charles was too slow. Dempsey reached him as he was standing up and sank his fangs into Charles's crotch.

Maris screamed, a high, thin scream, as Dempsey clamped his powerful jaws on his testicles. The other dogs, driven to a frenzy by the blood they smelled on Charles, launched their attacks.

One dog bit hard into Charles's leg, shaking it like a rat. Another buried his teeth in Maris's hand, severing two fingers.

Dino waited for Charles to fall, then went for his throat, cutting off Maris's shrill screams and severing the carotid artery. Blood sprayed everywhere as Charles's massive heart beat its last.

Berger staggered to his feet, retrieving his .38 and going for LaDonna, who was oblivious to the carnage. He picked her up, almost passing out from the pain in his shoulder; it began to bleed again.

Each step seemed like a mountain, but Berger finally reached the basement where Maris had kept the dogs. He spilled LaDonna from his arms and slammed the steel door on the savage mutilation going on below.

He sat with his back to the door, too tired to move. The overwhelming feeling of failure consumed him. He hadn't been able to save Rose, he thought. He closed his eyes and wanted to cry, but he even failed at that.

It seemed so clear to him now. There was only one way out. He took the .38 from his pocket. It had been useless to save Rose, but it would help him now. He put it to his temple and cocked it. It was all so simple.

His finger tightened on the trigger.

LaDonna stirred and looked up at him.

"Father B," she whispered.

# Epilogue

The day had been unusually warm for December 24, but the setting sun dropped the temperature into the thirties. Ira Berger put on the black cardigan sweater that had belonged to Franklyn Davis and rolled up the sleeves. The sweater was much too big for him, but he liked to think he'd grow into it someday.

It had been a little more than a year since Rose's death and he still felt the emptiness. But the crushing grief and desolation had faded. He was certainly busy, he thought, looking around what had been Davis's study. My study now, he thought, marveling that he had been pushed into the job by Sonny LoBianco. It had taken two months of cajoling, but Berger had finally agreed to take the job temporarily. That had been six months ago.

He shivered and turned up the thermostat. The shelter could afford the oil, he thought, now that LoBianco had become its chief benefactor. He supposed it was wrong to take Sonny's tainted money, but when he looked into the faces of the children . . . he didn't know anymore. He supposed he was an emotional and moral cripple now, not capable of distinguishing between right and wrong.

The twenty-inch Sony TV was playing softly in the corner of the redecorated study. Gone was the cheap plaid furniture and rickety table, replaced by expensive couches and chairs, paid for by LoBianco.

"Hey, Pat," Berger said to the television. "What's a four-letter place? Give up? Hell."

Vanna White winked and "Wheel of Fortune" carried on without him. Life carried on without him, he thought.

"You got it wrong, Pat," he said to a smiling Pat Sajak. "Life is not a wheel, it's a seesaw. It all happens too fast for a wheel. One day you're on top, next day you're on the bottom. What does it matter?"

He supposed it did matter. After all, it had only been a year ago that he had been in Maris's disgusting basement, wounded, on the verge of suicide. But LaDonna's blind trust in him had somehow gotten him through.

When he had summoned the strength, he had taken her upstairs and called 911. He had often wondered if he had made the right decision. Could any good grow from such monstrous evil?

Restless, he walked to the window, now rimmed with frost, and looked out. A patrol car cruised by slowly. One thing about Sonny, he provided more police protection for the shelter now that he was on the other side of the law than he ever had as a cop.

"Father B!"

Berger winced. He couldn't convince LaDonna or the other children he wasn't a priest. For a man who had forgotten religion and who had never particularly wanted children, he was somehow a celibate father. Rose, he thought, poor Rose. How she would have doted on these children. How she had yearned for a child of her own.

"Watch this," LaDonna said. "Go ahead, Shawndell."

The little boy walked up to Berger, put one hand on his stomach, the other behind his back, and bowed. "Pleased to meet ya," he said happily.

Berger smiled.

"I'm teaching him more manners," LaDonna said. "Pretty good, huh?"

"Well done, both of you," Berger said, thinking about the incredible resilience of the child. She had had nightmares for a month, then, amazingly, had settled back into her old routine. Curious, Berger had read her file and was appalled at the history of abuse and neglect she had suffered. Compared with that, being kidnapped by Charles Maris was only one dreadful episode in her truly horrible life.

Berger stared back into the darkness, seeing Maris's face. Why hadn't he turned out to be as strong as LaDonna? Charles, his nephew, had been completely insane, so insane he had dressed up as his mother and dropped the grotesque hand at Berger's apartment, so insane he had dragged Rose into his nightmare. Or had Rose only used Charles to get her baby back?

He rested his forehead on the icy window. How had Rose been able to keep the fact that she had given birth to an illegitimate baby from him? How had she existed all those years, knowing her baby had been killed? She had always seemed so normal. But if she wouldn't confide in him her deepest secrets, had their marriage been a sham? Had he been married to some counterfeit Rose, a persona she had created for him and the world? Had she loved him? At all?

His thoughts were interrupted by the buzzing of the high-tech closed-circuit camera and intercom Sonny had had installed.

Berger looked into the small black-and-white TV screen and saw the blurred face of a truck driver. "Yes?" he said.

"Fadda Davis Shelta?" the driver asked.

"Yes."

"Delivery."

"From who?"

"Mr. LoBianco."

Berger sighed. He pushed the button that automatically opened the gates. On the screen he could see the truck roar up the driveway and he went outside to meet it. Despite his orders, half the kids accompanied him. "It takes a truck this big?" Berger asked, eyeing the sixty-foot-long Ryder truck.

"Yeah," the driver said. "Merry Christmas."

Berger looked at the driver closely. "Jack? Is that you?"

"No, it's the baby Jesus," Rotten Jack Murphy said. "Happy Birthday to me."

"What's all this?" Berger asked.

"I'm atoning for my sins," Murphy said. Both cops had put in their papers back in January and both had ended up working for Sonny in one way or another.

"What's inside?" Berger asked.

"Send the kids to bed," Murphy said.

"Pornographic presents?" Berger asked.

"Good idea," Murphy said. "Next year, maybe."

"Father B, what's in the truck?" LaDonna asked, squeezing past the twenty kids clustered around the yellow truck.

"Okay, everybody, back inside," Berger said, and grumbling, the kids complied. "You too, LaDonna."

"Check this out," Murphy said, walking around the back of the truck. He raised the sliding gate. Inside were forty-three fifty-five-gallon oil drums, freshly spray-painted red and green. Each was wrapped with a large bow in a contrasting green or red, each had the name of a kid stenciled in white.

"Excess, thy name is LoBianco," Berger said.

"Same kind of cans we used on Jimmy Hoffa," Murphy said.

Berger shook his head.

"Inside each drum is about half a department store. Compliments of Sonny and Company," Murphy said. "Where you want us to dump 'em?"

"The garage," Berger said. "Sonny's old apartment." He wondered how Franklyn Davis would have reacted to this latest extravagance, considering the source. But he wisely decided not to pursue the matter. No one looks a gift truck in the mouth. "Come in, Jack," he said. "Sonny's coming over."

Murphy gave directions to the two men accompanying him. "Do what the priest says."

Berger growled. Everybody was a wiseacre.

Murphy was on his third eggnog laced with Irish whiskey when LoBianco's black Mercedes drove through the open gate.

"Amateurs," Murphy said, closing the gates behind LoBianco's car. "You've got to remember to lock this thing." He looked around, but Ira was gone.

Berger was already at the door of the rectory, welcoming LoBianco and Lucy Velez, who had been living with Sonny for the last few months.

Sonny had put on some weight, Berger thought. His once athletic grace was gone. The bullets he had taken in the legs had left him with a stiff-legged gait that made Berger shake his head sadly. The twenty-five-hundred-dollar suit he wore did a lot to smooth out the paunch he had acquired.

Berger greeted Sonny and Lucy, fending off the kids who swarmed the visitors, all talking at once. Berger had to threaten to cancel Christmas if they didn't go to bed quietly.

Once they were all in the study, LoBianco asked, "Everything all right?"

"Did you send enough presents, Mr. Rockefeller?" Berger asked. "Barrelsful yet. This I don't believe. Jesus taught that it is easier for a camel to pass through the eye of a needle than for a rich man to get to heaven."

"Jesus yet," LoBianco said. "I think you've been here too long, Ira. Besides, what these presents set me back has left me a poor man.

"Seriously, Ira. All okay?"

"I'm doing all right," Berger said. "I go to the cemetery once in a while. Rose, her sister, the child, they're resting comfortably."

"That's good," Sonny said. "Anything you need here?"

"Since the day you walked away from the department, Mr. Capone, and I don't know how you got away with beating up half the population of Brooklyn, to the day you bought this property, you've treated us royally. Sometimes I think it's too much," Berger said.

"Have you ever been forgotten on your birthday?" LoBianco asked.

Berger shook his head.

"Think about it," LoBianco said.

"How are you doing?" Berger asked him.

"Fine," LoBianco answered automatically.

"You're not in a courtroom, under oath. You can tell the truth. I read the papers," Berger said.

Sonny laughed. "I got a couple of problems."

"If twelve federal indictments are a problem, what's real trouble?" Berger asked.

"A year ago," LoBianco said. "How about that?"

"How about Angela?" Lucy said. "She's suing you for a bundle."

LoBianco shrugged.

A year ago LoBianco would have made some nasty wisecrack, Berger thought, but Sonny had changed. He rarely spoke now, unless it was to give an order.

They were silent for a moment.

"You damned cops," Lucy said. "You miss it, don't you?"

"Life was simpler, maybe," Murphy said.

"Life is never simple," Berger said. "But what choice do you get?"

"There's always a choice," LoBianco said.

"Sure," said Rotten Jack Murphy. "There's always death." He knocked back another eggnog and smiled.

Suddenly it was much colder in the room than it had ever been.

"SANDFORD GRABS YOU BY THE THROAT AND WON'T LET GO!"
—ROBERT B. PARKER

*NEW YORK TIMES* BESTSELLING AUTHOR

# JOHN SANDFORD

### __SILENT PREY  0-425-13756-2/$5.99

Davenport's ex-lover Lily Rothenburg of the NYPD wants him
to help her track down a group of rogue cops responsible for
three dozen murders. The cases couldn't be more clear-
cut—until they merge in unexpected and terrifying ways . . .

### __EYES OF PREY        0-425-13204-8/$5.99

They're killers working in concert. One terribly scarred. The
other strikingly handsome, a master manipulator fascinated
with all aspects of death. Lieutenant Lucas Davenport knows
he's dealing with the most terrifying showdown of his career.

### __SHADOW PREY       0-425-12606-4/$5.99

A slumlord butchered in Minneapolis. A politician executed in
Manhattan. A judge slain in Oklahoma City. This time, the
assassin is no ordinary serial killer...But Lieutenant Lucas
Davenport is no ordinary cop.

### __RULES OF PREY       0-425-12163-1/$5.99

The killer is mad but brilliant. He kills victims for the sheer contest
of it and leaves notes with each body, rules of murder: "Never
have a motive." "Never kill anyone you know." Lucas Davenport
is the clever detective who's out to get him, and this cop plays by
his own set of rules.

For Visa, MasterCard and American Express orders ($15 minimum) call: 1-800-631-8571

FOR MAIL ORDERS: CHECK BOOK(S). FILL
OUT COUPON. SEND TO:

**BERKLEY PUBLISHING GROUP**
390 Murray Hill Pkwy., Dept. B
East Rutherford, NJ 07073

NAME_____

ADDRESS_____

CITY_____

STATE_____ZIP_____

PLEASE ALLOW 6 WEEKS FOR DELIVERY.
PRICES ARE SUBJECT TO CHANGE WITHOUT NOTICE.

POSTAGE AND HANDLING:
$1.75 for one book, 75¢ for each ad-
ditional. Do not exceed $5.50.

BOOK TOTAL            $ _____

POSTAGE & HANDLING   $ _____

APPLICABLE SALES TAX $ _____
(CA, NJ, NY, PA)

TOTAL AMOUNT DUE     $ _____

PAYABLE IN US FUNDS.
(No cash orders accepted.)

303b